THE MOUNTAIN BETWEEN US

ALSO BY CHARLES MARTIN

The Dead Don't Dance

When Crickets Cry

Maggie

Chasing Fireflies

Wrapped in Rain

Where the River Ends

Thunder and Rain

Unwritten

A Life Intercepted

Water from My Heart

Long Way Gone

THE MOUNTAIN BETWEEN US

CHARLES MARTIN

B \ D \ W \ Y
Broadway Books
New York

FOR CHRIS FEREBEE

This is a work of fiction. Names, characters, places, and incidents either are the product of the author's imagination or are used fictitiously. Any resemblance to actual persons, living or dead, events, or locales is entirely coincidental.

Published in association with Yates and Yates, LLP, attorneys and counselors, Orange, CA, www.yates2.com.

Published in the United States by Broadway Books, an imprint of the Crown Publishing Group, a division of Penguin Random House LLC, New York.
crownpublishing.com

Originally published in hardcover in the United States by Broadway Books, an imprint of the Crown Publishing Group, a division of Penguin Random House LLC, New York, in 2010.

Library of Congress Cataloging-in-Publication Data
Martin, Charles, 1969–
The mountain between us / by Charles Martin.
p. cm.
1. Survival after airplane accidents, shipwrecks, etc.—Fiction. I. Title.
PS3613.A7778M68 2010
813'.6—dc22
2009039928

ISBN 978-1-5247-6247-6
Ebook ISBN 978-0-307-59249-1

PRINTED IN THE UNITED STATES OF AMERICA

Book design by Gretchen Achilles

10 9 8 7 6 5 4 3 2 1

2017 Paperback Edition

PRELUDE

Hey . . .

I'm not sure what time it is. This thing should record that. I woke a few minutes ago. It's still dark. I don't know how long I was out.

The snow is spilling in through the windshield. It's frozen across my face. Hard to blink. Feels like dried paint on my cheeks. It just doesn't taste like dried paint.

I'm shivering . . . and it feels like somebody is sitting on my chest. Can't catch my breath. Maybe broke two or three ribs. Might have a collapsed lung.

The wind up here is steady, leaning against the tail of the fuselage . . . or what's left of it. Something above me, maybe a branch, is slapping the Plexiglas. Sounds like fingernails on a chalkboard. And more cold air is coming in behind me. Where the tail used to be.

I can smell gas. I guess both wings were still pretty full of fuel.

I feel like I want to throw up.

A hand is wrapped around mine. The fingers are cold and callused. There's a wedding band, worn thin around the edges. That's Grover.

He was dead before we hit the treetops. I'll never understand how he landed this thing without killing me, too.

When we took off, the ground temperature was in the single digits. Not sure what it is now. Feels colder. Our elevation should be around

11,500. Give or take. We couldn't have fallen more than five hundred feet when Grover dipped the wing. The control panel sits dark, unlit. Dusted in white. Every few minutes the GPS on the dash will flicker, then go black again.

There was a dog here somewhere. All teeth and muscle. Real short hair. About the size of a bread box. Makes angry gurgling sounds when he breathes. Looks like he's jacked up on speed. Wait . . .

"Hey, boy . . . Wait . . . no. Not there. Okay, lick, but don't jump. What's your name? You scared? Yeah . . . me too."

I can't remember his name.

I'm back . . . was I gone long? There's a dog here. Buried between my coat and armpit.

Did I already tell you about him? I can't remember his name.

He's shivering, and the skin around his eyes is quivering. Whenever the wind howls, he jumps up and growls at it.

The memory's foggy. Grover and I were talking, he was flying, maybe banking right, the dash flashed a buffet of blue and green lights, a carpet of black stretched out below us, not a lightbulb for sixty miles in any direction, and . . . there was a woman. Trying to get home to her fiancé and a rehearsal dinner. I'll look.

. . . I found her. Unconscious. Elevated pulse. Eyes are swollen shut. Pupils are dilated. Probably a concussion. Several lacerations across her face. A few will need stitches. Right shoulder is dislocated and left femur is broken. It didn't break the skin, but her leg is angling out and her pant leg is tight. I need to set it . . . once I catch my breath.

. . . It's getting colder. I guess the storm finally caught us. If I don't get us wrapped in something we'll freeze to death before daylight. I'll have to set that leg in the morning.

Rachel . . . I don't know how much time we have, don't know if we'll make it out . . . but . . . I take it all back. I was wrong. I was angry. I never should've said it. You were thinking about us. Not you. I can see that now.

You're right. Right all along. There's always a chance.

Always.

CHAPTER ONE

SALT LAKE CITY AIRPORT

TWELVE HOURS EARLIER

The view was ugly. Gray, dreary, January dragging on. On the TV screen behind me, some guy sitting in a studio in New York used the words "socked in." I pressed my forehead to the glass. On the tarmac, guys in yellow suits drove trains of luggage that snaked around the planes, leaving snow flurries swirling in their exhaust. Next to me, a tired pilot sat on his flight-weathered leather case, hat in his hand—hoping for a last chance hop home and a night in his own bed.

To the west, clouds covered the runway; visibility near zero, but given the wind, it came and went. Windows of hope. The Salt Lake City airport is surrounded by mountains. Eastward, snowcapped mountains rose above the clouds. Mountains have long been an attraction for me. For a moment, I wondered what was on the other side.

My flight was scheduled to depart at 6:07 p.m., but given delays was starting to look like the red-eye. If at all. Annoyed by the flashing DELAYED sign, I moved to a corner on the floor, against a far wall. I spread patient files across my lap and began dictating my reports, diagnoses, and prescriptions into a digital recorder. Folks I'd seen the week before I left. While I treated adults too, most of the files on my lap belonged to kids. Years ago Rachel, my wife, convinced me to focus on sports medicine in kids. She was right. I hated seeing them limp in, but loved watching them run out.

I had some more work to do, and the battery indicator on my digital recorder was flashing red, so I walked to the store in the terminal and found I could buy two AA batteries for four dollars or twelve for seven. I gave the lady seven dollars, replaced the batteries in my recorder, and slid the other ten into my backpack.

I had just returned from a medical conference in Colorado Springs, where I had been invited to join a panel on "The Intersection of Pediatric Orthopedics and Emergency Medicine." We covered ER procedures and the differing bedside manners needed to treat fearful kids. The venue was beautiful, the conference satisfied several of my continuing ed requirements, and most important, it gave me an excuse to spend four days climbing the Collegiate Peaks near Buena Vista, Colorado. In truth, it was a business trip that satisfied my hiking addiction. Many doctors buy Porsches and big homes and pay for country club memberships they seldom use. I take long runs on the beach and climb mountains when I can get to them.

I'd been gone a week.

My return trip took me from Colorado Springs to Salt Lake for the direct flight home. Airline travel never ceases to amaze me; flying west to end up east. The crowd in the airport had thinned. Most folks were home by this time on a Sunday. Those still in the airport were either at their gate, waiting, or at the bar, hovering over a beer and a basket of nachos or hot wings.

Her walk caught my attention. Long, slender legs; purposeful gait, yet graceful and rhythmic. Comfortable, and confident, in her own skin. She was maybe five foot nine or ten, dark-haired, and attractive, but not too concerned about it. Maybe thirty. Her hair was short. Think Winona Ryder in *Girl, Interrupted*. Or Julia Ormond in Harrison Ford's remake of *Sabrina*. Not a lot of fuss, yet you could find the same style up and down Manhattan with girls who'd paid a lot of money to look like that. My bet was that she had paid very little. Or she could have paid a lot to make it look like she paid a little.

She walked up, eyed the crowd across the terminal, and then chose a spot ten or fifteen feet away on the floor. I watched her out of the corner of my eye. Dark pantsuit, a leather attaché, and one carry-on. Looked like she was returning from a business overnight. She set down her bags, tied on a pair of Nike running shoes, then, eyeing the terminal, sat on the floor and stretched. Based on the fact that not only her head, but also her chest and stomach could touch her thigh and the floor between her legs, I surmised that she had done that before. Her legs were muscular, like an aerobics instructor's. After she stretched a few minutes, she pulled several yellow legal pads from her attaché, flipped through pages of handwritten notes, and started typing on her laptop. Her fingers moved at the speed of hummingbird wings.

After a few minutes, her laptop beeped. She frowned, stuck her pencil between her teeth, and began eyeballing the wall for an outlet. I was using half. She was holding the swinging end of her laptop's power cord.

"Mind if I share?"

"Sure."

She plugged in and then sat cross-legged with the computer on the floor, surrounded by her legal pads. I continued with my files.

"Follow-up orthopedics consultation dated . . ." I studied my calendar, trying to resurrect the date. "January 23. This is Dr. Ben Payne. Patient's name is Rebecca Peterson, identifying data follows. Date of birth, 7-6-95, medical record number BMC2453, Caucasian female, star right wing on her soccer team, leading scorer in Florida, highly recruited by teams around the country, at last count she had fourteen Division I offers; surgery three weeks ago, post op was normal, presenting no complications, followed by aggressive physical therapy; presents full range of motion, bend test 127 degrees, strength test shows marked improvement, as does agility. She's good as new, or in her words, better. Rebecca reports movement is pain free, and she is free to resume all activities . . . except skateboarding. She is to stay off the skateboard until she's at least thirty-five."

I turned to the next file. "Initial orthopedics consultation dated January 23. This is Dr. Ben Payne."

I say the same thing each time because in the electronic world in which we live, each recording is separate and, if lost, needs to be identified.

"Patient's name is Rasheed Smith, identifying data follows. Date of birth, 2-19-79, medical record number BMC17437, black male, starting defensive back for the Jacksonville Jaguars and one of the fastest human beings I've ever been around. MRI confirms no tear in the ACL or MCL, recommend aggressive physical therapy and that he stay off the YMCA basketball court until he's finished playing professional football. Range of motion is limited due to pain and tenderness, which should subside given therapy during the off-season. Can resume limited strength and speed training with cessation in pain. Schedule two-week follow-up and call the YMCA and tell them to revoke his membership."

I slid the files into my backpack and noticed she was laughing.

"You a doctor?"

"Surgeon." I held up the manila folders. "Last week's patients."

"You really get to know your patients, don't you?" She shrugged. "Sorry, I couldn't help but overhear."

I nodded. "Something my wife taught me."

"Which is?"

"That people are more than the sum of their blood pressure plus their pulse divided by their body mass index."

She laughed again. "You're my kind of doctor."

I nodded at her pads. "And you?"

"Columnist." She waved her hand across the papers in front of her. "I write for several different women's magazines."

"What kind of topics do you cover?"

"Fashion, trends, a lot of humor or satire, some relationships, but I'm not Jane Doe and I don't do gossip."

"I can't write my way out of a wet paper bag. How many will you write in a year?"

She weighed her head side to side. "Forty, maybe fifty." She glanced at my recorder. "Most doctors I know loathe those things."

I turned it in my hand. "I'm seldom without it."

"Like an albatross?"

I laughed. "Something like that."

"Take much getting used to?"

"It's grown on me. Now I couldn't live without it."

"Sounds like a story here."

"Rachel . . . my wife, gave it to me. I was driving the moving truck to Jacksonville. Moving our life back home. Joining the staff at the hospital. She was afraid of the schedule. Of finding herself on the couch, a doctor's widow, a gallon of Häagen-Dazs and the Lifeway channel. This . . . was a way to hear the sound of each other's voice, to be together, to not miss the little things . . . between surgery, making rounds, and the sound of my beeper at two a.m. She'd keep it a day or so, speak her mind . . . or heart, then pass the baton. I'd keep it a day or two, or maybe three, and pass it back."

"Wouldn't a cell phone do the same thing?"

I shrugged. "It's different. Try it sometime and you'll see what I mean."

"How long you been married?"

"We married . . . fifteen years ago this week." I glanced at her hand. A single diamond decorated her left hand. Absent was the wedding band. "You got one coming up?"

She couldn't control the smile. "I'm trying to get home for my rehearsal dinner party tomorrow night."

"Congratulations."

She shook her head and smiled, staring out across the crowd. "I have a million things to do, and yet here I am making notes on a story about a flash-in-the-pan fashion I don't even like."

I nodded. "You're probably a good writer."

A shrug. "They keep me around. I've heard that there are people who buy these magazines just to read my column, though I've never met them." Her charm was magnetic. She asked, "Jacksonville still home?"

"Yep. And you?"

"Atlanta." She handed me her card. *ASHLEY KNOX*.

"Ashley."

"To everyone but my dad, who calls me Asher. He wanted a boy, was mad at my mom when I appeared with the wrong equipment, or lack thereof, so he changed the ending. Instead of ballet and softball he took me to tae kwon do."

"Let me guess . . . you're one of those crazy people who can kick stuff off the top of other people's heads."

She nodded.

"That would explain the stretching and chest to the floor thing."

She nodded again, like she didn't need to impress me.

"What degree?"

She held up three fingers.

"I worked on a guy a few weeks ago, put a few rods and screws in his shin."

"How'd he do it?"

"Kicked his opponent, who blocked it with an elbow. The shin kept going. Sort of folded it the wrong way."

"I've seen that before."

"You say that like you've been cut on."

"I competed a lot in my teens and early twenties. National championships. Several countries. I broke my fair share of bones and joints. There was a time when my orthopedist in Atlanta was on speed dial. So is this trip work, play, or both?"

"I'm returning from a medical conference, where I sat on a panel, and . . ." I smiled. "Got in some climbing on the side."

"Climbing?"

"Mountains."

"Is that what you do when you're not cutting on people?"

I laughed. "I have two hobbies. Running is one . . . it's how I met Rachel. Started in high school. Tough habit to break. When we moved back home we bought a condo on the beach so we could chase the tide in and out. The second is climbing mountains, something we started while attending medical school in Denver. Well, I attended, she kept me sane. Anyway, there are fifty-four peaks in Colorado higher than 14,000 feet. Locals call them 'fourteeners.' There's an unofficial club of folks who have climbed them all. We started checking them off in medical school."

"How many have you climbed?"

"Twenty. Just added Mt. Princeton. 14,197 feet. It's one of the Collegiate Peaks."

She thought about that a minute. "That's almost three miles above sea level."

I nodded. "Close, but not quite."

"How long does something like that take?"

"Normally a day or less, but conditions this time of year make it a bit"—I shifted my head back and forth—"tougher."

She laughed. "You need oxygen?"

"No, but acclimating helps."

"Was it covered in snow and ice?"

"Yes."

"And was it bitter cold, snowing and blowing like crazy?"

"I'll bet you're a good journalist."

"Well . . . was it?"

"At times."

"Did you make it up and down without dying?"

I laughed. "Evidently."

One eyebrow rose above the other. "So, you're one of those people?"

"What type is that?"

"The 'man versus wild' type."

I shook my head. "Weekend warrior. I'm most at home at sea level."

She stared up and down the rows of people. "Your wife's not with you?"

"Not this time."

My stomach growled. The aroma from the California Pizza Kitchen wafted down the terminal. I stood. "You mind watching my stuff?"

"Sure."

"Be right back."

I returned with a Caesar salad and a plate-sized pepperoni pizza just as the loudspeaker cackled.

"Folks, if we can load quickly, we might beat this storm.

There aren't too many of us, so all zones, all passengers, please board Flight 1672 to Atlanta."

The eight gates around me read DELAYED. Frustrated faces populated the seats and walls. A mom and dad ran the length of the terminal hollering over their shoulders at two boys dragging Star Wars suitcases and plastic lightsabers.

I grabbed my pack and my food, and then followed seven other passengers—including Ashley—toward the plane. I found my seat and buckled in, the attendants cross-checked, and we began backing up. It was the fastest load I'd ever seen.

The plane stopped, the pilot got on the intercom: "Folks, we're in line for the deicer, and if we can get them over here, we might beat this storm. By the way, there's plenty of room up front. As a matter of fact, if you're not in first class, it's your own fault. We've got room for everyone."

Everyone moved.

The only remaining seat placed me next to Ashley. She looked up and smiled as she was buckling her belt. "Think we'll get out of here?"

I stared out the window. "Doubtful."

"Pessimist, are you?"

"I'm a doctor. That makes me an optimist with realistic notions."

"Good point."

We sat for thirty minutes while the attendants served us most anything we asked for. I drank spicy tomato juice. Ashley drank Cabernet.

The pilot came on again. His tone did not encourage me. "Folks . . . as you all know, we were trying to beat this storm."

I heard the past tense.

"The controllers in the tower tell us we've got about an hour's window to make it out before the storm closes in. . . ."

Everyone breathed a collective sigh. Maybe there was hope.

"But the ground crew just informed me that one of our two deicing trucks is inoperative. Which means we have one truck attempting to service all the planes on the runway, and ours is the twentieth in line. Long story short, we're not getting out of here tonight."

Groans echoed around the plane.

Ashley unbuckled and shook her head. "You got to be kidding me."

A large man off to my left muttered, "Son of a . . ."

The pilot continued, "Our folks will meet you at the end of the gate. If you'd like a hotel voucher, please see Mark, who's wearing the red coat and flak jacket. Once you reclaim your baggage, our shuttle will take you to the hotel. Folks, I'm really sorry."

We walked back into the terminal and watched as each of the DELAYED signs changed to CANCELED.

I spoke for everyone in the terminal. "That's not good."

I walked to the counter. The female attendant stood staring at a computer screen, shaking her head. Before I opened my mouth, she turned toward the television, which was tuned to the weather channel. "I'm sorry, there's nothing I can do."

Four screens over my shoulder showed a huge green blob moving east-southeast from Washington, Oregon, and northern California. The ticker at the bottom of the screen called for snow, ice, single-digit temperatures, and wind chills in the negatives. A couple to my left embraced in a passionate kiss. Smiling. An unscheduled day added to their vacation.

Mark began handing out hotel vouchers and ushering people toward baggage claim. I had one carry-on—a small daypack that doubled as my briefcase—and one checked bag in the belly of the plane. We were all headed to baggage claim whether we liked it or not.

I walked toward the baggage claim and lost Ashley when she stopped at the Natural Snacks store. I found a place near the conveyor belt and looked around. Through the sliding glass doors, I saw the lights of the private airport less than a mile away. Painted on the side of the closest hangar, in huge letters, was one word: CHARTERS.

The lights were on in one of the hangars. My bag appeared. I hefted it atop my free shoulder and bumped into Ashley, who was waiting on hers. She eyed it.

"You weren't kidding when you said you got in some climbing on the side. Looks like you're climbing Everest. You really need all that?"

My bag is an orangish Osprey 70 backpack, and it's got a few miles on it. I use it as a suitcase because it works, but its main function is best served hiking and it fits me like a glove. It was stuffed with all my overnight and cold-weather hiking gear for my climbs in the Collegiate Peaks. Sleeping bag, Therm-a-Rest pad, Jetboil stove—maybe the most underappreciated and most valuable piece of equipment I own, next to my sleeping bag—a couple of Nalgene bottles, a few layers of polypropylene, and several other odds and ends that help me stay alive and comfortable when sleeping above ten or eleven thousand feet. There was also a dark blue pin-striped suit, a handsome blue tie that Rachel gave me, and a pair of Johnston & Murphy's, which I wore once, for the panel.

"I know my limitations, and I'm not made for Everest. I get pretty sick above fifteen thousand. I'm okay below that. These"—I hefted the pack—"are just the essentials. Good idea to have along."

She spotted her bag and turned to run it down, then turned back, a pained expression on her face. Apparently the idea of missing her wedding was starting to sink in, bleeding away her charm. She extended her hand. Her grip was firm yet warm. "Great to meet you. Hope you can get home."

"Yeah, you—"

She never heard me. She turned, threw her bag over her shoulder, and headed toward the taxi lane where a hundred people stood in line.

CHAPTER TWO

I carried my bags through the sliding glass doors and flagged down the airport shuttle. Normally it would be busy taxiing people between terminals and the private airport, but given that everyone was trying to leave the airport, it was empty. The driver was thumping his fingers on the steering wheel.

I stuck my head in the passenger window. "You mind giving me a ride to the private airport?"

"Hop in. Got nothing better to do."

When we arrived in front of the hangar he said, "You want me to wait?"

"Please."

He sat in the van with the engine running while I ran inside. I pulled my collar up and tucked my hands into my armpits. The sky was clear, but the wind was picking up and the temperature was dropping.

Inside I found a red-hot space heater and a white-haired guy standing next to one of three planes, a small single engine. On the side of the plane it said *Grover's Charter*, and below that, *Fishing and hunting charters to remote locations*. The ID number on the tail read *138GB*.

He was facing away from me, shooting a compound bow at a target against the far wall. Maybe forty yards. As I walked in, he released an arrow that whistled through the air. He wore faded blue jeans and a shirt with snap buttons, with the sleeves rolled up. *Grover* was stamped across the back of his leather belt, he carried a Leatherman multi-tool in a holster on his hip, and he'd walked the heels down on his boots, giving him a bow-legged appearance. A Jack Russell terrier stood at his heels, sniffing the air and sizing me up.

I waved at the man. "Hi."

He relaxed, turned, and raised his brow. He was tall, handsome, had a strong, square chin. "Howdy. You George?"

"No, sir. Not George. Name's Ben."

He raised his bow and returned to his target. "Shame."

"How's that?"

He came to full draw and talked while staring through his peep site at the target. "Two guys hired me to fly them into the San Juans. Land them at a small strip down near Ouray." He released the arrow, sending it whistling downrange. "One of them is named George. Thought you might be him." He nocked another arrow.

I came up alongside him and stared at his target. The evidence around the bull's-eye suggested he'd spent a good bit of time shooting that bow. I smiled. "You look like you're new at that."

He laughed, came to full draw a third time, let out half a breath, and said, "I do this when I'm bored and waiting on clients." He released his arrow, and it slid into the target, touching the other two. He set his bow down on the seat of his plane, and we walked toward the target.

He pulled out the arrows. "Some guys retire only to chase a little dimpled ball around somebody's backyard only to beat the white off it with an expensive piece of metal." He smiled. "I fish and hunt."

I eyed his plane. "Any chance I could convince you to fly me out of here tonight?"

He lowered his chin, raised an eyebrow. "You running from the law?"

I shook my head and smiled. "No. Just trying to get home ahead of this storm."

He checked his watch. "I was fixing to close up shop, head home myself, and climb into bed with my wife." He noticed my wedding ring. "I 'magine you'd like to do the same." He smiled a broad smile, exposing white teeth. "Although not with my wife." He laughed. It was easy, and there was great comfort in it.

"Yes, I would."

He nodded. "Where's home?"

"Florida. Thought if I could get ahead of this storm, maybe I could catch a red-eye out of Denver. Or at least get on the first flight out tomorrow." I paused. "Any chance I could hire you to fly me to anyplace east of the Rockies?"

"Why the hurry?"

"I'm scheduled for a knee and two hip replacements in . . ." I checked my watch. "Thirteen hours and forty-three minutes."

Grover laughed. Pulled a rag from his back pocket and rubbed the grease around his fingers. "You might be a bit sore tomorrow night."

I laughed. "I'm performing them. I'm a surgeon."

He glanced through the hangar doors at the airport in the distance. "Big birds not flying tonight?"

"Canceled. One of their two deicing trucks broke down."

"They do that a lot. I think the unions got something to do with it. You know . . . they can reschedule surgeries." He chewed on his lip. "I've done that a few times myself." He tapped his chest. "Bum ticker."

"I've been gone a week. Medical conference. Sort of need to get back. . . . I don't mind paying."

He stuffed the rag into his pocket, fed the arrows into the quiver hanging on the side of his bow, and then slid the bow into a foam-lined compartment behind the backseat of the plane. He snugged the Velcro straps. Alongside the bow were three tubes extending back into the body of the plane. He tapped the ends. "Fly rods."

A hickory-handled something had been fastened alongside the rods. "What's that?"

"Hatchet. I fly into some remote places. Ain't much I can't do with what's right here." He tapped a stuff sack beneath the seat, compressing a sleeping bag. "Where I fly, it pays to be self-sufficient."

Behind the seat hung a vest covered with flies, small scissors, and a net that hung from the back collar. He waved his hand across all of it. "My clients take me to some wonderful places. I couldn't afford to get there on my own, so I use them as an excuse to do the things I love. My wife, she even goes with me from time to time." He looked early seventies with the body of a fifty-year-old and the heart of a teenager.

"You own the plane?"

"Yep. It's a Scout."

"Looks a lot like Steve Fossett's plane."

"Real similar. Powered by a Locoman zero-three-sixty that generates 180 horsepower. Top speed is 140 at full throttle."

I frowned. "That's not very fast."

"I gave up speed a long time ago." He put his hand on the three-bladed propeller. "She can land at thirty-eight miles an hour, which means I can put her down in a space about the size of this hangar."

The hangar was maybe 70 feet by 125.

"Which"—he smiled—"means I get to hunt and fish some

rather remote places. Makes me rather popular with my clients." He sucked through his teeth and stared at a large clock, calculating the time and hours. "Even if I get you to Denver, you may not get out of there tonight."

"I'll take my chances. Folks at the counter say that storm may dump enough snow to ground everything out of here tonight and tomorrow."

He nodded. "Won't be cheap."

"How much?"

"One-fifty an hour, and you've got to pay my way going and coming. Cost to you is about $900."

"You take a credit card?"

He sucked in through his teeth, squinted one eye, and considered me. Like he was having a conversation with himself. Finally he nodded, smiled out of the corner of his mouth, and extended his hand. "Grover Roosevelt."

I shook it. It was calloused and firm. "Any relation to the former president?"

He smiled. "Distant, but they don't claim me."

"I'm Ben Payne."

"You really wear a little white jacket that says *Dr. Payne* across the front?"

"Yep."

"And patients actually pay you to look after them?"

I handed him my business card. "I even cut on some of them." Across the bottom, the card read:

KNOW PAIN? NO PAYNE.
KNOW PAYNE? NO PAIN.

He tapped the card. "Jesus might get kind of pissed at you for stealing his slogan."

"Well . . . as of yet, he hasn't sued me."

"You operate on Jesus?"

"Not that I know of."

He smiled, pulled a pipe from his shirt pocket, packed it, and then pulled out a brass Zippo lighter from his front pocket. He flicked it open and sucked in on the pipe, drawing the flame downward and into the tobacco. Once the center was glowing red, he flicked the lighter shut and slid it back into his pocket. "Orthopedics, eh?"

"That . . . and emergency medicine. The two often go hand in hand."

He dug his hands into his pockets. "Give me fifteen minutes. Need to call my wife. Let her know that I'll be late, but that I'm taking her out for a steak dinner when I get back. Then . . ." He thumbed over his shoulder toward the bathroom. "I need to see a man about a horse." He walked toward the phone, talking over his shoulder. "Throw your bags in the back."

"Has this place got wireless?"

"Yep. Password is *Tank*."

I flipped open my laptop, found the network, logged in, and downloaded my e-mail, which included my business and personal voice mail, which had all been forwarded as audio files into my e-mail account. Because so much of my time was accounted for, I responded to most everything via e-mail. That done, I synced my recorder with my computer, then e-mailed the dictation file to our transcription office while copying two other servers in the event we needed a backup, or a backup of our backup. It's a CYA thing. Then I closed my laptop, figuring that I'd respond to all my unanswered e-mail during the flight, allowing them to automatically send when we hit the ground.

Grover reappeared a few minutes later, walking from the phone toward the bathroom. The picture of Ashley Knox, trying to get home, flashed across my eyelids.

"How many people can you carry?"

"Me and two more if they don't mind sitting hip-to-hip."

I stared at the airport over my shoulder. "You mind waiting ten minutes?"

He nodded. "I'll be working through my preflight." He stared outside. "But you need to hurry. Your window of opportunity is narrowing."

My friend in the shuttle van returned me to baggage claim and, as I was his only customer, once again offered to wait. I found Ashley standing on the curb waiting on the next taxi. She had zipped up a North Face down jacket over her suit coat.

"I've hired a charter to fly me to Denver. Maybe get ahead of the storm. I know you don't really know me from Adam's housecat, but there's room for one more."

"You're serious?"

"Should take a little less than two hours." I stuck out both hands. "I know this can look a little . . . whatever. But I've been through the whole wedding thing, and if you're anything like my wife you won't sleep for the next two days trying to make sure every detail is perfect. This is just an honest offer from one professional to another. No strings."

Skepticism shaded her face. "And you don't want anything from me?" She looked me up and down. "Because . . . trust me." She shook her head. "I've fought bigger people than you."

I spun my wedding ring around my finger. "On the back porch of my condo, where I sip coffee and stare out across the ocean, my wife placed three bowls to feed all the Dumpster cats that hang out in the parking lot. Now they drink coffee with me every morning. I've got names for them, and I've gotten used to that little purring thing they do."

A wrinkle appeared between her eyebrows. "You saying I'm a stray cat?"

"No. I'm saying that I never noticed they were there until she pointed them out. Started feeding them. Opened my eyes.

Now I see them most everywhere. It's sort of spread into the way I look at people. Which is good, 'cause us doctors tend to get a bit jaded after a while." I paused. "I don't want you to miss your wedding. That's all."

For the first time I noticed she was kind of hopping around like she had nervous feet or something.

"Will you let me split the fare with you?"

I shrugged. "If that'll make you feel better about going—but you're welcome either way."

She stared down the runway, shifting from foot to foot. "I'm supposed to take my six bridesmaids to breakfast in the morning, followed by a few hours at the spa." She looked at the shuttle and the hotel lights in the distance. She took a deep breath and smiled. "Getting out of here tonight would be . . . fantastic." She glanced back inside. "Can you wait three minutes?"

"Sure, but . . ." The green blob inched closer to the airport on the screen behind us.

"Sorry. Too much coffee. Was just trying to make it to the hotel. Figure the bathroom here is bigger than the one on that plane."

I laughed. "Chances are good."

CHAPTER THREE

Grover was sitting in the plane, headphones on, clicking buttons and turning dials in front of him. "You ready?"

"Grover, this is Ashley Knox. She's a writer from Atlanta. Getting married in about forty-eight hours. Thought maybe we could give her a lift."

He helped her with her bag. "Be my pleasure."

He stowed our luggage behind the rear seat, and my curiosity got the better of me. "Any storage space in the tail?"

He opened a small door near the rear of the tail and smiled. "Currently in use." He pointed to a bright orange battery-powered gizmo. "It's called an ELT."

"You sound like a doctor, speaking in acronyms."

"Emergency Landing Transmitter. If we crash-land, and that thing experiences more than thirty pounds of impact pressure, it sends out a tone on emergency frequency 122.5. That lets other planes know we've had a bit of trouble. Flight service picks up the signal, sends out a couple of planes, triangulates our position, and sends in the cavalry."

"Why'd it take them so long to find Steve Fossett's plane?"

"ELTs are not designed to survive impacts that occur at over 200 mph."

"Oh."

We climbed into the plane, and he shut the door behind us and cranked the engine while Ashley and I put on the headsets hanging above our seats. He was right. It was tight. Hip-to-hip.

We rolled out of the hangar, where he sat flicking more switches and moving the stick between his knees and adjusting knobs. I'm not a plane person, but Grover looked to me like he could fly that thing in his sleep. Two dash-mounted GPS units sat on either end of the control panel.

I'm naturally curious, so I tapped him on the shoulder and pointed. "Why two?"

"Just in case."

I tapped him again. "Just in case what?"

He laughed. "One quits on me."

While he was going through his preflight, I dialed my voice mail. One message. I held the phone to my ear.

"Hey . . . it's me." Her voice was low. Tired. Like she'd been sleeping. Or crying. I could hear the ocean in the background. The waves rhythmically rolling up on shore. That meant she was standing on the porch. "I don't like it when you leave." She took a deep breath. A pause. "I know you're worried. Don't be. In three months, this'll all be forgotten. You'll see. I'll wait up." She attempted a laugh. "We all will. Coffee on the beach. Hurry . . . I love you. It'll all work out. Trust me. And don't think for a minute that I love you any less. I love you the same. Even more. You know that. . . . Don't be angry. We'll make it. I love you. With all of me, I love you. Hurry home. Meet you on the beach."

I clicked the phone shut and sat staring out the window.

Grover glanced at me out of the corner of his eye and gently pressed the stick forward, rolling us down the blacktop. He spoke over his shoulder. "You want to call her back?"

"What?"

He pointed at my cell phone. "You want to call her back?"

"No . . ." I waved him off, slid it into my pocket, and stared out at the storm. "It's okay." I didn't know how he'd heard anything over the drone of the propeller. "You've got pretty good ears."

He pointed at the microphone connected to my headset. "Your mike picked up her voice. Might as well have been listening to it myself." He pointed at Ashley. "There are no secrets in a plane this small."

She smiled, tapped her earphones, and nodded, watching him work the controls.

He slowed to a stop. "I can wait if you want to call her."

I shook my head. "No . . . really, it's okay."

Grover spoke into his mike. "Control, this is one-three-eight-bravo, request permission to take off."

A few seconds passed. and a voice spoke through our headphones. "One-three-eight-bravo, you're cleared for takeoff."

I pointed at the GPS. "Does that unit show the weather radar?"

He punched a single button, and the screen switched to something resembling what we'd seen on the weather channel in the terminal. The same green blob was moving left to right, encroaching on us. He tapped the screen. "That there is a doozy. A lot of snow in that green cloud."

Two minutes later we were airborne and climbing. He spoke over the microphone to both of us. "We'll climb to 12,000 feet and cruise about fifty miles southeast across the San Juan Valley toward Strawberry Lake. Once she's in sight we'll turn northeast, head across the High Uintas Wilderness Area and then descend to Denver. Flight time is a little more than two hours. Sit back, relax, and feel free to move about the cabin. In-flight meal and entertainment service will begin immediately."

Sardines had more room than the two of us.

Grover reached into the door pocket, passed two bags of smoked almonds over his shoulder, and began singing "I'll Fly Away."

He cut the song midsentence. "Ben?"

"Yes."

"How long you been married?"

"Got married fifteen years ago this week."

Ashley piped up. "Tell the truth . . . is it still exciting or just ho-hum?" There was more to her question than just the question.

Grover laughed. "I've been married almost fifty years, and trust me, it gets better. Not worse. Not dull. I love her more today than the day we married, and I thought that impossible when I was standing in that July sun with sweat running down my back."

She looked at me. "How 'bout it? Got any plans?"

I nodded. "Thought I'd bring her some flowers. Open a bottle of wine and watch the waves roll up on the sand."

"You still bring her flowers?"

"Every week."

She turned sideways, lowering her head, raising one eyebrow, which pulled up one side of her lip—doing that thing women do when they don't believe a word you're saying. "You bring your wife flowers every week?"

"Yep."

Grover piped in. "'Atta boy."

The journalist in her surfaced. "What's her favorite flower?"

"Potted orchids. But they're not always blooming when you need them, so if I can't get her an orchid, then I go to this shop not too far from the hospital and buy whatever is blooming."

"You're serious?"

I nodded.

"What does she do with all the orchids?" She shook her head. "Please don't tell me you just pitch them."

"I built her a greenhouse."

A single eyebrow lifted. "A greenhouse?"

"Yep."

"How many orchids you have?"

I shrugged. "Last time I counted, 257."

Grover laughed. "A true romantic." He spoke over his shoulder. "Ashley, how'd you meet your fiancé?"

"The courtroom. I was writing a story about a celebrity trial in Atlanta. He served as opposing counsel. I interviewed him, and he invited me to dinner."

"Perfect. Where're you two going on your honeymoon?"

"Italy. Two weeks. Starting in Venice and ending in Florence."

Turbulence shook the plane.

She turned the questioning back toward Grover. "Just curious, Mr. . . . ?" She snapped her fingers.

He waved her off. "Call me Grover."

"How many hours have you logged in the air?"

He dipped the plane hard right, then pulled back on the stick, shooting us upward and sending my stomach into my throat. "You mean can I get you to Denver and your wedding without dipping the nose into a mountain?"

"Yeah . . . something like that."

He rocked the wheel, left then right, dipping each wing. "Including or not including time spent in the military?"

White-knuckled, I latched a death grip on the handle above my head.

Ashley did likewise and said, "Not."

He leveled out, smooth as a tabletop. " 'Bout 15,000."

Her hand relaxed. "And including?"

"Somewhere north of twenty."

I exhaled and let go of the handle. The inside of my fingers were red. He spoke to both of us. I could hear the smile in his voice.

"You two feel better now?"

His dog crawled out from under his seat, hopped up on his lap, and stared over his shoulder at us. Snarling and twitching like a squirrel on steroids. His body was one massive, rippled muscle, but his legs were only four or five inches long. Looked like somebody had cut him off at the knees. He commanded a lot of personal space, and reading his body language told me that this cockpit was his space.

Grover again. "You two, meet Tank. My copilot."

"How many hours has he got?" I asked.

Grover's head tilted, and he was quiet a minute. "Somewhere between three and four thousand."

The dog turned and stared out through the windshield. Satisfied, he hopped down off of Grover's lap and curled back into his hole beneath the seat.

I leaned forward slightly, staring over the top of his seat to watch Grover's hands. Gnarled. Meaty. Dry skin. Big knuckles. Wedding ring thin around the edges. It hung loosely around the base of his finger, but probably needed dishwashing soap to get it around the knuckle.

"How long will it take us to get there?"

He slid a silver pocket watch from his shirt, clicked it open with one hand. A woman's picture was taped to the inside of the cover. He then stared at his instruments. His GPS gave him the estimated arrival time, but I got the feeling he was double-checking his instruments. Something he'd done a lot. He clicked the watch shut. "Given our crosswind . . . right at two hours."

The picture I'd glimpsed was tattered and cracked, but even faded she was beautiful.

"You got kids?"

"Five, and thirteen grandchildren."

Ashley laughed. "You been busy."

"At one time." He smiled. "Three boys. Two girls. Our youngest is probably older than you." He glanced over his shoulder. "Ben, how old are you?"

"Thirty-nine."

He spoke again. "And you, Ashley?"

"Don't you know you're never supposed to ask a lady her age?"

"Well, technically I'm not supposed to put two people in that backseat, but I'm old-school and it's never stopped me and you two seem to be doing just fine."

I tapped him on the shoulder. "What's the deal with one or two people?"

"The FAA has stated from on high that I'm only allowed one person in that backseat."

Ashley smiled and stuck a finger in the air. "So this isn't legal?"

He laughed. "Define legal."

She stared out the glass. "So when we land . . . are we going to the terminal or to jail?"

He laughed. "Technically, they don't know you're on this plane, so I doubt they'll be waiting to arrest you. If they do, I'll tell them you kidnapped me and I'd like to press charges."

She looked at me. "I feel better."

He continued. "This plane is designed to fly low and slow. Because of that I fly under a VFR designation, meaning 'visual flight rules.' "

I didn't understand any of this. "Which means?"

"Which means I don't have to file a flight plan as long as I plan to fly by sight. Which I am. Which means what they don't know won't hurt them. So?" His head was cocked back, looking in Ashley's direction. "Your age?"

"Thirty-four."

He looked at his instrument panel and then eyed one of the two GPS units and shook his head. "Wind drift is killing us. This is a big storm coming in. It's a good thing I know where I'm going; otherwise we'd be way off course." He laughed to himself. "Youngsters. Both of you. Your whole life before you. What I wouldn't do to be thirtysomething, knowing what I know now."

The two of us sat quietly in the back. Ashley's disposition had changed. More pensive. Less charming. I wasn't all that comfortable knowing I'd just put her in a precarious position.

Grover picked up on it. "Don't you two worry. It's only illegal if you get caught, and I've never been caught. In a couple hours you'll be on the ground and on your way." He coughed, cleared his throat, and laughed some more.

The night sky shone through the Plexiglas above my head. The stars looked close enough to touch.

"All right, you two." Grover paused, checking his instruments. He coughed again.

I'd heard it the first time, but it was the second time that caught my attention.

He said, "Given that we're trying to outrun that storm over your left shoulder and given the wind drift and given that we've got a pretty good tailwind now and given that I don't carry oxygen, we've got to stay below 15,000 feet or you'll land with a headache."

Ashley said, "I hear a *so* coming."

"So," Grover continued, "hold on because we're coming up on the Uintas."

"You-what-as?"

"The High Uintas Wilderness. Largest east-to-west mountain range on the continent, home to 1.3 million acres of uncivilized wilderness, gets five to seven hundred inches of snow a year—

more in some of the higher elevations. More than seven hundred lakes, some of the best fishing and hunting anywhere."

"Sounds remote."

"Ever see the movie *Jeremiah Johnson*?"

"One of my favorites."

He pointed down. Nodded longingly. "That's where they filmed it."

"No kidding?"

"No kidding."

The ride was starting to get bumpy. My stomach jumped into my throat. "Grover? You know those 3-D theme park rides that move but don't go anywhere?"

He rolled the stick toward his left knee. "Yep."

"I call them vomit comets. Is this going to be one of those?"

"Nothing to it. Feels like little more than a roller-coaster ride. Nice and easy. You should actually enjoy it."

He stared out the glass and we did likewise. The dog jumped up on his lap.

"In the middle is a national forest that's designated a wilderness, which means there are no motorized vehicles of any kind allowed. Hence, it's one of the more remote places on the planet. More Mars than Earth. Tough to get out of and hard as nails to get into. If you robbed a bank and were wanting to hide, it'd be a great place to do it."

Ashley laughed. "You speaking from experience?"

Another cough. Another laugh. "I plead the fifth."

The wilderness spread out beneath us. "Grover?"

"Yep."

"How far can we see right now out the windshield?"

He paused. "Maybe seventy miles, give or take."

There was not a single light in any direction.

"How many times have you made this run?"

He tilted his head. "A hundred or more."

"So you could do it with your eyes closed?"

"Maybe."

"Good, 'cause if we get any closer to the snowcapped peaks beneath us, they'll scrape off the bottom of the plane."

"Naw . . ." He was playing with us. "We got a good hundred feet. Although it will pucker up your butt if you start looking at them."

Ashley laughed. Grover pulled a sleeve of Tums from his shirt pocket, popped two, started chewing, and coughed again. He tapped his chest, covered his microphone, and burped.

I tapped him on the shoulder. "Tell me about your bum ticker. How long you been coughing and popping antacids?"

He pulled back on the stick, bringing the nose up, and we climbed, rose up over what looked like a plateau, and skirted between two mountains. The moon appeared out the left glass. Shining down on a world blanketed in white.

He was quiet a minute, looking right, then left. "Beautiful, isn't it?"

Ashley answered for all of us. "Surreal."

"Doc," Grover started, "I saw my cardiologist last week. He's the one recommended the antacids."

"Did you have the cough then?"

"Yep, it's why my wife sent me."

"They run an EKG?"

"Yep. All clear."

"Do yourself a favor and go back. Might be nothing. But might be something, too."

"Think I should?"

"I think it'd be worth another look."

He nodded. "I live by a couple simple rules. One of those is that I stick to what I'm good at and I give people credit at sticking to what they're good at."

"So you'll go?"

"Probably can't get in tomorrow, but maybe the middle part of the week. That soon enough?"

I sat back. "Just get in this week. Deal?"

Ashley interrupted us. "Tell me about your wife."

We were rolling across mountaintops with precision. Grover was quiet a moment, then spoke, his tone lower. "A Midwest girl. She married me when I had nothing but love, dreams, and lust. Gave me children, stuck with me when I lost everything, believed me when I told her we'd be okay. No offense to present company, but she's the most beautiful woman on the planet."

"None taken. So, got any advice for a girl forty-eight hours from walking down the aisle?"

"When I wake up in the morning, she's holding my hand. I make the coffee, and then she sits with her knees touching mine while we drink it."

Grover liked talking, so we let him. Not that we had a choice.

He took his time. "I don't expect you to get all this." He shrugged. "Maybe one day. We've been married a long time, seen a lot, experienced much, but loving somebody gets better the more you do it. You might think an old man like me doesn't get fired up when she walks across the bedroom in a faded flannel gown, but I do. And she does for me, too." He laughed. "Although I don't wear flannel gowns.

"Maybe she ain't as perky as she was in her twenties, maybe her skin sags behind her arms and down the back of her butt. Maybe she's got some wrinkles she don't like, maybe her eyelids droop, maybe her underwear ain't as small as it used to be, maybe all that's true . . . but I don't look like the man in our wedding pictures either. I'm sort of a white-haired, wrinkled, slower, sunburnt reflection of that boy. It may sound cliché-ish, but I married a woman who fits me. I'm one half of a two-piece puzzle."

Ashley spoke again. "What's the best part?"

"When she laughs . . . I smile. And when she cries, tears roll down my cheeks." He nodded. "I wouldn't trade that for . . . for nothing."

The drone of the motor vibrated the plane as we rolled over mountaintop and across valley. Grover pointed at the GPS and then out the glass, waving his hand across the earth. "Spent my honeymoon down there. Hiking. Gayle loves the outdoors. We go back every year." He laughed. "Now we drive a Winnebago. Sleep under heated blankets. Electric coffeemaker. Really roughing it."

He shifted in his seat. "You asked me for some advice. I'm going to tell you the same thing I told my girls before they married. Marry the man who's going to walk with you through the next fifty or sixty years. Open doors, hold your hand, make your coffee, rub lotion on the cracks of your feet, put you up on a pedestal where you belong. Is he marrying your face and your bottle-blond hair, or will he love you when you look like whoever you're going to look like in fifty years?"

I broke the silence. "Grover, you missed your calling."

He chuckled, checking his instruments. "How's that?"

"Dr. Phil's got nothing on you. You should've had your own television show. Just you, a couch, and one audience member at a time."

Another laugh. "You two walked into my hangar tonight and saw a blue and yellow plane piloted by a crusty old man with age spots on his hands and an angry little dog at his heels. A quick hop to Denver so you can get on with your busy, scheduled, e-mailed, voice-mailed, text-messaged lives." He shook his head. "I see an enclosed capsule that lifts you up above the problems of the earth and gives you a perspective you can't get on land. Where you can see clearly."

He waved his hands across the landscape passing below us in shadows. "All of us spend our days looking through lenses that are smudged, fogged up, scratched, and some broken. But this here"—he tapped the stick—"this pulls you out from behind the lenses and for a few brief seconds gives you 20/20 vision."

Ashley's tone was quiet. "That why you love flying?"

He nodded. "Sometimes Gayle and I will come up here and spend two or three hours. Not saying a word. And not feeling like we need to. Not filling the air with a bunch of static. She'll sit back there, put her hand on my shoulder, and we'll skirt the earth. And when we land, all the world seems right."

We were quiet several minutes.

Then he coughed.

Grover grunted, something low and guttural. He grabbed his chest, leaned forward, pushed off his headset, and his head slammed against the side of the glass. He arched his back, then grabbed his shirt and pulled, tearing the shirt and popping off the buttons. He lunged forward, hunched over the stick, jerked the stick hard right, and then dipped the wing ninety degrees toward the earth.

The mountain rose up to meet us. It felt like we were falling off a tabletop. Just before we hit, he corrected her, pulled back on the stick, and the plane began to stall. Our speed slowed to almost nothing, and I remember hearing treetops brushing the underside of the plane.

Then, as if he'd done it a thousand times, he pancaked the plane against the mountain.

The tail touched first, then the left wing, which hit something and snapped off. The weight of the right wing pulled on the plane, tilting us and making an anchor of sorts. Somewhere in there Grover cut the engine. The last thing I remember was spinning, somersaulting, and the tail breaking off. Then I heard a loud crack, Ashley screamed, the dog barked and floated through the air. Snow peppered my face, followed by the sound of breaking tree limbs, followed by the impact.

The last image I remember seeing was the green blob inching across the bluish glow of the dash-mounted GPS.

CHAPTER FOUR

Having just met Ashley, who reminds me a lot of you, I was thinking about the day we met.

After school. I was standing on the track. A good bit warmer then than I am now. We were running quarters when the cross-country team came skimming across the field. Actually, the team was clustered in a group, several hundred meters behind a breakaway, single girl.

You.

You were floating. Barely skimming the surface of the grass. A concert of arms over legs controlled by some unseen puppeteer above. A sophomore on the cross-country team, I'd seen you before. Word was that distance was your specialty. Your hair was cut short, like Julie Andrews in The Sound of Music. *You jumped the trackside bench with little effort, then the high hurdle next to me. Your breathing was deep, rhythmic, purposeful. Somewhere over the hurdle, you shot a glance at me. The whites of your eyes rolled right and revealed the jade-green emeralds in the center.*

Your whipping arms and fingers slung sweat across my legs and stomach. I heard myself say "wow," then I tripped over a hurdle, causing a loud crash. In that single second you broke your concentration. Or allowed it to be broken. The corner of your lip turned up. Your eyes lit. Then your feet touched down, the emeralds disappeared, whites returned, and you were gone.

I watched you running away. Over obstacles. Seldom around. The ground rose and fell beneath you, having little impact on your up-and-down movement. Laser-beam focus, and yet your face seemed disconnected from the turret. Able to operate on its own. I think I must have said "wow" a second time, because my teammate Scott smacked me in the back of the head.

"Don't even think about it."

"What?"

"Rachel Hunt. She's taken, and you don't stand a chance."

"Why not?"

"Two words." He held up two fingers like a peace sign. "Nate Kelsey."

I had yet to take my eyes off you. A picture of Nate entered my mind. He played middle linebacker. Had no neck. And set the state bench press record—the last three years. You crossed the infield and the adjoining practice field and then ran out of view near the girls' lockers.

"I can take him."

Scott smacked me in the back of the head again. "Boy, you need a keeper."

But that was all it took.

Coach's wife worked in the dean's office. She was always trying to set me up. When I asked her for your class schedule, she gladly typed and printed it. Soon after, I discovered I had an insatiable desire to make a change in my third-period elective. My advisor was not persuaded.

"You want to take what?"

"Latin."

"Why?"

" 'Cause I think it's cool when people speak it."

"People haven't spoken Latin since Rome fell."

"Rome fell?"

He was not impressed. "Ben."

"Well . . . they should. It's time for the Latin Renaissance."

He shook his head. "What's her name?"

"Rachel Hunt."

He signed my change form and smiled. "Why didn't you just say that?"

"Next time I will."

"Good luck. You'll need it."

"Thanks."

He leaned around his desk. "You got health insurance?"

"Yeah. Why?"

"You seen her boyfriend?"

I got to class early and watched you walk in. If I hadn't been seated, my knees would've buckled. You looked at me, smiled, and walked straight toward me. Set your books on the table to my left. Then you spun, tilted your head, smiled, and stuck out your hand.

"I'm Rachel."

"Hi." Okay, okay. Maybe I stammered a bit.

I remember looking at your eyes and thinking I'd never seen green like that. Big, round. They reminded me of that snake in The Jungle Book *that was always trying to hypnotize people.*

You said, "You're Ben Payne."

My jaw fell open, and I nodded. In the hallway, one of my teammates was slapping a knee, laughing at me. "You know me?"

"Everybody knows you."

"They do?"

"Fast as you run, who doesn't?"

Maybe my dad wasn't such a bad guy after all.

You smiled, looked like you wanted to say something else, but shook your head, turned away.

Maybe I was just a tad self-conscious. "What?"

You turned your head sideways, half smiling. "Anyone ever told you you have a nice voice?"

My finger touched my voice box. My voice rose about eight octaves. "No." I cleared my throat. "I mean . . ." Lower this time. "No."

You opened a notebook, started flipping through it. You crossed one leg over the other. "Well . . . you do. It's . . . warm."

"Oh."

We spent the rest of the year as "friends," because I didn't have the you-know-whats to ask you out. Not to mention the fact that Mr. No-neck could break me in half—if he could catch me.

Junior year, I had just arrived at school, had about thirty minutes before the first bell rang, and we bumped into each other as you were walking out of the girls' locker room. Your hair was wet from the shower.

Your eyes had narrowed, and a deep wrinkle had creased the area between them.

"You okay?"

You turned, eyes wet, and began walking toward the track and bleachers. Away from school. Your fists were clenched. "NO!"

I took your pack, and together we walked out onto the track, circling the obvious. "What's wrong?"

You were exasperated. "I'm not getting any faster, that's what."

"You want help with that?"

Your nose wrinkled. "You can help me?"

"Well, yeah. Least I think so." I pointed at the cross-country coach's office. "I'm pretty sure he can't help you. If he could, he would have told you by now."

You weren't convinced. "Oh, and you can see something he can't?"

I nodded.

You stopped and threw up your arms. "What, then?"

"Your arms. Too much lateral movement. Not forward. And . . ." I waved my hand over your hip flexor. "You're too tight in here. Stride's too short. Your feet are fast, but you need to cover more ground with each stride. Maybe two inches would help."

Your lips turned down, like I'd just said you looked fat in that outfit. "Oh, really?"

Another nod. I was starting to look over my shoulder for your boyfriend. To my recollection, this was the longest period of time we'd ever spent talking alone and in public.

You put your hands on your hips. "And you can fix this?"

"Well . . . I can't really fix it. You do that. But I can run alongside you and help you see it differently. Maybe help you find a rhythm that will cause you to lengthen it. Like running down a sidewalk—you naturally either start trying to land on the crack or miss it. Run with someone who has a longer stride, and then let your brain kick in. Either way, your stride adjusts without your thinking about it."

"And you'd do that?"

"Well . . . of course. Who wouldn't?"

You crossed your arms. "Until now? YOU! You're the only one who won't give me the time of day."

I was still looking over my shoulder. I could almost hear him breathing down my back. "What about . . . number fifty-four? The guy with no neck."

"In case you haven't heard, Einstein, we stopped dating . . . last year!"

"Oh." I scratched my head. "You did?"

You shook your head. "You may be fast out here"—you waved your hand across the track, then tapped me in the chest—"but when it comes to this thing, I can run circles around you."

You still do.

CHAPTER FIVE

It was dark, and the pain had worsened. I pressed the light button on my watch. 4:47 a.m. Maybe six hours had elapsed since the crash. Another two to daylight. This high, maybe earlier. But in this cold, I wasn't sure I'd last another fifteen minutes. I was shivering so hard, my teeth were clattering. Grover was covered in four inches of snow. I was still buckled into my harness, and my seat had broken at the hinge.

Ashley lay on my left. I touched her neck and carotid artery. Her pulse was strong and elevated, but she was quiet. I couldn't see her in the dark. I felt around me. Snow and broken glass covered us. To my right I found the compression sack strapped to the underside of Grover's seat. I pulled, and the sleeping bag came out slowly. I unzipped the side and spread it over us as much as I could.

I could only move a little at a time because the pain in my rib cage left me breathless. I tucked the bag around her, slipping her feet into the end. The unnatural cant of her leg told me she was in a bad way. The dog tucked himself in with me. I pressed the light button again. 5:59 a.m. The light was a fuzzy green. The numbers a fuzzy black. Several feet in front of me, I saw the propeller protruding into the air. Caked in snow. Part of the blade was missing.

DAYLIGHT BROKE, AND I WOKE to the dog standing on my chest, licking my nose. The sky was gray and still dumping snow. Grover, a few feet away, had mostly disappeared beneath what looked like a foot of it. Somewhere an evergreen tree grew out of the earth, and one of its limbs extended into view. I tucked my hands under my armpits. The down sleeping bag was both good and bad. It was warming me up. Which was good. Increasing blood flow. Now maybe the cold wouldn't kill me. But with blood flow came more pain in my ribs.

Ashley still lay next to me, silent and unmoving. I touched her neck again. Her pulse was still strong and not as elevated. Meaning, her body had burned through the adrenaline that flooded her system when we crashed.

I sat up and tried to examine her. Her face was swollen and caked with blood due to the cuts above her eyes and on her scalp. I ran my hand along her shoulder. It looked like someone had stuffed a sock inside her down jacket. Her shoulder was dislocated, hanging low from the socket.

I slid my arm up her sleeve, pulled down, and let the tendons pull the bone back and snap it into the socket. Once in place, I manipulated the joint. It was loose and had a good bit of side-to-side movement, which told me she'd done that before, but it was back where it belonged. Shoulders are pretty good about going back into place if you start them in the right direction.

Without undressing her and talking to her, I couldn't get a handle on whether she had any internal injuries. I ran my hands along her hips. Fit, lean, muscular. Then her legs. Her right was fine. Her left was not.

The femur had broken when the plane smashed into a rock upon impact. Probably the source of the scream. Her thigh was grossly swollen, maybe twice its normal size, and her pant leg was taut. Fortunately, the bone had not broken the skin.

I knew I had to set it before she woke up, but before I could do that, I needed space to work. Currently, I felt like I was in an MRI machine with all the sides too close to my face. I sat up and found that we were encased in a snow and plane-fuselage cave. Which, from a certain perspective, was good.

The impact, along with the storm, had buried us in a snowbank, then mostly covered us up. That formed a snow-cocoon, and while that sounds bad, and it was, it also meant that we were more or less maintaining thirty-two degrees, which was better than whatever the outside temperature was. Not to mention that it kept the wind chill from cutting through us. The majority of the light was coming in through the Plexiglas atop the plane, filtering through the snow and letting me see to work.

While I worked to dig away the snow to make room to get at her leg, the dog whined and spun in circles. Then he climbed up on Grover's lap and started licking the snow away from his face. He wanted to know when this plane was taking off. I pulled at the snow with my fingers, but that only lasted a minute before my hands got too cold. I realized that if I kept it up my hands would be useless. I dug around in front of Grover and found a plastic clipboard wedged into the pocket of the door. I pulled off the papers and used the clipboard like a shovel. It was slow work, but I dug a cavity, or shelf, in the snow that was long enough for Ashley to lie in. It also meant that once I got her in there, I could get at her left leg.

I pulled the bag off of her, laid it flat inside the shelf, and then slowly slid and lifted her body across the seat and onto the shelf. The effort exhausted me, so I fell back against Grover's seat and sat there breathing. Still short and shallow, trying to lessen the pain in my chest.

The dog walked around me and hopped up on my lap, licking my face.

"Hey, boy," I whispered. I couldn't remember his name.

Thirty minutes passed before I had enough energy to return to her leg.

I sat up and spoke to her, but she didn't respond—which was good, because what I was about to do was going to hurt more than the initial break.

I took off my belt, wrapped it around her ankle and then my wrist, giving me an anchor to pull on. Then I took off my left hiking boot and slowly placed my left foot between her legs. I straightened my leg, pressing it against her, then tightened the belt and grabbed her foot with both hands. I took four or five deep breaths and felt her hand slide onto my foot. I looked up and saw that one eye was partly open. She patted my foot and mumbled, "Pull . . . hard."

I pulled, pushed with my leg, and arched my back, all at the same time. The pain shot through her, her head rocked back, and she uttered a muffled scream before losing consciousness. The leg popped loose, I turned it, let it straighten itself naturally, and then let go. When I let go, the left leg "hung" to the side in a mostly natural position that mirrored the right.

There are two keys to the healing of a broken leg. Setting it correctly and then holding it in place while the bones fuse. Neither is easy.

With the leg set, I began looking for a brace. Above my head hung two mangled wing supports, more than three feet long and about as big around as my index finger, that had ripped in two when the left wing became disconnected from the plane. I began working them both back and forth, weakening the metal, and they eventually snapped off.

When hiking, I carry two pocketknives, a Swiss Army knife and a folding single-bladed knife with a lock. Given that I had passed through security in the airport, both had been packed into my backpack to be carried in the belly of the plane. The pack lay behind us, mostly submerged in the snowbank. Only a corner was visible. I pulled away some snow, found the zipper, and slid my hand around inside until I found the knives.

My Swiss Army knife has two blades. Using the smaller, I slit Ashley's pant leg up her thigh to her hip. The leg was swollen, and much of the thigh was black and blue. A deep purple even.

The belt restraints on both seats were comprised of an over-the-shoulder harness system with a typical quick-release buckle. I loosened ours from our seat and used both pieces of one harness to secure the "poles" I'd just removed from the wings. The buckles, while bulky, gave me the opportunity to tighten and loosen the "brace." I secured the brace around her leg, tightened the straps so they were snug, and placed the buckle directly above her femoral artery.

Then I took a T-shirt from my suitcase, cut it in two, and wound each piece into a straight, taut, tubelike piece, which I placed beneath either side of the buckle. This allowed me to snug the buckles further, tightening the brace, while taking the pressure off the artery and giving her leg ample blood flow, which it was going to need.

Lastly—and while she may not have liked any of my former actions, she certainly was not going to like this—I packed the area around the break in snow. I had to be careful to bring down the swelling while not dropping her core temperature.

I reached further into my backpack and pulled out a pair of polypro long underwear and a wool sweater I wear when I'm on mountains. It's a little tattered, but it's lined with a wind-stopper fabric and it keeps me warm even when it's wet. I pulled off her down jacket, her suit coat, her blouse, her bra, and checked her chest and ribs for any evidence of internal injuries. No bruises had surfaced. I slid her into my long underwear and sweater, which was too big but dry and warm. Then I slid her back into her down jacket, but didn't pull her hands through the sleeves. I pulled the sleeping bag beneath her, wrapped her up like a mummy with only her left leg hanging out, then elevated and covered her left foot.

We lose half our body heat from our heads, so I pulled a wool beanie from my pack and slid her head into it, pulling it down over her ears and forehead but not covering up her eyes. I didn't want her to wake up and think she'd either died or was blind.

Once she was dry and warm, I realized how shallow my breathing and elevated my pulse had become. The pain in my ribs had intensified. I pushed my arms into my jacket, then lay down next to her to get warm. When I did, the dog walked across my legs, walked in two circles while his nose stretched to find his tail, and burrowed between us. He looked like he'd done that before. I stared across at Grover's snow-covered body.

I closed my eyes, and as I did, the fingers on Ashley's left hand extended through her jacket and touched my arm. I sat up in time to see her lips move, but I couldn't understand. I leaned closer. Her fingers squeezed around my palm, and her lips moved again.

"Thank you."

CHAPTER SIX

It's daylight. The snow is still falling heavy and I can see my breath. Blowing smoke. It's also really quiet. Like somebody hit the mute button on the world.

Ashley is not doing too well. She may have some internal injuries. I set her leg and her shoulder, but she'll need an X-ray on both and surgery on her leg when we get out of here. She passed out when I set her leg. She's been asleep since. Talking some in her sleep.

She's got several lacerations on her arms, face, and head, but I didn't want to move her any more than I had to. I need her to wake up and talk to me before I start sewing. I found a fly-fishing vest behind my seat filled with some monofilament that I can use for stitching.

Grover, the pilot, he didn't make it. Did I already tell you that? I can't remember. He landed the plane after his heart had stopped. I don't know how. Putting that plane down without killing all of us was nothing short of heroic.

Me?

I broke a few ribs. Maybe three. The pain on inhaling is sharp. Piercing. And I may have a collapsed lung. 'Course the elevation here is above 11,000 feet, so breathing isn't all that easy anyway.

I've been thinking about the possibility of a rescue, but I can't think of any reason we should expect one. We didn't tell anyone we were getting on the plane. Grover wasn't required to file a flight plan.

He never told anyone he had passengers, so the tower had no idea we were on the plane.

From the side, Grover sort of looked like Dad. Or like the better parts of him. Although Grover struck me as a bit kinder.

Some people said Dad was a jerk. Domineering. Others said I was lucky to have such a committed father. 'Course those folks wouldn't have lasted a day in my house. Mom didn't. He abused her, she crawled inside a bottle, and he made sure he had enough evidence to keep her hopping from one rehab center to the next, which allowed him to strip her of parental rights for good. He seldom lost. I don't know the whole story. He let me talk to her by phone. Stevie Nicks and Don Henley sing about leather and lace. My dad was handy with the leather. Our home had no lace—at least until you crept through the window.

From the moment he clicked on the light at 4:55 a.m., I had five minutes to be standing at the back door. Dressed. Two pair of sweats, running shorts, and shoes.

"Miles don't run themselves. Get your butt out of bed."

"Yes, sir."

Most nights I slept dressed. I remember the first time you snuck in and tugged me on the shoulder. You looked surprised. "Why you wearing all these clothes?"

I looked at the clock and then the door. "You stay here about four hours and you'll find out."

You shook your head. "No thanks." When you figured out I was wearing two pair, you asked, "Aren't you hot?"

"You get used to it."

You tugged on me. "Come on, let's get out of here."

To the lifeguard station and back. Six miles. I don't know why he chose six, but that was the number. He called it my warm-up. I think it had more to do with the doughnut shop than anything else. Cheating was impossible, because he'd drive to the shop, sit next to the glass, stare out over the ocean, coffee in one hand, doughnut in the other, paper flat on the table, checking my time as I trudged up the beach and slapped the red lifeguard's chair. If I was up a few seconds, or fast, he'd finish his doughnut, beat me home, and say nothing. But if I was slow, he'd run out of the shop and shout across the sand. "Down seven!" or "Down twenty!"

I learned how to run within myself, monitoring and gauging output and speed. Fear does that.

When I got home he met me on the beach, where I was allowed to pull off both pair of sweats before I started my speed work. Mondays we ran twelve 660s. As in six hundred and sixty meters. Tuesdays were 550s. Wednesdays 330s. And so on. Sunday was my only free day, but it was a mixed pleasure because Monday was just around the corner.

We always finished with a speed rope, sit-ups, crunches, push-ups, a medicine ball, and whatever other pain-inducing thing he could dream up. He had this piece of bamboo he'd hold out above my knees.

"Higher!"

I'd lift them, but they were never high enough.

He'd shake his head and speak softy. "Pain is weakness leaving your body."

I'd stand there, lifting my knees, staring down the beach and thinking to myself, "Good . . . why don't we let some out of your body. I'm about out."

I lost a lot of pain in his house.

By 7:00 a.m. I'd have run seven to ten miles depending on what day of the week it was. Then I'd go to school, try not to fall asleep in class, and then go to track practice or run with the cross-country team—both of which seemed mundane in comparison.

Dad was managing his firm, fifty traders, all reporting to him, and if they didn't pull their weight, he sent them packing. No mercy. Because the stock market closed at four, he would appear about four fifteen, loosened tie, stopwatch in hand, sunglasses, wrinkled forehead, staring at me over the fence.

Yeah, he was committed all right.

My freshman year I won the 400-meter dash in 50.9 seconds, anchored the 4 x 400 meter relay, and won the mile in 4:28. That made me state champion in three events.

Dad drove me home in silence. No celebration dinner. No day off. No moment. He parked the car. "Five o'clock will come early. If you're going to break four minutes by your senior year, you've got some work to do."

Somewhere in there it occurred to me that, to my dad, I was only as good as my last time, and in truth, no time was ever good enough.

When it came to school, Bs were not accepted. And an A- "might as well be a B+, so you'd better pull it up." I had few friends, and if I wasn't in school, I was either running or sleeping.

Then came my sophomore year. I'd broken several state and national records. That didn't necessarily make me the big man on campus—football players had that all wrapped up—but it did give me a reputation with folks who follow that stuff. Like cross-country runners.

Like you.

You entered the picture and lit my world with laughter and light and wonder. Welcome and warm. You ran by me, a dart of the eyes, a quick glance, flicking sweat off your fingertips, and I wanted to take a shower, wash off Dad, and bathe in you.

So much of what I am, he made. Forged it in me. I know that. But Dad used pain to rid me of pain. Leaving me empty and hurting. You poured in you and filled me up. For the first time, I felt no pain.

You gave me the one thing he never did. Love, absent a stopwatch.

CHAPTER SEVEN

It was dark when I woke. I pressed the light button on my watch. 12:01 a.m. An entire day had passed. Then I checked the date. It took a second to register. Make that two days. We'd slept thirty-six hours straight.

A billion stars stared down on me. Close enough to touch. The big green blob had come and gone, having spread a thick white blanket in its wake. The moon had appeared over my left shoulder. Big as Christmas. I squinted my eyes. If I could climb the mountain to my left, I could step right onto the moon and keep walking.

As sleep pressed in, I made a mental list, which included two things: food and water, and we needed both soon. With emphasis on water. If Ashley was fighting infection, I needed to get her kidneys working and I needed to get her hydrated. Shock has a way of burning up your fluids, and while I may not have been conscious of it, I had been in shock and running on adrenaline since the crash. Tomorrow would be difficult. Especially at this elevation. If I could get the GPS working, I'd try to figure out where we were, 'cause I knew better than to expect a rescue.

I considered the facts. We'd notified no one. And even if someone had known we'd gotten on the plane, we were—by Grover's own calculation—more than a hundred and fifty miles off course, thanks to the storm winds. It'd be weeks before a search grid brought anyone this far out, if at all. If an air rescue were coming, and they knew exactly where to look and what to look for, we'd have seen or heard something. We had not. Or worse, we'd slept through it. Our only hope was the ELT.

Daylight lit a blue sky. I tried to move, but I was so stiff it hurt to pick up my head. If you've ever been in a car wreck you know what I mean. The wreck hurts, but two or three days later the hurt really sets in. I sat up and leaned against a large boulder protruding from the snowbank. Given its location, I thought it might have been the rock that broke Ashley's leg.

Daylight and some clarity allowed me to see what had happened to the plane and us. When the plane touched down, we hit what looked like about eight feet of snow along with trees and the side of a huge rock. As we neared ground, a tree or rock outcropping ripped off the left wing. That left the plane heavier on the right, so with the right wing pointed toward the ground, we hit a second time, flipping us. Somewhere in the third or fourth flip, the right wing caught again and dug what remained of the nose into the snow, sort of corkscrewing us. That swept us into another rock outcropping, probably the one next to my head, which smashed the side of the plane and Ashley's leg. The result left a relatively intact fuselage buried into a ten-foot snowdrift packed up against a rock ledge and what looked like trees growing out of the rocks.

Bad news first. While Grover's plane was bright blue and yellow, all but the left wing was buried several feet down. Needle in a haystack came to mind. Not to mention that the tail disintegrated when it hit the boulder. I'd found bright orange pieces of plastic, but no ELT. Hence, no signal on 122.5. No triangulation. No cavalry. The truth was hard to swallow. I didn't know how I'd break it to Ashley.

The only good news—if you can call it that—was that this

"burial" gave us a measure of protection from the elements. Otherwise, we'd already be dead from exposure. Thirty-two degrees above zero is better than thirty-two below.

Ashley lay sleeping and her face was flushed, which probably meant fever, which probably meant infection. Neither of which were good, but both of which I expected. I had to get some fluids into her.

The best I could do was crawl, so I rolled to my backpack, dug out my Jetboil, and filled the canister with fresh powder from just outside the cave. I clicked it on, the blue flame erupted, melted the snow. As it melted, I added more. Either the noise of the burner or my movement woke her. Her face was puffy, swollen, and her eyes were slits. Her bottom lip was fat, and now that it was daylight, I needed to clean her cuts and start sewing the ones that needed stitches.

I held a cup of warm water to her lips. "Drink this."

She sipped. I had a bottle of Advil somewhere in my pack. I desperately wanted to down about four, but I knew she was in more pain and would need them more than I in the days to come. I found them in a side pocket, dumped four into my hand, and held one to her lips. "Can you swallow this?"

She nodded, I placed it on her tongue, and she swallowed. We repeated this three more times. Slowly. The snow around her leg had long since melted, so the swelling, while it might have gone down at one time, was back. And swelling brought pain. If I could reduce the size of her leg, I could also reduce the pain. The Advil worked from the inside, snow would work on the outside. I repacked her leg, gently, with snow and felt for the pulse around her ankle to make sure she was getting good circulation. I kept holding the cup to her lips until she finished the whole thing. That meant eight ounces. My goal for the day would be five more of those. Forty-eight ounces of fluid would remind her kidneys to get to work.

I refilled the cup and the Jetboil, taking some fluid myself. Ashley forced her eyes open as much as the swelling would allow. She scanned the cave, what was left of the plane, the dog, her torn clothing, the brace on her leg, and then her eyes settled on Grover's body. She stayed there a minute, then looked at me. "Is he . . . ?"

"He was gone before the plane touched down. Heart, I guess. I don't know how he landed it."

She reached up, walking her fingertips across her face and head. Her expression changed.

Slowly, I pulled her hand down. "I need to stitch you up."

Her voice was hoarse. "What day is it?"

I gave her the short version. When I finished, she didn't say anything.

I dug through Grover's fly-fishing vest and found some fine monofilament. I stripped one of the flies off the vest and removed all the stuff that made it look like a fly, exposing a single barbless hook. I needed to straighten the hook to more of a ninety-degree angle, but I needed a tool. Something to help me straighten the hook.

Grover's belt.

I dug through the snow around his waist and found the Leatherman. When I popped open the snap on the holster, his stiff body didn't move. I needed to bury him, but I also needed to get Ashley stitched up and I needed to find some food. He'd have to wait.

I straightened the hook, threaded the monofilament through the eye, and tried to flatten the eye with the pliers. When I looked back at Ashley, tears were rolling down her face.

She said, "I'm sure his wife is worried about him."

We hadn't talked yet about our predicament. The being-stuck part. One of the things I've learned both in medicine and climbing mountains is that you attack one crisis at a time. The next was her face and head.

I used the Leatherman and dug out a second shelf in the snow lower than the makeshift shelf on which Ashley now lay. In my practice, following surgery, I have a habit of going to my patients' rooms and checking on them. Oftentimes, I'll roll a stainless steel stool on wheels up to the side of the bed. The level of which actually puts me lower than most of them, allowing them to look down or at least straight at me. Ever noticed how it's hard to look up when you come out of surgery? Me too. This shelf next to Ashley accomplished the same sort of thing. Maybe it has something to do with bedside manner.

The wind gusted, scraping the branch across the Plexiglas. I was finally able to dig my sleeping bag out of my pack and spread it on the shelf next to her. Until now we'd been sharing; now we each had our own.

I held the cup to her lips, and she sipped. I wiped the tear from her face. "What hurts?"

She glanced at Grover's body. "Him."

"What else?"

"My heart."

"Physically or emotionally?"

She laid her head back. "Do you know how long I've wanted to get married? Looked forward to, even planned, my wedding. Like . . . all my life."

"How about on your body?"

"Everything."

"I'm not finished hurting you. I need to sew a few stitches."

She nodded.

Three places. The first required two stitches in her scalp, which were relatively painless. The second was along the top of her right eye, running through the middle of her eyebrow. An older scar had split upon impact. I pierced the skin with the hook and said, "There's an older scar here."

"Nationals. I was eighteen. Other kid caught me with a roundhouse. Never saw it."

I tied the first stitch and started on the second. "Knock you out?"

"No. Made me mad."

"Why?"

" 'Cause I knew it was going to mess up my prom pictures."

"What'd you do?"

"Caught him with a spinning back kick followed by a double round and finally an ax kick, which cockroached him."

"Cockroached?"

"We had names for the positions that people fell in when we knocked them out."

I distracted her. "Such as?"

"The porpoise, the white man's dance, the cockroach, a few others."

I tied the third knot and cut the line. I nodded at her eyebrow. "What I've done is good enough to hold you until we can get to a hospital and let a good plastic surgeon fix my Band-Aid."

"What about my pretty two-poled brace? My leg is killing me."

"It's the best I can do. I set it, but without an X-ray, it's hard to tell. Again, when we get to a hospital, they can take some pictures and check it. If it's not aligned, I'll recommend, and I'm sure they'll agree, that they rebreak it and give you a few presents that will set off the metal detector when you pass through security. Either way, you'll be good as new."

"You've just said 'get to a hospital' twice, but do you really think anybody is coming?"

As we looked up at the blue sky through the hole created between the leaning wing and the eight-foot snow wall, we saw a commercial airliner cruising at what looked like 30,000 feet. It'd been nearly sixty hours since our crash, and we hadn't heard a sound other than our own voices or the wind or a scratching limb. And that plane was so high, we couldn't hear it either.

I shook my head. "We can see them just fine, but I'm pretty certain they can't see us. Any evidence of our disappearance lies under three feet of snow. Won't be seen until July when it melts."

"Don't crashed planes send out some sort of SOS signal or something?"

"Yes, but the thing that sends it is lying all around us in about a thousand little pieces."

"Maybe you should crawl out and wave your shirt or something."

I chuckled. Which hurt. I clutched my side.

Her eyes narrowed. "What's up?"

"Couple of broken ribs."

"Let me see."

I pulled up my shirt. I hadn't seen it in the daylight and figured that the bruise would have set in by now. The whole left side of my rib cage was a deep purple. "Only hurts when I breathe."

We laughed.

She looked up at me, her head not moving, as I tied the sixth knot in her arm. She looked more worried. "I can't believe I'm lying here like this, with you sewing on me, in the middle of God only knows where, and we're laughing. You think there's something wrong with us?"

"Chances are good."

I turned my attention to the side of her arm. Either the rock or a branch had cut the skin on her non-dislocated shoulder, about four inches in length. Fortunately for her, when the plane came to a stop with her unconscious in it, she was pressed up against the snow on that shoulder. Pressure, mixed with snow, stopped the bleeding. It would need twelve or more stitches. "Give me your hand." She did. "I need you to slip your arm out of your sleeve."

She pulled slowly, wincing. "By the way, where'd I get this handsome shirt?"

"I changed you sometime yesterday. You were wet."

"That was my favorite bra."

I pointed over my left shoulder. "You can have it back once it dries out."

The cut on her arm was news to her. She looked down at it. "I didn't even know I had that one."

I explained about the snow and pressure and tied off another stitch.

She watched me work and spoke without looking at me. "What do you think our chances are?"

"You don't beat around the bush, do you?"

"What's the use? Sugarcoating it won't get us out of here any faster."

"Good point." I shrugged. "Let me ask you a few questions. Did you tell anyone you were getting on this plane?"

She shook her head.

"No e-mail? Phone call? No nothing?"

Another slow shake.

"So, nobody on planet Earth knows you stepped into a charter plane and attempted to fly to Denver?"

A final shake.

"Me either."

She whispered, "I imagine everyone thinks, or thought until yesterday, that I was still in Salt Lake. By this point they'd be looking for me, but where would they look? For all they know, I took a voucher and started toward the hotel."

I nodded. "Based on the way Grover was talking, I can't for the life of me think of any reason why anyone would come looking for us. There's no official record that we flew, 'cause he filed no flight plan, and according to him and something about VFR he didn't need to, and, here's the best one—my favorite actually—we, two professionals with probably twenty years of combined college and graduate schooling between us—never told a single living soul we were going." I paused. "It's as if this flight never existed."

She stared at Grover. "It existed all right." She paused, her eyes lifting upward. "I just thought it'd be a quick hop to Denver, outrun the storm, make two new friends in the process, and life would continue."

I cut the line. "Ashley, I'm really sorry." I shook my head. "You should be somewhere getting a manicure or pedicure or something, getting ready for a rehearsal dinner."

"Don't." She shook her head. "Don't beat yourself up over good intentions. I was glad you offered." She stared around her. "Not so much now, but was then." She laid her head back. "I was scheduled to go with my girlfriends to the spa and get a massage. You know one of those hot rocks deals? Instead I'm lying on ice with only one rock . . ." She nodded at her friend behind me. "And no heat. Somewhere out there is a dress with no girl and a groom with no bride." She shook her head. "Do you have any idea how much I paid for that dress?"

"It'll be waiting on you when you get there. Him, too." I held the cup to her lips, and she sipped a final time, finishing off twenty-four ounces. "Your sense of humor is a gift."

"Well . . . would you think it funny if I told you I had to pee?"

"From a certain point of view, that's good." I looked at the bag and her immobility. "From another, it's not."

"Which way are we looking at it?"

"We're looking at it from whatever way lets you go without putting pressure on that leg." I looked around. "What I wouldn't give for a catheter."

"Oh, no, let's don't. Those things give me the creeps. That part of me is not an innie, it's an out-only sort of thing."

I grabbed a Nalgene bottle out of my pack and laid it next to her. "All right, here's the deal."

"I'm not going to go like this, am I?"

"It's better than the alternative, and you get to stay right there, but I've got to help." I pulled out my Swiss Army knife and opened the blade. "I'm going to finish slitting your pantsuit on up to the side of your hip. That way, while you're lying there, you can lay it over you. Then, since there's about twelve feet of snow below you, I'm going to dig a hole beneath your butt big enough for my hand and this bottle. Then we're going to ease your underwear out of the way and you're gonna go in this bottle."

"You're right, I don't like this."

"We need to measure your urine output, and I need to see if there's any blood in it."

"Blood?"

"Internal injuries."

"Don't you think I have enough of those?"

"What, injuries?"

She nodded.

"Yes, but we need to make sure."

I slit her pants, pulled them aside, dug out the snow beneath her, held the bottle in place, and she used her one healthy arm to lift herself slightly, without changing the position of her leg. She looked at me. "Can I go?"

I nodded. She went.

She shook her head. "This has got to be one of the more embarrassing moments I've ever shared with another human being."

"Given that I blend orthopedics and emergency medicine, there are few days that go by that I don't study several people's urine. Even inserting the catheter."

She winced, stopping the flow.

"You okay?"

She nodded. "Just my leg." She relaxed and started again. The sound of a rush of liquid filling the empty bottle rose from beneath her. After a second she said, "Your fingers are cold."

"If it makes you feel any better, my fingers are too cold to feel anything."

"Gee, that's a relief."

I tried to deflect her discomfort. "Most of the folks I see in the ER have suffered some trauma, meaning an accident which usually means a substantial impact which means internal injuries which can mean blood in their urine."

She looked at me. "Are you trying to make me feel better?"

I pulled up on the bottle and studied the color. "Yep."

She looked at me, and then at the bottle. "That's a lot of pee."

"Yeah, and the color's good too."

"I don't know if I've ever had someone comment on the color of my pee before. I'm not quite sure how to take it."

I helped her dress, slid the sleeping bag back underneath her, and then covered her up. The process of doing so brought her skin into contact with mine. And while I was acting as her doctor, her nakedness, her total vulnerability, was not lost on me.

I thought of Rachel.

By the time we got it all finished, she was shivering and I felt like someone had stabbed me with a stiletto in the ribs. I lay down, breathing heavily.

She spoke down at me. "You taken anything for the pain?"

I shook my head. "No."

"Why not?"

"To be honest, if you think you're hurting now, just give it three or four days. I've only got enough Advil to get you through a week. After that you're on your own."

She nodded. "I like the way you're thinking, Doc."

"I've got a few prescription-strength narcotics somewhere in that pack, but I thought I'd save them for tonight when you can't sleep."

"You almost sound as if you've done this type of thing before."

"Rachel and I love to hike. One of the things we've learned is that while you may have a plan and a hope for what you'll do or how far you might go in a given day, conditions will determine what you do and how far you actually go. Hence, it pays to be prepared—while not carrying so much weight you can't move."

She eyed the hole in the snow where my pack was buried. "Got any red wine in there?"

"No, but I could make you a gin and tonic if you'd like."

"That'd be great." She eyed her leg. "Tell me about this contraption on my leg."

"Amongst doctors, orthopedists are known as the carpenters. Afraid that's true of me. Good news is this brace is rather effective. Or at least will be for the short term. You can't move around, you're stuck right here or wherever I move you to, but it will keep you from moving it some way you shouldn't and will help protect it. If the pressure gets too tight around your thigh or calf, let me know and I'll loosen it."

She nodded. "Right now, it's throbbing like somebody hit it with a hammer."

I lifted the top of the sleeping bag off her leg and repacked the snow beneath the break and around the side. "I'm going to keep doing this for several days. It'll speed recovery and help anesthetize the pain. Only problem is you're going to be cold."

"Going to be?"

I screwed the cap on the Nalgene bottle and started crawling toward daylight. "I'm going to take a look around and empty this bottle."

"Good. I'm going to clean up a bit around here, maybe order a pizza or something."

"I like pepperoni."

"Anchovies?"

"Never touch them."

"Got it."

I crawled out of the fuselage, or what was left of it, under the wing, around a tree, and into the sunlight. The temperature was probably in the single digits, but I had been expecting worse. I've had people tell me that a dry cold isn't quite as bad as a humid cold. But in my book, cold is cold. And nine degrees is nine degrees. Or whatever it was.

I took one step off the packed snow where the plane had landed, and my foot submerged all the way to my groin. The impact shook my chest and started me coughing. I tried not to scream in pain, but I'm afraid I wasn't very successful.

Ashley's voice rose up out of the plane. "You okay?"

"Yeah. Just wishing I had some snowshoes."

I dumped the bottle and looked around as best I could. Nothing but snow and mountains. We seemed to be on some sort of plateau with a few higher peaks to my left, but most everything else spread out below and before us. That meant we were higher than I thought. Maybe 11,500. No wonder it was tough to breathe.

I'd seen enough. I crawled back in and collapsed on the shelf next to her.

"Well?" she asked.

"Nothing."

"Really, you can tell me the truth. I can handle it. Just give it to me straight."

"Grover was right. More Mars than Earth."

"No, seriously. Don't sugarcoat it. I'm used to people shooting straight with me."

I stared up at her where she sat, eyes closed. Waiting.

"It's . . . beautiful. Can't wait for you to see it. The view is . . . panoramic. Unlike anything you've ever seen. One in a million. I've got two lawn chairs set up, and a little guy with umbrella-drinks will be back around in a few minutes. Had to go back and get some ice."

She relaxed and laid her head back. The first ear-to-ear grin I'd seen since we'd been in the snow. "For a minute there I was worried. Glad to hear it's not as bad as I thought."

Somewhere in there it struck me that Ashley Knox was one of the stronger human beings I'd ever met. Here she lay, half dead, probably in more pain than most people have felt in their entire lives, in the process of missing her own wedding, not to mention the fact that we had no probable chance of rescue. If we got out of here, it'd be up to us. Most people would be panicked, despondent, illogical at this point, but somehow she could laugh. What's more, she made me laugh. And that's something I actually hadn't done in a long while.

I was spent. I needed food and I needed rest, but I couldn't get food without rest. I put together a plan.

"We need food, but I'm in no shape to go find it. I'll go tomorrow. Right now I'm going to try and build us a fire without melting the cave around us, keep feeding us both warm water, and try and conserve my energy."

"I like the fire idea."

"Rescue people will tell you never to leave the site of a crash. And that's true, but we're high, real high, breathing less than half the oxygen we're used to, and we both need it to heal. Especially you. Tomorrow . . . or the next day, I'm going to start thinking about getting to a lower elevation. Maybe try and do some scouting. Right now . . ." I turned the mounting screws for the GPS and unplugged it from the dash. "I'm going to try and get a fix on where we are while this thing still has life in it."

She stared at me. "How do you know to do all this? I mean, what if you didn't?"

"When I was a kid, my dad realized I could run faster than most. He took that ability and turned it into his passion, his *raison d'etre* he called it, and I grew to hate him for it, because no time was ever fast enough and he was always measuring me with this stick that looked an awful lot like a stopwatch. Once Rachel and I were on our own, we gravitated to the mountains. I had, have, good lungs and pretty good legs, so when we could get away from class or the track, we started buying up gear and we spent the weekends in the mountains. Maybe I learned a thing or two. We both did."

"I'd like to meet her sometime."

I smiled. " 'Course . . . there was Boy Scouts, too."

"You're a Boy Scout?"

I nodded. "The one freedom my dad gave me away from him. Figured it was training that I needed that he didn't have to give me. He'd drop me off, pick me up."

"How far'd you get?"

I shrugged.

She lowered her head, gave me a disbelieving look. "You're one of those Hawks, or Ospreys or . . ."

"Something like that."

"Come on, what's it called?"

"Eagle."

"Yeah . . . that's it. Eagle Scout."

I got the sense that talking took her mind off the pain.

She lay back and murmured, "Guess we're about to find out if you really earned all those patches."

"Yep." I hit the power button, and the GPS unit flickered.

A wrinkle appeared between her eyes. "Did they offer an electronics badge?"

I tapped the unit. "No, but I think it's just cold. You mind warming it up inside your bag?"

She pulled back the sleeping bag, and I set it gently on her lap. "Electronics don't really like cold. Interferes with their circuits. Warming it up helps."

"Vince—my fiancé—wouldn't know the first thing about all this. If he had been in this plane, he'd be looking for the nearest Starbucks and cussing the fact that there was no cell service." She closed her eyes. "What I wouldn't give for a cup of coffee."

"I might can help with that."

"Don't tell me you have coffee."

"I have three addictions. Running. Mountains. And good hot coffee. And not necessarily in that order."

"I'll pay you a thousand dollars for one cup."

The Jetboil is seriously one of the greatest advancements in hiking technology, next to the compass. Maybe ever. 'Course, the down sleeping bag is pretty good too. I scooped snow into the Jetboil and clicked it on while I dug through my pack looking for my Ziploc bag of coffee. The good news was that I found it. The bad news was that there wasn't much left. Maybe a few days at best, and if we were conservative.

I slid the bag out of my backpack. Ashley saw it.

"Ben Payne . . . will you take a credit card?"

"A fellow coffee-lover. It's amazing what we value when we're at our lowest."

Jetboil makes an accessory that allows me to convert the canister into a French press. It only cost a few dollars, but I've used it a hundred times and always marveled at its simplicity and how well it works. The water boiled, I measured and dumped in the coffee, let it steep, and then poured her a cup.

She cradled it in her good hand, holding it just below her nose. The smile was genuine. It looked like for a brief moment she was able to push back on the world that was pushing down so hard on her. I was starting to learn that she used humor to ward off the pain. I'd seen other people do it. Usually something in their past had emotionally wounded them, and so they used humor or sarcasm to mask it. Take their mind off it.

Her pain was growing. Ramping up. I only had a couple of Percocet, but she'd need one tonight. And probably the next several nights. It'd been six hours, so with numb fingers, I fumbled with the Advil top, poured four into my palm, and handed them to her. She swallowed and then hovered above her cup.

She whispered, marking the moment. "It's amazing the moment a cup of coffee will allow you." She passed the cup to me. I sipped. And she was right. It was good.

She nodded at her attaché. "If you reach in there, you'll find a bag of snack mix I bought at the Natural Snack store in the terminal."

Filled with dried pineapple, apricots, and various types of nuts, it probably weighed a pound. I handed it to her. We both poured a handful and chewed slowly.

I nodded. "I believe this is the best snack mix I've ever tasted."

I gave the dog a handful. He sniffed it, then inhaled it, wagging his tail and begging for more. He leaned against me and put his paws on my chest, sniffing the air.

"How do you tell a dog that he's not getting any more?"

She laughed. "Good luck with that."

I gave him one more small handful, and when he returned a third time I pushed him off me and said, "No." Dejected, he turned his back on me and curled up at the foot of Ashley's sleeping bag.

We sat in the silence for a long time, drinking the entire pot.

When we finished, she said, "Save the grounds. We can use them twice and then, if we're desperate, we can chew on them."

"You're serious about your coffee." I touched the power button, and the GPS flickered to life. "You got any kind of pad or paper in your briefcase?"

She nodded. "Should be right in front."

I pulled out a yellow legal pad and a pencil, found the screen that showed our location, and tried to copy the map as best I could. Including the coordinates down to the minute. Once I had a relatively detailed drawing on par with a kindergartner, I said, "Be right back."

I climbed up and out of our hole and compared the picture on the screen with that before my eyes, marking mountains and making mental notes of mountain crests and where they landed on the compass. That way, I knew north from south. Being lost is one thing. Staying lost is another. I might not have known where we were, but I could pick a direction and stick with it. I also knew the batteries wouldn't last forever, and whatever I could copy now would pay dividends in the days ahead. The more time passed, and the more our predicament sank in, the more concerned I became. Things were bad all around.

"YOU WANT THE GOOD news or the bad?"

"Good."

"I know where we are."

"And the bad?"

"Our elevation is 11,652 feet, give or take three feet, the nearest logging road is over thirty miles and something like five mountain passes"—I pointed—"that way. We're nearly fifty miles from the nearest thing that looks like civilization or a hard road. And to top it off, most of the snow out there is higher than I am tall."

She bit her lip, and her eyes wandered the white-walled cave. She crossed her arms. "You're going to have to leave me."

"I'm not leaving anybody."

"I can see the writing on the wall here. You can't get me out. You have a better chance alone. Give me the coffee, put those legs to work, and take my coordinates with you. Bring a helicopter on your way back."

"Ashley . . ."

"Okay, but you've got to recognize that it is a distinct possibility." Her eyes narrowed. "Don't you?"

"Look, we need a fire, we need some food, and we need to lose a few thousand feet in elevation, then we'll talk about what's next. One crisis at a time."

"But . . ." She was strong. She had toughness that matters. The kind you can't get in school. Her tone changed. "Let's keep the truth on the table, where it belongs. It is a possibility."

"I'm not leaving anybody."

The dog noticed my change in tone. He stood, walked up next to Ashley, and dug his head beneath her hand. He still hadn't forgiven me since the trail mix episode. She scratched his ears, and his stomach growled. He looked over his shoulder at me, then slowly laid his head back down.

"I heard you. I know you're hungry."

We sat, listening to the wind pick up and rattle my tarp. I lay back into my sleeping bag, getting warm. I looked at her. "Do you do that with all your friends?"

"What's that?"

"Prepare them for the worst."

She nodded. "If the worst is a possibility, then you keep it on the table. Don't hide from it. Don't run. It can happen. And if and when it does, you need to have thought about it ahead of time. That way you're not crushed when your worst thought becomes your reality."

I Jetboiled more snow and made us both sip to keep our fluids up. If nothing else, it would help keep the hunger at bay. We napped on and off through the afternoon. The trail mix had taken the edge off our hunger, but food was a real problem and I knew it. I couldn't function without it, and I needed energy to trudge through waist-deep snow to find it. Tomorrow would not be easy. Maybe the toughest day yet. The pain in my chest was spreading.

Night fell, as did the cold. With dusk leaving I crawled out, shimmied beneath the snow and the lower limbs of a pudgy evergreen, gathered several handfuls of dead pine needles, twigs, and branches, and piled them up beneath the wing. Doing this took three trips and left me gasping and clutching my rib cage for support. Ashley watched me with narrowed eyes.

Grover's door was a single piece of some sort of sheet metal hanging by a single hinge. Probably didn't weigh ten pounds. I pried it up using my foot, laid it flat beneath the wing, and then piled pine needles and twigs atop it. The problem with a fire in our current location was melting the more or less protective wall around us—not to mention the supportive base below it. The door would keep it out of the melting snow it created, and the cold air outside would keep our cave intact overnight. The temperature had dropped drastically the moment the sun started going down.

I needed a light. I could have used the Jetboil, but I needed to save as much of its butane as I could. Then I remembered Grover's lighter.

I brushed away the snow, slid my hand into his jeans pocket, and fingered out the brass Zippo lighter. I clicked it open, making a sound that reminded me of Dean Martin and John Wayne, and thumbed the wheel. It lit.

"Thank you, Grover."

I turned it in my hand. Years in his pocket had scratched and worn it smooth. I held it up and on one side I saw an engraving. It read: A LAMP UNTO MY PATH.

I lit the end of a twig, let the twig flame grow and climb toward my finger, and then fed it beneath the pine needles. Dead and dry, they caught quickly. Using the empty trail mix bag, I fed the fire, adding larger sticks as the fire popped and crackled and grew in size.

She watched the paper bag turn to ash. "That was good trail mix."

The dog sensed the warmth, walked down to the end of Ashley's sleeping bag, and curled up in a puffy spot some four feet from the flame. The fire was a welcome addition. It improved our general disposition, which had darkened given the absence of food and the slim hope of finding it.

I figured I could go a week and still function without food, provided we had water, but after that I'd be so weak I'd be no good to anyone. Years ago, when I saw that movie *Alive,* it grossed me out. Sitting there staring at Grover, it grossed me out more. I wasn't eating him. Having said that, if all options were honestly on the table, and it meant our living versus our dying, there was always the dog. Problem was, he'd only feed us once. Maybe the first time his size was ever an advantage to him. Had he been a Lab or a Rottweiler, I'd have thought more seriously about it.

WE STARED AT THE FIRE, letting our eyes grow lazy. Ashley broke the silence. "I've been thinking about what to get Vince for a wedding gift. I'm coming up blank. Got any ideas?"

I fed tinder into the fire. "First anniversary. A cabin in the Colorado Rockies. Snowed in." I forced a laugh. "A little like this. We were paying off school loans, didn't have two nickels to rub together, and, like our honeymoon, had agreed on a no-present anniversary."

She laughed. "What'd you get her?"

"A purple orchid."

She nodded. "Ah . . . hence, the orchid and greenhouse thing."

I nodded.

"I like the way you talk about your wife. Sounds like you 'do' life together." She laid her head back. "In the course of my job, I work with or meet a lot of people who don't. Who treat their spouse like a roommate. Somebody they cross paths with, split the mortgage with, maybe have kids with. Two people bent on individuality. It's refreshing to hear you talk about her. How'd you two meet?"

I rubbed my eyes. "Tomorrow. We need to try and get some sleep." I extended my hand. "Here, take this."

She held out her palm. "What is it?"

"Percocet."

"What's in it?"

"A combination of Oxycotin and Tylenol."

"How many do you have?"

"Three."

"Why don't you take one?"

"I'm not in that much pain, and you will be come tomorrow and the next day. Go ahead. It'll help you sleep. And up here—where the air is half as thin—taking one is like taking two."

"Meaning?"

"You'll feel the effects more."

"Will it help my headache?"

"Probably not. That's the altitude . . . mixed with the impact of the crash. But give that a day or so."

"Do you have a headache?"

"Yes."

She rubbed her shoulders and the back of her neck. "I'm starting to feel really stiff."

I nodded. "Whiplash."

She swallowed, and her eyes fell to Grover. He sat, frozen,

about five feet from the end of her bag, mostly covered in snow. "Can we do anything about him?"

"I need to bury him, but I can't move him. Moving me is tough enough right now."

"When you breathe, you sound like you're in a lot of pain."

"Get some rest. I'll be right outside."

"One favor?"

"Sure."

"I need to go again."

"No worries."

This time was faster, still no red tint, and there was a good bit of fluid—all good signs. I repacked snow around her leg, and she said, "You know, you can stop doing that anytime you want. I'm freezing."

I felt her toes and the pulse in her ankle. "Hang in there. If I let your leg warm up too much, we'll fall behind the pain curve and . . ." I shook my head. "You don't want that. Not out here." I dug out some snow on her good side, creating a flat spot long enough for me, and laid my bag down alongside hers. "The temperature is dropping, and if we can share body heat, we'll both sleep better and live longer."

She nodded. "What time is it?"

"A little after six."

She lay back down, staring up. "I should be walking down the aisle."

I knelt next to her. Our breath was making smoke. "Ever been married before?"

She shook her head, her eyes tearing up.

I held out my sleeve, and she leaned forward, wiping her tears on it. I checked the stitches on her head and eye and then pulled her cap gently back over her ears. Her eyes were sunken, not quite as swollen, and her face had lost some of its puffiness.

"You will. We are going to get off this mountain, and you are going to have your wedding–just a little later than you planned."

She smiled and closed her eyes. It was little consolation.

"You'll look beautiful in white."

"How do you know?"

"We had a small wedding. . . ."

"How small?"

"Me, Rachel, and her folks."

"You're right, that is small."

"But the moment that door opened . . . and she stood there, that white dress sweeping the ground . . . It's a picture a groom never forgets."

She turned her head.

"Sorry. Thought I was helping."

An hour later, when her breathing had slowed, I crawled out and pulled the recorder from my pocket. The sky had leaned down, fire and crimson to a sea of white etched with veins of silver, and was threatening to kiss the earth just as soon as the last rays of sun disappeared and tucked themselves behind the west. The dog followed and walked around me. He was light enough to walk on top of the frozen snow, but he didn't like it. He walked a few circles, lifted his leg next to a small tree, kicked some snow behind him like a charging bull, and then stared off across the plateau and mountaintops. After two or three seconds he shook his head, sneezed, and disappeared back down the hole to curl up with Ashley.

I pressed RECORD.

CHAPTER EIGHT

Long day here. End of day three, I think. We're alive, but staying that way is another thing. Ashley is hanging in there, but I don't know how or how long. If I had all the breaks and pains she had, I'd be curled up in the fetal position, begging somebody to thump me over the head or shoot me with enough morphine to numb a cow. She hasn't complained once.

Good news? I know where we are. Bad news? It's a long way from anywhere in terrain that's tough even with two good legs. Nearly improbable with one bad one. I haven't told her that. I know . . . I will.

I don't really know how we're going to get out of here. I can make some sort of stretcher out of pieces of the wing, but how far can I drag her on that? We need to find someplace lower where we can rest up either until help comes, which I know it's not, or until I can walk us out of here. And we need food. It's been forty-eight hours since I ate anything other than some snack mix.

Not to mention the dog, whose name I still can't remember. I know he's hungry, 'cause he's chewing on tree limbs. He spends all his time shivering. And he doesn't like the snow. He walks around like it hurts his feet.

I think I upset Ashley. I didn't mean to. I was trying to cheer her up. Maybe I'm out of practice.

Speaking of practice . . . you ever added up all the miles we ran together? Me neither.

Seems like every time we ran, you'd ask me about your stride, and I'd act serious like I was really paying attention, but in truth, I couldn't take my eyes off your legs. I figure you knew that too. I loved running behind you.

When I look back on us, on our beginnings, I am reminded that we did something we loved and shared it. We never had to think of a reason to hang out. And nothing ever divided us.

Once you got your driver's license, you'd drive to the beach, tap on my window at 4:00 a.m., and we'd take off running down the beach. Long runs. Ten to twelve miles. What we called LSD. Long-slow-distance. Where time didn't matter. No stopwatch. No measurement of our success or failure. If we didn't run on the beach, I'd pick you up at the end of your drive and we'd run the bridges downtown. Over Main Street, through the Landing, back over the Acosta, around the fountain and do it all over again. If one of us was tired, maybe fighting shin splints or just needing a break, we'd drive through Dunkin' Donuts, order two coffees, and tour the town with the top down.

I think that's when I taught you how to drive a clutch, and you gave me whiplash. Okay, so maybe it wasn't that bad, but you did wear out my clutch. And my neck was sore. But I'd gladly teach you all over again.

There was that Saturday morning. We were coming back up the beach after a long run. This kid on a surfboard out to our right caught a wave, the nose of his board dipped, and he started tumbling. He washed up onshore just in front of us. The two pieces of his board surfaced a few moments later. His forehead was cut, blood everywhere, shoulder out of socket, and he was disoriented and nauseous. I sat him down and put pressure on his head, he pointed to his house, and you ran to get his folks while I sat with him, helped him set his shoulder. When you returned, he was laughing, talking about what new board he was going to get. His folks thanked us, walked him home, and you turned to me, shading your eyes from the sun. You said it like you'd known it all your life. "You're going to make a great doctor someday."

"What?"

"You." You tapped me in the chest. "You're going to make a great doctor."

I'd never thought about it. To be honest, I'd never thought about doing anything other than getting out of my dad's house. But the moment you said it, something in me clicked.

"How do you know?"

"The way you care for people. Your"—you made quotation notes with your fingers—"bedside manner."

"What are you talking about?"

You pointed at the kid walking away. "Look at him. When I left, he was about to throw up. Now he's laughing, about to buy a new board. Can't wait to get back in the water. That's you, Ben. Something about the way you talk . . . soothes people."

"It does?"

A nod. "I should know."

That was the first time I clued in to the fact that you saw potential in the mundane. The insignificant. The ordinary.

The second time occurred when I came to see you at work. Volunteering after school as a candy striper at the children's hospital. Bald, sickly kids strewn everywhere. Oxygen tanks. Wheelchairs. Messy sheets. Uncomfortable smells. Disconcerting sounds. When I found you, you were rubber-gloved, holding a bedpan, laughing with the little girl who moments before was sitting on top of it. You were all smiles. So was she.

I saw sickness and misery tucked away in every room. Not you. You saw possibility and promise. Even in the improbable.

Somewhere in my junior year, I looked around and you had become my best friend. You taught me what it meant to smile. To live with a heart that felt alive. With every mile, you dug down into the quarry that had become me and chipped away at the scars and rocks piled up around my soul. You were the first to put together the pieces of me. When it came to love, you taught me to crawl, walk, run, and then, somewhere on the beach, beneath the moon and running into a head-wind, clipping away five-minute miles, you turned to me, cut the ties that held my wings, and taught me to fly. My feet barely touching the ground.

Staring out across this ice-capped landscape with nothing but the impossible staring back at me, I am reminded.

I see what is. You see what could be.

I need to get inside. It's getting colder. I miss you.

TWICE DURING THE NIGHT I repacked snow around Ashley's leg. She never woke, but she moaned a lot and talked in her sleep. I had been up a few hours by the time she woke with what sounded like a painful cry. Her eyes were slits.

"How do you feel?"

Her voice sounded thick. "Like I've been hit by a Mack truck." With that, she rolled on her side and vomited. She did that for several minutes. It was mostly dry heaves and stomach acid. Finally she sat back. Trying to catch her breath. She was in a lot of pain.

I wiped her mouth and held the cup while she sipped. "I've got to get some Advil in you, but I doubt your empty stomach is going to like it much."

Eyes closed, she nodded.

I added fuel to the fire and clicked on the Jetboil.

The smell of coffee opened her eyes. She was tired. Her energy was gone. "How long you been up?"

"Couple of hours. I did some looking around. While I like our cave, we need to get out of this hole. Nobody will ever see us, and it prevents me from lighting any kind of signal fire."

She eyed the contraptions to my left. "You make those?"

I'd taken the netting off the backs of the seats, disassembled the wire and metal frames using Grover's Leatherman, and designed something that looked sort of like showshoes. The frames were longer than they were wide, wider in the front and tapered in the rear. I double-folded the netting, stretched it over the frames, and attached the squares using several loops of Grover's fly line. They came together well. I held them up. "Snowshoes."

"If you say so."

"Most mornings during scheduled surgery, or late nights when an ambulance rolls in or LifeFlight lands, I'm faced with something far more challenging than a pair of these."

"Are you bragging?"

"No, I'm just saying that my day job prepares me for the unusual and unexpected."

I handed her one, and she turned it, studying it. She handed it back. "I think any movement at all sounds painful, but I'm game to get out of here. A change of scenery would be nice."

I poured coffee and handed it to her. "Go easy on that. We've got about two days left."

"You're not expecting anyone, are you? I mean, seriously?"

"No. I'm not."

She nodded and breathed over the plastic cup.

"I'm going to leave you for a couple of hours. Walk around a bit."

I dug Grover's flare gun out of the plastic box in the back where he kept his fishing tackle, loaded it, and handed it to Ashley. "If you need me, cock this and squeeze this. And when you do, make sure it's pointed out that hole. Otherwise you're liable to set yourself and this whole place on fire. There's still some gas in the tanks in the wing.

"I should be gone most of the day. If I'm not back at dark,

don't worry. I'm taking my sleeping bag, bivy sack, emergency blanket, couple other things. I'll be fine. Out here, conditions determine most everything. They can change quickly, and if they get bad, I might have to hunker down and wait it out. I'm going to try and find some sort of food and an alternate shelter or someplace I can build one."

"You know how to do all this?"

"I know how to do some of it. What I don't know, I'll learn."

I unstrapped Grover's compound bow from its case in the tail of the plane, along with one of his fly rods, his vest, and one of the reels stuffed in it.

"You can fly-fish?"

"I've done it once."

"How'd you do?"

"You mean did I catch anything?"

She nodded.

"Nope."

"I was afraid you were going to say that." She eyed the bow. "How about that contraption?"

"This I've actually done."

"So you can hit stuff with it?"

"Used to."

"You think your ribs will let you pull it back?"

"Don't know. Haven't tried yet."

"So . . . you're winging it?"

"Basically."

"Before you go, will you help me with something?"

Ashley went to the bathroom, and then I melted more water and got her covered up.

"Will you hand me my case?" She pulled out her cell phone. "Just for kicks." She turned it on, but the cold had killed it, too.

I shrugged. "You could play solitaire." I pointed at my small backpack that doubles as my briefcase. "You're welcome to use my computer, but I doubt it'll turn on. And even if it does, I wouldn't give it very long."

"Got any books?"

A shrug. "Not much of a reader. Guess you're alone with your thoughts—and the dog." I scratched his ears. He had grown comfortable with us and had quit trying to lick Grover on the lips. "Can you remember his name?"

She shook her head. "No."

"Me either. I think we should call him Napoleon."

"Why?"

"Just look at him. If ever an animal had a Napoleon complex, it's him. He's got the attitude of an angry bullmastiff shoved into a package the size of a loaf of bread. He's the poster dog for 'it's not the size of the dog in the fight, but the size of the fight in the dog.' "

She nodded. "Can we do anything for his feet?"

I looked at the backseat that was leaning over, broken off its hinges, half-deflated looking after I'd robbed it of part of its frame. I opened the Leatherman and cut four squares of the vinyl covering. A half inch of foam padding was stuck to the back. I cut slits in the corners, fed a piece of fly line through each, and tied them around Napoleon's feet. He looked at me like I'd lost my mind. He sniffed them, stood up, walked around on the snow, then leaned against me and licked my face.

"Okay, I love you, too."

Ashley smiled. "I think you made a friend."

I held out my hand. "The GPS."

She slid it from beneath her sleeping bag, and I slid it into the inside pocket in my jacket. Lastly, I unzipped a small pocket on the side of my backpack, grabbed my compass, and hung it around my neck. It's lensatic, or fluid-filled. Rachel gave it to me years ago.

Ashley saw it and asked, "What's that?"

I palmed it. The edges were smooth. Some of the green had given way to the dull aluminum beneath. "Compass."

"Looks used."

I shouldered my backpack, zipped up my jacket, pulled on my gloves, and lifted the bow. "Remember . . . when it starts getting dark and I'm not back, remind yourself that I am coming back. It may be tomorrow morning, but I'll be here. Coffee date, you and me. Deal?"

She nodded. I knew when it got dark and I hadn't yet arrived, she'd start getting concerned, and her worries would populate in the shadows. Darkness does that. It speaks fears that, left alone, remain unspoken, yet real.

"Even if it's tomorrow morning?"

She nodded again. I pulled out the Advil bottle.

"Take four every six hours. And don't forget to feed the fire." I crawled out of our den, and Napoleon followed. I knelt to strap on the snowshoes, and he climbed on me. "I need you to stay here and take care of her. Okay? Keep her company. I think she's lonely, and it's not a very good day. She's supposed to be on her honeymoon now."

Ashley hollered up out of the wreckage. "Yeah . . . someplace warm where some guy named Julio or Françoise wearing white linen pants and a bronze tan brings me tall drinks decorated with umbrellas."

I turned and began walking up the mountain.

CHAPTER NINE

My senior year, state championships. You watched me win the 400 in a new state record, breaking the fifty-second barrier. We'd set a new state record in the 4 x 400, I'd won the two-mile just seconds off a national record, and I was standing at the start line of the mile. They had rearranged the meet, holding the mile last to garner enough media attention. Somebody had started a rumor that I could run four minutes. Coaches from around the country were standing around Dad, patting him on the back. At last count, I had over twenty Division I scholarship offers. Full rides.

I had my piles, and Dad had his. His prized pile centered around MBAs in finance. "They'll pay for five years of education. Get your BA in two and a half. Then your MBA. Once you're out of school, you can write your own ticket. With your drive, you could run my agency."

I wanted nothing to do with him, his markets, or his agency. And I knew where he could stick it, I just never told him.

You had two Division I offers, and truth be told, I was more proud of yours than mine.

I could see his face out of the corner of my eye. The vein had popped out on the side of his head. Just above his right temple. Sweat was pouring off him. I'd run 4:04 several mornings on the beach, but that was on sand into a partial headwind. He was sure I could run

3:58. Toe on the line, I was spent. My legs were jelly. I'd be lucky to run 4:05. You hung on the fence. Hands clutched.

The gun sounded.

After the first lap, we were still together. A tight group. Some guy from down south was trying to elbow me out. I knew if I was going to do anything, I had to get away from these guys. By the start of the third lap, I was all alone. The organizers had offered a pacer, but Dad had declined. "He'll earn this himself." Three laps in, and I was on pace. I had it.

And I knew I had it.

People in the stands were on their feet. Screaming. I remember a lady shaking a milk jug filled with half a dozen pennies. Dad was stone-faced. Granite with inflatable lungs. A hundred meters to go, and I was looking at 3:58, maybe 3:57.

I watched him watching me. Everything I'd ever worked for was coming true in those few seconds. You were screaming at the top of your lungs. Jumping three feet off the ground. Watching you, watching him, it struck me that no matter what time I turned in, it wouldn't be good enough for him. National record or not. He would always assume that I had not tried hard enough. That I could always run faster.

Something about his Rushmore face cut something loose in me. I eased up. Slowed. I watched the clock roll through 3:53. Then 3:57. My official time would be 4:00:37. The place went crazy. I'd done something no other Florida runner had ever done. Four-year state champion in twelve events headed to the national championships and, because I also carried a 4.0 GPA, any college I chose.

I stood on the track, swarmed by my teammates. But I didn't care. The only face I wanted to see was yours. And then you found me.

I never saw my dad. I'm pretty sure I had another five seconds in my legs. And I'm pretty sure he knew that too.

We were going out. The whole team. To celebrate. I came home to change. We walked in. He was sitting in his chair. An empty crystal glass on his thigh. The bottle half empty next to him. Brown liquor. He seldom drank. Considered it something lesser, weak people did.

You peered around me. "Mr. Payne, did you see?"

He stood, pointed his finger in my face, poked me in the chest. Spit gathered in the corner of his mouth. A vein throbbed beneath his eye. "Nobody ever gave me nothing. You son of a . . ."

He shook his head, balled his fist, and swung. The blow broke my nose. Felt like a blood-filled balloon had exploded inside my face. By then, I was six feet two, two inches taller than him, and I knew if I swung back, I might never stop, but when I stood up, he was raising his hand over you. And judging by the look on his face, he blamed you for me.

I caught his hand, spun him, and threw him into the sliding glass door. Tempered glass, it shattered into a million square pieces. He lay on the deck, staring at me.

You drove me to the hospital, where they set my nose, scrubbed the blood off my face and neck, and congratulated me. One of the orderlies handed me the front page of the paper, covered with a full-page picture of me, and asked for my autograph.

Around midnight we drove to a Village Inn, a twenty-four-hour pancake place, and ordered one piece of French silk pie and two forks. Our celebration. Then I drove you home, where your mom met us and we all sat at the kitchen table talking back through the meet. You sat at the table, sleep in your eyes, wrapped in a terrycloth robe and your leg touching mine. Your legs had touched mine a hundred times at the track or in the car or anywhere. But this . . . this was different. This was intentional. This was not Rachel the runner's leg touching mine, this was Rachel the girl's leg touching mine.

Big difference.

I got home around one. A few hours later, 4:55 a.m. arrived and Dad did not. He never woke me again. I lay awake. Listening for footsteps. Wondering what to do. Who to be. I couldn't answer that, so I dressed and went for a walk on the beach—watching the sun come up over the shrimp boats. I walked through lunch. On toward dinner. The sun was falling when I quit walking at the jetties in Mayport. Some twenty miles north of where I'd started. I climbed on the rocks and then climbed out toward the end of the jetties. Some might say that's dangerous.

Your voice sounded behind me. "What're you running from?"

"How'd you get out here?"

"Walked."

"How'd you find me?"

"Followed the footprints."

"Kind of dangerous, don't you think?"

You smiled. "Knew I wouldn't be alone."

You climbed up another rock, fiddler crabs scurrying beneath you, stood, and pulled me to you. You lifted your glasses. Costa Del Mars. I'd given them to you. Your eyes were red. You'd been crying. Arms crossed, you stared out across the water, hands hidden inside the long gray sleeves of your sweatshirt. "You think they'll care that we cut class?"

"I don't." I palmed away a tear. "You've been crying."

You nodded.

"Why?"

You pounded my chest, then leaned against me."'Cause I don't want it to end."

"What?"

Your eyes welled again. A tear hung on your chin. I brushed it gently with the top of my hand.

"Us, dummy." You placed your hand flat against my chest. "Seeing you . . . every day."

"Oh . . . that."

Maybe that's what really had me walking up the beach. And in over twenty miles, I'd found no easy answer. We were both about to hurt a whole lot.

High school love was one thing, but choosing a college because of that high school love was something everyone cautioned you and me against. Remember? Sometimes I wish we'd listened to them. Then I shake my head and think. Not so. I don't blame us. I'd do it again. Honest, I would. If I could fly back in time, I'd make the same choice.

But . . . sometimes I wonder.

CHAPTER TEN

The storm had dumped three feet of snow. All fresh powder. Without the shoes I'd have been thigh-deep, wet, and the cold would be stinging my legs. Wouldn't be long before they were numb. I made a mental note that if things went bad and I started tumbling, don't lose the snowshoes. Given that, I stopped, cut two tethers or cords, and tied one end to the back of each snowshoe and the other end around each ankle. Sort of like a surfer's leash.

Despite the fact that we needed to lose elevation, I first needed to gain it to get a bird's-eye view of where we were in relation to everything else. Once I got a better view, I could turn on the GPS and start relating it to what I saw. The air was thin, the surface was covered with a slick sheet of ice, I had to keep taking off and putting on the snowshoes, and I was much weaker than I expected. I climbed through lunch and into the afternoon before I summited a small ridgeline that rose up over the plateau, maybe a thousand feet above the crash site. It was late afternoon by the time I got the view I'd been hoping for.

What I saw did not soothe me.

I was hoping for any sign of civilization. A light. Smoke from a fireplace. A structure of some sort. Anything to give me a direction. A reason for hope. I turned, scanning the horizon, and the truth set in.

We were in the middle of nowhere. I saw nothing that was man-made.

It was a desolate, snow-covered landscape, etched with jagged peaks and impossible routes that stretched sixty or seventy miles in every direction. Look up *remote* in the dictionary and you'd see a picture of me standing on that rock. I turned on the GPS and oriented myself, confirming what my eyes told me, using the compass to confirm the directions and degrees the electronic unit was telling me. The only surprise was the number of lakes and streams showing on the screen. There were hundreds. Maybe a thousand. All had to be frozen this time of year, but I noted the few that were closest and logged that away as tomorrow's investigation.

In the far southeast corner of the screen I saw a dim trail suggesting a logging road or snowmobile trail. It wound up or down a pass and between two mountain ranges. I stared off in that direction, but saw nothing but treetops and jagged rock. I oriented the GPS with the surrounding peaks and took a reading with my compass. At this distance, a miscalculation of only one degree can set you off course by several miles. I was in the process of zooming in when the screen on the GPS flickered to black. I tapped it on the side, as if that would do any good, but it was dead. The cold had killed it and drained the battery. I closed my eyes, tried to remember everything I'd seen on the screen, and added that to the sketch I'd made yesterday outside the wreck. It was incomplete and lacking, but better than a blank slate.

I started back after dark. I was tired, and all I wanted to do was lie down and sleep, but the thought of Ashley wide-eyed and worried kept me putting one foot in front of the other. No matter how much I tried to prepare her for my late arrival, I knew as soon as the sun went down she'd started listening for my return. And every minute that passed would feel like an hour. Waiting for somebody does that. It turns minutes to hours, hours to days, and days to several lifetimes.

CHAPTER ELEVEN

For a minute I thought we'd had our last conversation. This thing wouldn't turn on. No green light. No red light. No nothing. For the last five minutes I've been pressing every button it has. Jiggled the batteries, even pulled them out and turned them around. Finally I slid it inside my shirt and pressed it to my chest for several minutes. Warming it slowly.

If this thing had quit . . . I don't know. Not sure how I'd react. In football they call it "piling on." In track we called it "hitting the wall."

I remember calling the track coach and asking him to look at your tapes and your times. He didn't skip a beat. "Would that influence your decision to attend this institution?"

"Yes . . . it would."

I heard some papers shuffling.

"Funny. I just happen to have an extra scholarship lying on my desk."

Just like that.

I look back on college, and I think those were some of the best of days. My dad was out of the picture, and we were free to be us. To grow together. To laugh together. And you found your rhythm and became the runner I knew you could be. I was just glad to have a hand in it.

Our final year in school. Med school on the horizon. My track career coming to a close. Medals hanging on the wall or stuffed in a drawer somewhere. To my knowledge Dad never came to see me run. But, inside me, running had changed. It was no longer my thing. It was our thing. I liked it better that way.

You're the best training partner I've ever had.

Plus, we'd found the Rockies, and that gave us an outlet. Became our thing too.

You'd been quiet a few days. I thought you were busy. Distracted with school or exams or . . . I didn't know you were thinking about us. You and me. Honey, I can't read your mind. Couldn't then. Can't now.

We were home for spring break. Your folks were glad to have you back in the house. Dad had moved to Connecticut to run another firm. Kept the condo in Florida to maintain residency. I had it all to myself. We'd just finished running. The sun was going down. Breeze was picking up. Sweat trickled down your arms. One bead was hanging off the lobe of your left ear.

You sat down, took off your shoes, and let the water roll over your feet. Finally you turned to me. A wrinkle between your eyes. A vein throbbing in your neck and one on your temple. You stiffened. "What's your problem?"

I looked around. "Didn't know I had one."

"Well . . . you do."

"Honey . . . I'm . . ."

You turned away. Rested your elbows on your knees and shook your head. "What have I got to do?"

I tried sitting next to you, and you pushed me away. "What are you talking about?"

You started to cry. "I'm talking about us." You poked me in the chest. "You and me."

"I like us just the way we are. I'm not going anywhere."

"That's just it." You shook your head. "You're about as dumb as a bag of hammers."

"Rachel . . . what are you talking about?"

Tears were pouring down. You stood up, hands on your hips, and stepped back. "I want to get married. You and me. I want you all to myself . . . forever."

"Well, I do too. I mean, I want you."

You crossed your arms. "Ben . . . you got to ask first."

That's when it hit me. "Is that what this is all about?"

You palmed a tear and looked away.

"Honey . . . " I knelt. Held your hand. Waves rolling over my shins.

You started to smile. The minnows were nibbling on your toes. Tiny shells stuck to your skin. Laughter bubbled up. I tried to get the words out, but my tears got in the way.

"Rachel Hunt . . . "

The smile spread across your face.

"I hurt when I'm not with you. I ache in places I didn't know my heart went. I don't know what kind of man I'll be or doctor or husband, and I know I seldom say the words you need to hear, but I know I love you. With all of me. You're the glue that holds me together. Spend forever with me. Marry me? Please . . . "

You wrapped your arms around me, and we fell. The sand and water and foam swallowed us, and you kissed me. Tears and salt and laughter and you were nodding.

That was a good day.

A good memory.

CHAPTER TWELVE

It was midnight by the time I got back to the plane. Napoleon heard me, poked his head out, and then disappeared again. The temperature had dropped back down to single digits, which meant my pant legs were frozen. I was cold down to my bones. I snapped off some dead limbs, shook off the snow, and carried them back into the hole. The snow was starting again. I'd only peed once the entire day, and even then not much, which told me I'd not had enough fluid. I had some catching up to do.

Standing there, I watched Napoleon disappear and noticed how his covered feet made small indentations in the snow. Only then did I notice the larger tracks alongside his leading to and from our cave. I'm no expert on tracks, but my first thought was mountain lion. The tracks came out of some rocks above us, wound down a snowdrift and up to the entrance where I'd been crawling in and out. I also noticed a small, burrowed area where it looked like something had been sitting or lying down. As in "lying in wait." Didn't take me long to make sense of it. Dead people smell. Even frozen dead people. So do injured people and little dogs.

I had to get out of my wet clothes, so I stoked the fire, stripped, spread out my clothes, and climbed naked but for my underwear inside my bag. I was shivering, and my fingers were stiff, as though they'd been dipped in wax. I dropped some snow in the Jetboil and clicked it on.

Ashley watched me. Her eyes betrayed anxiety. I curled up in my bag and let myself shiver, trying to create some heat. "Hey."

Her eyes were tired. She was suffering, and it showed in her eyes. She took a deep breath. "Hi." Her voice was weak.

"Taken anything lately?"

She shook her head.

I placed a Percocet on her tongue, and she sipped the last of her water. "You don't look too good," she offered. "Why don't you take some of the Advil?"

I knew if I didn't I might not get out of my bag tomorrow. "Okay." I held up two Popsicle-ish fingers. "Two."

She poured them into my hand, and I swallowed.

"What'd you see?"

"There's a level one trauma center just a few hundred meters from here. I flagged down the EMTs. They're pulling a gurney down here now. I talked to the hospital administrator and secured a private room for you. Should have you up, showered, warm, and pumped full of IV pain medication in ten minutes or less. Oh, and I talked to Vince. He'll be waiting on you when you get there."

"That bad, huh?"

I slid down further into my bag. "Nothing but snow, ice, rock, and mountain as far as I can see."

"And the GPS?"

"Same picture."

She lay back and let out a deep breath. The one she'd been holding all day. I poured some warm water and started sipping.

"Got any ideas?"

"There are some lakes down below us. A few streams. I'm

sure they're all frozen, but I thought I'd see if I could make my way down tomorrow and find some fish. Tomorrow makes five days since the crash, and four with no food."

She closed her eyes and focused on her breathing.

"How's the leg feeling?"

"Hurts."

I slid over, packed snow around it, and saw that while the swelling had gone down, her skin was a deep purple from the top of her knee to the side of her hip. I clicked on my flashlight, checked her stitches and then her pupils—for responsiveness. They were slow and fatigued quickly. Which meant her body was weak and the elevation was starting to take a toll.

I fed the fire and felt her toes. They were cold. Which was bad. Circulation was becoming a problem. By treating the leg with constant ice, I was compromising the foot or toes. I had to get some blood flow in that foot.

I turned so we were face to toes. I unzipped my bag, and without moving her leg, sat pressing my chest and stomach to the bottom of her foot. Then I wrapped us both in the bag.

She focused on her breathing. Staring up through the tarp and tree limbs. Large flakes weighted everything and muted the world.

" . . . I was scheduled for a pedicure yesterday. Or was it the day before?"

"Sorry. Fresh out of polish."

"Rain check?"

I wrapped my palm across the top of her foot. "When we get out of here, and you're warm in some hospital bed and not lying on a bed of ice, provided you don't sue me for putting you in danger the day before your wedding, I'll paint your toenails whatever color you like."

"Funny you should mention that. I've been lying here since

you left, drafting my attorney's opening argument. 'Ladies and gentlemen of the jury . . .' "

"How's it coming together?"

She shrugged. "If I were you, I'd hire a very good lawyer, and even then I wouldn't get my hopes up."

"That bad?"

Her head fell to one side. "Let's see . . . you started with good intentions, then saved my life, and despite the fact that I've seen you cough up blood at least twice, you set my leg and really haven't left my side."

"You saw that?"

"Blood on snow . . . hard to miss."

"We'll both get better when we lose a few thousand feet."

Ashley stared at the compass hanging from my neck. "When did she give you that?"

"Loggerhead turtles lay their eggs along our beach, leaving these big mounds up in the dunes. Years ago Rachel nominated herself the Turtle Patrol. She'd circle the mounds with stakes and pink surveyor tape, and then mark off the days on a calendar. She was amazed every time the turtles hatched and knew, somehow, to head for the water. I've always been pretty good with directions. Can find my way around most anywhere. She gave it to me one year after watching a particular nest hatch."

"Why not just get a GPS like Grover's?"

"The problem with a GPS is that batteries run dead and they don't like cold weather. Most times, on long hikes, I'll walk with a GPS clipped to one strap and my compass hung around my neck."

"This may sound stupid, but how does a compass know which way to point?"

"Actually, it only points one way. Magnetic north. We find what we need off of that."

"Magnetic north?"

Her foot was starting to warm. "You didn't do Girl Scouts, did you?"

She shook her head. "Too busy kicking people."

"The earth is magnetized. The source of that is up near the North Pole. That's why it's called magnetic north."

"So?"

"True north and magnetic north are not the same thing. Down here that doesn't matter much. But try to use a compass near the pole and it'll mess with your head. I use it mainly to walk point-to-point."

"Point-to-point?"

"A compass can't tell you where you are. Only the direction you are headed, or have come from. A right-handed person, like me, will walk in a right-turning circle if given enough time without a compass. To walk in a straight line, you pick a direction, a degree on the compass, say 110 degrees or 270 or 30 or whatever, then pick a visual marker somewhere in front of you that lines up with that point on the compass. A tree, mountaintop, lake, bush, whatever. Once you get there, you pick another, but this time you also use the point behind you as a reference point—double-checking yourself. Hence, point-to-point. Not difficult, but takes patience. And some practice."

"Will that compass help us get out of here?" Her tone suggested something I'd not heard. The first outward sign of fear.

"Yes."

"Make sure you don't lose it."

"Check."

I lay awake until Ashley started snoring. The drugs did that. When I couldn't sleep, I slid out from underneath my bag, pulled on my long underwear, jacket, and boots, and walked outside. I opened the compass and let the needle settle beneath the moonlight.

Remember how elated we were to get that job offer in Jacksonville? We jumped at it. Back to the beach. The ocean. The smell of salt. Taste of sunrise. Sound of sunset. We were moving back home, closer to your parents.

But you were the activities coordinator at the children's hospital and couldn't stand the thought of leaving a week before your replacement arrived. So driving the moving truck—Denver to Jacksonville, from the Rockies to the beach—fell to me. All 1,919 miles.

I told you I'd buy you a condo, any house you wanted, but you said you liked the one I already had.

You hung on the truck door, swinging on squeaky hinges, left heel in the air, and pointed to the floorboard. "I left you a present. But you can't open it until you get out of the driveway."

On the floor in front of the passenger seat sat a cardboard box. A silver handheld tape recorder was taped to the lid. Attached to it was a piece of paper that read PRESS PLAY.

I backed out of the drive, put the stick into DRIVE, *and pressed* PLAY. *Your voice rose up out of the tiny machine. I could hear your smile.*

"Hey, it's me. Thought you'd like some company." You licked your lips like you do when you're nervous or being mischievous. "Here's the deal, I'm . . . I'm worried about losing you to the hospital. About being a doctor's widow, sitting on the couch, a spoonful of Rocky Road in one hand, the remote in the other, flipping through the plastic surgery catalog. I gave you this thing so I can be with you even when I'm not. Because I miss the sound of your voice when you're away. And . . . I want you to miss mine. Miss me. I'll keep it a day or two, tell you what I'm thinking, then give it to you. We can pass it back and forth. Sort of like a baton. Besides, I've got to compete with all those pretty nurses who will be swooning over you. I'll have to beat them off you with a stick. Or stethoscope. Ben . . . " Your tone of voice changed. From serious to playful. "If you need to hear someone swoon, get weak in the knees, flushed in the face . . . play doctor . . . just press PLAY. *Deal?"*

I nodded in the rearview mirror. "Deal."

You laughed. "There are a couple of things in this box that will help you on your trip. You're holding the first. The others are marked with numbers, and you can't open them until I say so. Deal? No kidding. If you don't agree, I'm clicking off. No more me. Got it? . . . Good. Glad we got that settled. I guess you can go ahead and open the second now."

I pulled out a small envelope containing a CD and slid it into my player.

Your voice continued. "Our songs."

You had little trouble communicating what you felt. You wore your heart on your sleeve, and what your heart felt your mouth could say. And did. Your folks had spent a lifetime teaching you to do that. My dad had spent a lifetime browbeating me whenever I tried to tell him how I felt. He said any expression of emotion was a weakness that needed to be ripped out. Douse it with gasoline and throw a match on it. The result made me a decent ER surgeon. I could act without feeling.

Over the next twenty-four hours, you held the recorder to your mouth and took me with you everywhere you went. Babbling with every step. You always had a thing with kids, so first thing, we drove to work—the children's ward—where you walked me into each room, called each child by name, snuggled with each or took them a teddy bear or played a video game or played dress-up. You never hesitated to get on their level. And in truth, much of what I know about bedside manner, you taught me. They saw the recorder and asked you what you were doing. You held the recorder, and each one talked to me. Their little voices exploding with laughter and hope. I didn't know much about their conditions or their doctors, but I could hear it in their voices. The effect of you on them was palpable, and they would miss you.

We went to the grocery store, checking off items on your list. To the mall to find some shoes and a gift for some party. To get your hair cut, where the stylist talked about her boyfriend's body odor problem.

When the stylist walked to the register to welcome another client, you whispered into the recorder, "If she thinks her boyfriend stinks, maybe she ought to run with you." You then took me to get a pedicure where the lady told you that you had too many calluses on your feet and you ought to run less. Then to a matinee where you crunched popcorn in my ear and told me to close my eyes 'cause the guy was kissing the girl. "Just kidding. You kiss better than him. He's gross. You ask me how I know about such things. Oh . . . " I could hear more smiling. "I know." After the movie, you walked me to the bathroom door where you said, "You can't come in here. Girls only."

As I drove through Alabama, you took me to our favorite diner where you smacked key lime pie in my ear and said, "Sounds good, doesn't it." It did, too. Then you said, "Look in the box and pull out the big one that says DESSERT." I did. "Now open it, but be careful." I lifted the lid and found a piece of key lime pie. "Thought I forgot about you, didn't you?" I pulled into a rest area, and we all ate key lime pie together. You took me to our room, lay down, where I was already asleep. Dead to the world. You lay next to me. Running your fingers through my hair. Scratching my back. "I'm going to sleep now. Next to you. But you can't go to sleep until you get to our condo by the sea. I'm wrapping my arms around your waist. You're skinny. You need to gain some weight. You've been working too much." Then you paused. You were quiet several minutes. I only knew you were still there 'cause I could hear you breathing. You whispered, "Ben . . . somewhere in miles gone by . . . somewhere between way back there and here . . . I gave you my heart . . . and I don't want it back. Ever. You hear me?"

I found myself nodding.

You interrupted me. "Hey . . . no nodding at the road in front of you. You've got to say it out loud."

I smiled. "I hear you."

It's snowing again. Ashley's in a lot of pain and starting to show the effects of elevation. I've got to get her down or she's going to die up here. I know . . . but if I don't try, we'll both die.

Grover?

I need to bury him, but I'm not sure I have the strength. He may already be buried. Plus there's something up in the rocks that's got me a bit worried.

I've got to get some rest.

The wind's picking up. When it blows out of the south, it funnels through the fuselage, sounding a low whistle, like blowing across the top of a beer bottle. It sounds like a train that never arrives.

I've been studying the compass, trying to find a way out, but it's mountains all around. Tough to know which way to go. If I choose the wrong degree . . . well, things are bad here. Real bad.

I want to tell people that Ashley was trying to get home. I wish they knew. But chances are good they never will.

CHAPTER THIRTEEN

I woke with the sun, groggy and sore. Rolled over, pulled the bag up over my face, and woke again around lunch. No matter how hard I tried I could not get out of bed. I don't ever remember sleeping through an entire day, other than the one after the crash. Evidently my adrenaline had finally given out.

Ashley seldom stirred. Elevation mixed with starvation mixed with a plane crash mixed with a lot of pain had taken its toll on both of us. Toward sundown I finally crawled out of my bag and stumbled onto the snow. I hurt everywhere and could barely move.

By daylight on day six, the fire had long since died out. But my clothes were dry, so I pulled them on, forced myself to pack my backpack, rekindled and restarted the fire to keep her warm, and dropped a few handfuls of fresh snow into the Jetboil for her when she woke. I tried not to look at Grover.

We needed food.

I shouldered my backpack, tied the bow onto the back of it, and stepped out into the sun. The air was crisp and dry with ice crystals floating on our breath. I threw fresh snow across the tracks at the entrance. It would let me know if anything visited while I was away. I tied on the snowshoes, pulled out my compass, took a reading, spotted a rock outcropping maybe a half mile in the distance, and set off. I didn't have the advantage of a mountaintop perspective, so the compass would prove invaluable.

For three hours I picked points and plowed through the snow. It was dry and frozen, rather than sticky and wet, but I had to keep stopping to tighten my gaiters around my knees. The first lake turned up nothing, so I walked the frozen perimeter until I found the creek that spilled out of it. While the surface of the lake was frozen, the creek was not. The water was clear, clean, and tasted almost sweet. It was cold, and I risked dropping my core temperature, but I was moving so I kept forcing myself to drink. Eventually my pee turned nearly clear. A good sign.

A mile later the creek made a hard turn left, creating a deep pool below a rock overhang. The banks were mounded with snow. I didn't put too much faith in my ability to work that fly rod with my hands. They were too cut up and cold to do anything effectively. And not having done much fly-fishing, I couldn't figure out why a fish would bite at a fly that it knows good and well can't live in conditions like these. Fish aren't stupid.

Grover had a small bottle of imitation salmon eggs. They looked like red or orange peas. I slid one over a hook, threaded line through the hook, and dropped that single "egg" into the water.

Twenty minutes later, no bites. I packed up and looked for a bigger pool. A mile later I found one. Same routine. Same outcome. Only this time I could see little black shadows darting in and out beneath the rock and into the swirling current. Lots of black shadows. I knew there were fish here, why wouldn't they bite?

I guess that's why it's called fishing and not catching.

Thirty minutes later, an ineffective Popsicle, I packed up and continued trudging through the snow looking for another pool. I was tired, cold, and hungry. This time I had to climb a small rise and then descend to another stream. With the elevation and the pain in my ribs, even a simple rise meant a lot of work. I was expending calories I couldn't afford. I climbed over, then descended and walked down to the bank of one more stream. This one was wider, maybe twice as wide, but more shallow and still running with a good volume of water.

The black shadows reappeared. A good number, too.

I brushed away the snow and lay on the rock, a facedown snow angel, salivating at the sight of mountain trout. This time I lowered Grover's hand net slowly into the water below the bait. The problem with this method was that it submerged one hand into water that was probably twenty-eight degrees. The pain was excruciating until it went numb—which didn't take long.

The shadows disappeared, then slowly returned. Swimming closer. Slowly, they approached the egg and began to nibble. Maybe it was the cold water, but they too were sluggish. I slowly raised the net and caught seven finger-sized trout. I dumped them into the snow several feet from the creek and buried my cold hand in the pocket of my down jacket. With the hatchet I cut a limb, lashed it to the net, and submerged both it and the egg, catching a couple more.

I ate everything but the heads.

When they were gone, I crept back to the bank and kept "fishing." I did that off and on for more than an hour. When the sun started casting my shadow on the snow, I counted my catch. Forty-seven. Enough for us tonight and tomorrow. I packed up and followed my tracks home. The packed snow, along with colder temperatures that had frozen the surface, made my return quicker. On the way back, I pulled an arrow from the quiver, nocked it, took a deep breath, and drew hard on the string. It resisted, then gave and released all the way to my face. The pain in my ribs was sharp, but I had the bow at full draw. I set the top pin on the base of a wrist-sized evergreen some twenty yards away and released. The arrow missed the base by about two inches and disappeared in the snow on the right. I dug around a few minutes and retrieved the arrow, embedded in the frozen earth. Drawing the bow was not something I could do quickly. But it was something I could do. And while I had not hit the tree, I was close. And at that distance, close was good enough.

It was well after midnight when I climbed back onto our plateau. Oddly, it was plenty light. I approached the last half mile slowly, keeping my eyes peeled for anything moving. I saw nothing, but the entrance to our cave told a different story. Beneath the moonlight there was no mistake. The tracks were closer. Parked right at the entrance, with a rounded indentation between them where something had lain down, resting its stomach on the snow. Chances were good that it was lying here as I walked up. Chances were also good that it was lying in wait less than a hundred feet from me now.

ASHLEY WAS WEAK, and her eyes hurt. Classic altitude sickness mixed with a concussion and lack of food. I found some more wood, stoked the fire, gutted six trout, and fed them onto a long slender stick, piercing them through the middle like a kabob. I cooked them and made coffee at the same time. Caffeine would help her digest and absorb the nutrients—not to mention fight the hunger. She drank and ate slowly as I held the cup to her lips and then peeled off a fish and held it while she chewed. She ate fourteen like that and drank two cups of coffee before she shook her head.

Napoleon sat quietly licking his face. I laid out six fish on the snow in front of him and said, "Go ahead." He stood, smelled them, wiggled his nose, and devoured them. Eating everything, including the heads.

I gave Ashley the last of the Percocet, packed and elevated her leg, and checked the circulation in her foot. She was asleep before I realized we hadn't said two words to each other since I'd returned. I sat up a few more hours feeding the fire, making myself eat, watching the color return to her skin, and listening as her shallow breaths deepened. Much of that time I sat in my bag with her foot pressed to my stomach. Just before midnight, I walked outside. As I did, a long shadow disappeared up a rock face and into some trees on my left. Napoleon stood next to me, snarling. He'd heard it too.

CHAPTER FOURTEEN

Caught some fish today. Sort of like big sardines without all the mustard sauce and aluminum can. Nothing to brag about, but we're alive. And I shot the bow. If it came to a pinch, I think I could hit what I'm shooting at. As long as it stayed inside twenty or twenty-five yards. I know, not many things will, but it's better than jumping around and waving my arms in the air.

Ashley is sleeping. I gave her the last of the Percocet, hoping she'll get some sleep. Maybe put some energy back in her tanks. I need to put together a plan. I know folks will tell you to never leave the crash site, but we've got to get down out of here. Even if a helicopter was hovering a hundred feet over us, I'm not sure they could see us. It's snowed almost four feet in five days. We're pretty well buried by now.

Speaking of which . . . I'm going to move Grover tomorrow. Get him someplace where he can see the sun come up and set. Where he can count the stars at night. Someplace a good distance from us. I'll have to make a stretcher of some sort, but I can use that again when I move Ashley.

You remember that cabin in the mountains? Our daytime hikes, nighttime fires, watching the snow stick to the windows as a mountaintop wind leaned against the door and whistled atop the chimney.

Our honeymoon.

The second night . . . we'd finished dinner and were sitting in front of the fire. Between our student loans and the cost of life, we didn't have two pennies to rub together. I think we'd paid for the cabin with a then-maxed-out credit card. Drinking a cheap bottle of Cabernet. You were wearing your robe . . . and my sweat.

Seems I remember that we'd agreed on a no-present wedding. Promised to do it again when we could afford it. Good thing I knew better than to put much stock in that. You reached behind the couch and handed me the box. Wrapped perfectly. Topped with a red bow. Every corner perfect. You raised both eyelids and said, "This is something you desperately need."

The firelight was dancing across your skin. The vein on your left arm.

"I thought we'd agreed no presents?"

And you said, "This isn't a wedding present. It's something you need if we're going to stay married for seventy years."

"Seventy years?"

You nodded. And then asked, "You sure you're going to love me when I'm old, wrinkly, and can't hear a word you're saying?"

"Probably more."

You crossed your right leg over your left, and the split in your robe climbed halfway up your thigh. Then you said, "You going to love me when my boobs sag to my belly button?"

There I was marveling at the picture of you, and you were thinking about sagging boobs. I still can't believe you said that.

I stared up into the pine rafters, shook my head once, and tried not to smile. "Don't know. Might be difficult. You're a runner. You don't have much to sag to begin with."

You slapped my arm. "You better take that back."

I laughed. "When I was a kid, I saw that very thing in National Geographic, *and it's not pretty. Cured me from wanting to look at girly magazines."*

You pointed at me. Your voice rising. "Ben Payne." Your crooked, double-jointed finger was pointing everywhere but at me. "You are flirting with the couch. You better watch it."

"Okay, but if you start sagging to your belt, we might consider a tuck here and a nip there."

You nodded. "Trust me, we'll be tucking and nipping long before that. Now open."

I remember staring down at the split and marveling at how comfortable you were at being with me. Your smile. The tired eyes. Sweat above your ears. Flushed cheeks. Firelight. Laughter, beauty, spunk. All of you. I remember closing my eyes for a brief second and burning the image onto the back of my eyelids because I wanted to take it with me.

And I did.

Rachel, you're still the measuring stick. No one else holds a candle.

You smiled. "The way I look at it, there's Eastern Standard Time, and then there's Ben Time. And Ben Time can be anywhere from fifteen minutes to an hour and a half behind. This could help that little problem."

You were right. I'm sorry I was ever late for anything.

I peeled away the paper, and there sat a Timex Ironman. You pointed at the face. "Look . . . it has no hands, so you can see exactly what time it is—down to the exact second. And to help you out, I set it thirty minutes fast."

"Have you ever thought that maybe everyone else is just randomly early?"

"Nice try, but . . ." You shook your head. "No." You curled up against me, your back to my chest, your head on my arm, and we talked and laughed as the coals turned white and the snow painted the windows.

An hour or so later, just before you dozed off, you whispered, "I set the alarm."

"What for?"

You pressed against me, pulled my arm tight, and we drifted off.

When the alarmed sounded, I was somewhere beyond a deep sleep.

I jumped and tried to focus. 3:33 a.m. I reached for my wrist and punched every button trying to get it to hush. Not wanting to let it wake you. Moonlight broke through the skylight and showered both of us, casting our shadow on the wall. Highlighting the tips of your hair. Finally I just stuffed the watch under my pillow 'cause I couldn't get it to shut up. It sounded for a full sixty seconds. You laughed, dug yourself deeper beneath the covers. The room was cold. Fire dim. Coals a dull red. My breath a misty cloud of smoke. I slid out, naked, on the floor. Goose bumps crawling up and down.

You tucked the cover beneath your chin. Studied me. Smiled. Tired eyes. You whispered. "You cold?"

My embarrassment was obvious. "Very funny."

I stoked the fire, added three logs. Slid back under the blanket—which, if I remember correctly, was a fake bear rug—and you slid your leg across mine, then placed your chest to mine. Warm. You cradled me. I asked, "Why'd you set it for the middle of the night?"

You wiggled, wedging yourself closer to me. Your feet were cold. You pressed your lip to my ear. "To remind me."

"Of what?"

"That you'd be cold."

Sometimes I wonder how you ever fell for me. You believe in things you cannot see and speak a language that only hearts know.

"Oh."

A while later, the first ray of daylight broke the ridgeline, crowned in blue. Red crimson spilling across a sea of black. You lifted my hand off your chest and pushed the button on the watch. Green light showering the space around us. You whispered, "When you push this, and the light shines back at you . . . you think of us. Of me." You laid your head against me, staring up, and pressed my hand flat across your chest, you in the center of my palm. Hiding nothing. Your heart pounding inside. You said, " . . . of this."

CHAPTER FIFTEEN

Napoleon's growling woke me up. Low and different. His tone told me he wasn't kidding. I opened my eyes to ice crystals hanging in the air on my breath. Ashley lay quietly. Her breathing had become labored again. The dog stood between us, staring at the entrance. Moonlight filtered in, casting shadows. It was bright enough to walk outside without a flashlight. Napoleon lowered his head and took two slow steps toward the entrance. Two eyes stared back at us. Crouched low, seemingly growing out of a shadow. They looked like two pieces of red glass. Behind the shadow, something waved. Like a flag. There it was again. This time more like smoke from a fire. I sat up on an elbow, rubbed my eyes, and Napoleon's growl grew deeper, louder, more angry. I put my hand on his back and said, "Easy."

Evidently, he didn't understand that. As if shot out of a cannon, he launched himself toward the thing staring back at us. The two collided, spun in an angry ball. A loud catlike roar erupted from the middle of the ball and then disappeared, leaving Napoleon standing at the entrance, barking and jumping two feet straight into the air.

I crawled toward him, wrapped my arms around him, and pulled him backward. "Easy, boy. It's gone. Easy." He was shaking, and his shoulder was wet.

Ashley clicked on the flashlight. My palm was sticky, red, and the snow was splattered red beneath us.

Didn't take me long to find the cut. It was deep from the side of his shoulder toward the top of his back.

I grabbed my needle and thread, and Ashley held him still while I stitched him up. He didn't like me poking him with a needle, but I closed it with four stitches and, given the location, he couldn't chew at it. He chased it, turning in a few circles, but gave up, stared at the entrance, then licked me on the face.

"Yeah . . . you did good. I'm sorry I ever thought about eating you."

Ashley cleared her throat. "What was it?"

"Mountain lion."

"Is it coming back?"

"I think so."

"What does it want?"

"Us."

She closed her eyes and didn't say anything for a while.

We slept in fits throughout the rest of the night. Napoleon curled up in my bag, but kept his eyes on the entrance. I scratched his head, and it didn't take him long to fall asleep. I perched the bow next to my bag, nocked an arrow, and propped myself against the tail of the plane.

Only when the sun came up did I finally drift off.

WHEN I WOKE, Ashley lay half turned, staring left, the flare gun in her hand.

Napoleon too was trained on the entrance.

Something was crunching the snow below us. I crawled out, grabbed the bow, and clipped my release onto the string. Compound bows look complicated, but in truth they're simple. The release is like a trigger. It takes the place of your fingers, so that the same thing happens exactly the same way over and over again. You draw, hold the pin on the target, and squeeze the release. The release lets go of the string, sending the arrow toward the target. Grover's bow was a good one. A Matthews. His draw was a bit longer than mine, but I could manage.

I crawled forward and saw some sort of fox hopping around the rocks below us. Snow white, it was one of the prettier things I'd ever seen. I held my breath, drew the bow, held on the fox, and released. The arrow flew over the fox, maybe two inches high.

The fox disappeared.

Through clenched teeth and a white-knuckled grip on the flare gun, Ashley whispered. "What happened?"

"Missed. Too close."

"How do you miss something that's too close? I thought you said you could shoot that thing."

I shook my head. "Shot over it."

"What was it?"

"Fox of some sort."

Things had turned for the worse.

CHAPTER SIXTEEN

It was weird owning the place that was the source of so many tough or bad memories, but you just shook your head and smiled. “Give me six months, let me remodel, paint, get some new furniture, and . . . I’ll give you new memories. Besides . . .” You put your hands on your hips. “Paid for *and* oceanfront *are both really cool.”*

So we gutted walls, repainted, retiled, re-did pretty much everything. Seemed like a totally different place. Dad liked closed blinds, dark colors, little lighting, no visitors. More like a cave. You went for cool blues, soft tans, open windows with the blinds rolled up, sliding glass doors cracked so the sound filtered through. Wave upon wave.

How many nights has the sea sung us to sleep?

You remember the night of that crash? I’d worked late because two Cadillacs, overflowing with people, had been hit by a tow truck. The ER was slammed. My shift ended at four the previous afternoon, but the first ambulance arrived just minutes before with promises of more to come. I’d stayed until we had everybody stable—at least those that could be stabilized. I was tired. Thinking about life and how short it is. How we’re always just a breath away from overturned in the ditch with a fireman cutting you out with the Jaws of Life. It was just one of those moments where I knew, really knew, that life is not guaranteed. That I take it for granted. I wake up each day thinking I’ll wake up tomorrow, too.

It's not necessarily true.

It was early. Maybe three a.m. The ocean was angry ahead of a storm. Sideways wind. Stinging rain mixed with sand. Frothy churn. Choppy waves. Thunderous noise. A storm was coming in, and any idiot could tell the undertow would be severe.

Anyway, I was standing at the glass wrestling with life's impermanence, staring out over the beach. You appeared, in a silk robe. Tired eyes.

You said, "You okay?"

I told you what happened. What I was thinking. You tucked your shoulder under mine, wrapped your arms around my waist. Minutes passed. Lightning spiderwebbed the sky.

"You owe me something, and I want to collect."

Seemed a strange way to start a conversation when I was sharing my deepest thoughts. Sort of irritated me. I guess my voice betrayed this. "What?"

Admittedly, I'm a bit of an emotional blockhead. I'm still sorry.

I don't know how long you'd been wanting to bring this up. Don't know how long I'd missed the signals. Looking back, you'd been firing shots across my bow for months, and I was too wrapped up in work to pick up on them. But you'd been patient. I'd kept telling you, "Just let me get through medical school."

I guess you figured it was time to ramp up your efforts. You stepped aside, untied your robe, let it slip to the floor, and started walking to our room. At the doorway, you turned. A candle in our bedroom lit one side of your face. "I want to make a baby. Right now."

I remember watching you disappear into the warm glow of candlelight, the flash of a shadow across the small of your back. I remember staring back into the glass and shaking my head at the idiot in the reflection staring back at me. I remember walking into our bedroom, kneeling next to our bed, and saying, "Forgive me?" I remember you smiling, nodding, and pulling me toward you. A while later, I remember you lying on my stomach, your chest pressed to mine, your tears trickling onto my chest, a tired smile, trembling arms. And I remember that moment, when I knew. That you'd broken loose in me the stuff that only love breaks loose. That you'd given me all of you. Unselfishly. Unreservedly.

Something about that gift struck me. Something about the enormity of that touched me down where words don't live. Where expression fails. Where there are no secrets. Where there's just you and me and everything that's us.

And I remember crying like a baby.

That's when I knew. When I knew for the first time what love was. Not what it felt like. Not how it made me feel. Not what I hoped it was. But what it was. And what it was when I didn't get in the way.

You showed me. It'd been there all along, but something about that night, those people, the sense of gain, loss, heartbreak, and joy, all those things swirled into that moment and . . . I'd lived my whole life wanting to love but never able to do so apart from the pain I'd carried. The pain of my dad. Of my mom's absence. Of running but never being fast enough. Of never measuring up.

But there . . . that night . . . that moment, it was the first time I'd ever been cut free. When I took a breath deep enough to fill me. All of my life, I'd struggled in the waves, tossed, turned, thrown about like a rag doll, forever trying to surface, screaming for air, but somewhere some unseen hand held me beneath the foam and froth. But in that moment, you held back the waves, lifted me above the surface, and filled me.

CHAPTER SEVENTEEN

Grover was stiff when I tried to move him. Frozen in a sitting position. His head tilted a bit to one side. One hand still holding the stick. His eyes were closed.

Ashley turned her head.

I popped off a section of the wing, laid him on top of it, and slid-pushed him out the entrance. I pulled him across the snow to a boulder covered in lion tracks. I brushed the snow off, sat him on the rock, and leaned him backward.

I backtracked, counting. Eighteen steps.

I nocked an arrow, aimed at the snowdrift a few feet away from Grover, and released. This time I didn't shoot over. The distance was far enough to allow the arrow to flatten out while not so far away that I couldn't hit what I was aiming at.

Napoleon kept running back and forth between Grover and me. He'd started limping, and his circles had developed a hitch. He looked up at me.

"I won't let anything happen to him."

Napoleon walked back into our disintegrating cave. Everything about this location was bad. I needed to get us out of here, but I had two problems. First was my energy level. I'd have less tomorrow and even less the next day. Secondly, having spent part of my residency on the West Coast where mountain lions thrive and having seen what they can do to unsuspecting people, and having seen how often they do it, I had no intention of spending the next few days looking over my shoulder.

I crawled in.

Ashley's face was wet. She was breaking down. "What're you doing?"

"Hunting."

"Are you using Grover as bait?"

"Yes."

She didn't say anything.

"But, if it works the way I'm thinking, then nothing will happen to him."

"Not to point out the obvious, but nothing has worked out the way you'd hoped since we met in Salt Lake."

She was right. I had no response. I nodded. I just knew I wasn't going to sit in our cave and wait for that thing to come back. Using Grover helped tilt the odds. Maybe not in my favor, but not in that thing's either.

If it went my way, then Grover would never know it and would be no worse for it. If it didn't, well, he was dead already, and I'd bury him before Ashley had a chance to see what had happened.

We didn't say much the rest of the day. Or that night. Or the next day. By the time the second night came around, I hadn't slept soundly in forty-eight hours and was running on fumes. So was Ashley.

The cold had intensified. I couldn't say for sure, but it was crisp and painful, suggesting that it had fallen into the negatives. Clouds moved in, blocking out the moon, and that was bad. I needed the moon. Without it, I couldn't see the sight pin.

Midnight came and brought snow. I was sleepy. Fading in and out. I could see the outline of Grover just across the snow.

Based on the layer covering him, we'd had another three inches of snow.

I must have fallen hard asleep, because I jerked when I woke. Napoleon lay next to me. Crouched. His eyes were focused on Grover.

Something was leaning on Grover. And the thing was big. Six plus feet in length. My hands were nearly frozen, but I drew the bow and tried to find the pin. There was no way to see it in the dark. "Come on. Just a glimmer of light."

Still nothing. I swung the bow, knowing I only had another second or two. My arms were cramping and my chest felt like somebody had stuck me with a spike. I coughed, tasting blood. I was weakening. I needed light. My arms were shaking.

Next to me, something brushed my leg, then I heard a click and somebody shot a Roman candle out the entrance to the cave. The flare gun exited in a long space-shuttle arc and then hovered a metallic orange maybe a hundred feet above us. The light showered down, casting shadows. The cat had both his paws on Grover's shirt, like they were dancing. It looked up, arched its neck, I found the pin, leveled it on the cat's shoulder, and pressed the release.

I never saw the arrow.

I dropped the bow, fell back, clutching my side and trying to breathe. I coughed, tasted more blood, and spat on the snow next to me.

Ashley lay to my right, staring out. "It's gone."

"Did I hit it?" I had hunched over. Nursing my rib cage. The spasm was traveling around my back, further shortening my breathing.

"Don't know. It left in a hurry."

Somewhere in the darkness my hand found hers.

We lay there, catching our breath. I was too tired to carry

her back down to her bag, so I pulled her to my chest, wrapped us in my bag with my arms around her waist and chest. Within minutes, her head fell to one side and her pulse slowed.

MORNING WOKE US. Napoleon lay curled between us. I climbed out of my bag and saw what Ashley had done last night. Drag marks in the snow told the story.

I needed to check her leg, so I lifted the bag and ran my hand gently along the skin. The skin was dark, and the swelling had returned. The hair on her leg was stubbly. Ten days overgrown. The pulse in her ankle was good. The problem was the swelling. The skin was taut. Moving last night had been traumatic. Not good. She'd set herself back. The pain would be intense, but we were out of Percocet.

I tilted her head, placed two Advil on her tongue, and she sipped and swallowed.

I propped her head on my bag, dressed, tied up my boots, nocked an arrow, and stepped toward Grover. He'd fallen over. Or been pushed. And looked like he was asleep on his side. A trail of blood led away up the rocks. A constant trail.

It'd been several hours, which was either real good or real bad. If the mountain lion was mortally wounded, then those several hours would have given it time to die. If it was just sort of wounded, those several hours would have given it plenty of time to regather its strength and get angry.

I turned to Napoleon and held out my palm like a stop sign. "Stay. Take care of Ashley." He climbed inside her bag, only his nose sticking out. My breath was a thick cloud of smoke and bit at my nose. The cold was painful.

I climbed the rocks and followed the blood. It thinned, which was bad. A thin blood trail means a bad hit and probably an angry, injured lion. After a hundred yards I was down to following a drop here and a drop there. I stopped to think things over. The wind blew, cut through me, and blew snow dust into my eyes.

At a large outcropping, the drops increased in number, finally becoming a stream. After another hundred yards, it grew into a large puddle—suggesting that the thing had stopped there. A good sign. I dug at the snow with my toe. It was several inches deep in red.

That was good. At least for us.

The trail continued another two hundred yards up through some smaller rocks and toward some squatty trees. I saw the tail first, the black tip lying flat across the snow, sticking out from beneath the lowest limbs of the trees. I took a deep breath, drew the bow, and walked slowly toward the cat. Eight feet away, I set the front pin on its head, lowered it to account for the distance, and released the arrow. The arrow sliced through the neck. Only the fletching was visible. The cat never moved.

I retrieved the arrow, hung it in the quiver, and sat on the rock, staring at the cat. She was not big. Probably five feet from head to rump and maybe weighed a hundred pounds. I held her paw in my hand.

Small or not, she'd have ripped me to shreds. I checked her teeth. They were worn, which would explain why she'd started hunting easy targets.

I knew Ashley would be worried.

I retraced my steps and found her in a good bit of pain. She was shivering and on the verge of going back into shock. I stripped to my underwear, unzipped her bag, and pulled mine up alongside hers. I climbed in, pressed my chest to hers, and wrapped my arms around her. She lay shaking for close to an hour.

When she was asleep, I climbed out, wrapped both bags around her, stoked the good fire, fed it a little fuel, and returned to the cat. I caped it, which means I cut off the hide, and then gutted it. That left me with a mountain lion carcass of muscle and bone that weighed close to fifty pounds. Giving us maybe fifteen pounds of eatable meat. I dragged it through the snow, cut several green limbs, built a frame around the fire, and began hanging strips of meat.

The smell woke her.

She picked up her head, sniffed the air, and managed a hoarse whisper. "I want some."

I tore off a piece, tossed it between my hands like a hot potato, blew on it, and held it to her lips.

She chewed slowly, eating the entire thing. After a few minutes, she lifted her head, and I propped it up with part of her sleeping bag. Dark circles shrouded her eyes. I tore off another piece and held it while she took small bites. She laid her head back, chewing. "I just had the worst dream. You would never believe."

"Try me."

"I dreamed my flight out of Salt Lake was canceled, but then this stranger, a nice man, kind of homely looking but still nice, invited me to ride this charter flight with him on a short hop to Denver. So I agreed, and somewhere over this interminable forest, the pilot had a heart attack and crashed our plane. I broke my leg, and after nearly a week, all we'd had to eat was some trail mix, coffee grounds, and a mountain lion that had tried to eat us."

"Homely? Nice? 'Nice' was how we described girls in high school with good personalities."

"You're unlike any doctor I've ever met." She chewed slowly. "The strange part of the dream was that I agreed to get on a charter with a total stranger. Two, actually. What was I thinking?" She shook her head. "I need to re-examine my decision-making paradigm."

I laughed. "Let me know how that works out."

In the daylight I rechecked her leg. She was afraid to look. Which was a good call, because it wasn't pretty.

"You're lucky you didn't rebreak it. The bone ends are just now getting tacky enough to hold it in place, and there you go pulling some stunt with a flare gun. I don't think you moved the bone, but the swelling came back with a vengeance."

Her skin was pale, and she looked clammy. I repacked snow around the leg, adjusted and moved the braces to help circulation, then pressed her foot to my stomach to draw the warmth to it.

For the rest of the day we ate barbecued mountain lion and sipped warm water. I kept the snow packed around and under her leg and monitored the amount of fluid she was both drinking and expelling. She'd been lying still for ten days, breathing less than half the oxygen she was used to. I was worried about atrophy and infection. If she got one, I wasn't sure her body could fight it.

Once the protein hit my system, I rubbed down her right leg, her good leg, forcing the blood flow through it and stretching it as much as I could without jolting her broken leg. A delicate balance. Throughout the day, I continued cutting long strips of meat off the cat, feeding them through green bows from an evergreen and suspending them above the fire. Several times throughout the day I gathered fuel, taking me farther and farther from the cave, to keep the fire hot. By nightfall I'd carved off every available strip of meat I could find on the cat carcass and cooked it above the fire. It wasn't much, wasn't even all that good, but it would fill us, give us some protein, some energy, and, maybe just as important, it would travel. Which meant I wouldn't have to find food every day.

When I'd finished, late in the afternoon, the color had returned to Ashley's face and cheeks. Maybe more important, her eyes were moist and healthy.

With two hours of daylight remaining, I looked out the entrance, and my eyes fell on Grover, lying on his side. He looked like a toppled statue. I strapped up my boots. "I'll be right outside."

She nodded. As I passed by she reached out, grabbed me by the coat, and pulled me toward her. She stared up at me, then pulled my forehead to her lips. They were warm, wet, and trembling. "Thank you."

I nodded. This close to her face, I noticed how thin her cheeks had become. Even drawn. I guess shivering for a week mixed with prolonged periods of shock and the absence of much food would contribute to a hollow, gaunt look.

"I don't know how you managed what you did last night. It's a deep-down kind of strength"—I looked away—"I've only seen one other time." I pressed my palm to her forehead, checking for fever. "Tomorrow morning we're getting out of here. I'm not sure where we're going, but we're leaving this place."

She let go of my hand and smiled. "First flight out?"

"Yeah. First-class, too."

I crawled out. My stomach was full, and for the first time in ten days I was neither hungry nor cold. I looked around and scratched my head. Something was strange. Something I'd not noticed in a long time. Like something had crept up behind me that I'd not seen. I scratched my chin and it hit me.

I was smiling.

CHAPTER EIGHTEEN

You remember the turtles? I wonder how they're all doing. Where they are. How far did they swim? Did they ever make it to Australia? Especially your little friend.

You tapped me on the shoulder and said, "What's that sound?" Seems we found the female just as she was starting to build her nest. We climbed the dune, lay down, and watched her dig a hole. She was huge and dug a long time. Then she started laying eggs. Like she went into a trance or something. Must have laid a hundred eggs. When she finished, she covered the hole, crawled to the water's edge, and disappeared into the black water.

We slid down the dune and stared at the mound. It was one of the biggest we'd ever found. We carefully drove the spikes in a triangle, hung a line of pink surveyor's tape around the tips, and then you made me cut little flags to make sure that every beachcomber for a mile could see it.

Planes flying overhead could see that nest.

Then you started counting the days. Like a kid at Christmas. Marking the days on a calendar. I took a week's vacation, and at fifty-five days, we started camping out.

"Well, they don't know they're supposed to hatch at sixty days. What if they come early?"

We spread a blanket atop the dune, and you wore a flashlight on a strap around your head. Looked like a misguided coal miner. I tried to climb inside your sleeping bag, but you zipped up and pointed a finger at me. "Nope. Not now. What if they start hatching?"

Honey, when you get focused on something you are a piece of work.

So, we lay there. Watching the shadow of the moon cross the tape line. The beach was warm that night. A cool breeze came up out of the southwest, so the ocean was more of a lake than a raging torrent. Then came the fifty-ninth day. You were asleep. Drooling on your sleeping bag. I tapped you on the shoulder, and we hung our noses over the edge of the dune and watched the first baby shake the sand off his back and trek to the water. Wasn't long before the beach was crawling with loggerheads.

You were so excited. Counting quietly. Pointing at each one like you knew them by name. I remember you shaking your head. "How do they know which way to go? How come they don't get lost?"

"They have this internal compass inside. Tells them where the water is."

Then came our little friend. He crawled out, but unlike his one hundred and seventeen brothers and sisters, he headed the wrong way. Up the dune, toward us. He made it a few feet, then bogged down. Burrowing himself. The wrinkle grew on your forehead as you watched him dig his own grave.

"He's going the wrong way. He'll never make it." You climbed out, slid down the dune, scooped him up with two hands, and carried him to the water's edge. You set him down, he found his sea legs, and the first wave scooped him up. You gave him a little push. "There you go, little guy. All the way to Australia."

We watched as the moon shone down on his shell, making him look like a floating black diamond. The breeze was blowing your hair across your face. You were smiling. I think we stood there a long time, not saying much, just watching him swim out to sea. He was a good swimmer, too.

That was when you saw it. You turned around, stared at the dune where we'd been hiding, and the scrub oaks and wire grass. A FOR SALE *sign stood at the highest point, so folks could see it driving up or down A1A. You said, "Who owns that?"*

"Don't know."

"How much do you think they want?"

"Probably a good bit. It's been for sale awhile."

"It's a strange size lot. Be difficult to put a big house on it. The area where you can build is rather small, while the protected dunes are big. Might have a hundred feet of frontage on A1, and 800 feet of dune. Like a squashed triangle."

"Yep. And you're surrounded by state park on either side, so there are probably restrictions on what kind of house you can build, how big a footprint, et cetera. Most folks who spend a million dollars on a lot want to be able to build what they want."

You waved your hands across the sand. "Must be ten nests right here. There's enough pink surveyor's tape out there to mark the outline of a new subdivision. With all this activity, why doesn't the state buy it?"

I shrugged. "Money, I suppose."

You nodded. "We should buy it."

"What?"

You began walking up the dune. Studying the layout. "We don't need a big house. We could put it right over here. A beach house, back off the ocean. And we could build it with big glass windows where we could sit at night and watch the nests."

I pointed back down the beach. "Honey, we have a perfectly good condo right down there. We can walk down here anytime we like."

"I know, but the next person to come along might not like the turtles digging up their front yard. We do. We should buy it."

A week passed. I was back in the grind of work. I walked in, threw my stuff on the couch, and saw that the sliding glass door was open. I walked out and found you standing on the beach. The sun had gone down. It was my favorite time. That cool bluish light that falls before the darkness comes. You were standing there, a white sarong blowing in the breeze. You waved. You were so tan. Had tan lines drawn from your eye to your ear from wearing sunglasses so much.

I put on some shorts, grabbed my folder, and walked out. You were wearing a smile and holding a small wrapped box. You handed it to me. The breeze had turned and was pulling at your hair again. Streaking it across your cheek and through your lips. When I kissed it, you pulled it aside with your finger.

I opened the card. It read: SO YOU CAN FIND YOUR WAY BACK TO ME. *I opened the box. It was a lensatic compass. You said, "Read the back." I turned it over. It was engraved.* MY TRUE NORTH. *You hung it around my neck and whispered, "Without you, I'd be lost."*

"I got you something too."

She put her hands behind her back, turning side to side. "Yeah?"

I handed you the folder. You opened it, rifled through the pages. Looked like you were reading Greek. Your eyes narrowed. "Honey . . . what is this?"

"That is a land survey. And this . . . is a contract on a piece of property."

"What piece? We don't have the . . . " You stopped, stared at the survey, turning it sideways, then stared down the beach.

"You didn't."

"It's just an offer. Doesn't mean they'll accept it. I lowballed them."

You tackled me. An Officer and a Gentleman *right there in south Ponte Vedra Beach. You were laughing and screaming. "I can't believe you did that!"*

"Well . . . we don't know if they'll accept the offer. The property has some strong covenants and restrictions. There's a lot we can't put there. It's surrounded by state park, so . . ."

"Can we build a small house?"

"We don't own the property yet."

"Yeah, but we might, and when we do, can we build a small house with a glass front where we can watch the sun and moon rise over the beach?"

I nodded.

"How much is it?"

"A lot. We're not going to be able to build right away. It'll have to sit a few years."

"I can wait."

I loved giving you that piece of property.

CHAPTER NINETEEN

Grover deserved a proper burial. I studied the landscape, and just above him sat a rock outcropping. I climbed it, and the view stretched out for miles. Given his love of heights, he'd have liked it. I kicked away the snow, went back to the plane, pulled off a piece of the tail flap, and used it like a shovel. I dug a hole, which was more pushing stuff out of the way than digging through the frozen ground. I climbed back down, lifted Grover over my shoulder, and wound back up and through the rocks. I laid him in the hole and began collecting rocks the size of softballs.

I emptied his pockets and tried to take off his wedding ring, but it wouldn't budge. I unhooked his pocket watch and zipped all of that loose stuff into the pocket inside my jacket. Then I unlaced his boots, putting his laces in my pocket, pulled off his wool socks, and slid his belt out of the loops in his pants. Lastly, I took his denim jacket.

I stacked rocks under a cold sun that fell, turned a deep orange and then crimson. When finished, I stood up. Stood back. It was a good place. The wind had picked up. I supposed it would always be breezy up here. Maybe that was good. Maybe he'd feel like he was flying.

I took the wool beanie off my head. "Grover . . . I'm sorry

I got you into this mess. Guess if I hadn't hired you to fly me out here, you'd be home with your wife. I imagine you're in angel training right now. Make a good one, too. Probably on the fast track to getting your wings. Hope you get assigned to your wife, I imagine she needs you about now. If and when we get out of here, I'll go see her. Tell her what happened. Take your things to her." I turned my hat in my hands. "I don't know if I ought to be apologizing to you." I tried to laugh. "To be just gut-level honest, you did stick us out here in the middle of nowhere."

The wind blew hard against my face. "Unless God wants two more dead people up here, we're going to need a change in the weather. Blue skies and warmer temperatures would be nice. And since I don't know where we're going, we could use some help there, too. Maybe you could put in a word for us."

The world, blanketed in white, stretched forty miles one way and sixty in another. "I think Ashley would like to wear white, walk the aisle, get married. She's young. Whole life in front of her. She deserves to wear white."

The light faded, giving way to a cloudless, cold sky. A gray ceiling settled in. Stars started poking through. Overhead, maybe 40,000 feet in the air, a jet airliner flew southeast—a long white tail in its wake. "If that's your sense of humor, I don't think it's all that funny right now."

A second plane crisscrossed the exhaust of the first. "Or that. By the way . . . I'm lost, and since I'm lost, we're lost. Won't take much to kill us out here. We're circling the drain now. That big cat nearly did us in. You should know, you were dancing with it. I guess the rub is, if I die, she dies. Not to mention your dog . . . whose name I can't remember."

A cold wind cut through me, and I zipped up my jacket. "I'm not pretending to be more important than I am, but I'm not asking for me. I'm asking for that girl in there with the broken leg and the slowly breaking spirit. She thinks she's hiding it, but she's not. She's tough, but this up here . . . this'll break anybody." I looked around. "This is . . . a tough place. It'll strip your hope fast." A tear broke loose and fell down my face. My hands were cut, scabbed and cracking. I shook my head, my lip trembling. "You and I . . . we never really finished our conversation, but I can tell you this . . . living with a broken heart is living half dead, and that doesn't mean you're half alive. It means you're half dead. And . . . that's no way to live."

The mountains rose up around us, jagged, cold, unforgiving, throwing shadows. Grover lay beneath me, covered in stones and ice. "Once a heart breaks . . . it doesn't just grow back. It's not a lizard's tail. It's more like a huge stained glass that shattered into a million pieces, and it's not going back together. Least not the way it was. You can mush it all into one piece, but that doesn't make it a window. That makes it a pile of broken colored glass. Shattered hearts don't mend and they don't heal. They just don't work that way. Maybe I'm telling you something you already know. Maybe not. I just know that when half dies, the whole thing still hurts. So you get twice the pain and half of everything else. You can spend the rest of your life trying to put that stained glass back together, but it won't go. There's nothing to hold the pieces together."

I put my hat on, only to quickly pull it off again. "That's all I wanted to say." I held the compass, letting the needle spin and settle. "I need to know which way to go."

The two planes crossed and disappeared. Their exhaust caught my eye. I corkscrewed my head. The intersection of the two created an arrow, pointing southeast. One hundred and twenty-five, maybe a hundred and thirty degrees.

I nodded. "Given the fact that I don't have a better option . . . that'll do."

I WALKED BACK INTO the cave and slipped Grover's socks on her feet. They were medium weight wool. She looked at me with suspicion. "Where'd you get those?"

"Walmart."

"That's good to know. I thought you were going to say they belonged to Grover, and if I thought that, well . . . that might just gross me out."

She drifted off. Somewhere near midnight she caught me staring at the compass face. The tritium dots on the dial glowed neon green. "How do you know which way to go?"

"You don't."

"What if you choose the wrong direction?"

"You, me, and Napoleon will be the only ones who ever know it."

She closed her eyes, pulled the bag up over her shoulders. "Take your time . . . and choose wisely."

"Thanks, that's very helpful."

"Don't get me started on what would be helpful at this moment."

"Good point."

CHAPTER TWENTY

It's almost morning. We're heading out in a few minutes. Least, we're going to try. Don't know how far we'll get, but staying here is getting us nowhere.

I've packed up everything I can. I don't know how far we'll get, but I'm pretty sure every bump and jolt is going to be rough on Ashley. I hate to move her, but I can't leave her here. I don't know how long I'd be gone, and I'm pretty sure she'd be dead by the time I got back. Hope goes a long way toward keeping somebody alive. And . . . if I'm not here, I'm afraid her hope will fade. The longer I stick with her, the longer she'll make it.

Grover's resting in a good spot. He can watch the sun rise and set, which I think he'll like. I tried to say some kind words over him. He deserves better, but you of all people should know that verbal communication is not my strong suit. I told him I'd go see his wife if we got out of here. I think God should go ahead and make him an angel. He'd make a good one. He loves to fly, and he could watch over his wife. She's going to need him.

I spent much of last night staring at the compass, 'cause I know I don't need to tell you that a wrong heading could cost us. I know we're sitting in roughly sixty miles of wilderness. We might be thirty miles from the nearest town, but thirty miles as a crow flies is real differ-

ent from thirty miles up and down mountains pulling a hurt woman. One's possible. The other is not.

I guess if we got close and could see something, a trickle of smoke, a lightbulb in the distance at night, I could take off and bring back help, but every time I think about that, I remember when you and I watched The English Patient. *You kept shaking your head and pointing your finger at the TV and saying, "Don't leave her. Don't leave her. You're going to regret that." And you were right. They both paid the price. 'Course, the whole adultery thing didn't help much either. But leaving the girl . . . that's always bad.*

I'd better get going. Sun's cracking the skyline. It'll be a long day. We'll talk tonight. I hope.

CHAPTER TWENTY-ONE

Ashley was grinding her teeth when I shook her. "You ready?"

She nodded, sat up. "Any coffee?"

I handed her a mug of fluid that looked more like weak tea. "Go easy. That's the last of it."

"It's already a bad day, and we haven't even started yet."

"Think of it this way . . . every step away from this place is one step closer to a cappuccino at Starbucks."

She licked her lips. "I love it when you talk dirty to me."

I sat next to her. We took care of the whole bathroom thing and got her dressed. She zipped up her jacket. "I like all this personal service, but I have to say I am really looking forward to the day I can do all this by myself."

I emptied the Nalgene bottle. "Me too."

She crossed her arms. "Listen, I don't mean to overshare, but until now things have been okay as long as I've had to go number one. But that's soon to change."

I shook my head. "You've already done that."

"I have?"

"Twice. Once when I set your leg and later, when you were unconscious."

She looked embarrassed. "That explains a lot."

"Like?"

"Like why I haven't needed to 'go' in like a week."

"Oh . . ." I smiled. "You've 'gone.'"

"Well . . . back to my original question."

"Don't worry. Just give me a heads-up. We'll work it out."

"Not to beat a dead horse, but I seem much more freaked out by this than you."

"I was a first-year med student. Midnight shift. Changing bed-pans. For eight months. I was having a difficult time, really complaining. Had a bit of a lip about it, when Rachel got my attention. Told me that if I wasn't willing to do the dirty work, I'd better find another profession. That what folks need is a doctor who's willing to get his hands dirty and still look at them with compassion and dignity. You might say that 'attitude adjustment' became the basis of my bedside manner. Made me consider what people need versus what I, in my ivory tower, wanted to give them."

I shrugged. "Rachel tore down my tower. Made me set up shop down in the trenches where it didn't smell too rosy and people were suffering. So . . . while this may freak you out, cause you some discomfort, may even make you blush . . . it's what you need. And for lack of a better option, or even a second opinion, I'm your doctor. So . . . I'll tell you the same thing my wife told me when I tried to protest."

She raised both eyebrows. Waiting.

"Get over it."

She nodded. "I like this woman. A lot." She narrowed her lips, sizing me up and chewing on what she was about to say. "Have you won a bunch of awards? Like doctor of the year or something?"

I tilted my head to one side. "Or something."

"So, seriously . . . I'm in pretty good hands?"

"You're in my hands. But the best thing you've got going for you is your sense of humor. It's worth its weight in gold."

"How do you figure? It's not like telling jokes to the trees is going to hasten my escape."

"See what I mean?" I cinched a strap on my pack. "One night, late, maybe early morning, I was working the ER. Life-Flight brought in a guy who'd been shot in the side of the neck. Ordinary Joe buying ice cream for his wife. She was pregnant, sent him to the store—wrong place, wrong time. Got there just as a robbery went sour. When they brought him in he was still wearing his slippers. They opened the door, rolled him off the helicopter, and he was shooting blood from his carotid."

I touched her neck. "Looked like something out of a squirt gun. He'd lost a lot of blood, but was still coherent. Still talking. I put my finger on the hole, and we began running to the OR. We were about two minutes ahead of the reaper, who was gaining on us. I got down in his face and said, 'Are you allergic to anything?' He pointed to his neck and said, 'Yeah, bullets.' I thought *This guy'll make it*.

"Then, with all that chaos swarming around him, he grabbed my arm and said, 'Doc, you operate on me like I'm alive, not like I'm dying.' He let go, then jerked and said, 'And my name is Roger. What's yours?'

"He made it, too. Wife gave birth two weeks later. They paged me, called me into their room, and laid their son in my arms. Named him after me." I stared at her. "Textbooks will tell you that he should be doornail dead. No reason he's still with us. I think it had something to do with a DNA-level sense of humor mixed with a rather strong desire to meet his son."

I brushed her face and the edge of her smile. "You've got the same thing. Don't lose your sense of humor."

She grabbed my arm and pulled on me. Her tone serious. "I'm going to ask you a question, and I want an honest answer."

"Okay."

"Promise you'll tell me the truth?"

"Promise."

"Can you get us out of here?"

"Honestly?"

She nodded.

"No idea."

She lay back. "Phew. That's good to know. I thought you were going to say 'no idea,' and then we'd really be in a pickle." She shook her head. "And I'm not even going to ask you about the direction we're headed, 'cause I know you've got that figured out. Right?"

"Right."

"Seriously?"

"No."

Her eyes narrowed. She tapped herself in the chest, then me. "We've got to work on our communication."

"We were."

She shook her head. "I'm not asking you this stuff because I want honest answers. I want you to lie your butt off. Tell me we've only got a mile to go when there might be a hundred ahead of us."

I laughed. "Okay. Listen, if you'll quit talking, we can get going. There's a helicopter waiting for us just beyond that first rise out there."

"They bring Starbucks?"

"Yep. Orange juice, couple of egg sandwiches, sausage, muffins, raspberry Danish, and a dozen glazed doughnuts."

She patted me on the back. "Now you're getting the hang of it."

IDEALLY, I'D HAVE BUILT a sled of some sort. Something that would glide over the snow and not beat her to death. Problem was, that'd work great on the flat parts, but from what I could see, there weren't a lot of those. And given the angles we'd be traversing, I knew I couldn't handle a sled. If I got caught off balance, if the angle was too steep, or her weight started pulling against me, it could get away from me and I'd never recover. She'd survive the plane crash only to die on the stretcher.

I decided on a hybrid between a sled and stretcher. Something she could lie down in—facing away from me—that would glide behind me over those rare flat parts but, when needed, I could lift with two hands and pull behind me, giving me better control.

I started with the wing that had been ripped off. Given that its surface was some sort of material that was more cloth and plastic than metal, it was light, and maybe just as important, slick. Its internal structure was metal, and given that the wing had been ripped away from the fuselage, the gas tanks had drained via gravity. The problem with a wing was that it was, well . . . wing-shaped. Rounded on both sides. So I cut a woman-sized cavity lengthwise and reinforced the bottom with the support poles from the other wing.

The simplicity of it actually surprised me.

My next question: Would miles of dragging across rock, ice, and other rough objects tear the material? Obviously, yes.

I had to reinforce the bottom. Reinforcing would increase drag, but without it, we'd wear through the wing in no time. Where to find a suitable piece of sheet metal? Didn't take me long. The engine had been shrouded by sheet metal. One side had been bent severely upon impact. The other only scratched. And, thanks to some mechanic who invented a way to work on the engine, it was secured with removable pins. I removed it, tied it to the bottom of the wing, about where Ashley's butt would sit, and eyed my creation. It might work. Given what I had to work with, it had to.

I packed everything I could find into my backpack, including all the meat I'd cooked—more like jerky than filet mignon—and tied that bundle crosswise over the wing where it could elevate Ashley's leg.

I fed her four Advil and held the water to her lips. She sipped quietly as I explained my idea.

"I don't have a good fix on which way to go, but I do know that northwest, behind us, the mountains rise up, and we'd need to be part goat to get over them. That way . . ." I pointed. "The plateau rolls away southeast. The streams run that way too. It's pretty simple: we need to get lower, and fortunately for us, that's the only way down. So we're going to pick our way downhill. I lead. You follow. I'll have my hands on you all the time. When it's flat, I'll fix a harness that will allow me to use the straps and waist belt from my backpack to pull you. Any questions?"

She shook her head and chewed slowly on the meat. I checked her leg, wrapped her warmly, zipped up her bag, and pulled the wool beanie down over her ears. "For the first time, your leg is now down below your heart. It's going to swell during the day. Best we can do is ice at night. That's going to cause you . . . some discomfort."

She nodded.

"But"—I pointed—"nothing is going to hurt like getting you out of here."

She gritted her teeth. I put my hands beneath her arms, pulled gently, and began sliding her toward the stretcher, a few inches at a time. The sleeping bag slid rather easily over the snow and ice until it hooked on a rock or root, and when I pulled it jerked her leg.

She screamed at the top of her lungs, turned her head away from me, and threw up. Everything she had eaten, including the Advil, splattered the snow. I wiped her mouth and then her forehead where she'd broken out in a sweat.

"Sorry."

She nodded and said nothing. She was grinding her teeth.

I got her to the wing, slid her and her sleeping bag onto it, and then went back for Napoleon, who looked happy to see me. I picked him up and laid him next to her. She put an arm around him, but didn't open her eyes. She looked clammy.

I propped her head up with Grover's bag. I secured the bow and Grover's fly rods alongside. It was ridiculously overloaded, but I was operating on the principle that it was better to have it and not need it than need it and not have it. Even if it meant a little more weight. Although I did leave both our laptops, cell phones, and all paperwork related to either her or my work. Figured that was all dead weight.

I searched the site, double checking, then tied a tether of cord from her to me. If everything else failed, she'd be tied to me and me to her. This was only a bad idea if I fell over a cliff and took her with me.

I stared at the crash site, then up at the rocks where Grover lay, the rock where I'd had him perched and the faint blood trail from the wounded mountain lion leading away through the rocks. Then I took a long look down into the plateau where we were headed. I took a compass reading, because I knew as we descended or got mixed up in the trees below, my perspective wouldn't be as good. I zipped up my jacket, grabbed the makeshift handles behind me, took a step, then another, then another. After twenty feet, I said, "You okay?"

After a second she said, "Yes." The fact that her teeth were not gritted told me more than her actual answer.

I didn't know if we had ten miles to go or a hundred, but those first twenty feet were as important as any of them.

Well, almost.

CHAPTER TWENTY-TWO

The first hour, we said little. The snow was knee-deep most places. Deeper in others. Couple of times I fell to midchest and had to crawl out. This was good for Ashley and bad for me. It made my walking two or three times more difficult, but made her path across quite smooth. I focused on my breathing, my grip—or rather, making sure I had one—and took my time. The pain in my ribs was considerable.

We walked down off our plateau, toward the stream where I'd caught the trout and into a small forested area of evergreen trees. The limbs were thick with snow like frosting. If you bumped one, it'd dump several shovelfuls of snow down your back.

After an hour and what might have been a mile she said, "Excuse me, Doc, but we're not going very fast. You need to giddyup."

I collapsed in the snow next to her, breathing heavily. My chest rising and falling in the thin air. My legs were screaming.

She looked down at me and tapped me in the forehead. "You want me to get you a Gatorade or something?"

I nodded. "Yeah, that'd be great."

"You know what I was thinking?"

I felt the sweat trickling down the back of my neck. "There's no telling."

"I was thinking how great a cheeseburger would be right now."

I nodded.

"Maybe two patties. Extra cheese, of course."

"Of course."

"Tomato. Got to be a good tomato. Onion. Preferably Vidalia. Ketchup. Mustard. Mayo."

White, cottony clouds drifted overhead. Another commercial airliner streaked through the sky some 30,000 feet above us.

"And extra pickles," she added.

"And two orders of fries on the side."

"I think I could eat that whole thing twice right now."

I pointed up. "It's cruel, really. We can see them just fine, but I'm pretty sure they can't see us."

"Why don't you build a really big fire?"

"You think it'd do any good?"

"Not really, but it would make us feel better." She looked beyond us then, through the trees, in the direction I had been walking. "You'd better get to pulling." She tapped the wing-contraption in which she lay. "This thing's not battery-powered, you know?"

"Funny, I figured that out about an hour ago." I took a few steps. "I need you to do me a favor."

"Don't push your luck with me."

I handed her a clean Nalgene bottle. "We're going to need to drink. A lot. If, while I'm pulling, you could pack this thing with snow, then slip it inside your bag and let your body warmth melt it, it'll help us both keep hydrated, and we don't need to get into the habit of eating cold snow. You mind?"

She shook her head and took the bottle, scooping the mouth into the snow. She screwed the lid on. "Can I ask you something?"

The temperature was probably in the single digits, yet sweat was pouring off my forehead. I'd pulled off my jacket so I didn't soak it with sweat, and was pulling in a base layer and one shirt. My body was drenched. This was good when we were walking, but real bad when we stopped because I had no way to get warm and dry. As long as I kept moving I was okay, but when we stopped I'd have to immediately start a fire and start drying out my clothes. And this was before I could do anything to help Ashley. A tricky balance.

"Sure. Fire away."

"The voice mail. What's the deal?"

"What voice mail?"

"The one you were listening to as we were taking off."

I bit a piece of dead skin off my bottom lip. "We had a disagreement."

"About what?"

"About a . . . difference of opinion."

"You're not going to tell me, are you?"

I shrugged.

She smirked. "Is she right?"

I nodded without looking. "Yes."

"That's refreshing."

"What's that?"

"A man who admits when his wife is right about something that matters."

"I wasn't always this way."

"While I've got you talking . . . I've got a question for you. Have you talked about me in your recorder?"

"Only in a medical sense."

She held out her hand. "Give it to me."

I smiled. "No."

"Then you have." She raised a single eyebrow.

"My speaking into this box has little to nothing to do with you."

"So you admit it? Some of it includes me."

"As a doctor dictating a patient diagnosis."

"There's no personal opinion? No talking behind my back?"

No amount of conversation would convince her. I pushed the BACK button, then PLAY, rolled the volume wheel as loud as it would go, and laid it in her hand. My last recording to Rachel resonated through the air. Ashley hovered over it, listening intently.

When it finished, she clasped her fingers over it and gently handed it back. "You weren't lying."

I slid it into my pocket, close to my chest.

She watched me a minute, the question on the tip of her tongue. I knew it was only a matter of time. Finally she let it out. "Why do you clam up every time I bring up the recorder?" She raised an eyebrow. "What are you not telling me?"

I took a deep breath that did not fill me.

"Silence does not qualify as an answer."

Another shallow breath. "Rachel and I are . . . separated."

"You're what?"

"We had a fight. Kind of a big one, and we're working through . . . an issue, or two. The recorder helps to do that."

She looked confused. "She doesn't sound like she wants to be separated."

"What do you mean?"

"The voice mail."

"It's complicated."

"We've been stuck out here for what, eleven days now, you've set my leg, sewed up my head, even wiped my butt, and you're just now telling me you're separated from your wife?"

"I was acting as your doctor."

"What about the other 99 percent of the time when you were acting as my friend?"

"Didn't think it was relevant."

She held out a hand. "Give it here."

"What?"

She turned her palm up. "Put it in my hand."

"Are you going to hurt it, throw it, or cause it not to work in any way whatsoever?"

"No."

"Are you going to give it back?"

"Yes."

"Will it work when you do?"

"Yes."

I laid it in her hand. She studied it, then clicked RECORD.

"Rachel . . . this is Ashley. Ashley Knox. I'm the idiot who agreed to get in the plane with him. Your husband has many wonderful qualities, and he's a very good doctor, but he plays his cards close to his chest when it comes to talking about you. What is it with men and the whole stoic-controlled-I'm-not-talking-about-my-emotions thing? Huh?" She shook her head. "Why can't they just tell us what they're thinking? It's not rocket science. You'd think they'd find a way to just open up their mouths and say what's on their mind. Evidently it's not that easy. Well . . . I'm very much looking forward to meeting you, provided he gets me out of here. In the meantime, I'll keep working on him. I think the recorder idea is a good one. Now that I think about it, I may give one to Vince when I get home. But—" She smiled at me. "And I hate to be the one to break this to you—Ben may be a lost cause. He's one of the more tongue-twisted men I've ever met." She was about to click it off when she added, " 'Course, that's forgivable if a man is honest and can make a pretty mean cup of coffee."

I slid the recorder back into my pocket and stood up. I'd grown stiff. Cold filtered through my wet clothes, clung to me. We'd stayed too long.

She looked up at me. "I'm sorry I doubted you. You can delete my message if you like."

I shook my head. "No. I've already told her all about you, so . . . it'll help to add a voice to the story." I retraced my steps, backed up to the stretcher, lifted it, and began pulling.

"So . . . where does she live?"

"Just down the beach."

"How far?"

"Two miles. I built her a house."

"You're separated, but you built her a house."

"It's not like that."

"What's it like?"

"Complicated. The kids . . ."

"Kids! You have kids?"

"Two."

"You have two kids, and you're just now telling me?"

I shrugged.

"How old?"

"Four. They're twins."

"Names?"

"Michael and Hannah."

She nodded. "Good names."

"Good kids."

"I'll bet they keep you busy."

"I don't . . . don't see them much."

She frowned. "You must've really screwed up."

I didn't respond.

"In my experience, it's usually the guy. Always thinking with your plumbing."

"It's not that."

She didn't sound convinced. "Is she dating?"

"No."

"Come on . . . out with it. Why're you separated?"

I wanted out of this conversation.

"Still not telling me, are you?"

I didn't respond.

Her tone changed. "What if . . ."

I knew it was coming. "Yes?"

"What if we don't make it out . . . what then?"

"You mean, 'what good is it?' And given that possibility, why am I still talking into it?"

"Something like that."

I turned around, walked back to face Ashley. The snow was thigh-deep. Blue skies were giving way to gray, heavy clouds threatening snow.

I tapped my chest. "I've operated on thousands of people. Many were in bad shape. Much worse than us. Never once have I thought *They're not going to make it, they won't get better.* By design, doctors are some of the most optimistic people on the planet. We have to be. Can you imagine a doctor who wasn't? You'd sit there and ask, 'Doc, do you think I'll make it?' What if I shook my head and said, 'I don't think so.' I wouldn't make it in medicine very long because no one would come to see me.

"We have to look at very bad situations and find ways to make them better. Every day is a chess match. Us against evil. Most days we win. Some days we don't." I swirled my hand in a large motion in front of me. "And we do all of this because of one word." I tapped the recorder. "Hope. It circulates in our veins. It's what fuels us."

I turned away. A single tear trickled down my face. I spoke softly. "I will play this for Rachel. I will play the sound of your voice."

Ashley nodded, closed her eyes, and lay back.

I returned to the front, grabbed the handles, and began pulling.

From behind me I heard "You still haven't answered my question."

"I know."

WEATHER UP HERE IS FICKLE. Blink, and clouds will move in, cover you up, shower you in snow or ice. You can be cold all day, but come dark, you find your face and lips are sunburnt and peeling. Your cheeks are burned from the wind, your feet are blistered.

If water is available, people can normally make it three weeks without food. But up here, where we're burning twice as many calories just to breathe and shiver, not to mention pull a gurney through four feet of powder, that time is a bit less. This land is harsh and unforgiving, beautiful and magnificent yet unbending. Biting cold one second, hot the next, frigid the next.

Five minutes passed, clouds blew in, mist covered the mountain. Pretty soon the snow was blowing sideways. Even circling. It stung my face and made walking nearly impossible. We wouldn't last much longer in this storm. There was no place to hide. No shelter. I stared into that white darkness and made a tough decision.

I turned us around.

The walk back was disheartening. I hated giving up ground we'd already gained, but better to give it up and live than keep it and die. Four hours later, we were back at the crash. I could barely move. I got Ashley comfortable. Her face was riddled with pain. She said nothing. I forced my eyes open until she fell asleep.

I WOKE UP FOUR HOURS LATER. Shivering. I'd never pulled off my wet clothes. A costly mistake. The sleeping bag is designed to insulate the temperature inside it. Be that cold or hot. I was cold and wet—two conditions that deteriorate the bag's insulating ability, or R-value. I stripped, hung my clothes over a wing support, stoked the fire, and crawled back into my bag, shivering. It took me nearly an hour to get warm—which meant I wasn't sleeping but rather spending energy I didn't have and couldn't spare. Not only costly, but stupid. Mistakes like that will kill you when you're not looking.

CHAPTER TWENTY-THREE

She did not look impressed. "So what's today's adventure?"

Her voice rattled around my head. It took me a minute to remember where I was. I felt hungover. Disoriented.

"Huh?"

"You going to sleep all day? I've been trying to let you sleep 'cause I know you're tired, but I've really got to go and it's not like I can just cross my legs."

I sat up. "Sorry. You should wake me."

"You were sleeping really hard, so I tried without you, but I don't have enough hands and didn't want to soak my bag."

I nodded. Rubbed my eyes. "Good call."

"What day is this?"

I raised my watch and couldn't see anything on the face. I pressed the Indiglo button. Nothing happened. I pushed it again. Harder. Still nothing. I shook it and held it up to the daylight.

A deep, spiderwebbing crack spread across the glass from bottom left corner to top right. Condensation had gathered beneath.

"I don't know."

She noticed the watch. "That important?"

"Rachel gave it to me. Years ago."

"Sorry." She was quiet a minute. Her voice was softer. "How many days have we been doing this?

Napoleon was licking my ear. "Twelve . . . I think."

She nodded, calculating. "Florence. I think we'd be in Florence now. We reserved this suite in a hotel on the Arno River overlooking the Ponte Vecchio. The brochure said you could see the lights of the Duomo in the distance. . . . I've always wanted to see that."

When I sat up, the cold gripped my chest and reminded me I had stripped in the middle of the night. She studied the purple bruise on my rib cage. "How you doing?"

"Okay. It's not as tender."

She pointed to the key at the end of the wrist strap on my recorder. "You really need that out here?"

"You're kind of nosy, aren't you?"

"Well . . . if you're cutting weight . . ." She shrugged. "What's it fit?"

"Rachel's house."

"You mean the house you built her but don't live in, where she keeps the kids and you rarely get to see them."

"My . . . aren't we full of ourselves today."

"Just telling it like I see it."

I pulled my shirt down and began slipping into my cold, damp clothes. In doing so, I was able to see myself in the daylight. She did, too.

"You're skinny."

"It's this crash weight loss diet I've been trying out."

She chuckled, then started laughing. It was contagious. A good way to start the day.

I checked her leg, helped her take care of the necessities, and started melting snow in the Jetboil. I didn't know how much fuel we had left, but it had to be running low. The tank has no gauge, and it's designed to be portable, not endless in its supply. When

I shook it, it did not sound promising. At sea level, it would boil water in about seventy-five seconds. Up here, it was taking three to four times that long. Requiring more fuel and depleting the tank four times faster than normal. The fuel in Grover's lighter had nearly evaporated. While Zippo lighters look cool and sound cool, reminding me of the Rat Pack, James Dean, or Bruce Willis in *Die Hard*, they require filling. Often weekly. Again, it's a portable fuel supply. Not endless. Big difference. Any matches I'd had when we started were long gone. Our options were low, and we needed fire. I'd have to keep my eyes peeled for wood that I could use to make a bow drill.

It was midday. Given low clouds, an overcast sky, and dropping temperature, the snow had frozen on top. That created favorable walking conditions. Frozen snow meant that with my snowshoes I could spend more time on top of the snow rather than down in it. Requiring less energy. Allowing us, in theory, to travel farther.

I laced up my boots, strapped on my gaiters, and slid into my jacket. One sleeve was torn around the elbow, and little down feathers were slipping out. My hands were starting to take a beating. I cut strips from the sleeves of Grover's denim jacket and wrapped them around my hands.

Given that we'd packed yesterday, it didn't take us long to do it again. I loaded the "sled," gave Ashley a few pieces of meat to chew on, along with some water, and pulled her to the opening—remembering the painful bump at the entrance. I slid her gently over it and out into the open air. The temperature felt twenty degrees colder. I looked at the sled, studied my process of the day before, and realized I needed a harness. Something that kept my hands free, let me pull with my legs and chest, and yet kept me connected to the sled in case of a mishap. I crawled back inside, removed the seat belt harness from Grover's seat using his Leatherman. I attached a cord from the harness to the sled and buckled myself in. It made an X across my chest, allowed me to pull my arms free, and, given the quick release buckle, let me pop out of it in a hurry if I started slipping and needed to disconnect so I didn't drag Ashley down over the side of the mountain with me.

Dubious, she tilted her head. She had a mouthful of meat and was moving it from one side to the other. I pulled off my jacket, picked up Napoleon, and slid both inside the bag with her. If I wore my jacket in the harness, I'd be sweating in a matter of minutes, soaking the inside of my jacket and reducing the R-value to almost nothing. This way, she kept it warm and dry, so that when we stopped, I could slip it on, keeping warm. A crucial decision. I strapped myself in, leaned into the weight, and began pulling.

After an hour we'd gone maybe 500 meters, dropping maybe a hundred feet in elevation. Every three steps was followed by several seconds of rest. Then three more steps. Then more rest. It was painfully slow progress. But it was progress.

She was not impressed. "Seriously . . ." She took a sip of water. "How long do you think you can do this?" The good news was that she'd been eating and drinking at a slow, easily digestible pace nearly all day.

"Don't know." I watched her out of the corner of my eye.

"We can't do this. You can't." She pointed at the skyline with a piece of jerky. "Look around you. We are in the middle of BFE."

"BFE?"

"Bum-you-know-what-Egypt."

I stopped, sweat dripping off my face, breathing deeply. "Ashley?"

She didn't answer.

"Ashley?"

She crossed her arms.

"We can't stay up there. If we do, we'll die. And I can't leave you. If I do, you'll die. So we're walking out."

Her frustration at being helpless bubbled over. She screamed. "It's been twelve damn days and not a soul has come looking and we're maybe a mile from where we started. At this rate, it'll be Christmas before we get out of here."

"They don't know to look."

"Okay, then . . . what's your plan? How do you plan to get us out of here?"

This was fear talking. Not logic. No amount of talking would satisfy it. "One step at a time."

"And how long do you think you can keep that up?"

"As long as it takes."

"And what if you can't?"

"I can."

"But how do you know?"

"What's my choice?"

She closed her eyes, pulled Napoleon in close, and stared at the sky. I pulled out the compass, took a reading of 125 degrees, picked a small ridgeline in the distance as a marker, and started putting one foot in front of the other. Last night's snow had completely covered yesterday's tracks. There was no evidence we'd ever left the crash site.

We didn't speak for several hours.

My course took me slightly downhill and through the trees. The snow was heavy, as were the drifts. The ten to fourteen feet of snow beneath us meant we were walking through limbs that, come summertime, would be well above our heads. Evergreen limbs hold a lot of snow, although when you walk by and brush them, they don't try and keep it all to themselves. They dump as much as possible on you. I was constantly shaking out the snow from around my neck. I took my time, gauging my breathing and my energy level. I took plenty of rest between steps. If I started to get overheated, I'd slow down, take a few more breaths between steps. We were moving at a snail's pace. In a little over six hours, we'd come what I judged to be a little more than a mile.

It was nearly dark when I stopped.

I was soaking wet with sweat and exhausted, but I knew if I didn't start making my fire bow, I'd regret it. I slid Ashley beneath the limbs of an evergreen and up alongside a rock. The ground beneath her had been protected from the snow so it was actually dirt and dried evergreen needles. A squirrel had been here eating a pinecone. I pulled off my sweaty shirt, hung it on a limb, gathered several handfuls of dead pine needles along with some small twigs, and made a small fire next to Ashley. It lit quickly. And I was right about the Jetboil. When I clicked it to start the fire, it hiccupped. We had maybe a day left in the tank. I gathered more sticks, laid them in a pile next to her, and said, "Tend this. Don't let it die. I'll be within shouting distance."

"What're you doing?"

"Making a bow."

She stared at Grover's bow strapped to the end of the sled. "I thought we had one of those."

"I'm not making that kind."

I started making wide circles, looking for two pieces of wood. One piece, maybe three feet long with a bit of an arc, across which I could thread a shoestring or piece of cord and then a second straight piece out of which I could cut the spindle—something that would end up being about the size of the handle of a hammer. Maybe a bit shorter. Took me about thirty minutes to find both.

I slipped through the trees, the snow crunching under my makeshift snowshoes. Walking was a constant struggle. I stopped at a distance. Catching my breath. Maybe spying is a better word.

She was sitting up, tending the fire. The glow of the fire on her face. Even there, even then, she was beautiful. There was no denying that.

The difficulty of our situation was always on my mind. Always tugging at me. What faced us was nearing the impossible. But I hadn't really seen us through her eyes. Her sleeping bag. Her sitting there with nothing to do but tend the fire and scratch Napoleon's head. She was dependent on me for everything. Eating. Movement. Food. Water. Going to the bathroom. She couldn't do a thing, other than sleep, without me. If I'd had to be as dependent on someone else for the last twelve days as she was on me, I'd have been much more difficult to live with.

Doctors are used to sweeping into the midst of a problem, swooshing down like Zeus from on high, fixing it, and then getting out before the aftermath sets in. Nurses and RNAs do all the dirty work. Much of the true "doctoring." Ashley needed both a doctor and a "doctor." Being one was easy. Being the other was not. I didn't know how to make that any better. I just knew I wanted to.

I returned to the fire, slid into my bag, chewed on some meat, and made myself drink water. While the Jetboil was failing, I could still use the upper piece that we cooked in. Sort of a small coffee can sort of thing. At any rate, it was aluminum and would stand up to heat. So I filled it with snow and leaned it against the coals.

We drank and ate for the next hour while I worked on my bow. When I'd buried Grover, I'd unlaced his boots and stored the laces in my pocket. They were about to come in handy. I pulled out a lace, tied a knot in one end, threaded it through the groove on one end of the bow, pulled it tight, and slid it through the groove on the other end, securing it with a few loops and a knot. Not too snug, but tight enough so that when I twisted the spindle into it, there would be enough tension on the string to spin the spindle. It's sort of a touch thing and takes a few stringings of the bow to get it right. I cut the spindle to about ten inches, carved both ends into points—with one end wider for more friction—and then cut a groove in the middle that would help hold the shoelace in place.

That finished, I set it aside, drank the last of my water, and looked up for the first time in a long time.

Ashley was staring at me. "You can be intense when you want to," she said.

"I have a feeling we're going to need that tomorrow."

She crossed her arms. "I need an update. What you think. Where are we? That sort of thing."

"I think we made it about a mile from the crash site. Tomorrow morning I'm going to climb that small rise over there and see if I can tell what's in the other plateau on the other side. We'll stay on our current heading, as much as the mountain will allow, and we've probably got enough meat for several more days. So I think we just keep going. It'll help you to stay as hydrated as you can. Eat as much of the food as you like, and tell me when I jar you too much." I shrugged. "I'm sorry when I do. I know today was rough on you."

She let out a deep breath. "I'm sorry I jumped at you this morning."

I shook my head. "You're in a tough place. You can't do much of anything without my help. That'd be difficult for anyone."

I placed more wood on the fire, slid close enough to be warm but not set myself aflame, and closed my eyes. Sleep was falling on me fast. Then I thought of Ashley. I forced my eyes open. She was staring at me. "You need anything?"

She shook her head. Tried to smile.

"You sure?"

"No."

She was asleep in seconds.

CHAPTER TWENTY-FOUR

It was difficult to wake up knowing we'd been doing this for thirteen days. I shook off the sleep and was dressed before daylight. The fire was out, but a few coals remained. I fed it, blew on it, and fanned a flame in minutes. I fed it again, scratched Napoleon, and then headed up the small rise above us to get a view of our surroundings.

I took my time. Studying every indentation. Every seam in the mountain. I kept asking myself, does anything look man-made?

The answer was a resounding no. Everything was pristine and untouched. A nature lover's paradise. I loved nature as much as the next guy, but this was ridiculous.

I steadied the compass, let the needle settle, and took a reading. I stared across the face of the compass at the mountains in the distance. To get to them we'd have to travel all day, maybe two, through tall trees and deep snow. Wouldn't be easy, and once in them, I'd lose all sense of bearing. Never make it without the compass. In the trees, I'd lose all sense of perspective. Direction. Maybe life is like that.

My bearings would take us through a gap and hopefully to a lower elevation. Staring out at the immense wilderness reminded me. I could lose most everything and still have a chance. But not without the compass. I tied it to a piece of nylon cord and tethered it around my neck.

When I returned, Ashley was sitting up, stirring the fire. She started on me before I had a chance to say good morning. "How'd you know you wanted to marry your wife? I mean, how'd you *know*?"

"Good morning."

"Yeah, yeah, yeah. Good morning yourself. Let me know when it gets good."

"I see you're feeling better."

I knelt next to her bag, unzipped the side, pulled it back, and examined her leg. The good news was that there was no real change. And the bad news was that there was no real change.

"Today at lunch we need to ice that . . . okay?"

She nodded. "Seriously. I want to know."

I began stuffing my bag into its compression sack. "I wanted to spend every second with her. Wanted to laugh with her, cry with her, grow old with her, hold her hand, touch knees at the breakfast table, and since we'd been hanging out a couple years, I really wanted to have sex with her. And a lot of it."

She laughed. "Were you two still pretty active before you separated?"

"The best kept secret about the whole marriage thing is that the loving part gets better. You lose—at least I did—all the 'I've got to prove something' or whatever it is. I guess us guys get our ideas of what it ought to be through movies. When in fact, it's little or nothing like that. It's more of a sharing than a taking. Movies don't do a very good job of portraying this. They show the hot, sweaty side. And that's great, I'm not knocking it; I'm just exposing the myth that that's as good as it gets.

"Granted, there are a lot of folks whose fires die out, I get that, but I also think there are a lot of couples out there who have been married thirty, forty, fifty years that know a whole lot more about the loving part of marriage than we give them credit for. We think we're young, we've got the monopoly on passion." I shook my head. "Not so sure. They might give Dr. Phil a run for his money. Grover sure would."

"What about when one wants to and one doesn't."

I laughed. "Rachel liked to call that 'mercy loving'—and it's 99 percent of the time her having mercy on me."

"Mercy loving?"

"It goes something like, 'Honey . . . I can't sleep. Help.' "

"And . . . before the separation . . . did she 'help' you?"

"Sometimes. Not all the time."

"What do you do when she doesn't?"

"Tylenol PM."

"I guess I'm getting pretty personal."

"You are."

"So . . . how's that work in the separation?"

I took a deep breath. "It doesn't."

"How long have you two been separated?"

"Long enough for me to buy my Tylenol PM in the bulk section at Costco." I began strapping stuff to the sled. "Listen, I need to get you to stand up. I don't want you putting weight on that leg, so we'll take it easy, but I want you to start bearing weight on the good leg. Forcing circulation."

She held out her hands. I unzipped the bag, she braced her good foot on mine, and I lifted her slowly. She wobbled, got dizzy, leaned her head on my shoulder, and then finally stood up straight. "That feels good. Almost feel human."

"How's the bad leg?"

"Tender. More of a dull pain than sharp as long as I don't flex the muscles around the break."

I readjusted the straps on the brace. She put her arms on my shoulders, balancing on me. I steadied her by the hips. "Let's just give this a few minutes. The change in your blood pressure will be good for your heart. Put it under a load and force it to move the blood around your body."

She stared up into the trees, smiling. "My legs are cold."

"Well . . . that's what you get for walking around in your socks and underwear."

"You know, when I was in middle school, this was how we danced if we were 'going with someone.' "

"It's been a long time since I've heard the term 'going with someone.' "

"If we were serious, I'd put my hands on his shoulders and he'd put his hands on my hips, slowly wrapping them around my back when the chaperones weren't watching. The crude guys wrapped their hands all the way around you and cupped your butt or slid them into your jeans pockets. My dad wouldn't let me date those guys."

"Good call."

"Vince hates to dance."

"Can't say I'm much of a fan either."

"Why?"

"Got no rhythm."

"Okay, I've had enough. Put me down."

I settled her back inside her bag and zipped her up. She pointed. "Come on. Let me see. Show me what you've got."

"What? Dance?"

She nodded.

"You've lost your mind."

She swirled her finger at the ground beneath me. "Go ahead. I'm waiting."

"You don't understand. I have the hip movement of a toy soldier. I can't even do the 'white man dance.' "

"The what?"

"The white man dance. You know, the dance that black guys do to make fun of white guys who can't dance. Only problem is you've got to have rhythm to mimic guys who have none. I don't even have enough to do that."

She crossed her arms. "I'm waiting."

"Why don't you spit in one hand and wish in the other and see which one gets full the quickest."

She scratched her head, then smiled. "Where'd you hear that?"

"Something my dad used to say when I'd ask him for money for the weekend."

"Sounds like a rough relationship."

"A bit."

"So, are you going to dance or what?"

I turned, did my best John Travolta "Staying Alive" imitation followed by that weird mop-bucket thing that guys do with their arms and hips. I topped it off with my YMCA imitation and a Michael Jackson moonwalk, spin, and hat tilt. When I finished, she was doubled over in her bag, laughing so hard she couldn't talk. Finally she held out a hand. "Stop . . . don't . . . I think I just peed a little."

The laughter felt good. Real good. And as much as I wanted a satellite phone, a helicopter ride out of there, and a surgical suite to fix her leg, the laughter was worth all of that put together. Napoleon looked at us like we were nuts. Especially me.

She lay back, breathing. Half laughing.

I zipped up my jacket. "Rachel made us take lessons."

"What?"

"Yep. Swing. Tango. Waltz. Viennese waltz. Jitterbug. Foxtrot. Even a line dance or two."

"You know how to do all those?"

I nodded. "Rachel said that due to all the running, my hip flexors are rather tight, making me somewhat rhythmically challenged. So I signed us up for dance lessons. A year's worth. Some of the most fun we ever had on dates."

"So you really can dance?"

"With her."

"If I'm lucky, I'll get one dance out of Vince at our wedding. That's about it."

"I learned that I like dancing with my wife. Once I learned what to do, how to lead . . ." I laughed. "Once she let me . . . it wasn't so bad. Wasn't so embarrassing. Took the worry out of it, let us have fun. 'Course, after that she wanted to dance at every party we ever attended."

"And did you?"

I nodded. "I called it mercy dancing, and 99 percent of the time it had to do with me having mercy on her. But, it had its trade-off." I raised my eyebrows.

"You need to talk to Vince when we get out of here."

"I'll see what I can do." I gave her my jacket, which she stuffed inside her bag, stepped into the harness, and buckled myself in. "Come on, we're burning daylight."

"I've heard that before." She snapped her fingers. "Where's that come from?"

"John Wayne. *The Cowboys.*"

She slid down in her bag. "You are getting more interesting with every day that passes."

"Trust me, my rabbit's hat is just about empty."

"I doubt that."

I strapped on my snowshoes and leaned into the sled, and it gave way across the frozen snow. I took two steps, and she called to me.

"Can I see that little dance move one more time?"

I shook my hips, mopped the floor, tossed the pizza, spun the Q-tip, and spelled YMCA.

She was howling, gently kicking her one good leg.

We pulled out through the trees, bathed in the smell of evergreens and the sound of her laughter.

CHAPTER TWENTY-FIVE

By lunchtime we'd walked a mile and a half, and I was toast. My left foot was frozen, a bad sign, and because the last half mile was slightly uphill, the straps had been cutting into my shoulders, making my fingers numb. It's a good thing I wasn't scheduled to operate on anybody.

We stopped for an hour alongside a small creek whose banks were frozen and swollen with snow. I pulled Ashley up beneath a tree, pulled off my wet shirt and hung it to dry. Letting the shirt freeze was actually good because it was easier to shake off ice than wring out sweat in this temperature.

The tree's branches canopied out over the ground, protecting it from snow. It created a bowl effect. I slid Ashley down inside, flattened her out, and slid one of the branches slightly askew to let in more light. Then I climbed into my bag where, warm and quiet, I slept for an hour. When I woke I dressed, nibbled on some jerky, and stepped back into the harness. I dug a ramp of sorts to pull her out of the bowl beneath the tree. Once I got her up on flat ground again, I stamped my foot five or six times. It felt wet. Wet meant cold. And cold was bad. Especially for toes. I'd need to watch this.

Late in the afternoon the sun poked through, heated things up slightly, which turned the snow more toward mush—wet and sticky. I'd take two or three steps, fall, bury myself in snow, climb out, take two or three more steps, bury myself again. . . . This went on for a couple of hours.

By nightfall we'd come maybe two and a half miles. A total of three and a half or four from the crash site. Sometimes I'd take a minute rest between steps, and yet it wasn't enough. Clouds spilled over the mountains, nighttime fell quickly, and I could barely move. I was cold and soaking wet, but I didn't have the energy to make a fire. The little voice inside my head was telling me I couldn't keep this up for long. I needed to find a place to hole up tomorrow and rest a day.

Ashley too was tired. She'd been bracing herself all day against the what-if or possible fall. That was taking its toll on her.

We camped at a rock outcropping. A ledge that, given years of use by critters, had made somewhat of a cave. Good protection from the wind and snow, while also offering a one-in-a-million view. I propped Ashley up against the wall, giving her the full effect of the panorama. She cracked her eyes open and said, "Wow. Never seen anything like that."

"Me either," was all I could mutter. I sat down. Totally zonked. "Would it be all right with you if we didn't have a fire tonight?"

She nodded.

I stripped out of my wet clothes and tried to hang what I could along the inside of the rock ledge. Even though the outside temperature was in the teens, my inner layer of Capilene was dripping with sweat. I pulled on my only pair of boxer shorts, slipped into my bag, closed my eyes, and only then thought of my boots. If I didn't get my left boot dry, tomorrow would be a miserable day.

I climbed out. Put my jacket back on. Grabbed handfuls of dead pine needles and small twigs and built a teepee about a foot tall. I stacked the dry needles inside, along with a few branches still holding on to their dead needles. I knew I would only get one shot at this.

I took out Grover's lighter, rubbed it between my palms for some reason that I can't explain, stuck it inside the teepee, and struck it. It sparked, but no flame. I shook it.

"Come on, just one time."

I struck it again. Nothing.

"Last time."

I struck it, a flame appeared, grabbed the pine needles, and was gone. The flame didn't last more than a second. But it was long enough to light the needles—which are incredibly flammable. If you've ever set a Christmas tree on fire you know what I mean. I slowly fed more twigs into it, blowing lightly at the base. The fire grew, I fed more tinder into it, and once I felt like it had caught, I searched for larger sticks. Maybe even a log.

Dead on my feet, I found enough wood to feed the fire for a few hours, and stacked rocks alongside the edge to insulate it while creating an opening in the back so the heat could escape and waft in our direction. I set my boots at the base of a crack between two of the rocks. Close enough to dry but not melt the rubber. Peeled off my jacket. Climbed into my bag and fell asleep seconds after my head hit the ground.

My last thought was knowing that Grover's lighter was finished. It had given us its last flame. Conditions continued to worsen. Wet clothes, wet feet, blisters, and little energy. We had the cooked mountain lion, but even at our current rate of eating it sparingly, we might have two days left.

That included Napoleon. If we didn't feed him, maybe three.

Problem was, I couldn't not feed him. Intellectually and in different circumstances, say the warm comfort of my office or operating suite, I might talk about how I'd eat Napoleon in dire conditions. But in truth, now that I was in those dire conditions, I couldn't eat him. Every time I looked at him, he licked my face and wagged his tail. And every time the wind blew he stood up, facing into it, and growled. Anything with that tough a spirit deserves a chance.

Others might have already carved him into dog steaks and filled up, but I just couldn't. He was probably tough as old shoe leather anyway. But, to be honest, every time I looked at him, I saw Grover. Maybe that's reason enough.

SIX OR SEVEN HOURS LATER, with the first hint of daylight crawling across the gray and white mountains before us, my eyes cracked open to the unexpected sound of a hot crackling fire. The meaning of the sound registered in my brain, and I shot upright—fearful that I'd set us on fire.

I had not.

Ashley was tending it. And had been, for several hours. My clothes were warm, dry, and oddly enough, folded on top of a rock a few feet from the fire. She was poking at the fire with a long green evergreen limb, which she got from I don't know where. The ground around her sled was bare. She'd picked it clean. Anything within arm's reach had been thrown into the fire to keep it going. Now she was using the last of the sticks I'd gathered, which explained the crackling. My boots had been turned, and the leather was dry. As were my socks. I stood there rubbing my eyes, my boxers falling off my hips now that they were two sizes too big.

"Hi." She pointed with her stick—the end of which was smoking. "You might think about buying down one or two sizes when we get out of here. Those are kind of big. And"—she made a little circle with her stick—"buy some with a button fly. You selling hot dogs?"

I covered up, rubbed my eyes, and lay back down. "I'd like some coffee, a cinnamon bun, six eggs over medium, a New York strip, some hash browns, more coffee, some orange juice, a piece of key lime pie, and a bowl of apple—no, make that peach cobbler."

"Can I have some?"

I sat up. "You didn't sleep much, did you?"

She shrugged. "Couldn't. You were pretty tired, even talked in your sleep. And your clothes were dripping wet. I can't do much, but this . . ." She circled the fire with her stick. "I can do."

"Thanks. Really." I dressed. Pulled on my warm boots, which brought a smile to my face, and grabbed the hatchet. "I'll be back."

I returned a half hour later, arms full. I made three more trips. I'd heard that wives and mothers in African tribes can spend three to ten hours a day, depending on conditions, searching for water and firewood.

Now I understood why.

I cranked the fire up, melted some snow, heated up some jerky, and fed both Ashley and Napoleon. She chewed quietly, pointing at the dog. "His ribs are showing."

"Yeah . . . I think he'd like to be out of here."

Her voice softened, betraying both humor and seriousness. "Me too."

We were quiet awhile. The fire felt good.

"How's the leg?"

She shrugged.

I knelt, unzipped her bag, and ran my hand along her thigh. The swelling had decreased and the purple had quit spreading. Both good signs. She looked up at me while I stared at the stitches in her face. "I need to pull those out before the skin grows over them."

She nodded. I pulled out my Swiss Army knife, snipped each stitch, and then began the rather painful and unpleasant experience of pulling them out. She held out her palm, and I laid each stitch into it. She winced but never cried out.

When I'd finished, she crossed her arms and asked, "How do I look?"

"Nothing a good plastic surgeon can't fix."

"That bad?"

"Neosporin or vitamin E oil would be helpful once we get home. Lessen the scars."

"Vitamin E oil?"

"Yeah. Rachel used to have me put it on her stomach to reduce the stretch marks when she was pregnant with the twins."

"I'll bet they miss you."

"I miss them."

She changed the subject. "Don't know if you've had time to think about it yet, but what's the plan?"

"Shelter and food." I unconsciously looked at my watch, forgetting it was dead, and said, "We're on a bit of a plateau here. It continues another mile or so through trees like this, then drops off, if I remember right. I'd like to get there tonight. If it drops off, it drops off to something. I'm thinking a water source. Lake, stream, something. Maybe we can hole up there a few days and give me a chance to find some food."

She eyed the bow, strapped to the top of the sled. "Are six arrows enough?"

I shrugged. "Don't have much choice." I rubbed my chest. "My ribs feel better, but if I pull that thing all the way back, it stings a bit. Grover's draw length was longer than mine, so it's harder for me to pull it and hold it back than it should be."

"His what?"

"Draw length. Each bow fits the person shooting it. Like shoes. To a point, you can wear the wrong size, but it's not real comfortable." I stared out at the dark clouds rolling in across the peaks opposite us. "Looks like snow today. And lots of it. I'd like to get through those trees before the worst of that drops on us."

She nodded. "I'm game."

We packed quickly, something we'd gotten good at, and I was back in the harness before I had time to dread it. I'd just strapped on my snowshoes and taken the first of several steps when she called from behind me. "Ben?"

I stopped, not looking back. "Yeah."

She said it quieter this time. "Ben?"

The tone of voice was different. I turned and walked back to the sled, tangling myself in the straps. "Yeah."

She stared up out of the bag. The scar above her eye would heal, but it was pink and needed antibiotic ointment. She reached out, grabbed my hand. The denim strips from Grover's jacket were fraying and hung like dirty rags off my hands. My gloves had numerous holes, and my right index finger was sticking out. She grabbed my hand, rewrapping the denim strip around it. "You okay?"

She was asking about more than just my feet or my stomach.

I knelt and let out a deep breath. "I'm okay as long as I don't think past the next step." Shook my head. "Just one at a time."

She nodded and braced herself for the constant shifting and banging on the sled.

THE SNOW DIDN'T HOLD OFF. It began dropping quarter-sized flakes in the first hour. Walking the mile through the trees took us more than three hours. We emerged where a steep slope fell off into a valley of sorts. 'Course, I was just guessing it was a valley, because given the total whiteout conditions, I had no real idea.

We pulled up under the snow-weighted limbs of an evergreen, and I pulled out the sketch I'd made of the area. I guessed we were some eight miles from the crash site, on the edge of a valley. I knew we'd walked down a 125-degree line, but we were also dodging to the right and left to skirt around rocks, ledges, small peaks, downed trees. We were probably two to three miles off our original azimuth, or line. This was to be expected, and there was little I could do about it. Walking a straight line in the wilderness is seldom possible. Walking in a straight direction is. But there's a big difference between straight line and straight direction. Both will take you in the same direction, but not to the same place.

People experienced with reading compasses, and who take it seriously, who engage in what's called orienteering, can overcome the side-to-side adjustments required by conditions and return to a straight line, allowing them to arrive at an actual predetermined point. I wasn't that good.

Think of it this way: When we started, I set out on a given degree, 125. I then quickly bumped into a small peak that I could not climb, so we walked around. Once we got to the other side, I continued on our original heading—although we were now over a mile from that original line. It's something like walking on a grid. We can walk down one line, turn right, walk three squares, then turn back left and continue in our original direction. Only now we're three squares off our original line. While we were now eight to nine miles from the crash site, we'd probably walked close to twice that, given the back-and-forth that the conditions forced upon us.

My sketch suggested we were fifteen or twenty miles yet from the single line I'd seen on the GPS that might have been a logging road or hiker's trail or something. We were fourteen days into this and moving at a snail's pace. As much as I wanted to keep going, I needed to make a shelter and not move until we had more food. Without fuel, we wouldn't make it another few days. After that, I'd be too tired to hunt for it.

With the hatchet, I cut into the tree that hid us and pulled down some limbs, giving us an entry on the lee side, and then laid those limbs on the windward side to give us more protection. I cut more limbs from a nearby tree, stacking them like vertical boards against the others, and hand-shoveled snow against the base. I fed the tips inside the limbs of our tree to hold them up, then inserted more cut limbs inside the limbs of our tree, sort of like rafters in an attic. Within an hour, we had a fair shelter.

Ashley nodded. "Not bad."

"I wouldn't want to live here, but it'll do in a pinch."

I was dreading what came next. The bow drill. I gathered tinder, needles, and small twigs and even shaved some fuzz off one of my socks. I strung the bow and slowly began turning the spindle on the hearth board. Once I'd developed the hole and cut the notch, I gave myself to fully working the bow. At this altitude it took several minutes to get smoke, but once I got it, I kept tugging on the bow. Five minutes in, I had a lot of smoke and felt like I might have enough to make a coal. I set down the bow and spindle, picked up my hearth board, and studied my coal. It might work. I lifted it, blew gently, and a small red ember appeared. I blew again and blew too hard. It scattered like dust.

I started over.

This time I pulled on the bow for eight or nine minutes, making sure I had ample dust to create a coal. Anyone who's ever done this will tell you that eight or nine minutes is a long time. Experienced bow drillers can do this whole thing from start to finish in two minutes or less. I was not that experienced.

I set down the bow, lifted the hearth, blew gently, blew again, and this time smoke curled up. I blew some more, turning the coal red, then placed it gently inside my handful of tinder, needles, and sock fuzz while trying not to scatter the dust that was my coal. I blew some more. Blew some more. Blew some more.

Finally, a small flame. I blew into it, the flame spread and grew, and I set the handful of coal inside my teepee of sticks and twigs.

We had a fire.

Ashley lay there shaking her head. "You're better than Robinson Crusoe. You just made a fire without a match or gas or anything. How do you know how to do all this?"

"When I was in my residency in Denver . . ."

"Learning how to cut on people?"

"Actually, I'd already learned that on cadavers, but I was doing a good bit of it." A smile. "Rachel and I were spending more and more time in the mountains. Might call it cheap entertainment. Anyway, she had this wild idea that on one of our next trips, we weren't taking anything with us that could make a fire. No matches, no lighter fluid, no gasoline, no camp stove. And certainly no Jetboil. She said we were doing this the old-fashioned way. If we couldn't make it hot, we were staying cold. So I bought some books, read up on it, looked at the pictures, and tried it out a few times. Even called a local scoutmaster to give me some lessons. We went camping, and I figured out what did and didn't work. In part, I learned how to make a fire."

"Remind me to thank her when I meet her." Ashley pointed at me. "Where'd you learn to hold your mouth like that?"

"What do you mean?"

"Whenever you're concentrating on something, you make this face . . ." She flexed one side of her face. Looked like a string had been threaded through her right eyebrow down through her cheek and secured to the corner of her lip, then pulled up about three inches. "Like that."

"Does it look as painful as when you do it?"

"I don't know. Does it look painful?"

"Very."

"Probably not. You make it look more . . . stupid looking."

"Thanks. I'll remember that next time you need help with the necessaries."

She laughed. "Do your nurses make fun of you?"

I turned up the right side of my face. "They can't see it beneath the mask."

She lay back, closing her eyes. Quiet settled around us, and I realized that I had grown used to the sound of her voice. And for the first time, the silence caused me to wonder if I missed it when it wasn't ringing through the air.

SINCE OUR SHELTER was made entirely from evergreens, it smelled fresh, clean. "This is about the most eco-friendly house I've ever stayed in."

She laughed. "Yep. Real green."

It was warm and comfortable, and the limbs above did a good job of providing shelter while also drawing the smoke out. It was late afternoon now, but with two hours of daylight left, I pulled on my jacket, tied on my snowshoes, and grabbed the bow. "I'm going to take a look about."

"Be gone long?"

"An hour maybe."

I looked at Napoleon. "Be right back. Keep her company." He turned in a circle and hid himself in her sleeping bag.

One problem with a shelter like the one I'd just made is that the people who make them get inside, get comfortable, make a fire, and then set the whole thing aflame, bringing it down on top of themselves. Given her leg, Ashley wouldn't be able to dig herself out, making a really bad situation.

I pointed my finger at her. "Mind the fire. Don't let it get too big. You do, and you'll set our Christmas tree on fire, which would include you because I doubt you could dig yourself out. You're pretty well barricaded in here. And keep that snow close at hand. If the fire gets too big, throw a few handfuls on top. Not too much. Don't want to kill it. Just scale it back a bit. Agreed?"

She nodded, made a snowball, and threw it at me.

I climbed up a small ridge. The lee side was sheltered from the wind, so the snow cover was less. Sprigs of dead grass and ice-covered rock spotted the snow like bubblegum on a sidewalk. Maybe bird droppings was more like it.

My lungs told me we were still above 10,000 feet. The air was thin, and even though we'd been at this for two weeks, I wasn't used to it. Still caught myself taking deep breaths when sitting still. I guess that comes from living at sea level. It was easier, but it wasn't easy.

The snow had quit and clouds had flown through. The sky was gray, but the ceiling was high and I could see the whole valley stretched out before us. The ridgeline I was on made a half moon, which circled a larger valley below. Maybe ten to fifteen square miles in total. Frozen creeks and small streams creased between the trees, making wrinkles in the earth's face. Except for the occasional rise or roll and pitch of a hill, it was mostly flat. "Flat" around here was a relative term, but it was certainly better than where we'd been.

A couple hundred yards from our shelter, I reached a small ledge, sat down, zipped up my jacket against the wind, and studied the landscape. I cupped my hands around my eyes to help me focus and scanned every square acre, asking myself if anything I saw hinted at the possibility that it might be man-made. I did this until I grew cold and the light start growing dim.

Just as the last light was fading, I caught a flash of something brown. It looked like the trunk of a tall tree except it was horizontal near the treetops. I squinted, even stared out of the sides of my vision trying to get a better view. It was hard to make out, but worth a second look. I opened my compass, took a reading of ninety-seven degrees, and turned the plastic marker on the face of the compass to ninety-seven degrees. It paid to be redundant.

I started back to camp as darkness was falling. Twenty yards in front of me, something white flashed across my trail. I nocked an arrow and waited for any sign of movement. Five minutes I waited. Then a small hop. Followed by another. There, a small white rabbit. Big ears, big feet, hunched over and hopping beneath the trees.

I drew, settled the first pin in the middle of the rabbit, let out half a breath, and squeezed the release. Just as the arrow left the bow, the rabbit hopped maybe six inches. My arrow sailed by harmlessly and buried itself in the snow. The rabbit bounced twice and disappeared.

I searched for my arrow, but digging in the snow was painful to my blistered and cracking hands. I decided to leave it until tomorrow.

ASHLEY HAD THE FIRE warm and crackling when I returned. She'd even managed to boil some water and heat up what was getting close to the last of our meat. Maybe a day left. She eyed the bow and the single arrow missing. "What happened?"

"It hopped."

"And if it hadn't?"

"I'm pretty sure we'd be eating rabbit tonight."

"Maybe from now on you should let me hold them still while you shoot them."

"If you can catch them, I'm game for anything."

She laughed.

"Say, do you feel like taking a walk?"

She raised both eyebrows. "Seriously?"

"Yeah. If you can lean on me, I think we could make our way up to this ridge. I need your eyes."

"See something?"

"Maybe. Maybe not. Hard to say. I'm not willing to risk it without both of us looking at it."

"What are we risking?"

"I had thought we'd keep trying to lose elevation, but this thing I'm looking at would keep us up on the plateau for a few miles. It's a two- or three-day change in direction, followed by another three or four to make up for lost ground. Seven days out of the way if I'm wrong."

I didn't need to tell her that we were flirting with the edge as it was. Another week could kill us. We might be dead already and not know it.

"What is it?"

"Not sure. Looks something like a tree, only it's lying flat at the level of the treetops. It's a horizontal line in a sea of verticals."

"Is it safe for me to walk?"

"No, and the sled would never make it. We'll take it slow. One step at a time."

"I trust you. If you think we ought to."

"It's not about trust. It's about four eyes are better than two."

"When you want to go?"

"First light. The rising sun may be our best chance."

Taking Ashley to the ledge was risky, but so was deciding our direction. When we first left the crash site, it was anybody's guess. But now, now that we were committed and too far from the site to backtrack, we needed to make this together. Because I could see where the next week of walking would take us, our living or our dying rested to a great extent on which direction we headed.

I also knew we needed a break.

WE CLIMBED INTO OUR BAGS and watched the flame light the underside of the tree limbs. It was the first time I'd been overly warm and had to unzip my bag. Once I got some food in me I moved my attention to Ashley's leg. Swelling was down and knotting and scar tissue were discernible around the break. All good signs.

I sat opposite her, placed her good foot on my lap, and began rubbing deep into her arch, then her calf, and finally her hamstring and quadriceps to force the circulation.

She looked up at me. "You sure you didn't study massage?"

"You've been lying prostrate for two weeks. We need to get the blood flowing. You try to stand up on these things, and you're liable to look like a Weeble."

"A what?"

"A Weeble. You know, 'Weebles wobble, but they don't fall down.' " I worked my thumb into the side of her right buttock. It was painful, and she winced, finally letting out a deep breath, and the muscle relaxed. You can look at someone and think one thing, but you put your hands on them and you really get to know what they're made of. Ashley was all muscle. Long, lean, limber muscle. Which probably saved her life. A normal person would have folded in the fuselage.

I gently moved to her left foot, careful not to torque her leg. I just needed to get into the muscle of her foot and calf, forcing blood flow. "I'd hate for you to get angry and kick me when your leg heals. You're nothing but one big muscle."

"Don't feel like much of one lying here."

"It'll come back. A few weeks and you'll be good as new."

"Your wife a good runner?"

"First time I saw her in high school, I thought it was the most fluid thing I'd ever seen. Like watching water walk. Just floated across the infield. Her toes barely touched the ground."

She flinched as I worked deep into her calf. "When we get back, you've got to teach Vince how to do this." She tossed her head back and held her breath. Letting it out, she said, "Seriously, how'd you learn to do this?"

"Rachel and I continued to run races through med school. By default, we became each other's trainer. Which she needed, because she inherited some funny feet from her mom."

"What do you mean?"

I touched the outside of her foot, just below her big toe. "Bunions."

"You actually rub that woman's bunions?"

I drove my thumb hard into her arch, curling her toes. "You find that hard to believe?"

She shook her head. "That's some seriously sick love right there."

"Vince doesn't rub your feet?"

"Not even if I gave him rubber gloves."

"I better talk to that man."

She snapped her fingers. "That's a good idea. And while you're making a list, add that little thing you did with the stick and making the fire."

I shook my head and smiled. "Nope."

"Why not?"

I slid her sock back on and placed her foot inside the bag. "Because I think I'd convince him to do something else first."

"What's that?"

"Buy a satellite phone."

I'm not sure which was better, the fire or the sound of her giggling.

CHAPTER TWENTY-SIX

Warmed by the fire, I lay awake, staring at the ironic sight of another jetliner at 30,000 feet. Ashley was out. Slightly snoring. A gentle breeze filtered through our tree, pulled on the limbs above us, and added extra twinkle to a sky lit by ten billion stars. Tomorrow's decision was worrying me. Had I really seen something or, after fifteen days, had I wanted to so badly that my mind convinced my eyes that I had?

The sound woke me. Feet crunching snow. Sounded like two people standing outside our tree, grunting. Smacking their lips. Whatever it was had to be heavy, too, because when it crunched snow, it really crunched the snow. Packing it hard. I reached out to touch Ashley, but her hand met mine in the middle.

I climbed out of my bag, grabbed the bow, nocked an arrow, and crouched between Ashley and the door. Her hand rested on the back of my neck. My smoke blew white misting clouds that filtered up. The cold had returned. Goose bumps crawled up and down my skin. Less than five feet away, the thing circled around behind us, sniffing, grunting, and then I heard the knock of something hard on something else.

Antlers.

I heard antlers rubbing against the tree limbs. I took a deep breath and relaxed. Ashley picked up on it and took her hand off my neck. The thing snorted, snorted again, then grunted loudly, scaring us both, and took off running.

I laid down the bow and climbed back into my bag.

Ashley broke the silence. "Ben?"

"Yeah."

"You mind sleeping over here?"

"Sure." I picked up my bag and slid it over next to her right side. She slid down in her bag, only her eyes and lips exposed, and drifted off. I lay awake listening, watching my breath rise like smoke signals. It reminded me of Disney's *Peter Pan* and the song "What Makes a Red Man Red?" I guess I sang it a little while, making myself laugh. It must have been the altitude mixed with the hunger.

Sometime later, I woke again. There was hair in my face. Human hair. And it smelled of woman. Single hairs were tickling my nose. Others felt silky on my face. My first tendency was to move. Slide over. Respect her space.

But I did not.

I lay there, breathing in. Stealing the aroma. Slow inhales followed by long, quiet exhales. Remembering what a woman smelled like.

And I liked it.

Ashley turned her head, pressing her forehead to mine. Her breath on my face. I pressed in and slowly filled my lungs. Then, careful not to wake her, I did it again. I did that a long time.

Somewhere in there I drifted off, feeling guilty and filled with longing.

IT WAS DARK WHEN I WOKE. The moon was high and bright because it filtered through the evergreen limbs above me and cast a needled shadow across the snow. The fire had died, but coals remained. I blew on them, turning them red, added tinder, and had a flame in seconds.

Ashley stirred. The firelight threw finger-shadows across her face. She was thin and had lost a lot of weight. Maybe twenty pounds. Her eyes were sunken, circled in black, the whites of her eyes were red road maps, and her breath was bad—meaning, her body was eating itself from the inside out.

Mine wasn't any better.

I dressed, helped her do the same and, once I had her bundled, slid her out the entrance. I could only pull the sled about a hundred yards before the angle grew too steep and I had to lift her to a standing position. She wrapped an arm around my neck. I put her on my right side, so her bad leg was between us.

She winced as the weight of her foot pulled on the break. "That does not feel good."

"You want to sit down, go back?"

She shook her head. "No. Let's keep going."

We took our time. One step, then another. Napoleon trailed behind, hopping in our footsteps. Happy to be out.

Ashley wrapped her right arm around my neck and clung to my right hand with hers, locking us stride for stride. What had taken me twenty minutes took us nearly an hour, but we made it without incident. I sat her on the ledge, the view spread out before us, and she scanned the sixty or seventy square miles looking back at us. She nodded. "Under different circumstances, this would be beautiful."

I leveled the compass on my leg, let the needle settle, then pointed across the carpet of evergreens toward a distant mountain ridge. "See that brown-looking thing? Sort of flat, stretched left to right, sitting on top of the trees, just left of that white-capped ridgeline."

Napoleon hopped up into my lap, staring down in the valley.

She cupped her hands around her eyes. "They're all white-capped."

I waited while she studied the horizon. We were looking at a speck some eight to ten miles distant. The proverbial needle. "See it?"

She nodded. "Yeah." She was quiet a minute. "How in the world did you see that in the first place?"

"Don't know."

"It's hard to make out."

"Give it about ten minutes. When direct sunlight starts coming over the ridges, it'll light on whatever that is. If it's man-made, we'll get some sort of reflection that's unnatural."

So we waited. Trying not to look at it so much that it lost all meaning. Like a word you say over and over until you're only hearing what it sounds like and you've forgotten what it means. Sunlight crawled down the mountain summit and into the valley, pushing a dim shadow before it.

As it did, it uncovered what lay before us. An immense valley, hemmed on three sides by steep and jagged mountains. In the middle floated an evergreen sea crisscrossed by streams and small frozen lakes and ponds. Many of the trees were dead. Thousands, naked of bark and whitened by the sun, stood as silent sentinels. Those that had fallen spread across the forest in an angled, twisted maze of biblical proportions.

"What's the name of that game where you take a handful of straws, stack them up straight, then just let them fall in a messy pile?"

"Pick-up sticks."

"That's it." I waved my hand across the green sea before me. "Looks like God was playing a giant game of pick-up sticks and got called away right as it started."

She laughed.

Just before the sun grew too bright and the reflection off the snow obscured the image we were looking at, the brown thing glimmered. Or shimmered. With, maybe, a sparkling reflection below it.

I asked without turning my head. "You see that?"

"Yeah. I'm not sure whether it was a reflection off ice and snow or something else."

"Okay . . . look right. You see that clearing?"

"Yep."

"Could be a frozen lake."

"What's your point?"

"Well . . . if it was me, and I was to build a mountain house or camp or something, and I really wanted to get away, I'd come up here to this plateau, preferably near a lake, and build."

"I can see that."

The sun rose, grew bright, and the glare painful, obscuring our view. I prompted her. "What do you think?"

I pointed down our original line, which would take us to lower elevation and out of the valley we were looking into. "Going that way is lower elevation. Probably warmer. Certainly breathe easier. I just don't know where it leads or how long it will take us to get there."

I swung a wide arc left, across the valley toward the image in the distance. "Across the valley of pick-up sticks is a lot of deep snow, trees, frozen creeks hidden beneath the surface that could swallow me. If that thing over there is nothing, then it is going to cost us the distance of going over, then trudging a vector back across the other side of this thing to the break in the mountains where it looks like we can get down to a lower elevation."

"This is called a dilemma," she said.

I nodded.

"How much food do we have?"

"If we stretch it?"

"Yes."

"Maybe a day's worth. Day and a half if we don't mind being hungry."

"How long can you make it after that runs out?"

"I can keep breathing for maybe a week, but my energy level will be fading. If I'm pulling the sled . . ." I shrugged. "I'm not sure."

"Sounds to me like, absent another sudden influx of food, we've got enough energy to get into the valley and then across it on what's stored up inside you right now. And if we make it to the other side without finding food, then it might be a good place to curl up and go to sleep for a long time."

"If you want to put it that way."

"You got a better way?"

"Not really."

"What if you left me here and scouted it out on your own?"

"I've thought about that. Granted, I could get there a lot quicker, but there's no guarantee that I can do it safely or that I can get back to you. If I fall, get hurt, get eaten by a mountain lion, then you'll never know, and we'll both die alone with a lot of unanswered questions. I'm not willing to risk that."

"What if I am?"

"It's not your choice."

"How do you figure?"

" 'Cause I'm the one who has to walk across that. Then walk back. Not you."

"What if I asked you to?"

"I'd refuse."

"Why?"

"Let's say I get over there, stand on top of that ridgeline, and see a house or a road or something, anything, on the other side. Then I've got to make the decision to head for that. Taking me several more days from you. By the time I found help and returned, you'd never know it because you'd be dead."

"But you would have made it."

I shook my head. "I won't risk that."

"I thought we were in this together."

"We are, which is why I'm not leaving here without you." I stared at her. "Ashley, this is no game we're playing. We . . . both of us, are either going this way or that way. It's either-or, not maybe-and-what-if."

She closed her eyes, squeezing out tears, then she spoke without looking at me. "We've been at this for fifteen days. At some point, we're just prolonging the inevitable. If that's the case, and you can go a lot further without me, then you've got to try it. One of us making it is better than both of us dying."

"That's where you're wrong. I won't do it."

"What if I won't go with you? What if I fight you?"

"Then I'll thump you on the head, strap you to the sled, and haul you out under objection. Now, that's enough. I'm not leaving you."

We sat side by side. Staring out over a painful future. She hooked her arm inside mine and laid her head on my shoulder. "Why are you doing this?"

"I have my reasons."

"One of these days you've got to help me understand them, because they don't make any sense."

I stood and pulled her up on two feet. "That depends."

"On what?"

"Whether you're looking at this through my eyes or yours."

We began walking back down. Gingerly she set one foot in front of the other, clinging to me. Halfway back, I let her rest while I dug out my arrow.

"We look like two people in a potato sack race," she said through a running nose.

I nodded, watching where she put her foot. If she slipped, her reflexes would kick in and she'd attempt to brace herself with the broken leg. If she did, she'd pass out from the pain. I was hoping to prevent that.

She clung to me, breathing deeply. Two weeks on her back had caught up to her. "I've got to stop," she said. She turned and faced me. Two kids dancing.

She laughed. "Are you going to slide your hands into my jean pockets?"

"No, but we do make a good team."

She nodded. "If Vince and I had tried walking from here to that ledge, we'd have ended up on our backs with me in a lot of pain, trying to choke him by shoving snow down his throat for letting me fall."

"Not to pry, but every time you talk about him, you tell me how you two are different, not alike. Not compatible. What's up with that?"

"We're different, all right. But I enjoy him. He makes me laugh. And we have a lot in common."

"People go to the rescue shelter and choose dogs for similar reasons. Not seventy-year soul mates."

"Okay, Dr. Phil, what reason would you choose?"

"Love."

She shook her head. "That kind only happens to the select few. The rest of us better get what we can while we can. Otherwise . . ."

"Otherwise what?"

"Otherwise we end up waiting on a fairy tale that never comes true."

"But . . . what if you could have the fairy tale . . . but getting it meant waiting for it?"

"What, like *Pretty Woman*? Somebody has been trying to sell me that my whole life. I've looked for him, waited, tried to be selective, not hopping on the first train that came through the station. But I'm just not buying. All the good ones are taken. Guys like Grover, and you . . . I've never had much luck finding one of them."

"I'm just saying, I think you're . . ."

"I'm what?"

"Selling yourself short if you settle for a marriage that is less than what you'd hoped for. You deserve more. Better."

"Ben Payne . . . are you flirting with me?"

"No, I'm just saying I think you're quite remarkable, and if Vince isn't, if he's not remarkable and he doesn't light you up, then, with all due respect to him, don't marry him."

"That's easy for you to say. You've been married fifteen years and don't have to look at the prospect of shopping in a market where demand is high and supply is low. And it's not that Vince doesn't light me up . . ."

"I never said it was easy. I just think you deserve . . . something, or someone, stellar."

She smiled. "Thank you. I'll remember that." She reached up and scratched my beard. "You've got some gray in there."

"Time does that. Along with . . ."

"With what?"

"Hard miles on the chassis."

We reached the shelter, and I replayed our conversation. My words hit me like a brick. The tables had turned. Time and mileage had done that, too.

I packed the sled, got her settled back in her bag and strapped in.

Ashley stopped me. "You okay? You look pale."

I nodded, but didn't look at her. My face would have betrayed me.

CHAPTER TWENTY-SEVEN

We left the shelter and set out. The snow was frozen, hard on top, making my pulling easy. Ashley was quiet. Tired. She didn't look good. Gaunt. Hollow. She needed nutrients. Her body was working double time trying to survive and feed the wounds inside her.

In the light I studied the tracks outside, and they confirmed what I'd thought. Moose. I cursed myself for not slipping out and trying a shot with the bow. Even a small moose could have fed us for weeks.

Ashley heard me and said, "You didn't know what it was. What if it had been a grizzly bear?"

"I'd probably be dead."

"Then you were right in your decision."

"Yeah, but we could be eating right now."

She nodded. "Yep, and that grizzly could be licking his claws after he had you for dinner and me for dessert."

I stared at her. "Do you watch horror movies?"

"No, why?"

"You're kind of morbid in your thinking."

"I started out as a writer for a local rag covering the crime beat. Guess I've seen too many pictures of what happened to people who suspected it was not what it was. Sometimes it's better not to go investigate the noise down the hall."

I set Napoleon on her chest, and he kissed me on the face. I adjusted the little bootie things around his feet and scratched his head. He turned, dug himself into the bag, and disappeared. I turned, fastened my harness, and began pulling. Of all the days we'd had thus far, this promised to be the longest.

Toward lunchtime we'd made maybe two miles. A good distance but it had taken its toll on me.

Ashley broke the silence. "Hey, why don't you rest awhile?"

I stopped, hands on my knees, breathing down into my belly, and nodded. "Sounds good." I unbuckled myself and then pushed the sled over toward a small flat area beneath two trees.

I stepped, and had no time to react.

The false top gave way, bent both snowshoes nearly in two, and swallowed me to my neck. The impact knocked the wind out of me, jolting my ribs. Water rushed over my feet, shins, even my knees. My lungs felt full even though I was out of breath.

Reflexively, I turned and grabbed for anything to stop my falling. I caught the sled. Doing so turned it on its side and threw Ashley and Napoleon out of it, screaming and whimpering.

I pulled, dragging myself from the sucking hole and the stream beneath. Every foothold gave way, and whenever I pulled with my right side, the pain in my chest peaked and sent spasms through me. I paused, gathered myself, and pulled once. Then again. Then again. Slowly inching myself from the hole. The wet snow acted like quicksand.

I pulled my body up on top of the snow, beaching myself. Ashley lay several feet away, breathing deeply, tense, hands fisted, knuckles white, lips taut. I crawled to her, studying her pupils. Shock would show up there first.

She darted a glance, then returned her attention to some

speck in the sky she had focused on. Something she learned in tae kwon do.

I was drenched from the waist down. We were hurt, had no fire, I couldn't get dry, and we couldn't get across this valley of hell for at least another day. I could walk in wet clothes. They'd freeze, which was better than clinging to me wet. But wet boots were another thing. I turned, looked at the sled. There was a hole in it. When I'd grabbed it, flipped it over, and thrown Ashley out, it had caught on something that tore a large hole in the area just beneath Ashley's shoulders.

I propped her head up, unzipped her bag, and carefully studied her leg. The throw had not rebroken it, the angle of her foot had not changed, but it had torqued all the tender attachments and tacky bones that had slowly been resettling and regrowing. It was swelling right before my eyes.

Our options were few.

I could dig a snow cave and we could get in, crawl into our bags, and hole up, but that only delayed the problem. When we crawled out, my clothes and, more important, my boots would still be wet or frozen, we'd be no further along and that much hungrier. My core was okay, my jacket was wadded up nicely inside Ashley's bag, but I had no spare pair of socks because both of mine were currently on my feet, keeping me warm. Or were. And the bottom, most critical part of the sled now had a hole in it. If I tried to pull her, the sled would dig in, becoming a plow.

If I could get dry feet, get them warm and keep them dry, I could walk through the cold in my legs. The only other pair of dry socks was currently on Ashley's feet. The question then was how to keep them dry and, more important, how to fix the sled.

I sank my head in my hands. If our situation had been bad an hour ago, maybe even dire, it was now circling the bowl of unimaginable.

I didn't have a solution, but I knew I had to get moving. My teeth were starting to chatter.

I sat up, pulled off my gaiters, then my boots and both pairs of socks. "I know you probably don't feel like talking to me right now, but can I borrow your socks?"

She nodded. Her knuckles were still white.

I slipped them off her feet, wrapped her feet in my jacket, and then zipped her gently back inside her bag.

Both sleeping bags came inside what are called stuff sacks. With down bags, it's paramount to keep them dry or they lose all insulating ability. So most good bags come stuffed inside a "dry sack," which is almost entirely waterproof.

I pulled both sacks out of my pack, stuffed my sleeping bag back into the backpack, slid on Ashley's socks, slid my feet into the dry sacks, tightened the compression straps around my calves, loosened the laces on my boots, slid my feet in, laced them up, and then put my gaiters on beneath my pant legs. A poor solution, but the only one I could think of at the moment. I took a few steps. It felt like I was walking in moon boots.

I looked at my snowshoes and decided they were not salvageable. Both had bent in the middle, crimping the frames. They were one step from breaking in two. The sled was a much larger problem.

Ashley's leg had to remain flat. I couldn't just pick her up and carry her because the pressure of my forearm beneath her femur, aside from being excruciatingly painful, could rebreak it. A sled was essential.

I needed something to patch the hole. I had nothing but a backpack and two bent snowshoes.

The snowshoes caught my eye. The nets I'd used as the base of the snowshoes had been double folded when I'd first made them, in order to support my weight. If I unfolded them . . .

I did, and fastened the sides to either side of the sled. Doing so prevented Ashley from slipping through the hole, but it did not prevent snow from gushing through. My only option was to lift one end of the sled and tie it to me via the harness. This lifted Ashley's head and shoulders off the snow and meant I dragged the back end—making two deep drag marks in the snow. Like railroad tracks.

Compared to sliding the sled along the snow, this was several times harder. And, maybe the worst part, it was harsh and bumpy for Ashley, which meant painful, and slower by a large margin.

I didn't see any other way.

I pulled out the last of our food and split it with her. "Here, this might take your mind off the pain. But go easy. This is the last of it." I ate my three pieces, which only made me more hungry. I strapped the sled higher on the harness, buckled myself in, and put one foot in front of the other. I readjusted the straps, then did it again. And again.

I didn't stop until I could go no further.

I REMEMBER KNEE-DEEP SNOW, stumbling a thousand times, crawling on my elbows, pulling at tree trunks with my blistered and frozen hands, and the quagmire of more snow than I'd ever hoped to see. I remember walking through the afternoon, through dusk, through the first of night when the moon rose. I remember it shining down and casting my shadow on the snow. I remember starlight and then low clouds moving in. I remember blowing bitter-cold breath. And I remember walking a while longer. The compass dangled about me. I held it in my palm, let it settle, and just kept following the arrow. Bright green and glowing in the dark. Rachel had paid a hundred dollars for it a decade ago. Now, it was worth ten thousand.

I WOKE UP FACEDOWN in the snow. It was pitch-dark, no moon, no stars, and my right cheek was cold but, thanks to my beard, not frozen. My hands had cramped from holding on to the front of the sled behind me, trying to prevent Ashley's head from beating about. The straps were cutting into my shoulders and I couldn't really feel my legs.

I stood, pushed into the snow, and sank for the ten-thousandth time up to my thighs. I had stayed warm because I'd kept moving. But I could move no more, and my core was cold. Ashley was either asleep or unconscious. I unbuckled, lifted the harness over my head, crawled beneath an evergreen, kicked away the snow to make a flat section wide enough for two people, and pulled Ashley in underneath. I rolled out my bag, stripped, and climbed inside.

The tunnel narrowed, and I realized that I did not expect to wake up.

CHAPTER TWENTY-EIGHT

The sun was high when I opened my eyes. I was sore in places I'd forgotten were part of my body. I wasn't hungry, but I was so weak that I didn't want to move. Other than a few crumbs, our food was gone. My face felt tight. Sunburned. My lips were peeling, and my two-week beard offered little protection against the reflective burn of the sun.

I picked up my head, rolled over, and took a look around. Ashley was looking at me. Her eyes spoke two things: compassion and resolution. As in, resolved to the fate we faced. Even Napoleon looked weak.

My clothes lay in a crumpled wet pile next to me.

The reality of last night returned in a wave of hopelessness. Ashley leaned over me, a strip of meat in her hand. "Eat."

Spread across her lap, wrapped in the cups of her bra, lay several strips of meat. My thinking was cloudy. It didn't register. "Where'd you get it?"

She tapped my lip. "Eat."

I opened my mouth, she set a small bite on my tongue, and I began to chew. It was tough, cold, mostly sinew, and may have been the best thing I'd ever put in my mouth. I swallowed, and she tapped my lip again. We didn't have that much food yesterday. "Where'd you . . ."

Clarity came with a rush. I shook my head.

She tapped me again. "Eat this and don't argue with me."

"You first."

A tear dripped off her face. "You need this. You still have a chance."

"We've had this discussion."

"But . . ."

I pulled myself up on one elbow and reached out to grab her hand. "You want to die out here alone? Let the cold creep in and take you?" I shook my head. "Dying alone is no way to die."

Her hand was trembling. "But . . ."

"No buts . . ."

"Why!" She threw the gnarly piece of meat at me. It ricocheted off my shoulder and landed on the snow. Napoleon jumped up and devoured it. Her voice echoed off the mountains rising up around us. "Why are you doing this? We're not going to make it!"

"I don't know if we're going to make it or not, but either *we* are or *we* are not." I shook my head. "No other option."

"But . . ." She turned, pointed. "If you kept going, you might see something. Find something. What if it got you one step closer to finding a way out?"

"Ashley . . . I will not live the rest of my life staring at your face every time I close my eyes."

She curled up, crying. I sat up, staring at my frozen clothes. The only thing warm and dry was my jacket. I needed to take a look around. Figure out where we were. I pulled on my long underwear, then my pants, sinking my feet back into my boots. My feet were badly blistered. Sliding them in was painful, but not as painful as those first few steps. I pulled my jacket on over my bare skin. If I could keep my core warm and not sweat, I'd be okay.

We'd slept in the open and were lucky it had not snowed.

I turned in a circle, studying the top of the bowl-like valley in which we'd walked. I needed to get a bird's-eye view. Dark, heavy clouds were spilling in across the mountains to the north. I wasn't sure how long the snow would hold off.

I knelt next to her and touched her shoulder. Her face was buried in her bag. "I'm going to look around."

One of the unique things about the trees around us were the limbs. They were straight, sturdy, started near the ground, and were spaced like ladder rungs up the trunks. I walked a hundred yards or so, found one I thought I could climb, slipped off my boots, pulled up, and started climbing. I was tired, my muscles ached, and my arms were telling me I weighed a thousand pounds.

At thirty feet, I took a look around. I was amazed at how far we'd come since the evergreen shelter of yesterday. The ridgeline off which we'd seen the valley and made our decision lay a long way behind us. We'd traveled nearly the whole valley. Maybe eight to ten miles. That meant we had to be close. I cupped my hands around my eyes. We needed a break. We were due one. "Come on. Please be something."

Being down in the valley changed our perspective, which was part of the reason it took me a few minutes to find it. Once I did, I actually laughed. I pulled out my compass, checked my reading, turned the bezel to mark the degree—because I was tired and chances were good I'd forget or get confused—and climbed down.

Ashley was weak and wouldn't look at me. The resignation had grown. I stuffed my bag into the backpack, strapped everything onto the sled, and buckled myself into the harness. Doing so took energy I didn't have. The first step sent pain spasms through me. The second was worse. By the tenth, I was numb. Which was good.

I hadn't peed since yesterday, and given the amount that I'd sweated in the last twenty-four hours, I was dehydrated. I stuffed a Nalgene bottle with snow and handed it to Ashley. "I need you to hold this, try and melt it for me. Okay? I've got to try and get some fluid in me."

The snow was wet, thick, and I felt more like a plow than a man walking. The trees obscured my view, so I had to trust the compass. Every few feet I'd stop, check my bearings, pick a tree a short distance away, walk to it, pick another, and so on. Every ten minutes, I'd turn, ask for the canister, and take two or three sips. That continued for two or three hours.

When we finally broke through the tree line, the snow started in earnest. Quarter-sized flakes. Some as big as half dollars. The frozen lake spread out before us, stretching an oval mile toward the mountains that rose up behind it. The snow obscured my vision, but the sight at the other end was one of the more beautiful things I'd ever seen. I collapsed, hit my knees, and tried to catch my breath. My wheezing was deep and my ribs were throbbing.

Lying in the sled, Ashley was facing away. Continually looking behind us. It's the nature of a gurney. She needed to see this. I crawled around, elbow-deep in snow, and spun the sled. Her head was laid back and eyes closed. I tapped her on the shoulder. "Hey? You awake?"

She stared at me. "Ben . . . I'm sorry . . ."

I put my fingers to her lips and pointed across the lake.

She craned her eyes, staring through the snow, which was thickening. When she tilted her head and the picture made sense, she started crying.

CHAPTER TWENTY-NINE

It was late afternoon. 4:17 to be exact. I'd just finished up in surgery and returned to my office when my nurse said, "Your wife's waiting on you."

You never just appeared. And you never "waited" on me. "She is?" I asked.

They nodded but said nothing. They knew. I walked in, and you were looking at a color wheel. One of those things that looks like a fan, maybe two inches thick, eight inches long and covered with rows of every shade of every color in the spectrum. You were staring at it, hand on your chin, looking at it, then up at the wall, back at the color wheel and then back at the wall. "Hey," you said.

I pulled the blue booties off my feet and threw them in the trash. "What're you doing here?"

You held the fan thing up to the wall. "I like this blue. What do you think?"

A masculine striped pattern papered the wall. The wallpaper you'd picked out a year earlier when we'd "done" my office. I ran my hand along the paper. "I still really like this."

You were in another world. You flipped to another section of the fan. "Of course, we could use this tan, too."

I scratched my head. "You like it better than this $67-a-square-yard paper we picked out last year?"

You picked up a catalog off my desk. Flipped open to a paper-clipped page. "And I like this color of wood. It's masculine, yet not too dark. It's something we can grow with."

I looked around my office at the $6,000 worth of swanky, fashionable, modern office furniture we'd bought in San Marco about the same time we'd papered the walls. I began thinking about the money we could make if we sold all that stuff on Craigslist. I said nothing.

Then you pulled out a large portfolio. Like those large briefcases that designers carry their drawings in. You laid it open across my desk, then starting flipping through several prints you had on loan from Stellars Gallery. "These . . . " You pointed. Tapping each one. ". . . I like. They remind me of Norman Rockwell; and then here are a few Ford Rileys and even a Campay." You shook your head. "I know they are each different, but I like them all." You chewed on a fingernail. " I just don't know if we have the wall space for all of them."

"Honey?"

You looked at me. Eyebrows raised. Your facial expression told me it made total sense to you.

Admittedly, I was tired and had been on my feet for twelve hours. Four surgeries. One that almost went south. "What in the world are you talking about?"

You said it so matter-of-factly. "The nursery."

Your words echoed through my office in slow motion. Nurrrr-serrrr-ieeee. I remember thinking "Didn't they have one of those in Peter Pan*?"*

"Ben?" You tapped me on the shoulder. "Honey, have you been listening to anything I've been saying?"

Maybe a dumb look crossed my face because you took my hand, slid it beneath your shirt, and pressed my palm to your stomach. "The nursery."

If that other night during the storm you held back the waves, lifted me to the surface, and filled my lungs with air—then in this moment, leaning against my desk, color swatches and prints scattered around, my hand pressed to your stomach, your butterflies fluttering beneath my palm . . . you took my breath away.

CHAPTER THIRTY

I couldn't risk walking across the middle. I had a pretty good feeling the lake was frozen several feet deep, but I had no way of knowing, so I kept to the shoreline. It was flat, free of debris, and the easiest walking to date. In comparison, it felt like we were speeding. The distance to the far shore was nearly a mile. We crossed it in a little over thirty minutes.

I pulled her up the small incline and into the trees that lined the bank. Again I turned her so we could both look.

The A-frame construction rose up some forty feet in the air. The front of it, facing the lake, was entirely glass. A few of the shingles on the roof were missing, but on the whole, the building was doing fairly well. The front door faced the lake, had been painted yellow, and because the prevailing winds came from behind the building, it was only half covered with snow.

I pulled the sled up to the front door and spent several minutes pulling away the snow and making a ramp. The door was tall and thick and looked imposing. I grabbed the hatchet and was about to strike the lock when Ashley spoke. "Why don't you see if it's unlocked first?"

I pushed on the door, and it swung easily on its hinges.

The supports for the A-frame were built entirely of lodgepole pine, the floor was concrete, and the inside of the building was one huge room—nearly as large as a basketball court. On the sides, the roof went all the way to the floor, and the only windows were the ones at either end. A fireplace—big enough for two people to sleep in—sat off to our right. A huge iron grate filled the middle. Stacked ten feet high in the corner sat a pile of wood that could supply the two of us for an entire winter. Maybe six or seven truckloads.

Beyond that, down the center of the building, two dozen pews, all worn and faded, were mounded on top of one another. Several silver canoes lay atop the pews, awaiting summer and the thaw. Off to the left was a kitchen area, and at the far end, a set of stairs rose to the second floor. The second floor took up only half the length of the building and was open to the area above the fireplace. Huge, forearm-thick cables hung from the apex of the building and supported the floor, which was made of one-inch plywood and cross timbers. Constructed across the length of the second story were fifty or sixty bunk beds, all covered with carvings, pencil drawings, and every manner of name and lettering detailing who loved who. A squirrel had eaten a pine cone on the middle of the floor and left a mess and something else had chewed on a piece of Styrofoam and didn't clean up after itself. Along the windowsill lay a hundred dead flies, wasps, and other flying insects. A good layer of dust covered most everything, and there were no lights and no light switches.

Napoleon hopped off the sled, ran down into the room, barked, barked again, then turned in four circles, and returned to me, wagging his tail and snotting all over my leg.

Slowly, I pulled the sled down the ramp and onto the concrete floor. We stared, awestruck. I pulled Ashley over to the fireplace and began stacking wood for a fire. Then I scoured the place for anything small to start the fire. I started laughing when I found a box of fat lighter next to the pile of wood. I built the fire, small sticks on the bottom, larger pieces on top, tore strips of old newspaper out of an old box, and then pulled my bow drill out of the sled and began working the spindle across the hearth.

Ashley cleared her throat. "Uh . . . Ben?"

"What . . ." I was starting to get smoke and didn't want her distracting me.

"Uh . . . Ben."

"What!"

She pointed above the fireplace, off to a side shelf. A can of lighter fluid sat next to a box of strike-anywhere matches. I dropped the bow, grabbed the can—which was nearly full—quickly doused the wood and paper, struck a match, and threw it onto the wet paper.

When I first took a job with the hospital and began making a doctor's salary, I started taking longer showers. Even shaving in the shower. Admittedly, it's a luxury, but I loved the steam in my lungs, the hot water on my back, and the way the heat allowed me to relax.

We sat mesmerized and . . . bathing.

I was drenched. Every piece of clothing I had on was wet and cold. My hands were chapped, cracking, and the denim strips were torn and little good.

I knelt, hands held out, and began peeling off the fraying denim. Neither of us spoke. With my hands free, I pulled off my wet coat and jacket, sat next to her, put my arms around her shoulders, and hugged her.

We'd caught a break, and doing so had pushed back the hopelessness that was crowding in, choking the life out of us.

AFTER THE FIRE BLED out the cold, I climbed the stairs and searched the bunks. All were empty except one. A single twin foam mattress, six inches thick and partially chewed around the edges, lay wedged and half folded over in a corner. I dusted it off, beat it against the railing, filling the air with dust, dragged it downstairs, turned it over, and laid it in front of the fire. Napoleon immediately took his place at the end closest to the fire and curled into a ball.

In the three minutes I'd been gone, the fireplace had heated the area around it.

I pulled out my bag, laid it on the mattress, then unzipped Ashley's bag and slowly helped her lift herself from her bag to mine. She was weak and needed help to get across. I propped her head on my pack, unbuckled the leg brace, helped her out of her clothes, and hung them across a pew.

With Ashley dry and warm, I started pulling off my wet clothes and spreading them across the pew. Then I dug in my pack and pulled on the only dry piece of clothing I had. A pair of Jockey athletic underwear Rachel had given me years ago. She'd given them to me as a joke, but they functioned well.

Then I eyed the kitchen.

It filled an area of space to the left of the stairs and contained two large black cast-iron woodburning stoves. A single black pipe led from the back of each and out through the wall. Several long preparation tables sat in the middle, and a long stainless steel sink lined the other wall, ending in a tall, white, gas hot water heater. The whole thing looked like it was effective at serving large amounts of food for lots of people.

I tried the faucet, but the water had been turned off, and when I looked beneath the hot water heater the pilot light wasn't lit. I tried to shake the hot water heater, but it was full and wouldn't budge. I grabbed the matches from the fireplace, turned on the gas, smelled propane, and lit the pilot light. I stacked the stove with wood, lit it, and adjusted the damper to feed air to the fire. I filled a huge pot with snow, packed it tight, and filled it again, then placed it atop the stove.

On the far left wall stood a rather menacing-looking door. Large hinges, bolt, and padlock gave the do-not-enter impression. I pulled. No luck. I returned to the fireplace, grabbed the steel poker, which was every bit of six feet long and thicker than my thumb, and wedged it into the lock. I put my weight into it, pulled once hard, pulled a second time harder, then repositioned it and pulled again. While the lock didn't break, the hinge did.

I swung open the door.

On the left side there were a few paper napkins, a couple hundred paper plates, and maybe a thousand paper cups. On the right I found an unopened box of decaffeinated tea bags and one two-gallon can of vegetable soup.

That was it.

I tied on an old apron that looked like it had been used at one time to clean the stoves and scanned the can of soup for the expiration date. Not that it really mattered, but it was still a few months from expiring. Ashley lay in front of the fire, propped on one elbow. Thirty minutes later she snapped her fingers, whistled, and waved me over. I stepped out of the kitchen area.

"Yes."

She waved again. I walked within a few feet. She shook her head and waved me over. "Closer."

"Yes."

"That . . . is the sexiest thing I have ever seen."

"What . . . me?"

She turned up a lip, waved me out of the way, and pointed at the stove. "No, dummy. That!"

I turned and looked at the kitchen. "What?"

"The steam coming off that pot of soup."

"You need help."

"I've been telling you that for about sixteen days."

AN HOUR LATER, slowly chewing each piece of potato and savoring each chunk of steak, she looked at me, soup dripping off her chin, and mumbled, "What is this place?"

I'd given Napoleon a bowl of soup with a few chunks, which he'd inhaled. He now lay curled up at my feet, contentment on his face.

I shook my head. "Some sort of high alpine camp. Boy Scouts maybe."

She took a sip of tea and turned up her lip. "Who would make, much less drink, decaffeinated tea? I mean, what is the use?" She shook her head. "How do you think they get up here?"

"Don't know. All this stuff had to get up here somehow, and I'm pretty sure they didn't stick those iron stoves on their backs and just pack them up here. When my clothes dry, I'll see if I can get into the other buildings. Maybe find something."

She took another bite. "Yeah, like more food."

Two bowls later, we both lay in front of the fire. Not hungry for the first time in several days. I held my cup in the air. "What should we toast?"

She held out her cup, too full to sit up. "You."

She was still really weak. Tonight's dinner was good, but we'd need a few more days to start making up for what she and I had spent getting here. I stared out the window. The snow was falling thick. A total whiteout. I set down my cup, rolled up my jacket, and placed it behind her head for a pillow. She grabbed my hand. "Ben?"

"Yeah."

"Can I have this dance?"

"If I try and move, I'll throw up all over you."

She laughed. "You can lean on me."

I hooked my arms beneath her shoulders and lifted her gently. She slid up underneath me, finally standing. She wasn't too steady so she hung on me, leaning her head against my chest. "I'm dizzy."

I moved to set her back down. She shook her head and extended her right hand into the air. "One dance."

I'd lost so much weight that my underwear was hanging low on my hips. Reminded me of some of the swimmers I'd seen. She was wearing a baggy T-shirt that needed to be burned, and her underwear sagged where her butt used to be. I held her hand and we stood without moving. Her head pressed against me. Our toes bumped.

She laughed. "You're skinny."

I held her hand high, slowly walking a circle around her. I studied us in the firelight. My ribs were showing. Her left leg was badly swollen, nearly half again the size of her right. The skin was taut.

I nodded.

Eyes closed, she was swaying. She didn't look too steady on her feet. I stepped closer, wrapped my arms around her waist, holding her. She put her arms around my neck, wrapping them around my head. Her weight pressed down on my shoulders. She was humming a tune I couldn't understand. She sounded drunk.

I whispered, "Let's not hear any more of this nonsense about me leaving you . . . going on alone. Deal?"

She stopped swaying, turned her head sideways, ear to my chest. She let go of my hand and rested it between her chest and mine, pressing it flat. She was quiet several minutes. "Deal."

The top of her head came just above my chin. I leaned in, touched my nose to her hair, and breathed.

After a few minutes, she said, "By the way . . ." She threw her eyes at me and tried not to smile. "What exactly . . . are you wearing?"

The underwear Rachel had given me was bright, neon green.

They were meant to be supportive and fit more like athletic briefs or bike tights, but given my weight loss, they hung a little loose. Now more boxer than brief. "I'm always . . . or was always making fun of Rachel and the underwear she chose to wear. I wanted Victoria's Secret, something with a little imagination. She liked Jockey. All function and no form. One year for her birthday, I bought her this awful pair of granny panties. Couple of sizes too big, covered up half her torso, they were just gross. In retribution, she actually wore them . . . and to top things off, bought me these things."

Ashley raised both eyebrows. "They come with batteries?"

The laughter felt good.

"When Rachel gave them to me, she addressed the card to Kermit."

"I don't think Kermit would be caught dead in those things."

"Yeah . . . well, I wear them sometimes."

"Why?"

"To remind myself."

She laughed. "Of what?"

"Among other things . . . that I have a tendency to take myself a little too seriously, and that laughter can heal the hurt places."

"Then . . . I'd wear them, too." She nodded and chewed on her bottom lip. " 'Course, you might want to get a T-shirt that says JUST SAY NO TO CRACK."

WHEN SHE GREW TIRED, I laid her down on her bag, propped her head up, and poured her some more tea. "Drink." She sipped a few times. I elevated the broken leg, hoping to alleviate the swelling. It needed ice.

I needed to look into those other buildings, find some food, maybe a map, maybe anything, but I was dead on my feet, it was dark outside, more snow was piling up against the window, and the fire had heated me to my core. I pulled on dry clothes. Finally, I was warm. And dry. And full.

I laid my bag out across the concrete, patted Napoleon, who was snoring, and lay back.

I was dozing off when it hit me that during all that dancing, when Ashley's body leaned against mine, when the feeling of her as friend and woman had warmed me, that I hadn't once thought of my wife.

I stood, crept barefooted to the door and out into the snow, where I vomited from my toes. It was a while before I got up my nerve to talk.

CHAPTER THIRTY-ONE

Kermit here. Ashley says my underwear looks like it came with batteries. Given my recent weight loss, they're a little big. Hanging off my hips a bit. They weren't too flattering before, and they're no better now.

At three months the "pooch" started giving you trouble. I'd catch you staring in the mirror, looking at yourself out of the corner of your eyes. Not quite sure what to make of yourself. Hesitant to wear baggy clothes, but hesitant to wear anything tight either. Sort of that midway place. Not totally pregnant, but not not-pregnant either. A volleyball stuffed beneath your belly button. The Tom Hanks movie Castaway *had come out, so we started calling the baby Wilson.*

Then it got really active. Doing laps on the inside of your rib cage. You'd page me. I'd call you back from the ER, a blue mask hanging off one ear. "Yes, ma'am."

"Wilson wants to talk to you."

"Put him on."

You'd place the phone to your stomach. I'd talk to our son or daughter or whatever he or she was going to be. Then you'd tell me, "Ooh, I just felt a kick. I think we've got a soccer player in here." Or, "Nope, nothing. Sleeping right now."

Four months in, I came home late on a Friday night. You were craving fried snapper. Hence, our reservation at The First Street Grill. I found you standing in the shower, rinsing shampoo out of your hair. You didn't see me. I leaned against the doorframe, loosening my tie. Taking it in. The whole wet, pregnant, glowing picture that was you . . . and was mine.

It was the sexiest, most beautiful thing I'd ever seen.

You caught me looking. "You better not let my husband catch you looking at me like that."

I smiled. "He'll understand."

"Yeah? Just who are you?"

"I'm . . . your doctor."

"You are?"

"Yep."

"Have you come to doctor me?"

I smiled, raised both eyebrows. "I'd say somebody already doctored you."

You laughed, nodded, pulled on my tie.

Rachel . . . when I look back across my life, and look for the one moment where all the good moments culminated into one, it was there.

And if God would open up time, let me go back, and live in one moment, it'd be that one.

Well, the next one was pretty good too.

CHAPTER THIRTY-TWO

Dawn outside. Day seventeen. New snow piled high. Pulling on warm, dry clothes was worth its weight in gold. Ashley lay sleeping. Her face was flushed and she was muttering in her sleep, but she looked warm and, for the first time in weeks, not uncomfortable. I found the lever on the wall that supplied the hot water heater with water, broke it loose, and turned it on. Brown, rusty water spilled into the sink. I ran it until it turned clear, then cut it off and turned up the heat.

A bath sounded like a good idea.

I slid the hatchet into my belt, grabbed the bow, and set out in search of the other buildings. Well rested, Napoleon beat me to the door, nudged it, and jumped out into the snow. In the fresh powder, he sank to his belly, then lay there grounded like a car stuck in ruts. I picked him up and cradled him. He growled at the snow as we walked. Flakes would land on his face, and he'd snap at them. I scratched his stomach and told him, "I like your attitude."

The morning was crisp, bitterly cold, and in some places had frozen the top layer of snow, which I broke through, knee-deep with every step.

I made a mental note to start thinking again about snowshoes.

There were seven buildings in all. One was a bathroom, split evenly between men's and women's. I found a few bars of soap and several rolls of toilet paper. None of the toilets or faucets worked, and if there was a water valve I couldn't find it.

Five were cabins—one-room A-frames, two stories, each with a woodburning stove, carpet on the floor, and a loft. One even had a reclining chair. All were unlocked.

The seventh was a two-room cabin. Maybe the scoutmaster's—or whoever was in charge. The back room had three bunks, each covered with a foam mattress. A thick, green, wool blanket lay folded at the end of each bed. Six in all. One even had a pillow. In a closet I found three folded white towels and a thousand-piece jigsaw puzzle. The picture had been ripped off the cover, but I shook the box and it felt heavy with pieces. On the floor sat a steel lockbox, locked with two padlocks and secured to the floor.

I hit it hard with the hatchet, busting one lock. I hit it again, busting the other. I lifted the lid. It was empty.

In the front room sat two wooden chairs, a woodburning stove, and an empty desk with a squeaky chair. I opened the top drawer to find a tattered game of Monopoly.

It took three trips to haul everything we needed—including the reclining chair. I was closing the door on the third trip when I noticed the most important piece.

A bas-relief map hung thumbtacked to the wall. It wasn't a map you'd use to navigate from place to place, didn't even give distances—was more like something put together by a city municipality advertising the national parks or forests in its area and their proximity to nearby towns. It was a 3-D map with raised, white-capped, plastic mountains. Across the top it read in large letters HIGH UINTAS WILDERNESS. Along one side it read WASATCH NATIONAL FOREST. And in the right-hand corner were the words ASHLEY NATIONAL FOREST.

Fitting, I thought.

A small dialogue balloon with an arrow pointed to the center of the Ashley. It read FOOT AND HORSE TRAFFIC ONLY. NO MOTORIZED VEHICLES OF ANY KIND ALLOWED AT ANY TIME.

Along the bottom, it read 1.3 MILLION ACRES OF WILDERNESS EXCITEMENT FOR THE WHOLE FAMILY.

Evanston, Wyoming, sat in the top left-hand corner with Highway 150 leading due south of it. In small letters across the highway it read CLOSED IN WINTER.

Around the edges were animated pictures of guys on snowboards, kids skiing, girls on horseback, a father and son hunting moose, couples on snowmobiles, and several hikers with backpacks and walking sticks. It looked like something you'd print if you wanted to advertise all the outdoor activities in your area. Interstate 80 bordered the top of the map, running west to east from Evanston to Rock Springs. Highway 191 led due south out of Rock Springs to a town called Vernal. Highway 40 led west out of Vernal and ambled along the bottom of the map through several small towns before turning up, or northwest, and intersecting Highway 150, which ran north to Evanston.

Somewhere in the middle of that plastic-capped mess inside the Ashley National Forest someone had stuck a thumbtack, marked an X, and written WE ARE HERE in black pen.

I pulled it off the wall, and Napoleon and I returned to the A-frame and the fire.

As we were coming into the building, Napoleon spotted something on the snow and took off after it. I never saw it, and he was gone before I had a chance to tell him not to. He ran off into the trees snarling, his feet spewing snow.

Ashley was still sleeping, so I dumped my goods, slid the chair in close to the fire, and checked the door for Napoleon, but all I could hear was a distant bark. I figured I didn't need to worry too much about him. Of the three of us, he was probably the most able to take care of himself. In one sense, we were holding him back.

I returned to the kitchen and built a fire in one of the cast-iron stoves. The sink had been welded out of either stainless steel or zinc and sat on legs as big around as my arm. The basin was deep and big enough to sit in. In fact, it was big enough for two people. The whole thing looked strong enough to support a house.

I washed out the basin and filled it with water as hot as I could stand. When I sat in it, steam was rising off the top. It was one of the more magnificent moments I'd had in the last few weeks.

I bathed, scrubbing every part of me twice. When I stepped out and dried off, the difference in pre- and postbath smell was noticeable. I stoked the fire, added wood, increasing the heat, plunged our clothes in the water, scrubbed each piece, and then hung them over the pew. I poured two mugs of tea and returned to Ashley, who had just begun to stir. I knelt, helped her sit up, and she sipped, cradling the mug between both hands.

After her third sip, she sniffed the air. "You smell better."

"Found some soap."

"You bathed?"

"Twice."

She set down her mug and offered me both hands. "Take me to it."

"Okay, but the hot water will increase the swelling. So we'll need to ice it when you get out. Okay?"

"Agreed."

I helped her hobble to the sink. She caught sight of her own legs and shook her head. "You didn't happen to find a razor around here, did you? Even a rusty one would do."

I helped her sit on the edge and lowered her in. The water came up over her shoulders. Slowly, she bent her left knee, laying it flat across the prep area of the sink. She leaned her head back on the built-in dish drainer, closed her eyes, and held out a hand, her finger hooked where the mug would be.

I brought her tea and she said, "I'll be with you in a little while."

It's amazing how a bath can improve your disposition.

I walked off, turning just before I reached the fireplace, hollering back toward the kitchen. "Oh, and you'll never believe the name of the national forest we're in."

"Try me."

"It's called the Ashley National Forest."

She was laughing as I stepped out the door.

CHAPTER THIRTY-THREE

Ashley's in the bath. I'm standing outside. The wind's picking up. I don't know if things are getting better or if we're just prolonging the inevitable.

So then you were four and a half months. You were lying on the table, and the nurse came in and squeezed the goo, as you liked to call it, on your stomach and started rubbing it in with the wand.

I handed her an envelope and said, "We'd rather you not tell us right now. We've got a date tonight, so if you don't mind, just write whether it's a boy or girl, and then seal it. We'll open it at dinner."

She nodded and began showing us the head, the legs, even a hand. It was the most magical thing. I'd seen dozens, but none had ever affected me like that one.

Then she started laughing.

We should have picked up on it, but we didn't. I asked her, "What?" She just shook her head, wrote on the card, licked the envelope, and handed it to me saying, "Congrats. Mom and baby are healthy. You all have a fun dinner."

So we did. I drove you home. You kept asking me, "What do you think? Boy or girl?"

I said, "Boy. Definitely a boy."

"What if it's a girl?"

"Okay. Girl, it's definitely a girl."

"I thought you just said it was a boy."

I laughed. "Honey, I have no idea. I don't care. I'll take whatever kid comes out of the oven."

Our favorite restaurant. Matthew's. Catty-cornered to San Marco Square. They seated us in a booth in the back. You were glowing. I don't know if I'd ever seen you like that.

Ever.

I don't remember what we ordered. I guess it was the chef's special, 'cause Matthew came out of the back, said hello, and sent us some champagne when he left. We sat there, champagne bubbles bubbling, candlelight flickering off your eyes, and the envelope lying on the table. You pushed it to me. I pushed it back to you. You pushed it back. I pushed it back and kept my hand on top.

"You do it. Honey, you've earned it."

You picked it up, slid your finger beneath the seal, pulled out the note, and pressed it to your chest. Laughing. Neither one of us could talk. Then you slowly opened the card and read it.

I guess you read it two or three times, because it was about three weeks before you said anything to me. "Well . . . " I asked. "What is it?"

You laid the card on the table and grabbed my hands. "It's both."

"Honey, come on. Quit kidding. It can only be one." Then it hit me. I stared at you. Tears were streaming down. "Really?"

You nodded.

"Twins?"

You nodded and buried your face in your napkin.

I stood, grabbed my champagne glass, banged it with my knife, and spoke to the other fifteen couples in the restaurant. "Ladies and gentlemen, excuse me, folks . . . I'd just like to announce that my wife . . . is giving me twins for Christmas."

We bought champagne for the entire restaurant, and Matthew made his signature apple cobbler thing that just absolutely melts in your mouth. Everybody in the restaurant had some.

Driving home, you didn't say a word. Your head was spinning with nurseries, colors, a second crib, a second of everything. We walked in the door, and you disappeared to the bathroom. Seconds later, you called me. "Honey?"

"Yeah."

"I need help."

I walked in to find you standing in your underwear and bra staring in the mirror and holding a bottle of vitamin E oil. One hand on your hip. You handed me the bottle. "Your job from here to Christmas is to make sure I'm not swallowed up in stretch marks and that my belly doesn't sag to my knees. So, get pouring."

You lay on the bed, and I dumped the whole bottle over your stomach. You screamed. "Gross!"

"Honey . . . I'm just trying to cover every square inch."

"Ben Payne!"

I rubbed it on your stomach, your back, legs, pretty much anyplace there was skin. You shook your head. "I feel like a greased pig."

"You do smell kind of funny."

I remember the laughter that followed, and I remember sliding around.

We had fun, didn't we?

Somewhere in the hours that followed, you stared at the ceiling, one foot bouncing on a knee, and said, "You thought about names?"

"Not really. Still getting over the sticker shock."

You crossed your hands over your stomach, crossed the other ankle over the other knee, your foot dancing up and down, and said, "Michael and Hannah."

The moment you said it, it clicked. Like pieces of a puzzle snapping together.

I rolled over, pressed my lips to your tightening stomach, and whispered their names. A soccer kick followed by a punch settled it. From then on, it became the four of us.

Maybe that was the moment. Maybe if I could go back and start over, bathed in laughter, warmth, the crazy thought of two of everything and the slide and smell of vitamin E oil, I'd go there.

Because I'm pretty sure I wouldn't go much beyond that.

CHAPTER THIRTY-FOUR

Napoleon had been gone awhile, which had me a bit worried. When my clothes dried, I grabbed the bow, zipped up my jacket, and stepped outside. The wind was blowing over my back, out across the lake. I whistled, but heard nothing. I pulled my collar up and followed his footprints up a hill, then along a ridgeline overlooking the lake. The zigzag pattern told me he'd been chasing something. His tracks were hard to follow, as the snow was filling them. I crossed a second hill and saw him down near the lake, lying still in a red section of snow. I walked closer and realized the snow wasn't the only thing red. I nocked an arrow and walked slowly up behind him. When I got close enough for him to hear me, he growled, but didn't look. I walked around in a wide circle so he could see me. I checked the trees around us and over my shoulder. I spoke softly, "Hey, boy. It's just me. You okay?"

He quit growling, but lay hunkered over what looked like a once-white-now-red ball of fuzz. I knelt, several feet in front of him.

Napoleon had not been attacked, but rather was the attacker. Part of a rabbit lay beneath him. A couple of feet and a few bones were all that was left. I nodded, checking over my shoulders. "Good job, boy. How would you feel about finding two more just like that and dropping them off at the big house up there."

He looked at me, ripped, chewed, swallowed, snorted, and licked the sides of his face and nose.

"I don't blame you. I'm hungry, too." I stood up. "Can you find your way back?"

Apparently feeling like I was too close, he picked up what was left of the rabbit and carried it further from me.

"Suit yourself."

Walking back gave me time to think. While we were warm, dry, and protected from the elements, we needed food—and a way out. Now more than ever. If I thinned it, the soup might last a day more. Beyond that, all we'd done was find a warm, dry place to die.

I took a different route back. Away from the lake. Several times I crossed moose tracks. More than one moose. And one larger than the other. Many times I crossed rabbit tracks, which are easy to spot because they hop, making a distinctive pattern. Moose are easy to spot because they are so big and press deep into the snow.

I needed practice with the bow, but if I missed the target, the arrow would penetrate several feet down into the snow and I'd never find it. Wouldn't take me long to lose all the arrows.

I returned to the A-frame, stoked the fireplace, and checked on Ashley, who was frolicking about like a dolphin and told me to go away. I went to one of the other cabins and pulled up a piece of carpet. Back at our place, I folded it once, then folded it again, and then again. I laid that over the top of one of the pews and tacked a paper plate to the center of it. In the center of the plate, I cut a hole about the size of a dime.

The A-frame room was more than forty yards long. I only needed about fifteen. I counted off the steps, backed up, and drew a line in the dust with my toe. I nocked an arrow, drew, settled the site, told myself, "Front sight, front sight, front sight" and then, "Press." I gently squeezed the release, sending the arrow toward the target. It struck the paper about three inches above the hole. I nocked another and followed the same slow, easy movement. The second arrow struck just a hair to the right of the first. I shot a third arrow with the same result.

I needed to make an adjustment, so I pushed the peep site down. The peep site was the little circle inside the string through which your eye looked. It required you to look from the same spot every time, making the release the same every time. At least, in theory. Pushing it down would bring the arrow's impact down.

It did. Just not far enough. I adjusted it again, bringing the impact too far. I readjusted, and brought the arrow up. Within thirty minutes, I could hit the hole from fifteen yards. Not every time, I'm not that steady, but every third or fourth shot, if I held true and still, I could hit the hole.

Ashley had heard the commotion. "What's all that racket?"

"Just me trying to improve our chances at getting some dinner."

"How about helping me out of here."

She'd washed her T-shirt and underwear and spread them across the dish drainer grooves behind her head. She reached out her hands, and I helped her climb out. She wrapped a towel around herself and tucked it in the front like women do. Then she closed her eyes and reached for my shoulders. "I'm dizzy."

She leaned against me, trying to regain her balance. She spoke with her eyes closed. "I'm told that guys are visual. Seeing naked women excites them. So, how're you doing with all this?"

I turned her and started leading her toward the fire. "I'm still your doctor."

"You sure? Doctors are human too." She was smiling. Acknowledging the elephant in the room. "I can't get much more naked."

Her hands and feet were pruny, but she too was clean and smelled better. She toweled off, and I lifted her arm around my shoulder and allowed her to use me as a crutch. This time I got her to the reclining chair, which by its very design would elevate her leg, taking the pressure off it. I'd fed the fire too much, and the room was actually hot. I cracked the door to cool it off, which also didn't take long.

She raised a finger. "Ben? You didn't answer my question."

"Ashley, I'm not blind. You're beautiful, but you're not mine." I fed the fire. "And . . . I do still love my wife."

She raised a finger. "I'm half naked and I've seen you naked a half dozen times. Every time I go to the bathroom, you're literally right here. So . . . how are you doing with all this? Is being this close to me difficult for you?"

I shrugged. "Honestly?"

"Honestly."

"No."

She looked surprised. Almost deflated. "So, you're not excited by me at all?"

"Didn't say that. I can be plenty excited by you."

"Then what are you saying?"

"We've all seen movies where two strangers are lost in some vast wilderness. And then just like *An Officer and a Gentleman,* they end up rolling on the beach. Mad, passionate love that solves all their problems. Movie ends, and they walk off into the sunset. Weak-kneed and googly-eyed. But this is real life. I really want to get out of here and back home. And I want to do it with my heart intact. The part of my heart that needs to be filled with that has already been filled. By Rachel. It's got nothing to do with whether you could or couldn't. Do or don't."

"So in the all this time, from airport to plane crash to here, you haven't once thought about having sex with me?"

"Sure I have."

"You're confusing me."

"Being tempted and doing it are two different things. Ashley, don't get me wrong. You're remarkable. Incredibly good-looking. You've got the body of a Greek goddess—although I really wish you'd shave your legs—and you're certainly smarter than me. Every time we talk I end up tongue-twisted and sounding stupid, but somewhere out there is a guy named Vince who, when I do meet him, is going to wish I'd treated you a certain way. And after I meet him, I'm going to wish I had. I'd like to be able to look him the eye and hide nothing. Because, trust me, hiding stuff hurts." I stared at her.

"When we get out of here, you and I are going to look back on this, and we're both going to wish I'd treated you a certain way. I want to be able to look back and know I did." I fumbled with my thumbs. Nervous. "I'm separated from my wife because of something I did. Or, put another way, didn't do. I'm living with that. Sex with you, or anyone else, would further that separation. And as good as that sex could or might be, it can't hold a candle to the pain of being separated. I try to remind myself of that whenever . . ."

"Whenever what?"

"Whenever . . . I think something that your doctor ought not to be thinking."

"So you are human."

"Very much."

She was quiet a minute. "I envy her."

"You remind me of her."

"How so?"

"Well . . . physically, you're lean, athletic, muscular. I imagine you could knock me out with one kick."

She laughed.

"Intellectually, I don't want to argue with you. Emotionally, you don't hide from anything. You put stuff on the table rather than dance around it—tend to face what's facing you. And you have a deep reservoir of strength, evidenced by your sense of humor."

"What's her greatest weakness?"

I didn't want to answer.

"Okay, don't answer that. What was her greatest weakness prior to the separation?"

"The thing that's also her greatest strength."

"Which is?"

"Her love . . . for me and the twins."

"How so?"

"She put us first. Always. Making herself a distant third."

"And that's a weakness?"

"Can be."

"Is that the reason you guys separated?"

"No, but it didn't help."

"What would you prefer?"

I chose my words. "I'd prefer she was selfish like me."

I grabbed a piece of plywood, three feet square, dusted it off, laid it flat across her lap, and handed her the box containing the jigsaw puzzle. "Found this. The picture's worn off, so I don't know what it's supposed to be, but . . . might help occupy you."

She wiggled off the lid and dumped out the pieces, immediately flipping them over and separating those with straight edges. She said, "You want to help?"

"Not a chance. Makes me dizzy just looking at it."

"It's not that bad." Her fingers smoothly flipped the pieces. "Just take your time. Eventually, it'll come together."

I stared at the mess dumped in front of her. "What if it doesn't?"

She shrugged. "It will. Maybe not like you think, but it will."

"I don't have the patience."

"I doubt that."

I shook my head. "No, thanks."

GIVEN THE CONTINUING SNOW, the light outside stayed dim and gray and the temperature changed little. High in the A-frame, ice crystals formed on the window, spreading like spiderwebs across the glass.

The size of Ashley's leg did not encourage me. She shook her head. "You might as well start calling me Thunder Thigh."

I carried our large pot outside, made a dozen tightly packed snowballs about the size of softballs, and then sat down next to her left leg. I set the puzzle aside, folded a towel and set it beneath her leg, then began gently rubbing one snowball at a time in circles around the break.

She squirmed, her hands behind her head. "I don't like this."

"Just give it a few minutes. Once it turns numb, it'll be better."

"Yeah, but right now it's not fun."

Four snowballs later and she'd quit complaining. She lay back and turned her head, staring up through the window. I iced her leg for close to thirty minutes. Other than turning her skin bright red, the effect on her leg was minimal.

"Every hour on the hour. Got it?"

She nodded. She still didn't look good. Her eyes were bloodshot, and her face looked flushed. It could have been the bath, but I had a feeling it wasn't.

"Any idea where we are?" she asked.

I spread out the "map" and showed her the X that marked our spot.

About then Napoleon scratched at the door, pushed his way through, and sauntered over like he owned the place. He walked over to his corner of the mattress, circled, flopped down, curled up, tucked his face beneath one paw, and closed his eyes. The sides of his muzzle were still red, and his stomach was rounded and full.

"Where's he been?"

"Eating breakfast."

"He save any for us?"

"I talked to him about that, but he wasn't having any."

"Couldn't you have taken a little bit? Snuck a piece out the side?"

"You want to put your hand anywhere near his mouth when he's eating?" I shook my head. "Probably draw back a nub."

She rubbed his tummy. "He does seem to have a rather short fuse." She looked up at me. "So . . . what's the plan?"

"I'm going to do some scouting around today. See if I can't find us some dinner."

"And then?"

"Well . . . we've got to eat. And we need it to quit snowing."

"And then?"

"We're going to eat until we can't eat anymore, pack up, and head out."

"Where are we going?"

"Hadn't gotten there yet. I'm only tackling one crisis at a time."

She laid her head back and closed her eyes. "Let me know when you get it all figured out. I'll be right here."

I made a dozen more snowballs, packing them tight, and set them away from the fire on the far side of the chair. I cut strips out of one of the wool blankets and wrapped them around my hands. I grabbed the bow. "If I'm not back in an hour, ice that leg. Remember, thirty minutes on, sixty off."

She nodded.

"And keep drinking."

"Yes, sir."

"I'm not kidding. Thirty on. Sixty off."

"You sound just like my doctor."

"Good."

I STEPPED OUTSIDE. The wind had picked up, swirling the snow off the ground, sending miniature twisters up through the trees where they rattled the limbs and played out. I climbed through the trees and up the hill behind the camp. The ridgeline circled the lake. Lake on one side, another valley on the other.

I stared at the layout of the camp. People, Boy Scouts, somebody had to get here from somewhere, and on something. They didn't just drop in out of helicopters. It was conceivable that they only got here via foot or horseback, but where were those trails? If we were in fact inside the Ashley and they only allowed foot and horse traffic, we couldn't be too far inside it. Otherwise, they'd never get up here.

I circled south, and it didn't take me long to find it. A narrow, winding, snow-covered footpath, wide enough for two horses abreast, that led down away from the lake, through the notch in the valley behind us. Certainly, if they were escorting boys up here carrying packs, they didn't make them walk across the state to get here. A few miles maybe, but no more. Unless this was a Boy Scout camp for Eagle Scouts only, and I doubted that. It was too big. Designed to serve large numbers of people.

I was getting cold. While the wool worked better than the frayed denim, the strips were doing little to ward off the cold. I needed to get back to the fire.

Ashley slept on and off most of the day. Regardless, I continued to ice her leg. Sometimes she woke. Sometimes not. Sleep was the best thing she could do. Every minute spent sleeping was like a deposit in the bank that she'd have to draw on when we decided to pull out of here. Which I had a feeling was sooner rather than later.

Late in the afternoon, as the light dimmed from gray to more gray, more dim, I slipped out with the bow and returned to the ridgeline where I'd seen the majority of the tracks. I pulled myself up into the arms of an aspen and sat down. The cold made it difficult to sit real still. Toward dark I saw a white flash out of the corner of my eye. I studied the snow. When it moved again, the picture came into focus.

Six rabbits sat within fifteen yards of me. I drew slowly, aiming at the closest. I came to full draw, let out half a breath, focused on my front site, and pressed the release. The arrow caught the rabbit between the shoulders, sending it tumbling. When the others didn't move, I nocked a second arrow, came to full draw, focused again on my front site and let the arrow fly.

I walked in with two rabbits' bodies skewered on a green aspen limb and hung it over the fire.

Ashley sat with the jigsaw across her lap. "Just two?"

"I shot at three."

"What's the problem?"

"One moved."

"So?"

"You know . . . if you hit with this percentage in the major leagues, they put you in the Hall of Fame."

"I can let it slide this time."

I slow-cooked the rabbit and even happened to find some salt in the pantry.

Ashley hovered over a leg, her lips greasy, rabbit in one hand, a bowl of soup in the other, a smile from ear to ear. "You cook good rabbit."

"Thank you. It is pretty good if I say so myself."

"You know . . ." She chewed, tasting her food up near the front of her mouth. "It doesn't really taste like chicken."

"Who told you it did?"

"Nobody, it's just that everything tastes like chicken." She tossed her head and pulled out a small bone. "Nope. That's not entirely true." She pulled out another small bone. "Since I've been hanging around with you, nothing really tastes like chicken."

"Thanks."

THIRTY MINUTES LATER, the only thing between us was a plate of bones and two empty bowls. We lay flat, savoring full stomachs. Of everything, I enjoyed the salt best. And given the amount of exertion and sweat I'd expended since the crash, I needed all the electrolytes I could get. For now, straight sodium would have to do.

She nodded at the Monopoly box on the table. "You play?"

"Not in a long time."

"Me either."

Three hours later, she owned three-quarters of the board, had hotels on most of her property, and I was close to broke, since I had to pay rent most every time I rolled the dice. "You're tough."

"We played some as kids."

"Some?"

"Okay . . . maybe more than some." She rolled. "So what's your plan?"

"Well, I thought we'd let the snow stop and then see if . . ."

She counted as she moved her piece down the board. "I'm not talking about our plan to get out of here. I'm talking about the one when you get home. The plan with you and your wife."

I shrugged.

"Come on. Spit it out."

"I . . ."

"Stuttering will get you nowhere."

"If you'll just let me get a word in edgewise."

"I am. Now spill it. What'd you do, and what are you going to do about it? Nice guy like you can't be all that bad."

"It's complicated."

"Yeah? Welcome to Earth. Everything here is complicated. So what did you say?"

"Said some words."

"Yeah, you and everybody else. What kind?"

"The kind I can't take back."

"Why not?"

" 'Cause they're . . . she . . ." I closed my eyes and took a deep breath.

"Were they true?"

"Yes, but that didn't make them right."

She nodded. "Sooner or later, you've got to quit playing your cards so close to your chest. I'm trying to help you." She pointed at the recorder. "You're a lot better at talking to that thing than you are to me."

"I told you that in the beginning."

"You haven't been talking into it very much. What's up?"

"Maybe I'm running out of things to say."

"You know . . . whatever you said, you can always take it back. I mean, what could possibly have been that bad? They're just words."

I turned, poking at the fire and staring into the flames. My whisper was low. "Sticks and stones may break my bones, but if you want to hurt someone . . . way down deep, use words."

ASHLEY SLEPT IN FITS, talking in her sleep. After midnight I stirred, added wood to the fire. I slid the bag off her leg, running my hand along her thigh. The swelling had gone down and the skin was not as taut. Both good signs. Alongside her, spread across the plywood, portions of the puzzle were starting to take shape. The picture was fuzzy, but one section looked like a snowcapped mountain.

She lay in the firelight. Long legs. One elevated. The other flat out. Relaxed. The growth of prickly hair on her calves and fuzzy hair on her thighs told the story of how long it'd been since the crash. Her head lay tilted at an angle. T-shirt rested on her collarbone. Underwear lying loosely across her hipbones.

I touched her temple. Pushed her hair behind her ear. Ran my finger down her neck, along the line of her arm. Down the tips of her fingers. Bumps rose on her skin.

"Ashley . . . ?"

She didn't stir. Made no response.

The crackle from the fire was louder than my whisper. "I . . ."

Her head turned, a deep inhale, followed by a long, slow exhale. Her eyes were moving left and right behind her eyelids. The truth wouldn't come.

CHAPTER THIRTY-FIVE

A week later we were back at the doctor's office. You were throwing up in every trash can between the car and the office. I felt pretty low. Every time I told you that, you nodded. "You should. You did this to me."

It's hard to argue with that.

Twins required more ultrasounds more often. The 3-D kind. Your doctor wanted to make sure we were on track. And given my place at the hospital, they were, in a sense, taking care of one of their own. A nice perk.

They called us back. More goo squirted from a tube. Another wand smearing it across your tummy. They strapped the monitor around your stomach, and we could hear both heartbeats. Dueling echoes. Everything normal. Right?

Wrong?

The technician paused, backed up, ran the wand over you a second time, and then said, "Be right back."

Ninety seconds and three hours later, your doc, Steve, strode through the door, having done a poor job of masking his concern. He studied the picture, nodded, swallowed, and then patted you on the leg. "Sheila here is going to run a few tests. When you finish, come see me in my office."

I spoke up. "Steve . . . I can read doc body language. What's up?"

He was elusive. More bad news. "Maybe nothing. Let's run the tests."

I'd have said the same thing if I was trying to figure out how to communicate bad news. Both heartbeats echoed strongly in the background.

You turned to me. Both hands spread over your stomach. "What's he saying?"

I shook my head and followed him into the hall.

He turned. "Just let her run the tests. I'll see you in my office."

I didn't need to. His face told me plenty.

We sat down opposite him. He was in pain. He stood up, walked around his desk, and pulled up a chair. The three of us sat in a triangle. "Rachel . . . Ben . . ." His eyes darted back and forth. He didn't know who to look at. He started sweating. "You . . . have a partial abruption."

Rachel looked at me. "What's that mean?"

He spoke for me. "It means your placenta has torn away from the uterine wall."

You crossed your legs. "And?"

"And . . . I've seen larger tears, but it's not small either."

"So . . . you're saying . . . ?"

"Total bed rest."

You crossed your arms. "I was afraid you were going to say that."

"Let's give it time. If we can slow it down or even stop it, everybody will be fine. No need to panic."

In the car on the ride home, you put your hand on my shoulder. "So, what's this really mean, Doc?"

"You need to take up needlepoint and find about a hundred movies you've been wanting to see. Maybe read several dozen books."

"Will we make it?"

"If it doesn't tear anymore."

"And if it does?"

"We're not there, so let's leave that for then."

"But . . ."

"Honey . . . one hurdle at a time, okay?"

CHAPTER THIRTY-SIX

Daylight filtered through the tree limbs, lit upon the snow, and found me slipping along the ridgeline. The snowfall had not lessened. We were approaching three feet of fresh powder. Moving was slow and difficult. Without the snowshoes, it would have been impossible. Currently, the snow was dry and fluffy. It was still too cold to be sticky. If it grew warm, conditions could become near hellish.

I walked an hour, but saw nothing. Returning, I came down the ridgeline and walked up through the trees. Approaching the back of the A-frame, I spotted an eighth building I'd not seen before. Smaller, more like the shape of a shed. The only thing showing was the top of a pipe chimney rising up through the snow. The rest of the building was buried.

I circled it, trying to decide where the door would be, and then started pulling at the snow. When I hit a cement block wall with no door, I walked to the other side and dug in again. I didn't find a door, but I did find a window. I dug it out, tried to lift it and couldn't.

I kicked it, and the single pane shattered and crashed on the floor inside. I knocked off the sharp edges with the hatchet and crawled in through the hole.

It was a storage room of sorts. Old saddles, bridles, and stirrups hung on one wall. Zebco fishing reels with no line. Some tools, hammers, files, and a few screwdrivers. A rusty knife. Several jars of rusty nails, all sizes. A fireplace with a bellows where it looked like a blacksmith could shoe a horse. It looked like the workshop necessary to keep a camp like this up and running. On the other wall hung several old tires that looked like they could fit a four-wheeler. Some tubes, even a chain. I scratched my head. If that was true, if they brought four-wheelers up here, then we had to be on the outside border of the Ashley. Which meant we were closer to a road than I'd previously thought.

Part of me wanted to get excited. To let my heart race. To run down the rabbit trail of all the possibilities. But if I did, and if Ashley read it on my face, and she too got excited, and none of my hopes were true, then . . . false hope was worse than no hope at all.

I kept looking. Even that still didn't explain how they hauled everything up here. What actually carried all the stuff? Pots, pans, food, supplies. Then I looked up.

Above my head, in the rafters, lay six or eight blue plastic sleds made for hauling equipment behind a snowmobile or four-wheeler or horse. Several lengths and widths. I pulled one down. It was about seven feet long, plenty wide enough to lie in, had runners along the bottom to track more easily in the snow, and didn't weigh fifteen pounds.

I turned it at an angle, slid it out the window, and was in the process of climbing out when I looked up a final time. There, lying on top of the other sleds, were several sets of snowshoes. I'd almost missed them. This time my heart did race. Someone had put them there, which meant someone might have used them to walk up there, and if they could do it, well . . .

Four pairs in all. They were dusty, old, and the bindings were stiff and cracking, but the frames were strong, as were the supports. And they were light. I found a pair that fit, strapped them on, and returned to the A-frame, pulling the sled.

Ashley stirred, stared over her shoulder. "What's that?"

"Your blue chariot."

"Is there a really fast horse attached to the other end?"

"Very funny."

I pulled the harness off the old sled and anchored it to the new one. Between the wool blankets and sleeping bags, I felt like I could make Ashley a good bit more comfortable. "You get to ride forward in this one."

"That means I've got to look at your backside the entire time."

"Well . . . what remains of it."

"If you ain't the lead dog, the view never changes."

It was good to hear the humor return.

THAT AFTERNOON WE CONTINUED our game of Monopoly. Or rather, Ashley continued swallowing up real estate and charging exorbitant rental rates. At one point she was shaking the dice in both hands, saying, "You're going down, sucker." She rolled an eight, which bounced her completely over my few, pitiful properties.

"Has anyone ever told you that you're just a little bit competitive?"

She sat back, triumphant. "No, what makes you say that?"

By late afternoon I had mortgaged every piece of property I had and was just hoping I could pass GO one more time and collect $200 before she, the bank, foreclosed on everything I owned and took the shirt off my back.

I never made it. I landed on Park Place, and she laughed like a hyena for ten minutes.

An hour before dark, I set the puzzle in her lap and said, "I'll be back." I strapped on the snowshoes and began slipping along the ridgeline in search of something to eat. The snow wasn't falling as heavily, but it was still falling. Still accumulating. The entire world was muted. Every sound deafened. Silence was the loudest noise I heard.

I considered how different life had become. No phones, no voice mail, no beepers, no e-mail, nobody paging me over the hospital intercom, no news, no radio. No noise other than the crack of the fire, the sound of Ashley's voice, and Napoleon's nails scratching the concrete floor.

Of all those, I caught myself listening for one sound in particular.

I walked thirty minutes, maybe a mile, where I found a lot of tracks merging into a ravine. The snow was all torn up. I set up under an aspen and waited. Didn't take long. A fox appeared, ran through the ravine, and disappeared before I could draw. A doe soon followed, but it winded me, threw its tail in the air, blew loudly through its nose, stamped the ground, and took off at light speed. That's about when I figured my hide beneath the aspen wasn't all that great, given the prevailing wind. Either that, or the animals were smelling the soap. This hunting stuff wasn't as easy as it looked on TV.

It was almost dark so, rather than move, I stayed put five more minutes. One rabbit appeared and began hopping down into the ravine and up the other side. It hopped twice going up the other side, stopped, caught a whiff of me, and I let the arrow fly. Fortunately for us, I did not miss.

An odd light shone through and across the snow as I retraced my steps, returning to Ashley. Napoleon was gone again, and Ashley was asleep in the chair. The puzzle on her lap. I boiled some water, steeped the tea bags for what was certainly the last time, and sat alongside her while I turned the rabbit above the fire.

When I'd sufficiently burned it, she woke, and we ate slowly.

Chewing every bite longer than normal. Savoring what we could. It was barely enough to feed one, much less two.

Napoleon returned shortly thereafter. I had really grown to like him. He was tough, tender when needed, and did a pretty good job of taking care of himself. He walked in, licking the sides of his muzzle. His face was red and stomach taut and rounded. He walked back to his section of mattress, walked in a circle, rolled over, and stuck his feet in the air. I rubbed his tummy, and he started involuntarily kicking one leg.

Ashley spoke. "I'm glad he's putting some meat back on his bones. I was starting to worry about him."

When I leaned over, my recorder slipped out of my shirt pocket. She noticed it and spoke without looking at me. "How are the batteries holding up?"

"Thanks to the airport, batteries are not a problem."

"The airport seems like a long time ago. Another life even."

"Yes, it does."

She smiled. "Those batteries the same size you use for your shorts?"

"Very funny."

"So . . . what are you telling her?"

I didn't respond.

"Is that too personal?"

"No."

"What then?"

"Well . . . I have described the snow and the crappy situation in which we find ourselves."

"You saying you don't like having me as a traveling companion?"

"No. Other than having to haul you halfway across Utah, you're a great traveling companion."

She laughed. "I'll give you that. Why don't you tell her what you miss about her?"

The moon must have been shining behind the clouds, because an eerie and bright light shone. More of a glow, it cast down through our window and threw a shadow on the concrete floor.

"I've done that."

"Certainly, you haven't told her everything."

I turned the recorder in my hands. "I've told her a good bit. Why don't you tell me what you miss about Vince."

"Let's see . . . I miss his cappuccino maker, and the smell of his Mercedes, and the sparse cleanliness of his bachelor's penthouse . . . the view off the balcony at night is really something. If the Braves are playing you can see the lights of Turner Field. Boy . . . a hot dog would be good right now. I'd even settle for one of those big pretzels. What else? I miss his laughter and the way he checks on me. He's very good at calling me even when he's busy."

"You're hungry, aren't you?"

"No . . . what makes you say that?"

After she fell asleep, I lay awake a long time, thinking. She had told me very little about Vince.

CHAPTER THIRTY-SEVEN

A month passed. You were ready to climb the walls. Couldn't wait for the next ultrasound. We got to the hospital, and Steve met us in the room. The attendant squirted the goo and Steve squinted, watching the screen.

The attendant stopped circling and looked at him. A blank stare. You were the only one who didn't know. You said, "Somebody better start talking to me."

Steve handed you a towel and looked at the technician, who left the room. I helped you wipe the goo off and sat you up.

Steve leaned against the wall. "The tear has worsened. A lot." He fumbled with his hands. "This doesn't mean you can't have more kids, Rachel. It's an anomaly. You're healthy, you can have more children."

You looked at me, so I translated. "Honey . . . the abruption has . . . worsened. Sort of hanging by a thread."

You looked at Steve. "Are my babies okay?"

"For the moment."

"Getting nutrition?"

"Yes, but . . ."

You held up your hands, two stop signs. "But are they, as of this moment, okay?"

"Yes, but . . ."

"But what? What else is there to talk about? I stay on bed rest. I rent a room in this hospital. I do something. Anything."

Steve shook his head. "Rachel . . . if it tears . . ."

You shook your head. "But as of this moment, it hasn't."

"Rachel . . . if you were in the OR right now, and I was scrubbed for surgery, and it tore, I'm not sure I'd have enough time to get them out and stop the bleeding before you bled to death. Your life is in danger. I need to take the babies."

You looked at him like he'd lost his mind. "Where are you going to take them?"

He shrugged. "You know what I mean."

"I'm not letting you do any such thing."

"If you don't . . . none of you will make it."

"What chance do I have? I mean, in percent?"

"If I wheel you into surgery right now, real good. Beyond that, the numbers fall off a cliff."

"And if not . . . ?"

"Even if we monitor you, we won't know it until it's too late. Once it tears, the internal bleeding will . . ."

"But it is conceivable that if I can lie real still for the next, what . . . four weeks, then I can have a C-section and we can drive home with a happy family, two cribs, two baby monitors, and two very tired parents? Well? Is it conceivable?"

"With total bed rest, it is conceivable, but not likely. You have better odds in Vegas. You need to understand that this is like walking around with a cyanide tablet in your stomach. Once it's broken, we can't unbreak it."

"My children are not cyanide."

"Rachel . . ."

You held a finger in the air. "Is there a chance we could make it?"

"Technically, yes . . . but . . ."

You pointed at the screen. "I've seen their faces. You showed them to me with your fancy 3D hi-def television that you're so proud of."

"You're not being reasonable."

"I'll not sleep the rest of my life looking at their faces on the backs of my eyelids. Wondering what if I let you 'take' them, when in reality you were wrong and they'd have made it and if it weren't for you and your dire predictions, they'd be right here."

He had no comment. Just looked at me. He shrugged. "Rachel . . . at this point, they're just . . . clumps of cells."

You took his hand, pressed it to your stomach. "Steve, I'd like to you meet Michael and Hannah. They're pleased to meet you. Hannah plays piano. She could be the next Mozart. And Michael, he's a math wizard, and a runner like his daddy. He thinks he can find a cure for cancer."

Steve shook his head.

You two were getting nowhere. Not that I was much help.

I piped in. "How long do we have? I mean, realistically, to make this decision . . . when everyone's emotions aren't so high."

Steve shrugged. "I can push it to first thing tomorrow morning." He looked at you. "You can have more children. This is not something you will incur again. It's a fluke. An accident of nature. You can start again right away."

You placed your palm across your stomach. "Steve . . . we didn't have an accident. We made babies."

The ride home was quiet. You sat with your hands on your stomach, legs crossed.

I parked and met you on the porch. The breeze was tugging at your hair.

I spoke first. "Honey, let me get you into bed."

You nodded, and I propped you up there. We sat staring out across the waves. The ocean was choppy. The silence was thick.

"Hey . . . your chances aren't real good."

"Like what are they?"

"I'd say less than 10 percent."

"What does Steve say?"

"He doesn't think it's that much."

You turned. "Seventy-five years ago this wasn't even an issue. People didn't have this much information."

I nodded. "You're right. But we're not living in the Great Depression. We're living now. And, either thanks to or in spite of modern medicine, we have technology, which is giving us a choice."

Your head tilted. "Ben . . . we made our choice. That night, about five months ago. It's the risk we took then, and it's the one we're taking now."

I bit my lip.

You placed my palm on your stomach. "I can see their faces. Michael has your eyes and Hannah has my nose . . . I know how they smell, which side of their lips turn up when they smile, whether or not their ear lobes are connected, the wrinkles in their fingers. They are a part of me . . . of us."

"This is selfish."

"I'm sorry you see it that way."

"Ten percent is nothing. It's a death sentence."

"It's a sliver of hope. A possibility."

"You're willing to bet on a sliver?"

"Ben, I will not play God."

"I'm not asking you to play God. I'm asking you to let him work it out. Let God be God. I've seen all the pictures. Jesus with all the children. Let him have two more. We'll see them when we get there."

You turned. "The only way he's getting these two is to make me part of the deal." You shook your head, turning back. The tears came in earnest. "Seriously, what percent is enough for you? If Steve had a different number, what would that number be?"

I shrugged. "Somewhere north of fifty."

You shook your head. Touched my face. "There's always hope."

I was angry. Bitter. I couldn't change your mind. The very thing I loved about you, your laser-beamed focus, anchored strength, was the very thing I was fighting. And at that moment, I hated it. "Rachel . . . there is no hope. You're playing God with you."

"I love you, Ben Payne."

"Then act like it."

"I am."

"You don't love me. And you don't even love them. You just love the idea of them. If you did, then you'd be in surgery right now."

"It's because of you that I love them."

"Forget them. I don't want them. Go away. We'll make more."

"You don't mean that."

"Rachel, if I had it my way, you'd be in surgery right now."

"Are you absolutely certain it'll tear loose?"

"No, but . . ."

"Are my babies alive right now?"

"Rachel . . . I've spent the last fifteen years of my life studying medicine. I come at this with some credibility. This is no kids' game. This will kill you. You will die and leave me alone."

You turned, amazement in your eyes. "Ben . . . there are no guarantees. This is the chance we take. The chance we took."

"Why are you being so stubborn? Think about someone other than yourself for a minute. Why are you being so selfish?"

"Ben . . . I'm not thinking about me. One day you'll see that."

"Well . . . you're certainly not thinking about me."

I changed, laced up my shoes, and tore out the door, nearly slamming it off its hinges.

I took off running. A half mile down the beach, I turned. You were standing on the porch, leaning against the railing. Watching me.

When I close my eyes, I can still see you.

And whenever I get to this point in our story . . . I never quite know how to talk about what comes next.

CHAPTER THIRTY-EIGHT

Two days passed. Three weeks since the crash. One moment, it seemed like a year. At another, like a day. It was an odd feeling. A place where time both sped and crawled.

I woke and found myself groggy, holding my head in my hands. In the last couple of days we'd eaten rabbit and two ground squirrels, but nothing bigger. We weren't wasting away as quickly, but we weren't putting much in the bank either. I needed a massive influx of calories if I hoped to get us out of here. In the A-frame, we were safe and warm. Stoking the fire, napping, and playing Monopoly required little energy. But as soon as I strapped on the harness and we stepped out the door, all bets were off. Between the cold, shivering, wind, driving snow, sweating, and physical exertion, I'd never make it on an empty tank.

We needed several days of stored food because of the simple fact that I couldn't pull, take care of Ashley, and hunt. I needed to hunt now, freeze the meat, preferably seven days' worth, and strike out. To set out before was to invite a cold, hungry death.

It might be anyway.

Ashley woke shortly after me. She stretched and said, "I keep hoping to crack open my eyes and find that you've hauled us out of this place, back to the world where train horns echo through the night and the smell of Starbucks lures me on my way to my office and my biggest struggles are road rage and a phone that rings more than I wish, and where . . ." She fidgeted, a grimace on her face. "Advil exists. And . . ." She laughed. "Disposable razors and shaving cream are found."

I had grown used to that laugh. I scratched my face. The beard had come in thick and grown past the place where it itched my face. "Amen to that."

She lay back. "I'd give a thousand dollars for some scrambled eggs, toast, cheese grits—heavy on the cheese, and spicy sausage." She stuck a finger in the air. "Bookended by a pot of coffee and finished with a cheese Danish."

I walked to the kitchen to boil some water. My stomach was growling. "You're not helping me."

I MASSAGED ASHLEY'S LEGS, and was encouraged by both the healthy blood flow and lack of swelling. I got her settled in the chair and told her, "I might be gone most of the day. Probably be dark when I get back." She nodded, pulled Napoleon up onto her lap, and I set the puzzle next to her. I packed my bag into my pack, buckled on the snowshoes, grabbed the bow and hatchet, and set off around the lake. I had gotten better at walking in the snowshoes, which meant I wasn't always beating the insides together. I brought along both of Grover's fly reels in the event I could make a few snares.

The wind had picked up and was swirling the snow. Tiny flakes, thick, blowing fast and stinging my face. I circled the lake, walking in the direction I'd spotted the cow moose and her yearling days before. The yearling would feed us for two weeks.

I walked the rim of the lake, setting two snares in areas where the tracks suggested animal traffic. I cut limbs and spread debris, further narrowing the lane of travel, and hung loops just off the surface of the snow.

When I reached the other end of the lake, I found the snow torn up and moose tracks everywhere. Not directional tracks, but standing-around-eating tracks. Wasn't hard to figure out. The moose stood on the lake and ate the tree limbs extending out over what, during summertime, was water. The ice and snow allowed them to eat higher on the branches—essentially standing on the water.

I needed a blind, a place to hide. The lake was lined with lodgepole pine, spruce, Douglas fir, and aspen. I picked out an aspen close to the tracks with branches low to the ground, located about thirty yards downwind from where they fed. I cut limbs, inserted them into the tree to thicken it so nothing could see me from behind, then dug out the snow beneath the tree and packed it up into the underside of the limbs. Doing so blocked the wind and made for a cozy blind. Beneath the tree were several large rocks. I rolled one up against the base and used it as a chair, leaning against the trunk. I cut a small "window" in front of me to shoot through, nocked an arrow, slid into my bag up to my chest, and began the long wait. Around lunchtime I shot a rabbit, retrieved it, and buried it in the snow alongside me. By midafternoon I'd seen nothing, so I napped, waking an hour before dark.

Night fell, and I walked back. Wasn't hard finding my way; I just kept the trees on my right and the large white, open area on my left. The first snare remained untouched, the second had been moved but remained empty, suggesting something had bumped it. I reset it and trudged home, realizing I needed to increase my chances. Sort of like Bingo. If you really want to win, play more boards.

I cleaned the rabbit and threaded it through the rod hanging horizontally over the fire. I bathed my face and hands, and after an hour or so, we ate. Ashley was chatty. The consequence of my having left her alone all day. I was not. I'd been left alone with my thoughts and one or two questions I couldn't answer.

She picked up on it. "You don't want to talk, do you?"

I'd finished eating and I was stripping line off Grover's fly reels to make new snares. "Sorry. Guess I don't multitask very well."

"You run the ER at your hospital, right?"

I nodded.

"So, you deal with multiple traumas at once?"

Another nod.

"I imagine you multitask just fine. What is it?"

"Are you interviewing me for an article?"

She raised both eyebrows. Universal women's body language for *I'm waiting.*

The fly line was light green and blended in well with the branches. It should work. I'd cut twelve equal pieces of line, all about eight feet in length, and looped the ends with slipknots. I sat on my bag, legs crossed. "We're at a bit of a crossroads."

"We've been at one since our plane went down."

"True, but this one is a bit different."

"How so?"

I shrugged. "Stay or go. We've got shelter here, warmth, maybe somebody will stumble upon us, but I think it's more likely that'd be two or three months off. If we head out, we're taking our chances on shelter and food, and we don't know how far we have to go. If we could increase our food stores, we could cook it here, wrap it up, and probably last a week or two out there. The new sled will move easier, the snowshoes will work, but . . ."

"But, what?"

"We're left with one big unknown."

"Which is?"

"How far? We don't know if we're twenty miles or fifty or more. It's been snowing for I don't know how long, there's four feet of fresh powder, avalanches will be a constant concern, and . . ."

"Yes . . . ?"

"What if I walk you out into the middle of that mess only to get us both killed—when if we stayed here, we might get lucky and hold out."

She lay back. "Sounds like you're in a pickle."

"Me?"

"Yeah, you."

"I'm not deciding for us. We are."

She closed her eyes. "Let's sleep on it. You don't have to decide right now."

"I told you, I'm not deciding. We are."

She smiled. "I'm going to sleep. You can give me your decision in the morning."

"You're not listening."

She pulled Napoleon up underneath her arm and pulled the bag up around her shoulders.

It was dark except for the fire. I fed it with wood. Of which we had plenty.

"You let me know when you get around to voicing the thing that's really bothering you."

I could hear the smile in her voice. I scratched my head. "I just did."

"Nope. You did not. It's still in there." She pointed toward the door. "Why don't you go for a walk. And take your recorder with you. By the time you get back, you'll have figured it out."

"You . . . are annoying."

She nodded. "I'm trying to be more than just annoying. Now go for a walk. We'll be here when you get back."

CHAPTER THIRTY-NINE

Did you have something to do with this? I don't know how you did it, but I'd bet you put her next to me on the plane. I'm not sure what she's talking about. Well . . . maybe I do a little, but that doesn't make her right. Okay, it makes her right. There. She's right. And I'm right back here talking into this thing 'cause I can't get what I think out my mouth.

Both of you should be happy.

But what am I supposed to do? I haven't hunted seriously since Granddaddy took me in school. Well, maybe a bird hunt here and there. A few deer hunts. But it's never mattered. It didn't matter then. We were just hanging out. Granddaddy took me hunting because he should've taken Dad when he was a boy, didn't, and Dad grew up a jerk. I was the consolation prize. Which was fine with me; I loved him, he loved me, and we became pals, and it got me out from under Dad's thumb. But if we didn't shoot anything, neither of us died. We just stopped at Waffle House on the way home. Maybe McDonald's. Or Wendy's. Sometimes the seafood buffet. It was a social thing. Not a life or death thing.

Out here, if I miss, wound it, and can't find it, or just don't see anything 'cause it either smells me or sees me, then we die. Out here, it matters. A lot. I should have watched more TV. What's that guy's name? Bear Grylls? And Survivorman. What's his name? I'll bet either of those guys would already be out of here. If they could see me, they'd probably laugh at me.

I just didn't know when I got on Grover's plane that I was going to have to hunt my way out of this eternal wilderness. I know a lot of people have survived much worse conditions, but ours aren't getting any better. It's like . . . it's like being in hell when things froze over. It's not like I have any idea what I'm doing. And I'm scared that if I don't get it figured out, that girl in there is going to die a slow, painful death.

There. I said it. I feel responsible. How can I not? She should be back at her office, after her honeymoon, talking on the phone, e-mailing her friends, racing to meet a deadline, glowing in the post-wedding bliss. Not lying helpless out here in the middle of nowhere with a bumbling, tongue-tied idiot who's slowly starving her.

I've got nothing to offer her. And I've got nothing to offer you. Now you've both got me talking to myself. What is it with you women? Can't us guys not *have the answer? Can't we* not *know what we're doing or what's going to happen next? Can't we be . . . incapable and broken and worn down and disheartened? Can't we* not *know how we're going to help or fix the problems we encounter?*

But, you already knew that, didn't you? I'm not telling you anything you don't already know.

I'm sorry for yelling at you. This time . . . and the last.

I guess she was right. Guess I needed to get out here and get this off my chest. To vent a little. But I'm not telling her that. Of course, she already knows it. It's why she sent me out here. She's as bad as you. You two must be cut from the same cloth.

Okay, I heard you. I'll tell her. I know she's lying there with a broken leg in the middle of nowhere, dependent upon a total stranger. Although we're not as much strangers now as we once were. I mean, she hasn't been to the bathroom in three weeks without my help. Even in the A-frame I've got to support her leg. She's not any more happy about it than I am, but if I don't she can't bend or sit or put pressure on it. You ever tried squatting on one leg? Ain't easy. I tried it. So anyway, we're not strangers.

And yes, I've looked at her, and no, *it's not what you're thinking. If you know what I mean? Well, of course, I find her attractive. She is. She's . . . incredible. Honey, she's getting married, and I'm trying to get her home to her fiancé. I don't know if she likes him or not. Sometimes I think yes. Other times I think no.*

I'm not having this conversation with you.

Yes, she has legs like yours. No, she's . . . bigger. Not sure what size she wears. It's not like I'm checking bra tags. Well, of course, I've seen them. I had to take it off her after the crash.

No, I'm not having a tough time with all this. I'm . . . I'm missing you.

Honey, I'm her doctor. That's all. Okay . . . maybe it's a little tough. There, you want me to be honest. I said it. It's not easy. . . .

I will say this about her . . . her sense of humor is rare. Something I've found myself leaning on. Needing. It's a strength thing. Like yours. Comes from way down deep. She's tough. I think she'll make it. Provided I don't kill her first from starvation.

Will I? Honey . . . I don't know. Didn't think I'd make it this far, but I have. Could it get worse? Sure. This is not the worst thing. The worst thing . . . is . . . being separated from you. That's ten times tougher than being stuck out here.

I'm going to bed now.

And no, I don't know what I'm going to do about the "it's not easy" part. No, I'm not going to tell her. Absolutely not. Stop it. I'm not telling her. I'm not listening.

All right, I might tell her . . . it's a little tough. Fair?

No, I don't know how. I don't know . . . I'll be honest. Honesty's never been a problem. Selfishness? Yes. Honesty? No. But you already knew that.

And, yes, I'll tell her I'm sorry.

I'm sorry for raising my voice at you.

Both now . . . and then.

CHAPTER FORTY

The following morning, I was out early. Setting twelve snares took the better part of the morning. When I finished, it was after lunch. A dozen plus the two I already had made fourteen. I'd set them up all around the lake. Some on the bank, some inland a hundred yards or so. I could check them all going to and coming from my moose blind.

I got settled in my blind in the midafternoon, and sat three hours before I saw anything. A young moose, followed closely by its mother, came waltzing out onto the lake. It ran out a few feet, the snow above its knees, then turned and ran back to the trees and began feeding. It was too big to still be nursing on its mother's milk. Most animals that I know of give birth after the harsh winters. If this calf was born in May or June of last year, it might have been eight months old now. The cow, its mother, was huge. Probably seven feet tall at the shoulders, and weighed every bit of a thousand pounds. She could have fed us for a year. But we didn't need a year. If I took the calf, the cow would make it. If I took the cow, chances were good the calf would die anyway.

They fed to within forty yards, and my heart started beating pretty fast. The snow was blowing into my face, which meant the wind was blowing that way, too. The cow moved to within twenty yards, and I thought seriously about shooting her. In hindsight, I should have. The calf didn't let her get too far away and moved in closer. Getting within ten yards of me. Any closer and they'd hear my heart beating.

I drew slowly, and the mother popped her head up. One big eye looking at me. Or, rather, at the tree. She knew something was in here. She just didn't know what.

I settled the pin on the calf's chest, took a deep breath, let out half, and whispered, "Front sight, front sight, front sight . . . *press.*"

The arrow disappeared into the chest of the calf. It hopped, bucked, spun in a circle, and took off running behind me, out across the lake, followed closely by the cow. The mother's head and ears were held high. Full alert. Pounding through the snow.

I caught my breath, allowed my nerves to settle, and thought back through the release and the arrow flight. I'd intended to hit it in the heart area—causing it to die quickly—but I'd flinched and pulled the shot right, causing it to hit too far back on the ribs. A difference of maybe four inches. That meant the arrow had pierced the lungs, which meant that the calf, afraid and in pain, would run. It couldn't fight, so it took flight. That meant it would bleed itself to death, but in the process it might run a mile. The mother would follow the flight, and fight when needed.

Once it ran into cover, it would stop and listen for its mother. Seeing the mother and feeling safe, the calf would lie down and bleed to death. If I stepped out of my hide and traipsed off after it, I would scare it some more, and push it.

I waited almost an hour, nocked another arrow, and stepped out. The blood trail was a red brick road, trailing out across the lake. I was right. It had been a bad shot. The calf had run a straight path across the lake and up into the trees. I followed slowly, keeping a lookout for the mother. Cow moose are protective. They'd rather fight than run.

It quit snowing, a breeze pushed out the clouds, and a three-quarter moon shone above me. It was the brightest night I'd seen in a long time. My shadow followed me into the trees. The only sounds were my breathing and the sound of snowshoes crunching snow.

I took my time, and an hour later, I found them. The calf had made it nearly a mile from where I'd shot it, began climbing up a ridgeline and, too weak to continue, had toppled and rolled down. The mother stood over it, nudging it.

It lay unmoving.

The cow was standing straight up, as was her tail. I hollered, raised the bow high in the air, and tried to look bigger than I was. She looked at me, then back over her shoulder. While its nose is quite good, a moose's eyesight is poor. I walked within forty yards, approaching downwind, arrow nocked. I didn't want to shoot her, but if she charged me, I wasn't sure I'd have much choice.

I kept the trees close by. If needed, I could dive below one.

At twenty yards, she'd had enough of my encroachment. She charged as if she was shot out of a cannon. I stepped for the trees, but tripped on my own snowshoes. She caught me with her head and chest, launching me into the limbs of the aspen. I slammed against the trunk, then dove below the lowest limbs, wrapping myself into a ball down around the base. She could smell me, but given the limbs, couldn't see me. She snorted and made a deep bellowing sound, then shook the limbs with her chest, stamped her foot, and then stood back listening. Her ears perked up. She took one tentative step . . .

They came all at once.

Eight wolves spilled out of the trees higher up and descended upon the calf, tearing at it. She didn't even hesitate. Nine animals collided in a spinning whirl and mass of fur, teeth, and hoof above the dead calf.

I crawled out from underneath the tree, lay on my belly, and watched. She was standing over the calf, kicking. I heard bones crunching and saw wolves flying some twenty feet into the air. One jumped from somewhere, latched itself to her hindquarters and began tearing while another jumped onto her throat and clung to her windpipe and jugular. A third and fourth began tearing at her from underneath. Two more were still tearing at the calf. Two lay unmoving on the snow.

With little regard for herself, she kicked the two atop the calf, sending them spinning through the air like footballs. Then she turned her attention to those that had latched onto her. She bucked and kicked and filled the air with splattering wolf blood and shattered wolf teeth. Within seconds, the wounded wolves had retreated to the trees, whining. They stood off some sixty or eighty yards, considering their options. She stood in the moonlight, breathing heavily, her own blood dripping on the snow, straddling the calf, nudging it with her muzzle. Every few minutes she'd fill her stomach with air and sound a deep bellow. I crawled into my bag, sat on top of my pack, and leaned against the tree.

The wolves circled for another hour, made one feigned charge, then disappeared over the ridgeline, their howling echoing into the distance. In the hours that followed, she stood over the calf, shielding it from the snow that had returned. The field of red she had created slowly turned to white, burying the memory.

At daylight, when the calf was little more than a white mound beneath her, the cow bellowed one last time and wandered off. Quietly, I pulled the calf into the trees. Its hams, or hindquarters, were gone, having been eaten—or at least torn off, by the wolves. Its shoulders too had been chewed at, but some meat remained. I cut out the backstraps, pulled as much meat as I could off the tops of the shoulders and the tenderloins from inside, between the shoulder blades. Doing so gave me maybe thirty pounds of meat. Enough to feed us for a week to ten days. Or more.

I tied it down into my pack and went to retrieve the bow where I'd dropped it during the charge. It lay in pieces. The limbs had shattered, cams had broken, the string lay in a bird's nest of a mess, and all the arrows had snapped when she'd stepped on it.

I left it.

I strapped on the snowshoes and walked back to the lake. At the far end I could see the A-frame, the fire glowing bright through the glass. I doubted Ashley had slept.

I reached the red brick road and stopped. In the distance, the cow bellowed. She would probably do that all day and into tomorrow.

I wasn't sad for killing the calf. We needed to eat. If given the chance, I'd do it again. I wasn't sad that the cow was lonely. She'd have another calf. Most had twins or triplets when they gave birth.

The thing that had my stomach in knots was the sight of the mother, standing over her young.

I sank my hand into the snow, ran my fingers through the clumps of red. Fresh snow had covered most of it. Only a dim outline remained. In an hour, there would be no reminder.

Maybe it was my twenty-third morning, my weakened condition, my own weariness, the weight of the recorder pressed against my chest, the fading bellows of the cow, the thought of Ashley hurt and worried, maybe it was all of the above. I fell forward, landing on my knees, my pack driving me into the snow, which rose around my thighs. I scooped my hand beneath a red clump the size of my fist, lifted it to my nose, and breathed.

To my left stood a tall pine. Straight and spiraling upward

maybe sixty feet. The first limbs didn't sprout out until some thirty feet up the trunk.

I unbuckled my pack, pulled the hatchet from my belt, and crawled to the tree. With several good swings I cut a band, maybe two feet long, three inches wide, and an inch or two deep, into and around the base. Come summer, when the heat rose, drawing the sap up, it would ooze and trickle out the scar like tears.

Chances are, it would do that for several years.

CHAPTER FORTY-ONE

You were right . . . you were right all along.

CHAPTER FORTY-TWO

Ashley's face told me all I needed to know. I shuffled in and put down my pack. I didn't realize how drained I was until I tried to speak. I shrugged. "I tried to call, but the line was busy. . . ."

She smiled, squinted her eyes, and fingered me closer. I knelt next to her. She raised her hand to my left eye, gently brushing it. "You've been cut. Deep, too." Her palm brushed my cheek. "You okay?"

Next to her, the puzzle lay complete. The picture had come together. It was a panoramic view of snowcapped mountains and a sun behind.

"You finished it?" I turned my head, squinted my eyes. "Is it a sunrise or sunset?"

She lay back, closed her eyes. "I think that depends on the eyes of the viewer."

I SPENT THE DAY cutting strips of meat and slow-cooking them over the fire. Ashley held up a small mirror and flinched while I sewed up the skin above my eye. Seven stitches in all. We ate off and on all day. If we even thought about food, we tore off a piece and chewed. Napoleon, too. We gave ourselves permission.

We didn't gorge, but we weren't hungry either. By nighttime, we were content. All three of us.

She asked me to run her a bath, which I did. While she bathed, I packed the sled. We didn't have much left. My pack, our bags, the blankets, the hatchet, the meat. Anything that wasn't necessary, I left, lightening the load. I helped Ashley out of the bath, got her tucked into bed, then bathed myself, not knowing if and when I'd have another chance.

I was asleep by nightfall, and slept until just before daylight. Maybe twelve hours in all. The longest stretch since the crash. In truth, the longest stretch in years. A decade maybe.

Surgeons, especially trauma surgeons, are pretty good at making tough decisions, making them quickly and under a good bit of stress. I'd been struggling with ours. What to do? Go? Stay?

I didn't want to leave. I wanted to stay by that warm fire and hope somebody stumbled upon us, but we'd gotten lucky with the calf. I could hunt my whole life and not get that chance again. Not to mention the fact that the bow had been destroyed.

I thought about setting the A-frame on fire. Just torching the whole place. But there was no guarantee that someone would investigate. And if we got three days out and had not gotten anywhere, or seen anything of promise, we needed a retreat. I was not Columbus. We needed someplace to come back to more than we needed the possibility that someone might see and investigate the fire.

I cut the foam pad to fit into the bottom of the sled, laid two blankets atop it. Then I dressed Ashley in her clothes, strapped the brace back on her leg, zipped her up in her bag, slid her onto the sled, and lifted her head onto a third blanket I'd folded into a pillow. The sled was hollow in the middle, putting a pocket of air between her backside and the snow. That meant she'd stay warm. And maybe just as important, stay dry, because the plastic sled was totally impervious to moisture.

I tied the tarp down across the top of her to protect her from the snow. She thumped it from the underside. "Snug as a bug in a rug."

I tucked Napoleon in alongside her. He must have been worried too, because he licked her face more than usual.

I strapped on my gaiters, rolled up my jacket, and placed it inside the sleeping bag with her. I grabbed the matches and lighter fluid, buckled myself into the harness, took one last look at the warm fire, and pulled her out the door and back into the never-ending snow.

Surprisingly, I felt good. Not strong, but not tired and not as weak. If I had to guess I'd say I'd lost more than twenty pounds since the crash. Maybe twenty-five. A lot of that was muscle. Not all, but most. Losing it meant I'd lost some strength as well. The good news was that, with the snowshoes, I was a bit lighter on my feet. I didn't have as much strength, but I didn't have as much to haul around either. If you didn't count Ashley and the sled. I probably hadn't been this light since high school.

I tied a long tether from the harness around my shoulders and handed her the loose end. "If you need me, just tug that."

She nodded, looped the tether over her wrist, and tucked the tarp up under her chin.

We walked out into glowing daylight. Within minutes we were climbing up the ridgeline en route to the trail leading out of the valley and through the notch. I seldom felt much tension on the harness because the sled glided well over the snow. The snow was blowing into my face, landing on my eyelashes, blurring my vision. I was constantly wiping my face.

My plan was simple: start walking and keep walking. Logically, and based on a rudimentary reading of the 3-D map we'd found, I'd calculated we were probably looking at thirty or forty miles, fifty on the outside, from any kind of road or something man-made. I hadn't given much thought to how far I could pull this sled. I tried not to think about it. I guess I thought I could make thirty. I had my doubts about fifty. If it turned out to be more than that, our chances were slim.

Our path took us down small hills and up short rises, but on the whole I could tell we were losing elevation and, thankfully, the path was mostly clear. That meant I wasn't spending a lot of energy stepping over and under debris, which allowed me to put more of my energy into moving forward. And I was comforted by the idea that we were on a path. A route taken by other people. And those other people had to come from somewhere.

By lunch I calculated we'd walked three miles. By midafternoon we'd covered six. I wondered what time it was, and out of habit, stared at my watch. The cracked crystal and condensation beneath the glass stared back at me. Toward dusk the trail came down off a small hill and flattened out. I'd pushed it, and hard. I looked behind us, thinking back through each turn. Maybe we'd covered ten miles.

WE SPENT THE NIGHT beneath a makeshift shelter using our tarp, which had grown tattered, and some limbs I cut to help shed the snow. Ashley lay snug on the sled. She shrugged. "There's only room on here for one."

I lay on the cold snow, a wool blanket and my bag separating me from the snow. "I miss our fire."

"Me too."

Napoleon was shivering. "I don't think he's too happy about this either," I said, and pulled him up close to me. He sniffed me and my bag, then hopped across the snow and dug himself in with Ashley.

She laughed.

I rolled over and closed my eyes. "Suit yourself."

BY MIDMORNING WE'D COME DOWN another four or so miles, and the temperature was warmer. Maybe just around freezing—the warmest it'd been since the crash. On the hillsides, small shoots and twigs shot up through the snow, suggesting that the ground rested only a few feet beneath us rather than eight or ten. While we had lost elevation, down as much as 9,000 feet, the surface of the snow was wet and pulled at the sled, increasing the workload.

Around mile five the trail dropped down, widened, and straightened. Almost unnaturally. I stopped and scratched my head. I was talking to myself, pointing at the trail before me.

Ashley spoke up. "What's wrong?"

"This thing is wide enough to drive a truck down." That's about when it hit me. "We're on a road. There's a road beneath us."

To our right I saw something flat, green, and shiny sticking up a few inches through the snow. I brushed away the snow. Took me a minute to figure out what it was. I started laughing. "It's a road sign." I dug out around it. It said EVANSTON 62.

"I want to see. What's it say?"

I stepped back into my harness. "It says Evanston, this way."

"How far?"

"Not very."

"Ben Payne."

I shook my head and didn't look. "Nope."

"How far?"

"You really want to know?"

A pause. "Not really."

"That's what I thought."

She tugged on the tether. I stopped again.

"Can we make it?"

I leaned into the harness. "Yes. We can make it."

She tugged again. "Can you pull this thing as far as that sign says we need to?"

I tightened my buckle and leaned into the weight of the harness. "Yes."

"You sure?"

"Yep."

"'Cause if you can't, just tell me. Now would be a good time to come clean if you don't think . . ."

"Ashley?"

"Yes."

"Shut up."

"You didn't say please."

"Please."

"Okay."

We walked five miles, most of which sloped downhill. It was relatively blissful walking. Night came, but with colder temperatures the sled slid easier, so I walked a few hours more. Putting ten miles on the road. Twenty-five since the A-frame. Walking on the road was a lot like walking around the lake—keep the trees on either side and walk down the white stuff in the middle.

Sometime after midnight I saw an odd-shaped tree, or shape, to my right. I unbuckled and investigated. A building, eight feet square, with a roof and a concrete floor. The door had been left cracked open, so snow had spilled in. I dug out an entrance and slid the sled down into it. A laminated sign hung on the wall. I lit a match. It read THIS IS AN EMERGENCY WARMING HUT. IF THIS IS AN EMERGENCY, THEN WELCOME. IF IT'S NOT, THEN YOU SHOULD NOT BE IN HERE.

Ashley's hand found mine in the darkness. "Are we okay?"

"Yeah . . . we're good. I think we actually have someone's permission to be in here. Except . . ." I unrolled my bag and climbed in. The floor was hard. "I miss my foam mattress."

"You want to share mine?"

"Don't think I haven't thought about it, but I don't think there's room on that thing for two of us."

She was quiet.

"How's the leg?" I asked.

"Still hurts."

"Differently or the same?"

"Same."

"Let me know if it starts feeling different."

"And when it does, just what will you do about it?"

I rolled over, closed my eyes. "Probably amputate. That way it'll quit hurting."

She slapped my shoulder. "That's not funny."

"Your leg is fine. It's healing nicely."

"Am I going to need surgery when we get out of here?"

I shrugged. "We need to look at it under X-ray. See how it looks."

"Will you do the surgery?"

"No."

"Why?"

" 'Cause I'll be sleeping."

She slapped my shoulder again. "Ben Payne . . ."

"Yes."

"I want to ask you a question, and I want an honest answer."

"Good luck with that."

A third slap. "I'm not kidding."

"Okay."

"If we needed to, could we get back to the A-frame? I mean . . . if conditions were worse . . . is going back still an option?"

My bag had become tattered, having lost some of its down insulation. Cold spots appeared. Sleep would not be easy. I thought back through the miles since the A-frame. Most had been slowly losing elevation. I was pretty sure I could not make it back.

"Yeah . . . it's still an option."

"Are you lying to me?"

"Yes."

"So, which is it? Yes or no?"

"Maybe."

"Ben . . . I still have one good leg."

"No."

"So, there's . . . no going back? We'll never see the A-frame again?"

"Something like that." I stretched out flat, staring up at the ceiling. Clouds had moved back in, so it was dark. Felt like we were in a hole, which, given the eight feet of snow banked against the walls around us, we were. After a few minutes, she quietly slid her hand inside my bag and placed it flat across my chest.

It stayed there all night.

I know.

CHAPTER FORTY-THREE

We started again at daylight. Ashley was chatty and I was feeling the effects of yesterday. Not to mention the fact that our road was slowly turning upward. Gradual at first, it turned ugly four miles into the morning, gradually snaking and twisting its way up the mountain I'd been staring at for the last two days. Given the incline and the wet, sticky condition of the snow, pulling the sled became a lot harder. I tightened the straps on my snowshoes, dug my hands beneath the straps, and leaned into it. It took me three hours to walk the next mile. By lunch we'd made five miles total and probably regained a thousand feet in elevation.

And the road was still going up. And the snow was blowing into my face.

By dusk we'd made a total of seven miles, but I was spent and my legs were cramping. I needed several seconds' rest between steps. I kept hoping we'd find another warming hut, but we did not, and I could walk no further to find it.

We camped next to a spiraling aspen. I tied the tarp around it, anchored it to the end of the sled, rolled out a blanket on the snow, set my bag on top of it, and was asleep before my head hit the ground.

I woke in the middle of the night. Snow was falling heavy and weighing down the tarp. I pushed it up from underneath and dumped off the snow. I ate a bite of cold meat, sipped some water, and poked my head out. To the north, the clouds were clearing. I slipped on my boots, strapped on the snowshoes, and went for a walk, climbing up another several hundred feet. The road on the mountain was winding tighter toward the summit. The only encouraging thought was knowing that if we had to climb up it, then we also got to come down it. The road turned left sharply, and I bent over, catching my breath. My legs were sore and cramped quickly.

Standing straight, I stared out across the darkness. The clouds were low, tucked down into the mountains. More cotton on a wound. Beyond that, maybe thirty or forty miles, it cleared. I squinted. It took me a second to realize what I was looking at.

I untied the tarp, folded it, and startled Ashley. She jerked. "What? What's going on?"

"I want you to see something."

"Right now?"

"Yep."

I buckled up and began pulling. What had taken me fifteen minutes alone now took an hour. I walked faster, hoping it would stay clear just a few minutes longer. Hoping she would get a chance to see it. My stomach muscles and the muscles on the front of my neck were sore, I was winded, and the straps were cutting into my shoulders.

We rounded the corner, I pulled her up to the ledge, and we waited for the clouds to clear again. The wind cut through me. I slipped on my jacket and hid my hands inside my sleeves. After a few minutes, the clouds rolled off and the view cleared. I pointed.

A single lightbulb sparkled some forty-plus miles in the distance. Beyond that, further to the north, a single trail of smoke.

She clutched my hand, and neither of us said a word. The clouds came and went. Rolling in and out on the wind. I took a reading on the compass, careful to let the needle settle and get an exact reading. Three hundred and fifty-seven degrees, almost due north.

She said, "What're you doing?"

"Just in case."

We stared at it for the rest of the night, hoping for more holes in the clouds. It had an orangish glow, which made me think it was some sort of street or utility light. Something big enough to be seen this far away. We finally lost sight of it when the sun rose in the east and the world became a white-capped carpet once again.

The road had brought us back up to around 11,000 feet. I needed sleep, but I knew I couldn't. I was too excited. We trudged across the snow quietly. Thinking about the picture in our minds. The thought of a world out there with electricity, running hot water, microwavable food, and coffee baristas.

The mountain plateaued. We walked several miles across what felt like the top of the world. The wind was steady, straight on, burned my face. The air was thin, and the snow stung my cheeks. I leaned into it, numb, wanting more air, counting the miles in my head. Maybe forty-five to go.

I walked, counting backward. Talking to myself. "Forty-two to the lightbulb . . . forty-one to the lightbulb . . ."

When I got to forty, we came down into a saddle atop the mountain. A bowl protected from the wind. Halfway through it, we discovered another warming hut. This one bigger. One room, three metal bunk beds with mattresses, a fireplace, and enough wood for an entire winter. Above the door it read RANGER'S CABIN. Inside I found the same laminated sign.

Given the lighter fluid we'd stolen from the A-frame, getting a fire going was easy. I stacked the wood, doused it, and lit the outside. The flame caught, traveled inward, and blazed. Once I was sure it had caught, I pulled out of my wet clothes and hung everything on the bunks. I got Ashley situated, then fell into my bed and didn't remember falling asleep.

CHAPTER FORTY-FOUR

She shook me. "Ben . . . you in there?"

"Yeah."

The day was full. Overcast but not snowing. Not yet. I didn't know what time it was, but it had to be close to lunch.

"You slept a long time."

I looked around, trying to remember where we were.

My legs were sore. My feet felt like hamburger. In truth, all of me was sore. I sat up, but my legs and stomach muscles quickly cramped. I stretched, easing the knots out. Ashley handed me a Nalgene bottle mostly full of water. It was body-temp warm and felt good going down my throat.

I ate, sipped, and wondered how far we could get today. Thirty minutes later, I was leaning into the harness, pulling.

She tugged gently on the tether. "Ben?"

I spoke over my shoulder. "Yeah."

"Do you happen to know what day it is?"

"Twenty-seven."

"Four weeks ago tomorrow?"

I nodded.

"So . . . today is Saturday?"

"Yeah . . . I think so."

I pulled on the harness, pushing my legs into the snowshoes.

Ashley jerked the tether again. "You know, I've been thinking."

"Yeah?"

"This losing weight stuff has been so easy that I think we need to capitalize on this whole deal."

"How so?"

"We need to write a diet book."

"A diet book?"

"Yeah . . ." She sat up. "Think about it. We've eaten almost nothing but meat and drunk only water and a few cups of coffee and tea since the wreck. I mean, look at us. Who's going to argue that it doesn't work?"

I turned. "I think our current diet is sort of a derivative of the Atkins or South Beach diet."

"So?"

"Well, what would we call it?"

"How about the North Utah diet?"

"Too blah."

She snapped her fingers. "What's the name of these mountains?"

"The Wasatch National Forest."

"No, the other name."

"The High Uintas."

"Yeah, we could call it the High Uintas Crash Weight Loss Diet."

"Well . . . it sure has worked for us. No arguing that, but I think it's too strict, and too expensive, for most people."

"How so?"

"Well . . . we've eaten mountain lion, trout, rabbit, and moose and drunk only water, tea, and coffee. I just don't think the average American is going to pay good money for a 300-page diet plan that I just gave you in one sentence. Not to mention the fact that you can't get mountain lion at your local meat counter."

"Good point."

I knelt and tightened one of my boots. "The whole thing is too simple. Needs to be more complicated, and you need to make people think it either originated with astronauts in space or actors in Hollywood."

"Well, you can make it more adventuresome by crashing people into mountains, then letting them walk out with nothing but a dead pilot, a compound bow, an angry dog, and a messed-up girl who missed her own wedding."

"I can pretty much guarantee that they'd lose more weight that way."

She paused. "Are you going to go see Grover's wife?"

"Yes."

"What will you tell her?"

"The truth, I guess."

"Do you always do that?"

"What?"

"Tell the truth."

"Yes . . ." I smirked. "Except when I'm lying."

She stared up at me. "How can I tell when you're lying?"

I tightened the buckles, leaning forward, breaking the sled loose from the grip of the snow. "You'll know 'cause I won't be telling you the truth."

"How will I know that?"

"Well . . . if I look at you in the next two or three days and tell you I've just ordered a pizza and that it'll be here in fifteen minutes, you'll know I'm lying."

"You ever lied to a patient?"

"Sure."

"What'd you tell them?"

" 'What I'm about to do won't hurt a bit.' "

"I've heard that one." She probed. "Ever lied to your wife?"

"Not about stuff that mattered."

"Like?"

"Well . . . when we first started taking dance lessons, I told her we were going to a movie. We didn't. We went to this studio where this guy made me wear funny shoes and attempted to teach me how to dance."

"I'd call that a good lie."

"Me too, but it's still a lie."

"Yeah, but it's justified. It's like the Jews in your basement thing."

"What do you mean?"

"The SS knocks on your door. They ask, 'Are you hiding Jews?' You answer, 'No, I'm not hiding Jews.' When in truth, there are three families tucked down in your basement. Quiet as a church mouse. Or synagogue mouse. Anyway, it's a justifiable lie. The kind God understands." She jerked the tether and held it, not letting the tension go. "Ben . . . ?"

I knew what was coming. She'd been beating around the bush and was finally getting to it. I relaxed, and the tension in the harness went slack.

"Ben?"

I was looking forward. "Yes?"

"You ever lied to me?"

I turned, and this time I looked at her. "Depends."

THE ROAD FLATTENED, then turned right and started descending off the plateau. Every few minutes the clouds would blow over, momentarily clearing, and I could see the road winding down below us for what looked like eight or ten miles. It looked like we were soon to lose several thousand feet of elevation.

The problem with such a drastic elevation change meant steep pitches and the possibility of the sled getting away from me.

The first four or five miles were blissful. Gradual decline, easy walking. At one point the sun broke through and we saw blue skies. But late in the afternoon, around mile six, the road corkscrewed, and looked like it dropped off a tabletop. I took it slow and easy. Winding my way down. If I started moving too fast, the sled would pick up speed and get away from me. With an hour to go before dark, the road descended and turned right in a huge horseshoe that curved some ten miles in the distance. It bent around a valley off to our right. The hillsides were steep, but the valley was only a half mile across.

I weighed the difference—ten miles versus a half mile. If I worked us slowly down the steep incline, lowering Ashley with the rope slowly before me, then anchoring on another tree, moving tree to tree, we could be across the valley before nightfall and cut ten miles out of our trip. Ten miles. With luck, we could make the lightbulb tomorrow or the next day.

I turned to Ashley. "You up for a little adventure?"

"What'd you have in mind?"

I explained. She eyed the distance, the valley, then the steep incline that dropped off a quarter mile to our right and then the valley below. "You think we can get down that?"

We had been down steeper when we left the crash site, but we had yet to traverse anything this steep that was this long. "If we take it slow."

She nodded. "I'm game if you are."

There was a little voice inside my head whispering, "Shorter is not always better."

I should've listened to it.

I CHECKED THE HARNESS ROPES. The sled was secure. I slipped off the snowshoes, tied them to the sled, and began easing down the incline. I needed my boots to cut down into the snow, giving me leverage to hold the sled back. I lowered Ashley over the ledge, and she slowly slid down, pulling the harness tight. Then I began picking my way downhill, using the trees as my anchors.

It actually worked quite well. I'd step down, dig a foot thigh-deep into the snow, anchoring myself, grab a tree or branch; we'd move forward, then I'd do it again. In ten minutes, we were halfway down. That meant in ten minutes I'd cut out nearly half a day's worth of walking.

Napoleon was sitting on Ashley's chest, staring at me. He didn't like it at all. If I could have asked his opinion, I have a feeling he'd have told me to walk the ten miles.

Two weeks of constant snow meant it had piled high. At times I was waist-deep with another ten feet below me. It didn't take much to set it loose.

I don't remember it letting go. I don't remember tumbling and rolling. I don't remember the harness snapping. And I don't remember coming to an abrupt stop where, even though my eyes were open, all the world went black.

The blood was rushing to my head, so I knew I was upside down, half turned, and the snow was pressing in on me, allowing only shallow breaths. The only part of me free of the snow was my right foot. I could move it freely.

I tried to clench my fists. Pulling in. Pushing out. Trying to make room. I tried moving my head back and forth, but it was no good. I wasn't getting much air, and I knew I didn't have long. I began pulling my arms in. Shoving. Jerking. I knew I needed to get out and find Ashley. I began kicking my right foot trying to clear away from snow. Above me, along my torso, I could see a faint light. Screaming was no use.

Five minutes later I'd worked myself into a frenzy, which produced absolutely no helpful result. I was stuck, and chances were good I was going to die upside down, frozen and suffocating in the snow. When they found me, I'd be a blue Popsicle.

We were so close. Why go through all we'd been through to end here? None of it made sense.

Something with really sharp teeth began biting my ankle. I heard snarling and began kicking at it, but it wouldn't let go. Finally I kicked it loose. Seconds later, I felt a hand on my foot. Then I felt snow being pulled away from my leg. Then more snow. I could move my whole leg. The second came free. Then the snow around my chest, and finally a passageway to my mouth.

Her hand shot in, pulled out the snow, and I sucked in the sweetest, largest breath of air I'd ever known. She worked out one arm, and with it, I righted myself, pulled myself out of that snowy grave and rolled onto my side. Napoleon, seeing me emerge, jumped onto my chest and began licking my face.

It was almost dark, causing me to question what dim light I'd seen moments before. Ashley lay to my right. She was off the sled, out of her bag, and lying on the snow. She was lying facedown, trying not to move. Her hands were cut and bloody. Her cheek was swollen. And then I saw her leg.

We didn't have long, and I knew I couldn't move her.

THE AVALANCHE HAD CARRIED us down to the base of the hillside. I'd been buried in the snowbank. The harness to the sled had evidently saved my life, because while the sled surfed the topside it kept me, albeit only for a few seconds, from being totally swallowed by the snow. When the ropes broke, Ashley shot off the top like a missile careening down the mountain and collided with a huge boulder laid there by the last ice age.

She'd worked her way back up to me, crawling. Her leg had rebroken, and this time the bone had pierced the skin. It was poking up underneath her pants. She was in shock, and any movement, absent drugs, would send her back into unconsciousness.

"I'm going to turn you."

She nodded.

I did, and she screamed louder than I'd ever heard a woman scream.

I crawled out across the snow and found the sled. Stripped clean. Her sleeping bag lay crumpled where she left it when she climbed out of it. One wool blanket lay twisted around the sled. Everything else was gone. No pack, no food, no tarp, no water bottles, no lighter fluid, no down jacket, no snowshoes, no fire drill, and no fire.

I unzipped her bag and laid her in it. Blood had soaked through her pants, spilled around her, and painted the snow. I pulled the sled up next to her, laid the wool blanket across the bottom, slid her on top of the sled, and wrapped the blanket over her. I wanted to cut away her pants and look at her leg, but she shook her head and managed a whisper.

"Don't."

She lay still, unmoving. Her bottom lip was shaking. I'd kill her trying to set the leg in place, and even then there was no guarantee. She'd lost blood, but not much. The bone had come out the top outside of her thigh, which was better than the inside. If it had gone the other way, through the femoral artery, she'd have been dead a long time ago. As would I.

Clouds had moved in, and the snow returned, hastening the return of the darkness.

I knelt, whispering, "I'm going for help."

She shook her head. "Don't leave me."

I tucked the bag around her. "You've been trying to get rid of me since we started this trip, so I'm finally doing what you asked."

She shook her head once more and said nothing. I leaned in, my breath on her face.

"I need you to listen to me."

Her eyes were still closed.

"Ashley?" She turned to me. The pain was rifling through her.

"I'm going for help."

She gripped my hand. Squeezed it tightly.

"I can't move you, so I'm leaving Napoleon here with you, and I'm going on for help, but I'm coming back."

She tightened her grip as another wave shot through her.

"Ashley . . . I'm coming back."

She whispered, "Promise?"

"Promise."

She closed her eyes and let go of my hand. I kissed her on the forehead, then the lips. They were warm and trembling, and both blood and tears had puddled there.

I tucked Napoleon in with her, stood and stared off down the road. Clouds were thick, and I could not see where it went.

CHAPTER FORTY-FIVE

I've spent my life running. One of the things I've learned is to look just a few feet ahead. Not more than four or five steps. It helps in long distance, because you're already in a lot of pain, and breaking it into small, doable pieces is about all you can handle. Others will tell you to keep your eyes up, focus on the finish line, but I've never been able to do that. I can only focus on what's in front of me. If I do that, the finish line will come to me.

So I put one foot in front of the other. The road wound down, snaking toward the valley in which we'd seen the orange light and single smokestack. I figured I had twenty-five to thirty miles to go, and if I was lucky I was averaging two miles an hour. All I had to do was run until the sun rose over my right shoulder.

I could do that. Couldn't I?

Yes.

Unless I came to the end of myself first.

That wouldn't be so bad.

What about Ashley?

What about Ashley.

I CLOSED MY EYES, and Ashley was all I could see.

IT WAS THREE, maybe four o'clock in the morning, day twenty-eight I think. I'd fallen a thousand times and pulled myself up a thousand and one. The snow had turned to sand. I could smell and taste salt. I heard a seagull somewhere. My dad was standing at the guard shack, a doughnut and coffee in his hand. A scowl on his face. I slapped the red lifeguard's chair, cussed him beneath my breath, turned, and kept running—picking up the pace. What if I beat him home? The beach stretched out before me, and every time I thought I was getting close to the house, it would fade, reset, and the beach would lengthen, and another event or moment would take its place. The past played before me like a movie.

I remember falling, pulling with my hands, standing and falling, again and again.

Many times I wanted to quit, lie down, and sleep. When I did, I'd close my eyes and Ashley was still there. Lying quietly in the snow, laughing over a leg of rabbit, chatting from the sled, yakking from the kitchen in the tub, embarrassed over a Nalgene bottle, shooting the flare gun, sipping coffee, pulling me out of the snow. . . .

Maybe it was those thoughts that got me up and helped me put one foot back in front of the other. Somewhere under the moon, on a flat section with a concrete bridge and a river trickling below me, I fell, eyes wide open. The picture changed. I saw her.

Rachel.

Standing alone in the road. Running shoes on. Sweat on her top lip. Trickling down her arms. Hands on her hips. She motioned me forward and whispered. I couldn't hear her at first, but she smiled and whispered again. Still nothing. I looked down, tried to move, but the snow had frozen around my feet and clung to me. I was stuck.

She ran, held out her hand, and whispered, "Run with me?"

Rachel before me. Ashley behind me. Torn between the two. Running both ways.

I reached, pulled, took a step, and fell again. Then again. And again. Soon I was running. Chasing Rachel. Her elbows were swinging, her toes were barely touching the ground, and I was back on the track with the girl I'd met in high school.

The road led up to a gate and a sign of some sort. I don't remember what it said. She ran with me, up the hill, toward the sunlight, and when it cleared the mountaintop, I fell. Face forward for the last time. My body would not go. I could run no more. I had done something I'd never done. Reached the end of myself.

She whispered. "Ben . . ."

I lifted my head, but she was gone. I heard her again. "Ben . . ."

"Rachel?"

I could not see her. "Get up, Ben."

In the distance, a few hundred yards away, a single column of smoke spiraled above the trees.

IT WAS A LOG CABIN. Several snowmobiles parked out front. Snowboards leaning against the porch railing. Lights inside. A fire's reflection off the wall. Deep voices. Some laughter. The smell of coffee. And maybe . . . Pop-Tarts. I crawled up the drive, climbed the steps, and pushed open the door. Given my experience in ERs, I'm practiced at squeezing as much information into as few words as possible while still conveying what's needed. But as the door pushed open, all I could muster was a cracking whisper.

"Help . . ."

Moments later, we were screaming across the snow. My driver was wiry, on the short side, and his snowmobile was not slow. With the engine wound, I glanced around him at the electronic speedometer. The first time it read 62. The second time it read 77.

With one hand I held on for dear life. With the other I pointed up the road. He followed my finger. The other two guys followed us. We made it to the valley, and I pointed again. Ashley's blue sleeping bag lay flat and highlighted against the snow on the far side. She was not moving. Napoleon barked at us and spun Tasmanian-devil circles in the snow. The kid cut the engine. In the distance I could hear the helicopter.

When I made it to her, Napoleon was licking her face and looking at me. He was whining. I knelt. "Ashley?"

She opened her eyes to look up at me.

THE KIDS POPPED a green handheld flare, and LifeFlight landed in the road. I briefed the medics, they got her breathing oxygen, injected her with painkillers, loaded her onto a stretcher, started an IV, and slid her into the single patient bay of the helicopter. I backed out, they began winding up the propeller, and she reached for me. I gave her my hand, and she slid something into it. The helicopter lifted, dipped its nose forward, and shot across the mountains, blinking red lights fading in its wake.

I opened my hand. The recorder. It was warm where she'd held it close to her. The tether had broken, the frayed ends spreading across my hand. I must have lost it in the avalanche. I stared at it, pushing the power button, but it would not play. The red warning light for low battery was flashing, keeping time with the one on the tail of the helicopter.

The kid I'd ridden with slapped me on the back. "Dude . . . mount up."

My knees nearly buckled. I grabbed Napoleon, and we climbed on. Coming into town, the posted speed limit was 55. Tucked behind him, I peered around the kid's shoulders. The speedometer read 82, and he was laughing.

CHAPTER FORTY-SIX

It was a single room. She lay beneath a sheet of white, sleeping beneath a fog of sedation. Her vitals were good. Strong. Blue lights and numbers flickered above her. I turned the blinds, keeping daylight at bay. I sat, her hand resting in mine. Her color had returned.

LifeFlight had bypassed Evanston and rerouted her directly to Salt Lake, where in two hours the ER docs put in a few bars and pins. When I arrived at Evanston atop a snowmobile, they were waiting on me. I was loaded into an ambulance and, with a police escort, sped to Salt Lake. They started me on an IV and began asking me a bunch of questions. The answers surprised them. By the time we arrived in Salt Lake, camera crews were everywhere.

They put me in a room, and I asked for the chief of surgery. His name was Bart Hampton, and we'd met on more than one occasion at conferences around the country. He had been briefed on our situation, and when he learned it was me, he, along with the nurse feeding my IV, led me to a viewing room above the OR where we observed the last hour of Ashley's surgery. The intercom allowed the doctors to talk me through what they were seeing. What they were doing. She was in good hands. There was no need to interfere. My body was trashed, and my hands were little more than raw meat. I was in no condition to be a doctor.

They rolled her into her room and quickly left. I walked in, flipped the switch on the light, and viewed her X-rays pre- and post-op. I could have done no better. She'd make a full recovery. Tough as she was, probably better.

I turned. Blue light above her lit her forehead, showered the sheets. I pushed her hair back and gently placed my lips to her cheek. She was clean, smelled like soap, and her skin was soft. I slid my hand beneath hers. Blister to tenderness. I whispered in her ear, "Ashley . . . we did it."

Somewhere in there my adrenaline ran out. I was falling when Bart caught me. He laughed. "Come on, Steve. Time to get you to bed."

All I wanted to do was sleep. Something about his comment didn't register. "What'd you call me?"

"Steve. As in Steve Austin."

"Who's he?"

"The Six Million Dollar Man."

THE NEXT THING I knew it was daylight, and I was in a bed with white sheets, in a room filled with the aroma of fresh coffee, where the sounds of people talking echoed down the hall. Bart was standing over me, holding a Styrofoam cup. The perspective was odd. I was used to standing in his shoes. Not lying in mine. "That for me?"

He laughed.

It was good coffee.

We talked awhile. I gave him more of the details. He listened mostly, shaking his head. When I finished, he said, "What can I do for you?"

"My dog. Actually, he's not mine, but I've fallen in love with the little guy, and . . ."

"He's in my office. Sleeping. Fed him some steak. Happy as can be."

"I need a rental car. And I need for you to protect us from the media until she's ready to talk to them."

"She?"

"Yeah. I'm not."

"I suppose you have your reasons."

"I do."

"You know, when the details of this get out, they're going to want you two on every talk show in the country. You could be an inspiration to a lot of people."

"Anybody would have done what I did."

"Ben, you've been doctoring long enough to know that very few people on the planet could have done what you did. For more than a month you hauled that woman, in subfreezing temperatures, nearly seventy-five miles."

I stared out the window, at the whitecapped mountains in the distance. It was strange, looking at them from the other side. A month ago I had stood in the Salt Lake City Airport and wondered what was on the other side. Now I knew. I imagine prison bars are the same way. Maybe a grave.

"I just put one foot in front of the other."

"I called your people at Baptist in Jacksonville. They were elated, to say the least. Glad to know you're alive. They'd been wondering what happened to you. Said it was unlike you to just 'fall of the face of the earth.' "

"I appreciate it."

"What else? Seems like I ought to be able to do more to help you."

I raised one eyebrow. "In my hospital, we know our best nurses. They tend to stand out. If you could . . ."

He nodded. "Already took care of it. She's got them now and will have them around the clock."

I turned my empty cup. "Anybody around here make a latte? Maybe a cappuccino."

"All you want."

His answer rattled around inside my head. We were now back in a world where as much coffee as we wanted was available upon request.

The disconnect was almost audible.

LATE MORNING, SHE STIRRED. I walked down the hall, bought what I needed, and came back. When she cracked open an eye, I leaned in, whispered, "Hey."

She turned, slowly opening her eyes.

"I talked with Vince. He's on his way. Be here in a few hours."

Her nose twitched. One eyebrow lifted slightly. "Do I smell coffee?"

I pulled off the lid and held it beneath her nose.

"Can you just drip it into my IV?"

I held the cup to her lips. She sipped.

"Second best cup of coffee I've ever had." She laid her head back, tasting the beans.

I sat on the rolling stainless steel stool and scooted up next to her bed. "Your surgery went well. I consulted with your doctor. We've actually met before, sat on a panel together at a conference. Knows his stuff. I'll show you the X-rays when you want to see them."

Out the window, a jetliner was taking off from the airport in the distance. We watched it gain altitude, turn, and bank across our mountains.

She shook her head. "I'm never flying again."

I laughed. "They'll have you up and walking in about three hours. Good as new."

"Are you lying to me?"

"I don't lie about people's medical conditions."

She smiled. "It's about time you gave me some good news. I mean, how long have we been hanging out, and all you've had for me is one bad bit of news after another."

"Very true."

She stared at the ceiling, shuffling her legs beneath the sheets. "I really want to take a bath and shave my legs."

I rolled to the door and motioned for the nurse. She followed me in.

"This kind lady's name is Jennifer. I've explained to her where you've been the last month. She'll help you into the shower. Get you what you need. When you get cleaned up, there's another lady waiting outside your door. Something I promised you."

She stared at me out of the corner of her eyes. "What are you scheming?"

"I made you a promise awhile back. I intend to keep it." I patted her foot. "I'll check on you later. Vince lands in two hours."

She pushed back the sheet, reached for me. She held my hand. How do you explain to other people what we'd been through? How do you articulate that? We'd just walked through hell, a hell that had frozen over, and survived. Together. I didn't have the words. Neither did she.

I patted her hand. "I know. It takes some getting used to. I'll be back."

She squeezed tighter. "You okay?"

I nodded and walked out. An attractive Asian lady sat in a chair, waiting patiently. A bag on her lap.

"She's showering. Be ready in a bit. I don't know what color she likes, but you can ask her." I handed her a hundred-dollar bill. "This okay?"

She shook her head and started digging in her bag. "Too much."

I waved her off. "Keep it. Just take your time. That lady in there has had a rough go."

She nodded, and I walked downstairs to the Grille.

THE GRILLE WAS TYPICAL HOSPITAL SHORT-ORDER, but it'd have to do. I stepped to the counter. "I'd like a loaded double cheeseburger with a double order of fries. All the way."

"Anything else?"

"Can you please have someone deliver it to room 316 in an hour."

She nodded, I paid, and then I walked to my rental car and typed the address into the dash-mounted GPS.

CHAPTER FORTY-SEVEN

It was a simple house. Not too far from town. White with green shutters. White fence. Sitting up on a hill. Flowers all around. No weeds. The mailbox was marked by one of those flags they use at airports. The hollow kind that indicate wind direction.

She was sitting on the porch. Rocking. Snapping beans. A tall, handsome woman. I stepped out of the rental car. Napoleon jumped onto the ground, sniffed the curb, then tore up the sidewalk, flew up the stairs, and jumped into her lap, spilling beans across the porch. She laughed, hugged him while he licked her face, and said, "Tank, where on earth have you been?"

Tank . . . so that's his name.

I climbed the steps. "Ma'am . . . my name's Ben Payne. I'm a doctor from Jacksonville. I was . . . with your husband when his plane crashed. . . ."

She shook her head. Her eyes narrowed. "He didn't crash that plane. He was too good a pilot."

"Yes, ma'am. He had a heart attack. Landed the plane up in the mountains. Saved our lives." I opened a box and set it next to her. In it were his watch, his wallet, his pipe . . . and the lighter she'd given him.

She touched each item. The lighter last. She held it in her lap. Her lip trembled, and tears dripped off her face.

We talked for several hours. I told her everything I could remember, even where I'd buried him and what the view was like. She liked that. Said he would have too.

She opened their album, or albums, and told me their story. It was filled with tenderness. Hearing it hurt.

Several hours later, I stood to leave. What else could I say? I fumbled with the car keys. "Ma'am . . . I want to . . ."

She shook her head. Tank perched on her lap. She inched forward on the rocker, Tank hopped off, and she stood slowly. A bad left hip. She stood at an angle, then straightened. She gave me her hand.

I eyed her leg. "If and when you need a hip replacement, call me. I'll come out here and do it for nothing."

She smiled.

I knelt. "Tank, you're the best. I'll miss you."

He slobbered my face, then ran down into his yard and began peeing on every tree he could find.

"I know, you'll miss me too."

I gave her my card for if and when she ever needed me. I was unsure how to leave. Do I hug her, shake her hand? I mean, what's protocol for saying good-bye to the wife of the pilot who died saving your life? Not to mention that if I hadn't hired him to charter me to Denver, he'd have been home with her when he died, and I imagine she'd thought of that, too.

"Young man?"

"Yes, ma'am."

"Thank you."

I scratched my head. "Ma'am . . . I'm . . ."

She shook her head. "I'm not."

"You're not?"

Her eyes shone a clear, bright blue. "Grover didn't just fly anybody in that plane. He was picky. Purposeful. Turned away more clients than he accepted. If he took you flying . . . he had a reason. It was his gift to you."

"Yes, ma'am."

She leaned on me, hugged me, and squeezed my arms with her hands. Her skin was thin, hung off her, and her hair was a fine snowy white. She shook as she hugged me.

I kissed her on the cheek, soft with fuzz, and drove away. I glanced in the rearview mirror. She was standing on the porch, staring out across the mountain. Napoleon stood on the top step, chest out, barking at the wind.

CHAPTER FORTY-EIGHT

Vince was sitting with her when I walked into the room. He stood. A warm smile, warm handshake. Even a stiff hug. "Ashley is telling me what you did." He shook his head. "I can't thank you enough."

"Remember"—I patted her foot—"I'm the one who invited her onto the plane. You might ought to consider pressing charges."

He laughed. I liked him. She'd chosen well. They'd be happy. He'd marry above himself. As would any man who married Ashley. She was one in a million.

Color had returned to her face. Three empty coffee cups sat on the bedside table. The bladder bag hanging off the side of her bed was nearly full. And the color was good. Her new cell phone was ringing off the hook. Media crews had called. Everybody wanted the exclusive.

She asked, "What are you going to tell them?"

"Nothing. I'm ducking out the back door, going home." I looked at the clock on the wall. "Leave in ninety minutes. Just came to say good-bye."

Her expression changed.

"Don't worry, you two have plenty to talk about. A wedding to plan. I'm sure we'll be in touch." I walked to the opposite side of the bed.

She crossed her arms. "You called your wife yet?"

"No . . ." I shook my head. "I'm going to go see her soon as I get home."

She nodded. "I hope it works out, Ben."

I nodded.

She squeezed my hand. I kissed her forehead and turned to go. She held on and smiled. "Ben?"

I spoke without turning. "Yes?"

Vince patted her on the shoulder. "Be right back. I'm going to get some coffee." He put his hand on my shoulder. "Thank you. For everything."

He walked out. She was still holding on to my hand. I sat on the edge of the bed. Something was tugging at my insides. It most closely resembled an ache. I tried to smile.

"Can I ask you something?" she said.

"You've earned the right to ask me anything."

"Would you ever hit on a married or almost married woman?"

"I've only hit on one woman in my life."

She smiled. "Just checking. Can I ask you something else?"

"Yes."

"Why'd you ask me to get on the plane with you?"

I stared out the window. Thinking back. "Seems like a long time ago, doesn't it?"

"It does. Then . . . sometimes it feels like yesterday."

"Our wedding was one of the happier days either of us ever knew. On our own. It was a launching out. A beginning. We were free to love each other without interference. I think when two people really love each other . . . I mean . . ." My voice cracked. ". . . Way down deep . . . like where their souls sleep and dreams happen, where pain can't live 'cause there's nothing for it to feed on . . . then a wedding is a bleeding together of those two souls. Like two rivers running together. All that water becoming the same water. Mine did that.

"When I met you, I saw in your face the hope that yours might be that too. I guess meeting you was a reminder that I knew a precious, tender love at one time. And I think . . . if I'm honest, I wanted to brush up alongside that. To touch it. Come face-to-face with it. In doing so I thought maybe I could remember . . . because . . . I don't want to forget."

She reached up and thumbed the tear off my face.

"I think that's why I invited you on the plane. And for that . . . that selfishness . . . I'm both eternally sorry . . . and eternally grateful. Those twenty-eight days in the mountains with you reminded me that love is worth doing. No matter how much it hurts." I stood, kissed her on the lips, and walked out.

CHAPTER FORTY-NINE

The plane landed in Jacksonville just after two p.m. Media crews were waiting. My picture had circulated. So had the story. Problem was, they were looking for a guy thirty pounds heavier.

I had no bags, so I skirted the frenzy and walked to my car, which after more than a month and a half was still sitting there, covered in yellow pollen.

The lady at the ticket booth told me, with little or no facial expression, "Three hundred and eighty-seven dollars."

I had a feeling that arguing with her would have little effect. I handed her my American Express, grateful for the chance to pay my bill and go home.

The change in my environment was strange. Most striking were the things I was not doing: not pulling a sled, not staring out across snow, not starting a fire with a bow drill, not skinning a rabbit or moose, not dependent upon shooting an arrow to eat, not wiggling my toes or blowing on my fingers to keep them warm, not listening for the sound of Ashley's voice . . . not hearing the sound of Ashley's voice.

I drove south down I-95. Funny, I found myself driving slowly. Everybody was passing me. I crossed the Fuller Warren Bridge and passed the hospital where I live most of my life. My partners had all called, ecstatic to hear my voice. I'd check in with them in the days ahead. There was plenty of time to tell the story.

I turned south down Hendricks Avenue, drove through San Marco, then merged onto San Jose Boulevard and stopped at Trad's, a garden store and flower shop. I walked into the greenhouse and was greeted by two things. The first was the smell of manure. The second was Tatyana, an attractive Russian lady in her fifties, with filthy hands and beautiful cheek lines. She shouted at me across the tops of the plumeria.

There are a dozen flower shops in town, but Tatyana's accent is one in a million. Reminds me of everything James Bond and *Rocky IV*. Her voice is deep, guttural, scarred by either years of torture or years of alcohol or both. All the Ws are turned into Vs, all the Es are long, and she double-trills all her Rs. *Vodka* sounds like *wodka*. I don't even like the stuff, but when the word rolls off her lips, I'm ready for a Grey Goose or Absolut something.

She was probably a spy in her former life. Might still be.

She pushed her denim forearm across her sweaty forehead. "And just vere have you been?" The word *beeeeeen* echoed off the glass.

The truth would take too long. "Vacation."

Whenever she walked, it looked like she was marching. Brisk, stiff, and in a hurry. She fast-footed it around the corner, holding a purple orchid with a white stripe down the middle. The purple was deep, almost black in the middle, and the stem must have been four feet tall and had thirty blooms with thirty more on the way.

"I have joos the thing. Been saving it for you. Three people tried to buy it joos today, but I say, 'No, you can not have.' My boss, he think me crazy, threaten to fire me, but I say it is yours. You vill be back. And you vill vant this."

Rachel would love it. "It's remarkable. Thank you. I'll give it to her today. In just a few minutes."

She walked me to the cash register, looked both ways for the owner, then waved her finger in the air like a windshield wiper and said, "We have sale last veek. No sale zis veek. But, for you, sale goes on zis veek."

"Thank you, Tatyana." I held up the orchid. "And thank you for this."

Traffic was thick, stopping me at every light. Waiting for green, I looked right. Beyond the dry cleaners sat Watson Martial Arts. The front wall was mostly glass. Inside, a class of white-uniformed people with various colored belts were kicking and punching. I'd driven by it hundreds of times, yet never noticed it.

Until now.

The light turned green, and I accelerated. I drove south on I-95, east on J. Turner Butler Boulevard, then south on A1A. I stopped at the liquor store and bought a bottle of wine. I drove past Mickler's Landing, past my condo at South Ponte Vedra, then to Rachel's house. I'd fenced the property with a tall, wrought iron fence. I grabbed the orchid out of the passenger seat, walked beneath the towering live oak and up the stone steps, dug in the rocks for the hide-a-key, and unlocked the door. I had planted Confederate jasmine on both sides of the doorframe. It had grown up and filled in above the door. A few thicker vines hung down. I lifted the vines, pulled on the squeaking door, and stepped inside. To help it stay cool in the summer, I put in a marble floor. My steps echoed.

I talked to Rachel through the night. I poured the wine, pressed PLAY on the recorder, and stared out through the glass, listening to the sound of my voice and watching the waves crawl up and down the beach. I think parts were hard for her to hear, but she heard every word.

I gave her the orchid, placing it on a shelf along the glass where it would draw the morning sun. It'd be happy there. Once the blooms fell, I'd put it up in the solarium with the two hundred and fifty others.

It was four in the morning when my last recording finished. I was tired and had drifted off. The silence woke me. Funny how that works. I was rising to leave when I noticed the recorder. The faceplate was flashing blue. One file remained unplayed.

The recorder was electronic. I always recorded in the same file. I might have fifty recordings, but all under the same file number. For the first time, I noticed a third file number. One I'd not created. I pushed PLAY.

A faint whisper appeared. There was a lot of wind in the background. A dog whining. I turned up the volume.

Rachel, it's Ashley. We were caught in an avalanche. Ben went for help. He's running now. I don't know if I'll make it. I'm really cold.

There was a silence.

I wanted to tell you, actually I wanted to thank you. I know I'm a little chatty, but I've got to talk or I'll go to sleep. If I do, I'm not sure I can wake up again. . . . I write for several different magazines. Talk a lot about love. Relationships. Which is ironic, because I've had my share of bad ones. Hence, I'm a bit of a skeptic. I'm headed home to marry a man who is well off, good-looking, gives me nice things . . . but after twenty-eight days with your husband in this cold, white-capped world, I'm left wondering if that's enough. I'm left wondering . . . what about love? Is it possible? Can I have it? I once thought all the good ones were gone. The guys, that is. Now, I wonder. Are there other Bens out there . . . ? I've been hurt, I imagine we all have, and I think somewhere in that pain we convince ourselves that if we don't open up and love again, we don't have to hurt again. Take the Mercedes and the two-carat ring, the house in Buckhead, and call it a day, just give him what he wants when he wants it and everybody's happy. Right? I have thought that a long time.

But . . . this place out here is quiet. The silence has a ring to it. Even the snow makes a sound if you listen close enough. Somewhere a few days back, maybe when I first met him on the plane, I was attracted to this man I now know as Ben Payne. Sure, he's good-looking, but what attracted me was something else. Something . . . I wanted to touch, or be touched by, something tender and warm and whole. I don't know what to call it, but I know it when I hear it . . . and I hear it when he speaks to you in this recorder. I've listened many nights when he thought I was sleeping, but I stayed up just to hear his tone of voice and how he talked to and with you.

I've never had anyone talk to me like that. My fiancé doesn't. Sure he's kind, but in Ben, there's this palpable thing that is rich and I just want to sink my hands into it, bathe, and paint myself in it. I know I'm talking about your husband, so you need to know that in all the time we've been here, he has acted like a gentleman. Truly. At first my feelings were hurt, but then I saw that it had to do with this thing I'm talking about, with you . . . and it's deep-wired into his DNA . . . like you'd have to kill him to get it out. I've never seen anything like it. It's the truest thing I've ever sensed. Movies don't depict it, books don't narrate it, columns can't poke fun at it. I have lain awake at night, listening to him talk to you, share his heart, apologize for what I don't know and found myself aching and crying and wanting a man to hold me in his heart the way Ben holds you.

I know I'm not telling you anything you don't already know, but he says you two are separated . . . I guess I'm just wanting to go on the record for him to say that he can't love you any more than he already does. I didn't even think a love like this existed, but now I've heard it, seen it, felt it, slept alongside it, and if you won't have him, then what does he do with a love like this?

I've written a thousand columns where I've laughed at love, dared anyone to show me a love like Ben's existed, because, in truth, that's why I write. To build a wall around me, protect me from the hurts I've suffered, and dare anyone to show me a true love that's worth dying for. More than that, one that's worth living for.

He won't tell me the details. Plays his cards close to his chest, but he said you two argued. Said he said some things. I've thought a lot about that. What? What terrible words were spoken? What could he possibly have said that caused this? What thing? What act did he commit? What did he do to lose your love? If a love like Ben's can be had, if it's real, if a heart like Ben's exists and can be offered to another, then . . . I'm left wondering. What can't be forgiven? . . . What can't be forgiven?

Live or die . . . I want a love like this.

The recording ended and I rose, ready to leave, but Rachel beckoned me to stay. She had never wanted me to leave in the first place. I told her that many times I'd wanted to come back, return to her, but forgiving myself had turned out to be easier said than done.

Maybe there was something different in me. Maybe something different in her. I'm not really sure, but for the first time since our argument, I lay down, my tears dripping onto her face, and slept with my wife.

CHAPTER FIFTY

I tightened my cummerbund, straightened my bow tie, buttoned my jacket, then unbuttoned it and walked around the back of the country club. One of Atlanta's finest and most private. Lots of stone and grand timbers. I showed the guard my invitation, he opened the gate, and I walked up the winding walk. Designer lights lit the trees, giving the place a domed feel. A throng of people stood inside. Sparkly women. Powerful men. Much laughter. Drinks. The rehearsal dinner party. The night before the wedding. A happy occasion.

It had been three months. I had returned to work, put on a few pounds, told bits and pieces of the story, and deflected the attention. I had not contacted Ashley since I left the hospital. Figured it best. But it seemed strange to be so close for a month, so dependent upon one another, and then, in a second's time, end that. Cut that tie. It seemed unnatural.

I fell back into a routine, still working my way through the separation. Up before the sun, a long run on the beach, breakfast with Rachel and the kids, punch the clock at work, sometimes dinner with Rachel and the kids, then home, maybe another run or filter through the sand looking for sharks' teeth.

Putting one foot in front of the other.

ASHLEY STOOD ON THE FAR SIDE. The invitation had included a handwritten note along with a gift. The note read *Please come. We'd love to see you. Both of you.*

She went on to say that her leg had mended well and she'd been jogging. Even working out at the tae kwon do dojo and teaching youth classes, though she was only kicking at about 75 percent.

The gift enclosed was a new watch. A climbing watch made by Suunto. Called the Core. Her letter continued.

The guys at the store told me this is what all the climbers wear. Gives you temperature, barometric pressure, elevation. Even has a compass. You've earned it. Deserve it more than any.

I found myself staring at the letter. The *we* bothered me.

I stood staring from a distance. Her posture said her confidence had returned and that the pain was gone. She was beautiful. And for the first time in a long time, I felt okay thinking that.

Vince stood alongside. Seemed happy. He looked like a stand-up guy. In the wilderness, I'd conjured my own idea of what he looked like, how he held himself. I was off by a good bit. She'd make it. He got a good one in her. Were it not for her, Vince and I could have been friends.

I stood in the shadows, just outside, staring in the windows. I glanced at my new watch. I was late. Nervous, I turned the plastic package in my hands. I'd bought two new recorders. One for her. One for me. The latest technology, these contained a digital card with twice as much memory and battery life. At one time, that was appealing. Now, not so much. I removed them from the plastic packaging, inserted the batteries into one, and clicked it on.

Hey . . . it's me. Ben. I received your invitation. Thanks for thinking about me. Including me. Uh . . . us. I know you've been busy. . . . It's good to see you on your feet. Looks like the leg healed well. I'm glad. There are a lot of people here. All here to celebrate with you.

Just so you know, I kept my promise. I went to see Rachel. Took her an orchid, number 258, and a bottle of wine. I told her about the trip. Talked long into the night. I played her the tape. The whole thing. I slept with her. It'd been a long time.

It was also the last time.

I had to let her go. She's not coming back. The distance is too great. The mountain between us is the one mountain I cannot climb.

I thought you should know.

I've been spending a lot of time lately trying to figure out how to start over. The single life is different than I thought. Been taking a few notes off this website called "Flying Solo." Ironic, don't you think?

But it's tough. Rachel was my first love. My only love. I've never dated anyone else. Never been with anyone else.

I never told you this because it just felt wrong, but . . . even at your worst, no makeup, broken leg, sitting over a Nalgene bottle, stitches lining your face . . . well . . . being lost with you is better than being found and alone.

I wanted to thank you for that.

If Vince doesn't tell you that, doesn't put you on a pedestal, he should. If he forgets, call me and I'll remind him. I'm an expert on what a husband should have said.

After Rachel . . . I didn't know what to do, how to live, so I gathered all the broken pieces of me, shoved them into a bag, and hefted it over my shoulder like a bag of rocks. Years passed, dragging myself around in a bag behind me, buckled into my harness and leaning into the weight of the sled, the history of me slicing into my shoulders.

Then I went to this conference, found myself in Salt Lake, and for reasons I don't understand, you sat down. I heard the sound of your voice, and something emptied the bag, scattering the pieces of me. And there, laid bare and broken, I wondered, even hoped, that there might be an ending to the story of my life that I had not told. One not etched in pain, recorded in regret . . . echoing through eternity.

But here, hidden in the trees, I am torn. The pieces of me no longer fit together. I am reminded of all the king's horses and all the king's men. I cannot put me back together.

. . . Funny, I have loved two women in my life, and now I can't have either. Wonder what that says about me? I wanted to give you a gift, but what could I give you that would equal what you have given me?

Ashley . . . for that alone . . . I wish you . . . every happiness.

I STARED AROUND the dogwood tree and through the glass. She was laughing. A single diamond hanging around her neck. A wedding gift from Vince. She looked good in diamonds. She looked good in anything.

I left the recorder running, recording, emptied my pockets of my last two spare batteries, wrapped a rubber band around them, put all that in the box, closed the lid, tied the bow, left no card, slipped through the back doors, and slid it beneath the mound of a hundred other gifts. In thirty-six hours they'd be on a plane for two weeks in Italy. She'd find my gift upon their return.

I walked out through the unlit garden, started my car, and pointed the wheel south down I-75. The night was warm, and I drove home with the windows down. Sweating. Which was okay with me.

When I got home, I changed clothes, grabbed the second of my new recorders, and walked out onto the beach, stopping at the ocean's edge. I stood there a long time. Linus and his blanket. While the waves and foam washed over my feet, I turned the thing in my hands and wrestled with what to say, where to begin.

With the sun breaking the horizon, I clicked RECORD, took three steps, and threw the recorder as far as I could. It spun through the air and disappeared into the daylight and the foam of a receding wave and an outgoing tide.

CHAPTER FIFTY-ONE

I woke to the sound of cats on my porch. They had returned in force. Bringing friends. A beautiful black cat with white feet. I named him Socks. The second was playful, always purring in my face. Long tail, long whiskers, quick ears. Kept brushing along my leg and hopping into my lap. I named her Ashley.

I took the day off. Spent it at home. Leaning on the railing, cupping a warm mug, staring out over the ocean, listening to the waves, talking to the cats. Listening for the sound of laughter. Ashley was never far away. Neither the cat nor the memory. I thought back through the wilderness and drifted off to sleep sometime after dark. I dreamed of her sitting in a gondola with Vince somewhere beneath an afternoon sun in Venice. She was tucked up alongside him, his arm around her. They were tan, and she looked happy.

I didn't like the picture.

I crawled off the couch a few hours before daylight. The moon was full and hung low on the horizon, glittering on the crest of each wave, quietly casting my shadow across the beach. I laced up my shoes beneath a warm breeze. Pelicans in V-formation flew silently overhead, riding the updrafts, dragging their shadows across mine.

I turned into the wind, taking me south. Low tide, I had the beach to myself. I ran an hour, then two, weaving along the ridgeline edge of the water. A single path of turtle tracks led from the water to the dunes. She was laying her eggs.

When St. Augustine came into view, I turned around, slid my Oakleys down over my eyes, and turned for home. The sun was coming up, and the wind pressed against my back. Absent were the cold, the penetrating snow, the sight of white, the feel of snow, the taste of hunger, the weight of the sled, and, maybe most noticeable, the sound of Ashley's voice.

Halfway back, I intersected the mother turtle. Exhausted from her night's work. She was big, old, cutting deep grooves in her push to the water. The first wave reached her, she submerged, rinsed herself, then floated and began skimming the surface of the water. Her shell glistened. After a few minutes, she was gone. Loggerheads can live to be nearly two hundred years old. I let myself think she was the same one.

I watched her disappear, witnessing both sunset and sunrise.

Strange. I had not expected that.

I passed the entrance to Guana River State Park, and the condo came into view. I slowed, jogged, and finally walked. My ribs had healed. I could breathe deeply. I was healthy again. The July sun had climbed, harsh and bright. The water was blue, rolling glass. A few bottlenose dolphins were trolling near shore, but there was no sign of the mother loggerhead. But there would be. In the weeks ahead, the beach would be crawling with sign.

I DID NOT HEAR THE FOOTSTEPS. Only felt the hand on my shoulder. I recognized the veins, the freckles where she did not wear a watch.

I turned, and Ashley stood facing me. A windbreaker, running shorts, Nikes. Her eyes were red, wet. She looked as though she hadn't slept. She shook her head, pointed behind her, toward Atlanta.

"I was hopeful you would show. But when you didn't, I . . . I couldn't sleep, so I started picking through our presents, opening the ones that looked interesting. Anything to take my mind off . . . today." She held my hands in hers, then pounded me softly in the chest with her fist. Her left hand was naked. No ring. "My doctor says I should start running again."

"Be a good idea."

"I don't like running alone."

"Me either."

She picked at the sand with the toe of her shoe. She folded her arms, squinted against the rising sun, and said, "I'd like to meet Rachel. Will you introduce me?"

I nodded.

"Now?"

We turned and walked down the beach. Two miles. The house I'd built her sat up on the dunes, framed in scrub oaks and wire grass.

Since I'd returned, I'd marked ten turtle nests along the dunes with pink surveyor's tape.

Ashley eyed it. "Turtle nests?"

I nodded.

We wound up through the dune and up the walkway. The sand was soft. A lot like snow. I pulled the key from around my neck, unlocked the door, lifted the Confederate jasmine vine I had yet to trim, and opened the door.

To combat the summer heat, the entire house, walls, floor, sides, everything was lined with or made of marble. The solarium above thrived in summer. Many of the orchids were in bloom.

I led Ashley through the door.

Rachel lay on my left. Michael and Hannah on my right.

Ashley put her hands to her mouth.

I waved my hand. "Ashley, meet Rachel. Rachel, meet Ashley."

Ashley knelt, brushing the marble with her fingertips. She ran her fingers through the grooves of Rachel's name and the dates. On top of the marble lid, about where Rachel's hands would be folded atop her chest, sat seven digital recorders. All covered in dust. All but one. The one I'd carried in the mountains. Ashley touched it, turned it in her hand, and then returned it to its place among the others. On top, about where Rachel's face would be, lay my jacket, rolled up like a pillow.

I sat down, my back against Rachel, my feet resting against the twins. I stared up through the blooms and the glass above.

"Rachel was pregnant . . . with the twins. She had what's called a partial abruption. It's when the placenta begins tearing away from the uterine wall. We put her on bed rest for a month, hoping we could stop it, but due to no fault of her own, it worsened. She was a walking time bomb.

"I tried to reason with her, telling her that when it ruptured completely, it would kill the twins and her. Her doctor and I wanted to take the twins. She stared at us like we'd lost our minds and said, 'Where are you taking them?'

"I wanted Rachel, and if it meant the kids had to go to keep her, then the kids had to go. Send them to God. She and I, we could make more. I wanted us to grow old, laugh at our wrinkles. She wanted that too, but the problem was that there was a chance . . . a very slim chance . . . that, if we did nothing, the kids would make it. That they'd all be fine.

"She might have had better chances at a roulette table, but because it existed, she took a chance on the twins. I said, 'Give them to God. Let him sort it out.' She just shook her head. 'This is the chance we took.' I got angry, questioned her love, screamed, yelled, even threw stuff around the house, but she'd made up her mind. One of the very things I loved the most about her was now the very thing I was fighting.

"I shouted, 'How could God mind? How could he ever blame you? Surely he would understand.' She wouldn't hear it. She just patted her stomach and said, 'Ben, I love you, but I'm not living the rest of my life looking at Michael and Hannah on the back of my eyelids. Knowing they might have made it. Knowing there was a chance, and I didn't take it.'

"So I tied on my shoes, ran out the door. A midnight run on the beach to clear my head. When my cell phone rang, I . . . sent it to voice mail. I can't tell you the number of times I . . ."

I shifted, running my fingertips along the lettering of Michael's name. Then Hannah's.

"As best I can piece together, moments after I left, she ruptured. She managed to dial 911, but they were too late. Not that they could have done anything. Two hours later, I returned. Flashing lights. Police in my kitchen, talking into radios. The phone ringing. A call from the hospital. Strange people stood in my kitchen. . . . They drove me to the morgue. Asked me to identify her. In trying to save Rachel, they had performed an emergency C-section, delivering the kids. They had laid them out next to her. Kind of tucked them up alongside her. The voice mail you heard on the plane is the one she left me, just before everything went bad. I've saved it and resaved it so I could send it to myself. Most every day. To remind me that despite myself, she loved me."

I looked at Ashley. Tears were streaming down her face.

"You asked once, 'What can't be forgiven?' " I nodded. "It's words. Words you can't take back because the person you spoke them to took them to her grave four and a half years ago."

I looked around, waving my hand across the marble sarcophagus. "A simple tombstone didn't seem right, so I built them this. Laid them side by side. I put the solarium up there so she can see the orchids. And at night the stars. Knew she'd like that. I even had the tree limbs trimmed to let the light through. Sometimes you can see the Big Dipper. Sometimes the moon.

"Many nights I have come here, leaning against her, my fingertips resting on the twins, tracing their names and . . . listened to myself tell her our story." I shook my head and pointed at the recorders. "I've told it many times . . . but the end is always the same."

Ashley's lip was trembling. She held my hand between both of hers. Her tears had dripped onto the marble. Alongside ten thousand of mine. "You should've told me. Why didn't you tell me?"

"So many times I wanted to stop dragging that sled, turn around, and spill it, tell you everything, but . . . you have so much in front of you. So much to look forward to."

"You should have. You owe me that."

"I do now. I didn't then."

She placed her hand flat across my chest, then wrapped her arms around my neck and buried her face alongside mine. She placed both palms on my face and shook her head. "Ben?"

No answer.

"Ben?"

I opened my mouth, my eyes on Rachel, and pushed out the words. A whisper. "I'm . . . so sorry."

She smiled, shook her head. "She forgave you . . . the moment you said it."

Forgiveness is a tough thing. Both in the offering . . . and the accepting.

WE SAT THERE a long time. Through the glass above I watched a formation of pelicans fly over. And one osprey. Out beyond the breakers, bottlenose dolphins were feeding south, rolling in groups of six and eight.

Ashley tried to speak. Tried again and still could not find the words. Finally she wiped her eyes, pressed her ear to my chest, and whispered, "Give me all the pieces."

"There are a lot of them, and I'm not sure they'll ever go back together again."

She kissed me. "Let me try."

"You would be better off to leave me and . . ."

She half smiled. "I'm not leaving you. Not going it alone." She shook her head. "Not looking at the memory of you every time I close my eyes."

Something deep inside me needed to hear that. Needed to know I was worth that. That despite myself, love might snatch me back. Lift me from the fire. We sat for several hours, staring out across the ocean.

Finally I stood and kissed the stone above Rachel's face. The twins too. There were no tears this time. It wasn't goodbye. Only a pause. Just waving my hand through the mist—the smoke as it disappeared.

We walked out, locked the door, and wound through the dunes. I held her naked left hand in mine. She stopped me, a wrinkle between her eyes. She wiped her nose on her sleeve. "I gave Vince back his ring. Told him that I liked him very much, but . . ." She shook her head. "I think he was relieved to know the truth."

We stood atop the last dune, staring out over the beach. South, to our right, one of the nests had hatched. Hundreds of tiny tracks led to the water. The waves and foam were filling them. Erasing them. Far out, beyond the breakers and waves, shiny black circles of onyx floated atop the water's surface. Glittering black diamonds.

I placed her hand flat across mine. "Start slow. It's been a long time since I've run . . . with anyone. Not sure how my legs will respond."

She kissed me. Her lips were warm, wet, and trembling.

I pointed. "Which way?"

She shook her head, smiling. The sun lighting her eyes. "Don't care. You're a real runner and I'm not, so I don't know if I can keep up with you. How fast? How far?"

"LSD."

"What?"

"Long-slow-distance. Where miles don't matter. Only time. And in reverse. The slower the better."

She wrapped her arms around me, pressed her chest to mine, and laughed. "Okay, but we better route through Atlanta."

"Atlanta?"

She nodded, a sly smile. "You need to talk with my dad."

"I do?"

"Yep."

"Aren't you a little old for that?"

"Remember, I'm a southern girl, and my daddy's only daughter."

"How's he get along with doctors?"

A laugh. "Poorly."

"Poorly?"

She nodded.

"What's he do?"

"Plaintiff's attorney."

"You've got to be kidding."

"Don't worry, he likes you."

"How do you know?"

"He read the story."

"What story?"

"The one I wrote that hit shelves"—she stared at her watch—"this week."

"Where?"

A shrug. "All over."

"Define 'all over.'"

She rolled her eyes. "All over."

"What's it about?"

"A trip I took . . . recently."

"Am I in it?"

"Yep." She took off running, her laughter echoing. "We both are."

Her arms swung side to side, causing too much lateral movement. And her stride was too short by maybe three inches. And she put too much weight on her toes. She over-pronated. And she favored her left leg. And . . .

But she was a quick study. We could fix all that. And it wouldn't take long. Broken people just need piecing back together.

For so long I'd carried the pieces of me. Every now and then I'd drop one like a breadcrumb. So I could find my way home. Then Ashley came along and gathered the pieces and somewhere between 11,000 feet and sea level, the picture began taking shape. Dim at first, then clearer. Not yet clear. But these things take time.

Maybe each of us was once a complete whole. A clear picture. A single piece. Then something happened to crack and shatter us. Leaving us disconnected, torn, and splintered. Some of us lie in a hundred pieces. Some ten thousand. Some are edged with sharp contrast. Some dim shades of gray. Some find they are missing pieces. Some find they have too many. In any case, we are left shaking our heads. *It can't be done.*

Then someone comes along who mends a tattered edge, or returns a lost piece. The process is tedious, painful, and there are no shortcuts. Anything that promises to be one is not.

But somehow, as we walk from the crash site—away from the wreckage—whole sections start taking shape, something vague we see out of the corner of our eye. For a second, we stop shaking our heads. We wonder. *Maybe . . . just maybe.*

It's risky for both of us. You must hope in an image you can't see, and I must trust you with me.

That's the piecing.

ASHLEY RAN UP THE BEACH. The sun spilling down her back. Fresh footprints in the sand. Sweat shining on her thighs—condensation on her calves.

I could see them both. Rachel in the dunes, Ashley on the beach. I shook my head. I can't make sense of that. I don't know how.

I scratched my head.

Ashley returned. Breathing heavy, laughing, smiling. She raised her eyebrows, pulled on my hand. "Ben Payne?"

More tears I could not explain. I did not try. "Yes?"

"When you laugh . . . I want to smile. And when you cry . . ." She brushed the tears off my face. "I want the tears to roll down my cheeks." She shook her head once, whispering, "I'm not leaving you . . . won't."

I swallowed. How then does one live? A memory echoed from beyond the dunes. *Put one foot in front of the other.*

Maybe piecing is continual. Maybe the glue takes time to dry. Maybe bones take time to mend. Maybe it's okay that the mess I call me is in process. Maybe it's a long, hard walk out of the crash site. Maybe the distance is different for each of us. Maybe love is bigger than my mess.

My voice was slow in coming. "Can we . . . walk a bit first?"

She nodded, and we did. First a mile, then two. A gentle breeze in our faces. We reached the lifeguard chair and turned around.

She tugged on me. The breeze now at our backs. "Come on . . . you ready?"

So we picked up a jog. I was weak—using muscles I'd forgotten. Wasn't long and we were running.

And we ran a long time.

Somewhere in the miles that followed, sweat flinging off my fingertips, salt stinging my eyes, my breath deep, rhythmic, and clean, my feet barely touching the ground, I looked down and found the pieces of me melting into one.

A PERSONAL NOTE TO THE READER

Last February, as I stood in the High Uintas Mountains, midway between Salt Lake City and Denver, somewhere around 11,000 feet, I was staring at a view that spanned some sixty or seventy miles. Not a lightbulb in sight. It was cold and the snow was blowing in my face. Stinging my eyes. 'Course, tears do that, too. I was wrestling with some deep down DNA-level stuff. Questions I could not shake. Some of my hero's words came to mind. They echoed there, and followed me home. They are following me still: *I lift my eyes to the hills. From where does my help come . . .*

ACKNOWLEDGMENTS

This is not the first book I've written since *Where the River Ends.* For more on that period in my life, check my blog, The Truth About My Next Book. Having a manuscript rejected is . . . difficult. Something like giving birth only to watch the doctors and nurses stand back and shake their heads, "No . . . this won't do. We need to send this one back."

At the moment, that manuscript is a lot like a car on blocks in my backyard. I'm stealing parts and intend to rob it blind in the months and years ahead. Evidence to this rests in the pages that preceded this one. Thankfully, that wasn't the end of me, or rather my writing, and this book is in your hands. I have many people to thank.

Stacy Creamer. Thank you for the role you played in my work, development, and career—even the tough parts. I wish you great success in your new endeavor. You deserve it.

Michael Palgon. Given the year's events, I know full well you could have cut me loose. Set me adrift. Maybe the thought crossed your mind. It certainly crossed mine. Thank you for safe harbor.

All the talented folks at Broadway and Random House: Diane Salvatore, Catherine Pollock, Rachel Rokicki, Linda Kaplan and the foreign-rights department, and all the folks who've helped design or sell or market me and my stories that I've never met. I simply would not be here without you, and Christy and I cannot thank you enough.

Christine Pride. Thank you for your patience, your keen eye, your enthusiasm, and the great extent to which you have gone to bat for me. It is no doubt difficult to jump into the middle of a project. Like trying to catch a train at eighty miles an hour while standing flat-footed on the platform. You jump well. Thank you for how you did it. We're grateful.

L. B. Norton. It's nice to have you back. Thank you—for the fifth time. You make the process fun. Thank you for all the ways you help get me out of me and onto paper—so others can understand it. Oh, and yes, "anal-retentive" is hyphenated. I looked it up.

Bill Johnson. When I began the research for this book, I called one of my more adventurous friends, Bill Johnson, and asked him to fly to Utah with me and spend a week in one of the more remote and difficult places in the States—both the getting into and the getting out of. He was sitting behind his desk at Merrill watching a market in the midst of a freefall. He thought about it for maybe a half second (Google searches have returned slower) and said, "Okay." Friends like that are hard to come by. From Mitchell to the Uintas, you have proven yourself tough as nails—don't ever let anyone tell you different. And you possess absolutely no quit whatsoever—unless there's a dessert nearby, the smell of fresh coffee, or something cold with condensation running down the side, in which case we'll be taking a break. You laugh easily—a rare and true gift, one that you share liberally. We are all the better for it. You're welcome around my fire anytime. Especially if you bring your bow drill, or your Jetboil and French press.

Chris Ferebee. A decade ago, when I was just a dreamer from Jacksonville (little has changed), trying to get a manuscript noticed—maybe even published—a balding and washed-up ballplayer, with a weak fastball, pretty good curve, nonexistent changeup, and wicked slider, read my stuff and offered to represent me. That was ten books ago. You'll notice this book is dedicated to him. He's earned it. The reasons are many, but at the center are friendship, wise counsel, miles traveled, and dreams realized. Chris, you're a man among men.

Christy. When I said "Run with me . . . ," you did. You are—and always will be—the home for my heart.

READER'S GUIDE

ABOUT THIS GUIDE:

The following discussion topics are designed to enhance your reading of Charles Martin's *The Mountain Between Us*. We hope they will enrich your experience as you explore this captivating novel of extraordinary love.

QUESTIONS FOR DISCUSSION:

1. *The Mountain Between Us* is an adventure story, a story of survival, and above all a love story. By the end of the novel what do we learn about the author's views of love? Is there such a thing as a perfect marriage? What do Ben and Ashley learn from the pilot, Grover, about the nature of enduring love? Is that a lesson that stays with them throughout the book? In your experience does marriage get better? What makes a great marriage?

2. After the crash, Ben and Ashley are stranded at 11,500 feet, fifty miles from any kind of civilization with no hope of rescue, she with a broken leg, he with three busted ribs and a possible collapsed lung, and minimal supplies . . . yet they survive for more than four weeks in these extreme conditions. What skills and character traits do you think helped ensure their survival? Did you find the story credible?

3. Was Ben to blame at any point for what happened? Should he have hired the charter plane to take them out in the coming storm? During their time on the mountain, what choices did Ben make? Do you believe he made the right choices? What would you have done in his place?

4. We learn about Ben's wife mostly through the recordings she made on Ben's Dictaphone. Is she a strong presence in the book? What kind of person was she? What made her so special to Ben?

5. Ben refers to himself as "a bit of an emotional blockhead" (page 119). Why do you think he finds it so difficult to come to

terms with his "separation" from his wife, Rachel? What part did his childhood experiences play in his emotional development?

6. In the most difficult times on the mountain, when Ashley and Ben are losing hope of survival, how do they keep themselves going? What was the most difficult part of their ordeal? If you were in their position, what would you have done? Do you think you would have made it home alive?

7. How does Ben and Ashley's time on the mountain change their perspective on life? Does it make them see any more clearly? Are their lives irrevocably changed by the experience? In what ways?

8. Were you surprised by the revelation about Ben's family life at the end of the book? How did the discovery make you feel? Looking back through the book, did the author lay any clues for the reader along the way?

9. Ben uses his Dictaphone to communicate with his wife. What do you learn about Rachel from his recordings? Do you think this technique works as a narrative device? What does it say about the way we communicate with our loved ones today? Why did Ben throw the Dictaphone into the ocean at the end of the book?

10. What is the significance of the title? What is "the mountain between us"?

11. In the author's note, Charles references one of the most beautiful Bible verses: *I lift my eyes to the hills. From where does my help come* . . . What part does religious faith play in this novel? Do you think the author's own optimism is derived from his faith in God?

For more information about this novel and Charles Martin's other works, visit CharlesMartinBooks.com.

Share your thoughts on this book on Charles's Facebook page: http://www.facebook.com/author.charles.martin

ABOUT THE AUTHOR

CHARLES MARTIN is a *New York Times* bestselling author of eleven previous novels. He lives in Jacksonville, Florida, with his wife and their three sons.

ALSO BY CHARLES MARTIN

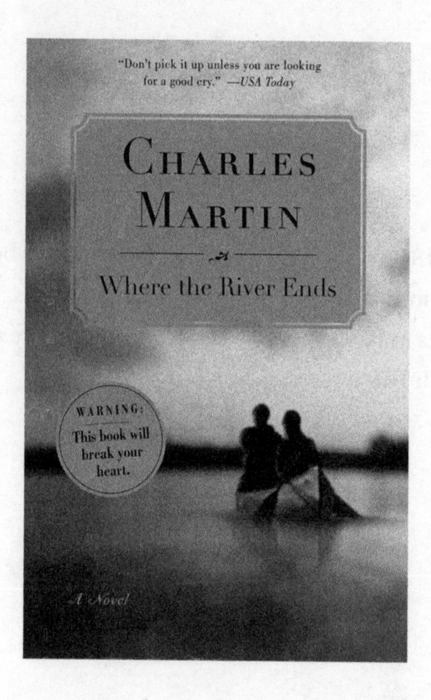

"In the tradition of Nicholas Sparks and Robert James Waller, Martin has fashioned a heartbreaking story."

—*Publishers Weekly*